GETAWAY

AN ESCAPE NOVEL

CASEY COX

SYNOPSIS

Ever woken up and realized you're in love with your childhood best friend?

I've got three big problems.

One, I'm in love with my childhood best friend.
Two, he hates any kind of change with a capital *H*.
Three, he thinks I'm straight.

To be honest, up until recently, I thought I was straight, too. But something's shifting in me. I don't know what it is exactly, but I can feel it. We tell each other everything, so I want to tell Cassius this.

I figure a tropical weekend getaway is the perfect time to do it. I mean, what could possibly happen that would change our lives forever?

GETAWAY is a best friends-to-lovers/gay-for-you rom-com style MM romance.

It features two childhood best friends, a luxury (clothing optional) resort, beach bonfire kisses, newly invented dance moves, dubious dietary claims, and some creatively named cocktails. You can expect more than a few gasps, giggles, and OMG moments on the way to a satisfying happily ever after that will make you feel like you've just returned from the best vacation ever.
(Suntan lotion and beach towels sold separately.)

GETAWAY is the first book in the super sweet, light and fluffy *ESCAPE* series. There are no cliffhangers (ew) and no cheating, either (double ew). You can read the books in whatever order your heart desires!

PROLOGUE - CASSIUS

ONE YEAR EARLIER...

Crunch, crunch, crunch.

The sounds of leaves and sticks crackling underfoot filled the crisp mid-October morning air as we made our way up the gently sloping trail. I looked back over my shoulder. "You guys all right back there?"

I was met with a chorus of low grunts and heavy breathing. I let out a pleased smile. It was as good a response as I could have hoped for. It wasn't easy getting a group of mainly teenagers to venture out of their natural habitat this early on a Saturday morning. And by natural habitat, I meant their beds. The fact that they were even here, walking behind me and, for the most part, awake, was a victory.

I peered over the tops of an array of colorful beanies and hooded sweatshirts to Michael, who was bringing up the rear. He gave me a small wave and a thumbs up, indicating that everything was fine with the group. I smiled and nodded back to him before turning back around for the final few minutes of our hike.

I took a deep breath of the fresh forest air as we continued making our way along the Hancock Hill trail. Though the Blue Hills were located only ten miles south of downtown Boston, civilization was the last thing on my mind as we trekked by majestic hemlocks, mountain laurel-covered slopes, and an Atlantic cedar swamp.

Ah, I loved hiking.

This trail was perfect for the group. It wasn't too long, about twenty minutes each way. It was relatively flat, with only a modest incline right before reaching the peak—enough to raise your heart rate and build up a bit of a sweat, but nothing that these kids couldn't handle. Plus, it was only a short five-minute drive from the center, which made it super convenient, too.

But the best thing about the hike, hands down, was the breathtaking view at the summit. The dense, rich forest opened up into an abundance of clear sky and a breathtaking view of Boston's city skyline.

I had walked this trail hundreds of times before and never got tired of it. Whenever I hiked it alone, I would get up at the crack of dawn. It was the only form of exercise I was willing to subject myself to, as well as the only time I would ever willingly get out of bed so early. I would time it so I'd reach the peak just as the sun rose over the mountains, lighting up the dark sky with spectacular splashes of magenta and orange-pinkish light, and with it, the promise of a new day.

But since my suggested start time of eight a.m. had drawn so many groans and protests from the gang, I didn't dare suggest an earlier start time.

I started the weekly Saturday morning hikes when I joined the Youth Accommodation Service Center three weeks earlier. The center was for youths aged between twelve and twenty-one who were either homeless or at risk of becoming homeless. This place was their last resort and, in many cases, the only thing keeping them from a life on the streets.

I was fresh out of college and was unbelievably lucky to score my first job as a social worker at a place like this. It had always been my dream to do something good with my life, and here I was, taking my first steps—figuratively and literally.

As I knew would be the case, it wasn't easy work and came with a lot of challenges. Hiking had always helped to clear my mind, so I hoped it might help the kids get a different perspective on some of the truly awful things they were experiencing in their lives. In the three short weeks since I had started, I had already heard a lot of heartbreaking stories.

The job also paid peanuts. Actually, less than peanuts. But I didn't care. I thought it was the best job in the world. I didn't care about money or having a fancy job title. All I wanted was a job where I could help others and make a difference. And in my own small way, that's what I was doing here.

My heart started beating faster in my chest and beads of sweat formed on my forehead. I felt the pressure building in my calves and legs as the incline increased. "Not long now," I yelled over my shoulder. "We're almost there."

"Yay!" a single voice cried out in return.

I couldn't tell if they were being sarcastic or not, proving, if nothing else, that it was possible to feel old at twenty-two.

"And you know what that means..." I trailed off, not needing to finish the sentence. It was a good thing they couldn't see the massive smile spreading across my face.

"Oh no, not a speech," one of them pleaded.

"He's gonna start talking again," another voice cried out amidst a rising chorus of exaggerated groaning.

"Oh, you know it's coming. And I think you secretly like it." There. That seemed to quiet them.

I knew it. Only three weeks into our weekly hiking adventures, and my speeches were already famous. Actually, that was probably underselling it. They were *legendary,* and in all honesty, probably the main draw of the hike. That, and the view.

A few moments later, we reached the peak, and it was, as always, spectacular. The sun was already hovering in the sky, but it was hidden behind a single long white cloud that stretched across an otherwise cloudless sky. It created an eerie stillness, one that allowed us to catch our breaths as we took in the wonder all around us.

The kids started settling in, finding a spot to sit down, either by themselves or with a friend. I kept my gaze fixed on the expansive sky, trying to take it all in.

"Oh god, he's going to start talking about the sky now," Jean, one of the oldest members of the group, said as she walked past me.

I shot her a wide grin. "Maybe I will, Jean, maybe I will. Don't worry, I won't keep you in suspense much longer. I'll just give everyone a minute to settle in."

Jean rolled her eyes but smiled playfully as she walked past me to sit on an empty bench. She'd been kicked out of her home when she came out to her parents as transgender. That was, of course, after her father tried to beat the living daylights out of her under the misguided notion that physical punishment would remind her that she's "really a boy."

It broke my heart to hear about these kids' lives and how much crap they had already gone through at such a young age. It wasn't fair.

I gazed out at the view, soaking up the serenity. When I came here alone, I would often bring my sketchpad and let my mind drift as I drew. Sometimes hours would pass, and the only thing that took me out of the tranquil state I was in would be my grumbling stomach, letting me know it was time to go. I was never organized enough to bring snacks, no matter how many times I told myself I should.

As the kids got settled in, I cleared my throat. "I'd just like to say a few words, and then I'll leave you be." I moved into a position in front of the group. Right on cue, the sun emerged from behind the cloud and lit up the early morning sky.

I knew they made fun and joked about it, but I also knew that they really loved it. In just a few short weeks, my speeches had become the stuff of folklore. And sure, my first speech may have included me putting on a terrible Scottish accent in an ill-thought-out attempt to recreate the pre-battle scene of *Braveheart*. My bad for thinking that these Gen Z-ers and millennials would have even heard of the movie.

And yes, last week I had to deviate from my original plan when I tripped over my own feet before I even started talking and almost face-planted in a completely undignified way in front of them. I told the group I was simply recreating Jennifer Lawrence's stumble on the way to accept her Academy Award and that I wanted to use my own fall as a teaching moment. They got the reference that time, but it didn't stop them from mercilessly making fun of me for it every single day for the past week.

Given that in some cases I was only a few years older than some of them, I didn't really have a wealth of life experience to draw on. I knew I had to earn their trust, so these speeches were my way of having some real talk with them without sounding like one of those aliens they often hated and distrusted—otherwise known as adults—who used terms like *real talk*.

I wanted to be approachable and relatable, and if that meant I had to publicly embarrass myself once in a while by acting like a total goofball, then I was totally fine with that. It's like I'd been practicing for it my whole life.

"From the very earliest dawn of time," I began in earnest, putting on my best David Attenborough impersonation. I was met with a series of groans and eye rolls.

"I'm just kidding, you guys." I chuckled at their totally predictable reaction. "I actually want to talk about something serious this time."

I stood perfectly still, feeling their eyes on me. "I'm not going to beat around the bush with you. You've had a pretty shitty start to life. It ain't all sunshine and rainbows, right?"

I saw heads bobbing. A few of them dropped their heads downward, feeling the truth of my words. "But here's the thing. Every single one of you is strong and brave, maybe even braver than you give yourself credit for. You had to be strong to make it here. And by *here*, I mean coming to the center, as well as this hike this morning. And guess what? You will be even stronger when you're ready to leave the center and start to live an amazing life, even though you may not necessarily have had the best start to it."

I let the words linger in the slowly warming air for a moment.

I wanted these kids to realize their power, that they could be whoever they wanted to be in life. I wanted them to know that they weren't bound to repeat the mistakes of their parents. They weren't victims of circumstances beyond their control. They didn't have to ignore their dreams and settle for less. They deserved to have the best lives possible, just as much as anyone did. I truly believed that with everything I had in me.

"In the words of one of the greatest wordsmiths of our generation, Rocky Balboa, it ain't about how hard you get hit—it's about how hard you get hit and keep moving forward."

Okay, that reference was met with a wall of blank stares. Note to self: start watching movies that were made in a year that started with two.

I walked over a few paces and picked up a small rock from the ground. "So before we leave here today, I'm going to ask you to pick up a stone. Think of somebody who has hurt you, somebody who has let you down. It could be a person who's lied to you or who wasn't there for you in the way they should have been, in a way that you needed them to be there for you. And then take the stone, throw it as far as you can over the edge, and let that person go. They held you back once. Don't let them keep holding you back."

"How far do we throw it?" a voice from the group asked.

"As hard and as far as you can," I replied.

"What if we hit a bird?" I recognized the voice. It belonged to Toby. I heard a half giggle escape his lips.

I rolled my eyes and sighed. "You're not going to hit a bird...unless you aim for one. So don't aim for one."

"I don't know how I could live with myself, having bird-killing on my conscience," Jean chimed in, and I knew I was losing the battle.

"Guys, no one's going to kill any birds today, okay? And if you do, it will be on my conscience—not yours."

"Can we get that in writing?" Jean asked with a wide grin.

"All right." I raised my palms in the air in defeat. "It's your call about the stone throwing. You can do it—or if you don't want to run the risk of being an accidental bird killer—you don't have to. It's your choice." I let out a breath. "Let's just hang out here for a few minutes and enjoy this beautiful view, okay?"

I placed the stone in my pocket and stepped back closer to the group.

"That speech actually wasn't too bad, man," Max said as I walked past him.

"Thanks, buddy," I replied cheerfully.

Max had come to the shelter about six months ago with a series of undiagnosed mental health conditions. We were slowly working our way through round after round of testing to firstly, diagnose his conditions accurately and secondly, get him on the right treatment plan.

"How are you feeling today?" I asked.

"Not too bad. I actually feel better up here than I did when I first woke up this morning."

"That's good to hear, Max. I'm glad." I patted him on the shoulder and kept making my way through the group. I wandered over to a bench near the edge of the peak, the city skyscrapers silhouetted in the distance.

Toby was sitting there, alone, looking out into the distance. His eyes were glassy and unfocused. His mother and stepdad were killed in a horrific car accident that also killed his half-sister. His closest relative was his biological father, who he hadn't seen since the asshole had walked out on them when Toby was just a baby. After the accident, Toby relocated halfway across the country to live with his father and his new family, only to be kicked out a short time later when his deadbeat dad found out he was gay.

"Today's the one-year anniversary of the accident," he told me as I sat down next to him.

"Oh, Toby, I'm so sorry." I put my arm around him to comfort him. "This must be a really hard day for you."

"It is." He wiped a tear away and looked away from me, as if embarrassed. He took a deep breath before speaking again. "But life goes on, right?" He tried to force a smile as he looked at me.

What could I say? What could anyone say? Nothing could undo what had been done, and there was no magic tonic for the pain he was feeling.

"You know, my dad died when I was twelve," I spoke softly, taking the smooth black stone I had picked up earlier out of my pocket and running it through my fingers.

"Really? I didn't know that. I'm sorry." Toby's eyes met mine. "What—what happened?"

"Heart attack. He was forty-six."

"That's terrible."

"Yeah, it is." I got to my feet, took a few steps forward, and hurled the rock as far and as hard as I could. I silently prayed I wouldn't hear any bird squawks filling the air. I waited for a few seconds, sitting down again once I heard nothing.

The memory of the last hike I ever went on with my dad came flooding back to me. It was a Sunday morning. He would always get up at the crack of dawn, filling our backpacks with snacks, water, and other essential supplies. He, unlike me, was always very well-prepared.

I, of course, was fast asleep and perfectly happy to stay in my warm bed and miss the hike. I mean, what twelve-year-old wants to get out of bed in the dark on the weekend? But he kept waking me up every five minutes until I was finally awake, dressed, and ready to go.

Not a day went by that I wasn't thankful that he dragged me along with him.

It had been raining during the night, so the ground was wet. We didn't go for a long hike, and as we made our way back to the car, I slipped on some wet leaves. He managed to grab me, and thankfully, the only thing that was hurt was my pride. I also ended up with a small scratch on my wrist. The pressure from where he had grabbed me had imprinted on my skin. But it didn't bleed, and it didn't hurt, so it was no big deal. I thought nothing more of it.

The next morning, while he was riding the elevator to his office, he suffered a massive heart attack and died.

I had never seen my mom cry as much as she did that day. I hadn't cried that much in my life since. That night as Mom was tucking me in, she noticed the small scratch mark on my wrist from where Dad had grabbed me to stop me from falling during our hike.

I barely slept a wink that night. Through tear-soaked eyes, I kept staring at the tiny scratches on my wrist. They were the only thing I had left of my dad.

When I turned eighteen, the first thing I did was go to a tattoo parlor—with my mom driving me—to get a tattoo on my wrist to remember him by. Whenever I hiked, which was pretty much every weekend, I always took a moment to look down at my wrist. I would run my fingers along the tattoo, a simple inscription of three letters—*DAD*— and every time I did, it made me feel like some part of him was still with me.

Life got hard after Dad died. Mom had to work three jobs, which meant that at the age of twelve, I was left to take care of my younger twin sisters, Cheryl and Emily. Or, as I had been trying unsuccessfully for years to call them, *Chemily*. Yeah, it didn't seem to stick, for some strange reason.

I never once complained about anything, though. How lonely I felt. How much I missed my dad and wanted him back. How hard it was to look after two very stubborn and determined eight-year-olds—making sure they did their homework, ate their dinner, and got washed and ready for bed by a decent hour. What right did I have to grumble about anything when my mom was working so hard to provide for us?

Despite how difficult those years were, I knew in my heart that I was lucky. I had a mom and sisters who loved me and a home that, while modest, was ours. We had each other, and we were safe. That was a whole lot more than what these guys had.

I shook my head free of thoughts of the past. "My dad used to say something to me that I never really got as a kid." I broke the silence and Toby turned to look at me. "Whenever he would tuck me in at night, I'd always say, 'I love you' to him, and then he'd always say, 'I love you, too' back to me. He'd then press his finger against the tip of my nose, lean in a little closer, and say, 'the real you.'"

"Wow." Toby studied me for a moment. "He sounds like a great dad."

I smiled, my mind filled with memories. "Yeah, he was."

I looked over at Toby, and some of the sadness in his face had lifted. He seemed a little lighter. It never ceased to amaze me the effect that taking some time out to just sit and reflect in nature had on a person.

"I'm going out to a bear bar tomorrow night," he announced, changing the subject completely. He'd just turned twenty-one a week earlier. "It will be my first time."

"Oh, that's great, Toby."

I tried to sound enthusiastic and as if I totally knew what a bear bar was. I had no idea. Even though I was gay, my knowledge of LGBTQIA+ culture was woefully absent. Worse than my speech-giving skills, even. But I didn't need Toby knowing that.

My mind tried to fill in the gaps. A bear...hmm, maybe that was a term for gay guys who were into *hunting* bears? Or did it have something to do with guys who liked being outdoors *near* bears? I felt like I was getting close, but nothing was hitting the jackpot.

Michael approached to let me know that he and some of the others were heading back. "Cool, I'll stay a while longer," I said.

"Me, too," Toby added.

Michael gave us both a nod, and as most of the group made its way back toward the trail, I glanced over and saw a few of them throwing a stone over the peak's edge. A happy feeling warmed my chest.

Once they were gone, I patted Toby on the shoulder and said, "When you go out into the world—whether it's to a bear bar, or a new job, or anywhere else that life takes you—remember, always be you. The *real* you."

Toby nodded, and a flash of determination crossed his face. "I will, Cassius. I will."

"You can be whoever you want to be, and you will find people who will love you. Don't settle for anything less."

He kept nodding as his lips curled upward into the first hint of a smile.

"Like you and Spencer?"

"Uh, yeah, sure," I said slowly. "Spencer's my best friend. You've seen him around, I take it?"

He wasn't able to contain the smile or the playful look in his eyes. "Yeah, I've seen him around. Are you sure you're *just* best friends?"

I was pretty open with the kids at the center. I tried to be real with them, and I knew that to do that, and do it well, I had to open up to them about myself and share parts of my life with them.

That's how most of them knew Spencer, who actually was my best friend, all innuendo aside.

Spencer and I had been best friends since the first day of school. I could still remember him arriving late because of his mother having some drama that day. Honestly, she was the reason for pretty much anything bad in Spencer's life.

He stood beside her by the doorway to the classroom, looking all cute and nervous, clutching his oversized school bag like his life depended on it.

There was a spare seat next to me, so I stood up and waved him over. Then he did the cutest thing ever—something he still does to this day. He stretched his arm out straight and slightly forward, then gave this frantic little hand wave. It was so weird, but so adorably precious at the same time, too.

We'd been inseparable since that day, even though we were the dictionary definition of polar opposites.

I was messy. Spencer was the neatest person alive.

I was disorganized and could barely remember what day it was. Spencer was the king of spreadsheets and had his life organized down to the very last detail.

Spencer was the fittest person I knew, whereas I would circle the parking lot until I found a spot as close to the entrance as possible.

Yet, somehow, we'd made it work. And I had literally lost count of the number of times that people had assumed—*incorrectly*—that Spencer and I were a couple. Because the thing that people forgot, the one little fact that everyone seemed to conveniently overlook, was that Spencer, unlike me, was straight.

Toby poked my arm gently, bringing me back into reality.

"Yes, I am sure, thank you very much," I said, answering his *are you sure you're best friends* question while giving him a gentle nudge.

"Alright." Toby stood up, the grin still plastered on his face. "I might head back, too."

"Cool. I'll stay for a few more minutes."

I watched as he made his way toward the trail, throwing a stone over the peak, before disappearing into the thick row of trees. The sun had risen higher now, revealing what promised to be a truly beautiful fall day.

My eyes shifted down as I grazed my wrist with my fingers. For a moment, my chest filled with memories of my dad. I felt the familiar sadness, but after all these years, it was joined by a sense of gratitude that I could still remember him and the hero that he would always be to me.

After a little while, my thoughts drifted to Toby's innuendo. I let out a sigh.

Why did everyone always think that Spencer and I were a couple?

FRIDAY

PRESENT DAY

1

SPENCER

I jumped out of the car, muttering a quick thanks to the driver as I closed the door. I bolted toward the entrance, keen to get out of the cold night air. I looked up at the building and felt a shiver run down my spine. It had nothing to do with the biting temperature and everything to do with the apartment building itself.

Cassius lived in the shittiest apartment in the shittiest apartment building in the shittiest part of town—otherwise known as Mattapan—and I hated it. For some reason, it didn't seem to bother him as much as it bothered me.

I pushed through the heavy front door and toward the staircase. It wasn't that much warmer inside. The walls had been white at some stage, I assumed; now they were a smoky, creamy color. A pungent smell of dampness coated the air and filled my lungs.

I held my breath as I raced up the stairs to Cassius' apartment, taking them two at a time all the way up to the third floor. Tiny beads of sweat formed on my forehead as I propelled myself up the staircase, doing my best to keep the flowers and chocolates I was carrying steady in my hands.

I reached the third-floor landing and let out a massive exhale. I glanced down at my watch.

Shit, I was late.

I was *never* late.

The last time I was late to anything, Megan Markle was still an actress, not a duchess.

It just so happened that the thing I was late for was a lunch date with my mother, who to this day made a point of acting surprised whenever I showed up on time. "Spencer, darling," she would drawl in an unwarranted way-too-loud voice and flashing her best *I'm totally surprised* look. "You made it"—cue exaggerated glance down at her watch—"and look at that, you're right on time for a change."

Seriously, I was late once, three years ago, and she still mentions it. Every. Single. Time.

Yep, that's my mom.

Cassius, on the other hand, couldn't give a shit if I showed up late. Not because he didn't care. He did. Deeply. But unlike my mom, he cared about things that mattered. You know, stuff like justice and equality for all, those sorts of things. But a little thing like showing up on time? Nah, he wouldn't even realize I was late. In the wonderful world of Cassius Draper, concepts like punctuality were about as abstract as any one of Mondrian's geometric compositions.

Me, on the other hand, I was a total time freak.

And neat freak.

And every other kind of organized freak you could be.

I once got thrown out of The Container Store for arguing with the manager about their aisle system. Excuse me, but kitchen drawer dividers do *not* belong in the office furniture aisle. That's just crazy, right?

I liked structure. A place for everything and everything in its place. It helped me be dependable, and I liked that quality about myself. People could trust me because when I said I'd do something, I always did.

There was no problem in the world that a spreadsheet couldn't fix. Sure, it might sound a little ridiculous, but for me, it gave me peace knowing that everything was organized and properly mapped out.

Well, except for one thing...

I wiped the beads of sweat off my forehead with the back of my flower-carrying hand and slowed my breathing down. My nostrils flared as they begrudgingly surrendered to the unpleasant aroma of the hallway. It smelled like...a meal cooked several days ago and left on the counter to go bad. And dirty socks.

I shuddered and squared my shoulders, trying to regain my composure. I quickly trudged down the dark, damp, and cold corridor to the third door on the left.

Apartment 3B.

The letter *B* had fallen off, leaving a faint outline of the letter on the door.

I hated that he lived here.

Twice before, I had offered for him to come and live with me in my three-bedroom apartment in Brookline. Even though I had a girlfriend at the time I made the offers, there still would have been plenty of space for all three of us.

Cassius and I shared a dorm in college, so we knew how to live well together. For some crazy reason, despite his messiness and propensity to interpret any empty space or surface as an invitation to leave his stuff on it—and his constant eye rolls at my color and material-coded laundry system, which would have earned me a gold medal if doing laundry were an Olympic sport (which it should have been)—we were the best of roomies. Just like we'd been the best of best friends ever since we'd met on our first day of school.

But when I made the offers for Cassius to move in with me, he politely declined. Both times. I guess he wanted to branch out on his own, which I could totally understand. We were both keen to get on our feet and start with this whole adulting thing. I just wished his job paid him more, so that he could afford to live in an apartment building that at least had proper heating in the winter.

The day we moved him in here, there were cops swarming all around the building. As it turned out, the guy who would have been his next door neighbor had been arrested for cooking up drugs in his bathroom tub, *Breaking Bad*-style, which was not only illegal, but also highly gross. I shuddered just thinking about it. Cassius being Cassius, he just shrugged it off. Like so many other things, it didn't bother him in the slightest.

It bothered me.

He deserved so much better than this. I wanted him to have the best of everything. I got that his career as a social worker wasn't about money. It was his lifelong passion, and I loved that he got to do what he wanted with his life. He was making a genuine difference, and I was so proud of him for that. I just wished his job paid a decent wage, that's all.

It wasn't fair that my job—which was much less noble than his —earned me so much money. Not to mention all of the perks that came along with it, like free tickets, complimentary meals, and kickass health insurance. But I guess that's the difference between working in PR-slash-marketing and being a social worker.

Sure, I worked hard and was passionate about getting the best results for my clients, but at the end of the day, I got paid a shit-ton of money as a reward. Cassius worked just as hard and made way more of an impact on people's lives, yet he didn't have all that much to show for it. It just wasn't right.

Again, something that bothered me a whole lot more than it bothered him.

Cassius had the innate ability to be happy wherever he was. One time, we were on a road trip to I can't even remember where, when it started to rain heavily. Of course, it was right at that moment that we got a punctured tire. We had to walk about two miles in the pouring rain just to reach the nearest, crappiest motel. The place was literally crawling with every insect known to humankind. It made his current apartment building look like The Ritz, which was really saying something.

I was totally freaking out and worried about what we would do, but Cassius wasn't stressed at all. We ended up buying beer, making nachos in a microwave that would have won the record for world's most disgusting and dirty kitchen implement, and staying up all night, getting slightly buzzed, talking shit, and playing with a sticky half-deck of cards we had found in the bedside drawers. It wound up being one of our funnest nights together.

That was one of the things I loved most about my friendship with Cassius: everything was just so easy and natural. It never bothered either one of us that he was gay and I was straight. If anything, I think it made our friendship stronger. We could talk to each other about literally anything and everything. There was never any judgment or fear of getting rejected. We were always up front and shared everything that was going on in our lives with each other.

At least, until six months ago.

I grimaced in the dark hallway. I'd stumbled upon something after my first, last, and probably only-ever girlfriend Natalie dumped me six months ago. It was a self-discovery of sorts, but one that not even a spreadsheet could fix. And believe me, I'd created one.

I'd called it *Spencer's Options—Sexuality*, or *SoS*. Appropriate.

As I knocked on Cassius' door, I played with the flowers and chocolate in my hands. Should I put them behind my back to surprise him? No, that would be stupid. This wasn't a romantic gesture, after all.

It was just...me.

And it was just him.

This was us.

After a few moments, the door swung wide open, and there was

Cassius, wearing his favorite white *Go With The Flow* T-shirt and a pair of loose-fitting gray sweatpants that clung low on his hips. He was holding a giant tub of ice cream in one hand and had a spoon hanging out of his mouth.

His face lit up, glowing due to the wide smile stretching his lips. It was a smile I had seen so many times in my life, but one that never failed to warm up my insides. The tightness in my chest lifted and my shoulders relaxed down my back.

"Spence," he said, in that rich, deep voice of his, taking the spoon out of his mouth.

"How ya doin', Cass?" I stepped in. He had ridiculously broad shoulders and strong arms that wrapped around me as he gave me his usual bear hug, squeezing me so tight I could feel the heat of his skin pressing against my chest.

"I'm doing good," he said as he pulled away from me and gave me a cheeky grin. There was music playing in the background, and he lifted his index finger. I paused. Then the moment he was waiting for arrived.

"I'm just chillin', chillin', mindin' my business," he riffed to the Salt-N-Pepa track I could hear playing in the background as I walked into the apartment, sidestepping his disastrous attempts at dancing. Or what I assumed he intended to be dancing.

"Nicely timed," I said with a warm smile. Just a few seconds with the guy, and I was instantly feeling a million times better. "Sorry I'm late," I added.

"You're late?" His forehead wrinkled, and he sent me a confused look. I knew it—he hadn't even noticed.

I shook my head and smiled. "What's that in your hands?"

"What's that in yours?" he whipped back.

I looked down at the flowers and chocolates I was holding and all of a sudden felt a little sheepish. "Oh, uh, we had these come in at work from a client we had worked for. Remember that Japanese fusion restaurant-slash-jazz bar I told you about?"

He nodded, even though he was looking down into the ice cream tub intensely, carefully scooping up his next mouthful.

"Their opening was a huge success which they said was largely due to the campaign we created for them. So they sent us, like, a million bouquets of flowers and enough chocolate to feed half the city. I grabbed these on the way out of the office and thought you might like them since you like nature and all that stuff, right?"

"Nature?" He glanced up, his light brown eyes sparkling with mischief.

"You know, like hiking...that's nature. Look, just shut up and take them." I shoved the flowers and chocolate into his chest.

"Thanks, Spencey," he said, juggling the ice cream tub, flowers, and chocolates in his hands. "I love them. They're beautiful."

I watched as he made his way over to the dining table, which was already buried beneath a mountain of clothes, books, and whatever else he had discarded onto it. He carefully placed the flowers and chocolates on top of the pile. It was like watching somebody playing Jenga in reverse. Instead of taking things away, he was just adding things on, until the pile collapsed—I assumed—and he was finally forced to do something about it.

My eyes traveled around the apartment. Gross hallway smells and former drug-making neighbors aside, Cassius had done a great job making the place feel snug. It was simple, but it felt warm and homey.

The lounge room had a sofa—more of a loveseat, really—a small wooden coffee table, a TV in the corner, and a packed-to-the-brim bookcase against the wall. A dining table took up the left side of the space, beyond which sat a small kitchen. The bathroom and single bedroom were off to the side of the kitchen.

As I glanced around, I picked up clues as to how Cassius' week had been. Not being one to put things back where they belonged— or having a place for things to belong to in the first place—meant that it was pretty easy to gather what he had been up to. His hiking clothes were slung over a dining chair with his hiking boots close by, so he'd gone for his weekly Saturday morning hike. Last week. Check.

There were a couple of still-unpacked grocery bags on the kitchen countertop, so he'd done his usual Thursday night grocery shopping. Check.

And he had made some more progress on the half-completed jigsaw puzzle that lined the floor between the bookcase and the TV, meaning he'd taken at least some time out for himself during the week. Check.

For all his laid-back charm and *Go With The Flow* T-shirt, Cassius was, in fact, a creature of habit. Big time. He didn't like change. Any change. At all.

I cleared my throat as a dark thought settled in my mind. *How would he react to what I had to tell him?* If Cassius had freaked out when Subway pulled roast beef from their menu, how would he react to my news?

I walked over to my favorite part of his apartment—the dining room wall which stretched all the way to the kitchen. It was filled with sketches. His sketches.

Despite never having taken an art class in his life, Cassius had an insane talent when it came to sketching. The drawings were of all sorts of things—views from his hiking expeditions, faces, vases, fruit, and men. Yes, naked men. I knew less than nothing about art, but these sketches were really beautiful. He had a cool way of shading the outline of the body so that it gave the sketch an almost surreal kind of depth. He was so talented, but, of course, he didn't think so.

"You know, you really should do something with these." I didn't know why I was starting a conversation we'd had countless times before.

"What, like throw them out?" he replied with a self-deprecating smile.

I flashed him my most serious *that's not what I mean and you know it* look. "Cass, I'm serious. These are good. Like, really good. You have to believe in yourself."

He was more intent at scooping out ice cream than in having the same conversation we'd had a million times already. Him not making use of his talent was something that bothered me more than it did him. As usual. I just wished he could see his art as the brilliant thing that it was. And something that deserved to be shared and seen by others. Not wanting to press it any further, I walked over and plonked myself down on the loveseat.

"Ooh!" His eyes lit up as a new track came on. "I love this song," He shimmied his way over to the speaker and cranked the volume up. "It's Friday night and I feel all right..." He mouthed the words to the early '90s Montell Jordan classic jam into his spoon-slash-microphone as he tried to coordinate his body to move to the rhythm of the music.

Keyword: *tried.*

I let out a massive smile. Whoever made up the stereotype that gay guys were good dancers had obviously never seen Cassius dance. It was tragically bad.

Then suddenly, out of nowhere, he started to bust out some new moves. His lower back and hips started doing things I hadn't seen him do before. It was a little...odd. Not good by any means, but definitely not as bad as his usual uncoordinated display.

My gaze traveled down to the top of his sweatpants, where his shirt had lifted and bits of his hairy stomach were peeking through. I cleared my throat and raised my eyebrows at him.

"I've been YouTubing old Miley Cyrus performances this week," he offered by way of explanation.

"Uh-huh." I settled back into the sofa, a funny feeling settling in my chest. "So...are you twerking right now, Cassius? Is this what I'm looking at?"

"Nope." He removed the spoon from his mouth and waved it at me, putting on a faux-serious expression. "Gay men were officially banned from twerking in 2016."

That year's second most shocking political moment.

"I'm a gay white dude, so I'm"—he dropped the tub of ice cream onto the coffee table and rapped his fingers against it in a drum roll—"gwerking."

"Gwerking?" I snorted, quickly covering my mouth. "Where do you come up with this stuff?" I took him in, looking all happy and silly and goofy. He really was one of a kind.

My heart did its own version of gwerking as a warm feeling settled in my chest. "You're a gwidiot, Cass."

He broke out into a hearty laugh, bringing his impromptu dance session to a close. He joined me on the loveseat, his feet grazing my legs as he tucked them under his body. He winced as he tried to get comfortable.

I patted my thighs, indicating for him to stretch his legs out onto me. He let out a relieved smile as he unfolded his legs. I grabbed them and gently positioned his feet on my lap.

We did this all the time. With all the hiking he did, plus the full-on nature of his job, Cassius' feet held a lot of stress. I began to press into the ball of his foot with my thumb and index finger, and he let out a contented sigh. The sound filled the space between us and sent a happy tingle up my spine. I loved seeing my best friend happy.

"I really want a dog," he said out of nowhere.

"In this place? Cass, dogs need cleanliness. Having a dog here would be...cruel." I was only half kidding.

"Hey, I live here, remember?" He was pretending—badly—to be slightly affronted.

"I do." How could I forget? "Why do you want a dog?" I asked seriously, turning to face him as my hands continued to massage the tightness out of his feet.

"I'm just lonely, I guess."

He scooped up another spoonful from the ice cream tub. "A dog would be a great companion. I'd take him on hikes. I could probably take him into work with me. It'd be nice."

"Hmm."

"Oh, god that feels good." He let out a soft moan as my fingers pressed firmly into the arch of his foot. "Keep going."

I smiled, applying even more pressure and watching in delight as his head rolled back in pleasure.

After a few moments, he brought another heaped spoon of ice cream and something that I couldn't quite distinguish to his mouth. "You never answered my question when I came in. What are you eating? Oh, and you do know we're going out to dinner, right?"

"Yeah I know. This is just a little pre-dinner...oh, geez, what's that thing called?" I could see his eyes searching for the word as he looked at me helplessly.

He ran his fingers through his thick mane of chestnut brown hair. "Entendre?" His brown eyes lit up like he had hit the nail on the head.

"You mean entrée, doofus," I corrected him, letting out a chuckle.

"Whatever." He waved his arm in front of his face. "I knew it sounded French. And don't worry, it's only ice cream and cereal. It's not like it's going to fill me up or anything."

"Wait, what? Did you say ice cream and *cereal*?"

"Uh, yeah. It's really good, Spence. You should try it sometime."

"Ice cream and cereal?" I repeated it again, slower this time, to give him a chance to correct me if I had somehow misheard him. He was looking at me as if I were the weird one here. "That's fucking weird, Cass. Even for you."

"What?" He raised both hands up in mock protest and flashed that dazzling wide smile of his. "I ran out of milk, and ice cream is basically frozen milk, right?"

I shook my head. There was no arguing with his logic, so I didn't even try.

"It's not fair. How can you eat all the shit that you do and still look like that?" I eyed him over.

His body made me completely jealous. He may have been a little shorter than me, but he had massively wide shoulders and a well filled out chest that tapered down to a slim waist. He had a flat stomach but didn't have visible abs, which I actually really liked for some reason. And all of it was covered in a light smattering of dark fuzz. It was all incredibly...manly.

"I just think about carbs, and I gain five pounds," I sulked, releasing his feet and folding my arms across my chest.

He let out a hearty laugh. "You look amazing, Spence. I wish I had a body like yours."

I let out a low grunt, but I couldn't deny that hearing him say that made me feel a teensy bit better. But it also didn't change the fact that I had to work out like crazy and eat super clean to avoid turning into a jar of lard. No ice cream and cereal for me.

Also, painful monthly trips to the salon to remove any signs of body hair that weren't on the top of my head. Unlike Cass. I didn't think he knew what the term *manscaping* even meant.

"Well"—my fingers returned to finding more pressure points on his foot—"make sure you still have room for dinner. It's meant to be the best Italian place in town. We're working on doing a brand refresh for them at the moment."

He shot me a funny look. "Does that mean I have to get dressed up?"

"It means you have to wear a shirt, yes. Preferably one with a collar."

Cassius groaned and rolled his eyes into the back of his head, but I knew that deep down, he liked going to fancy places with me. He just did a good job of hiding it.

"That's right, you're more of a drive-through kinda guy, right?" I teased.

"Uh, yeah." He wriggled his toes as I found a good spot on his foot. "I get a freshly cooked meal delivered in a matter of seconds, which I can enjoy in the comfort of my own car."

Now it was my turn to roll my eyes at him.

"You know my car has leather seats, Spencey?"

I looked over at him with a blank expression.

"*Leather*," he mouthed the word, whispering it in what I assumed was a terrible attempt at trying to look seductive. It was almost as bad as his shocking dance moves. Almost.

I shook my head, unable to suppress my smile. "You're such a doofus...and a doofus that needs to get a move on. The reservation is for eight."

"All right, let me just jump into the shower and find something to wear."

I glanced at my watch. "Okay, but be quick. I don't want to be late."

He swung his feet off my lap, getting up while still managing to stuff his face with another spoonful of ice cream...and cereal. I still couldn't get over that.

"I'm going, I'm going." He placed the ice cream tub onto the coffee table.

"Now that's a good boy," I said, putting on a *I'm talking to a puppy* voice.

Cass flipped me the bird as he walked away.

"What? I'm just practicing for when we get a dog." I was kidding, of course. We would never get a dog together. But the words did have a nice ring to them. Why couldn't two best friends get a dog together?

I cleared my throat and took my phone out of my pocket while I waited for him. I opened it again.

The spreadsheet.

S-o-motherfucking-S.

"Spencer."

Cassius' voice startled me as his head popped up right next to mine. He was so close I could smell the ice cream and cereal on his breath. It actually had kind of a nice fragrance. Maybe he was onto something.

"It's Friday night," he said, grabbing the phone from my hand.

"You shouldn't be working. No spreadsheets."

I quickly grabbed the phone back from him and stuffed it into my pocket.

"What would Montell Jordan do?" he asked, sporting a massive grin. He was clearly enjoying himself way too much.

"Hit up a party on the west side?" I answered without missing a beat.

"Exactly. Not checking work spreadsheets. All that shit can wait until next week. Just chill for a second. I won't be long. You know how I feel about showering."

"That it's something best to be avoided and done as infrequently as possible?"

"Exactly! I'll be real quick."

"Okay, fine." I sighed loudly. "I'll just sit here and wait in silence, shall I?"

"Now that's a good boy," Cassius said in his *I'm talking to a puppy* voice. He ran his hand through my hair, messing it up on purpose.

"Go," I growled, fiddling with my hair to fix it back into place.

"Okay, I'm really going this time." He backed away from me with a wide, shit-eating grin on his face. He loved to get a rise out of me...and I kinda loved it, too. Not that I would ever admit that to him.

Once he had left the room, I was tempted to grab my phone again. Why, I didn't really know. I'd stared at that damn spreadsheet for god only knew how many hours, and I was still no closer to figuring things out.

But this dinner would definitely help.

Cassius had no idea, but I had planned an awesome weekend getaway for us. I'd just finished working on a massive campaign for a luxury, all-male resort in Florida. The rebranding work my team had done resulted in one of the biggest successes for Crazy Red Man, the marketing and PR firm I worked for. As a thank you, the owner of the resort gifted me an all-expenses-paid long weekend at one of their newly renovated oceanfront villas.

Tonight's dinner at the fancy Italian restaurant I was taking Cassius to would be the perfect place to tell him all about it—and that we were going down next weekend. Over the years, I had learned of one of the most amazing and relatively unknown secret properties of pasta: it was a wonderful shock absorber for people who didn't like change or surprises thrown at them. People like Cassius.

And then, once we were there—sun-bathing by the pool, sipping on cocktails, relaxing and having a good time, eating more carbs—that's when I would tell him the other thing.

Yep. No *ifs*, *ands* or *buts* about it. One way or another, I would tell Cassius the truth...even if I didn't have the whole picture fully realized in my own head.

I shuffled on the loveseat to get a little more comfortable. As I moved, I felt something underneath my feet. I bent over and picked up a black sketchpad sticking out from underneath the couch. I opened it and saw Cassius' sketches. They weren't finished like the ones he had pinned on the wall, but they were still really, really good.

As I flicked through them, I noticed something. They were all of naked men. The funny thing was that while he had drawn clearly defined, almost complete bodies, all their faces were just a rough outline. Maybe it was easier to draw the body, and he was leaving the faces to the end? I literally knew nothing about art.

I continued thumbing through the sketches until I got to the last one.

My eyes widened as the sketch stared back at me. I blinked twice. I was looking at me, or at least my face, in full, clear detail. Unlike all of the other sketches, the body wasn't anywhere near finished, but the face was. He had totally captured every last part of me.

The light freckle on my right cheek.

My blue eyes.

My nose with the slight curve at the tip that I didn't like.

The level of accuracy was impressive. But for all the crafted care he had given to my face, the rest of the body was almost completely untouched, except for a faint outline.

I guessed it made sense. Even though we had known each other since we were six and had shared many a drunken adventure together during our high school and college years, Cassius and I had actually never seen each other naked.

Ever.

Not even once.

Not even by accident.

"Whatcha doin' there, Spence?" Cassius' voice boomed from behind me as I felt his strong hand resting on my shoulder. He startled me and I flinched like I had been caught doing something wrong.

"Uh, nothing. I just found your sketches under the couch." I snapped the sketchpad shut.

He walked around me and bent over to grab the ice cream he'd left sitting on the coffee table.

"What are you doing here? What happened to your shower?"

"Just needed to grab some supplies." He picked up the ice cream and poked his tongue out at me.

"Wait. You're going to be eating while you shower?"

"No, I am not," he replied with an exaggerated indignation. "But it takes at least five minutes to get hot water, so I'll be eating while I *wait* to shower. Important distinction, thank you very much." He flashed me his cheeky smile, which for some reason made me blush.

With the ice cream tub in hand, he once again set off for the bathroom. I watched him as he sauntered off.

"And hurry up," I yelled after him. "We're going to be late."

I *hated* being late.

2

CASSIUS

We showed up at the restaurant two minutes before eight.

Spencer tried to hide it and play it cool, but I knew that arriving on time—heck, arriving a little early—made his night. His eyes had been practically glued to his phone on the ride to the restaurant, and I had a feeling his "helpful" suggestions to the Uber driver would cost him a star rating or two.

Spencer hated being late, or having a hair out of place, or doing anything that could potentially piss anyone off in the slightest. Unlike me, he gave way too many fucks about what other people thought of him. But with a mother like his, I couldn't really blame the guy. In fact, it was a good thing he wasn't more damaged, given the upbringing he'd had.

But we were here now and with a whole two minutes to spare. "Look, Fred, we made it," I whispered, teasing Spence with a nickname I knew he hate-loved as we followed the server to our table.

"Don't call me Fred," he replied in a hushed tone as he walked in front of me. I could see his cheekbones rising, a sign that he was smiling, so he knew I was just ribbing him. Like I always did. Like he always loved.

"Promise me," he spoke over his shoulder, his eyes narrowing in semi-seriousness.

"Okay, I promise. I won't call you Fred again." I confirmed my intention with a friendly pat on the shoulder before my gaze turned downward to Spencer's hands, knowing what I'd see. His arms were by his side, and he was sticking his pinky finger out behind him. I couldn't help but giggle. Here we were, being ushered to our table at this super fancy restaurant, and I was pinky-swearing with my bestie.

I relented, dropping my pinky to meet his. Our fingers interlocked. He pulled his pinky around mine, held it for a moment, and gave it a tight squeeze before releasing it. The touch sent a warm spark to the center of my chest. I nibbled on the corner of my lip, determined to push the feeling away.

I came up with the nickname "Fred" after the *Scooby Doo* character, Fred Jones, because, well, Spencer was pretty much the real-life version of him. Golden blond hair, sparkling aqua blue eyes, and cheekbones so high they could cut glass. Or so sharp. Whatever the saying was about cheekbones.

As weird as it was to say about my best friend, he also had amazing muscular legs and a meaty ass that looked good in whatever pair of jeans he wore. While I followed Spencer and the server to our table, my eyes wandered from his shoulders, down the curve of his back, to the dark jeans he was wearing.

Now that was some tight-fitting denim.

The material clung to his ass with the grip of a rock climber hanging onto a mountain for dear life. My eyes shot back up as I shook my head, clearing away all thoughts of Spencer's ass.

What was I doing? I never checked Spencer out.

Instead, I used my eyes for less nefarious purposes—looking at other people's food choices and silently judging them for it. *Just kidding!* I never did that, either.

The restaurant was packed. A variety of enticing smells wafted through the air. Always a good sign. Not that I liked fancy food. I was more of a "burger and beer at the bar" kinda guy. Heck, even my latest invention of cereal and ice cream managed to hit the spot tonight.

Snooty servers, gold-encrusted cutlery, and fine wine never really impressed me that much. But Spencer loved it, and hey, if being a good friend meant that I tagged along as he checked out some of the finest restaurants and bars in Boston, then I would happily scarf down some fancy food for the guy.

Of course, I'd never let him know that I secretly enjoyed it a little bit. Hence my too-cool-for-school exterior when we hit up places like this.

The surprisingly friendly and not at all snooty server showed us to our table, and we sat down. When he left, Spencer looked at me. "So," he said, his eyes gleaming excitedly. "This place looks kinda cool, hey? Do you like it?"

I gave a one-shoulder shrug. "Yeah. This place looks...all right." I was sticking to my usual nonchalant routine.

He smiled warmly back at me, knowing full well what I was doing, but happy to play along anyway. "You actually scrub up all right, you know?"

"Thanks," I laughed. "When I'm wearing a shirt, you mean?"

He laughed back.

Okay, here's the thing about Spencer's laugh.

You know when sometimes you see a dog that's just so ugly that you can't help but feel sorry for it and it totally makes you see it as the most adorable dog ever? Spencer had the human-laugh version of the ugly-cute dog.

He hated being loud and drawing attention to himself, so his laugh was more like a whisper. He produced the softest *tee-hee-hee* sound, which he then proceeded to always cover up with his hand. He'd close his eyes sometimes, too, especially when it was something really funny, as if he was trying to hold it all in.

My mission in life was to, one day, have Spencer James Montgomery let it all out.

"Yes," he replied, straightening himself up. "I'm pleasantly surprised to see that you even own a clean shirt."

I pouted my lips as I discreetly gave him the finger, placing it against my chin as if I were scratching an itch. This was a fancy restaurant, after all. I wasn't going to completely embarrass myself. Not yet, anyway.

He was right, though. I had grabbed the only clean shirt that was hanging in my closet and paired it with the cleanest dark pants I could find and a pair of black Vans. Yep, lace-ups and relatively clean-ish clothing was about as dressed up as I got.

The server returned with a pitcher of water and began to fill up our glasses. "Can I get you anything to drink, gentlemen? Perhaps some wine?"

I smiled stupidly, the way I did whenever someone called me a gentleman. Yes, I knew it was just a thing polite service staff said to patrons, and yes, I shouldn't have made anything more out of it than that, but it got me every single time. Because the last thing I was, was a gentleman.

Spencer looked over at me, a flicker of acknowledgement registering in his eyes. I knew that he knew what I was thinking, but with the server standing right there, he didn't want to say anything.

"What do you think, Cass?" He lowered his face, studying the drink menu.

"Why not? It's Friday night. What would Montell do?"

Spencer leaned forward, a glint in his eyes. "Is that our mantra for the evening, then?"

"Yes. Yes, it is." I shot back with a wink.

The server grinned. "What sort of wine are you in the mood for? Red, white, or something bubbly?"

"Red," we replied at the same time.

"Just nothing too..." I rubbed the tips of my fingers together, trying to find the word I was looking for.

"Peppery?" Spencer offered.

"Yes." I snapped my fingers. That was it. Spencer always knew what I meant without having to use those pesky things known as words. "Maybe something like what we had at that place—"

Spencer's eyes lit up in recognition. "Oh yeah, the place where you had the four desserts," he interrupted, finishing my sentence for me.

"That's the one." I beamed, leaning back in my chair. It's not easy to eat four rich, decadent desserts, but somehow, I managed to do it. It was a crowning achievement in a long list of food-related experiences and one I was justifiably proud of.

The server's head swung from left to right as if he were at a tennis match, trying to keep up with our conversation. "You guys are so adorable," he said with a genuinely warm smile on his face.

Spencer cleared his throat. "We'll have the 2016 Highwood Hills cabernet sauvignon, thanks. What have you got in the way of specials?"

God, I loved it when he sounded so...*gentlemanly.*

The server rattled off a whole bunch of different types of pasta that I had never heard of. Spencer, seeing my blank face, thanked him and let him know we would need a few moments.

"Did you understand anything of what he just said?" I leaned in and hid my face behind the menu. "I thought pasta was just pasta. What the hell is cavatelli or gemelli?"

Tee-hee-hee. Spencer ducked his head behind the leather-bound menu, too, his bright blue eyes shifting from side to side. We must have looked as if we were two naughty children up to no good. "Let me guess, you just want some spaghetti bolognese?"

"Yeah." I gave a serious nod. "Do you...do you think they even have it here?"

His eyes crinkled around the edges as he lifted his menu to conceal his smile. "You're such a shit sometimes," he whispered, recovering slightly. "Yes, I'm sure they have spaghetti bolognese. But I can double-check for you."

The server returned to take our order.

"Now"—Spencer said, eyeing the menu—"would you happen to have any spaghetti bolognese for my taste bud-challenged friend over here?"

"Hey," I protested. I wasn't expecting to get thrown under the bus like that. "Spag bol is a classic, am I right?" I motioned at the server.

He smiled as he wrote it down on his pad. "It certainly is." He turned to Spencer. "And for you, sir?"

"I'll have the seafood salad, thanks."

"Huh?"

It must have come out a little too loudly because it drew the attention of the elderly couple seated at the neighboring table, who shot me the eye equivalent of an irritated *tsk*.

"Why aren't you getting some of that fancy-sounding pasta? You can get a salad anywhere, Spence."

"Actually, I can't." Spencer patted his stomach. "Gotta eat clean to stay lean."

I sighed at the server. "Do you see what I have to deal with here?"

He smiled warmly at me and leaned over to whisper, "My boyfriend is exactly the same. He won't even let *me* have dessert."

"Oh, he's not my—I mean, we're not..." I sputtered.

Spencer and I had been mistaken for a couple so many times over the years, I had literally lost count. But sometimes, like right now, it still completely surprised me. It almost felt redundant at this point to correct people. It honestly didn't bother me if people thought we were a couple, and I knew Spencer felt the same.

I looked over at Spencer. He was leaning back in his chair, this time happily displaying his shit-eating grin for the entire restaurant to see. He was clearly enjoying my unsuccessful attempt to explain our situation to the server. I looked around and assessed my options, but there was no discreet way to give him the finger. Dammit.

Once he had double-checked our order, the server turned and left.

"Thanks for helping me out with that," I said, hoping I'd picked up on enough sarcasm from the kids at the center over the past year to be able to pull it off myself. Judging by Spencer's amused reaction, I hadn't.

"Hey, you were doing such a great job, I didn't want to butt in." He was looking way too pleased with himself. "So, anyway, tell me about your week, Cass."

I looked over at my best friend just as his eyes lifted to meet mine. A rush of something warm and familiar surged through me. I didn't know how he did it, but Spencer just had a way of making me feel so...good. I loved every single moment I spent with him.

I began to prattle off my usual tales of what the kids were up to and the center's never-ending financial woes, before launching into the constantly growing list of maintenance items that were either breaking or in such a fragile state that they were about to break.

And as always, Spencer sat there, listening intently. And I knew that he was really listening and not just pretending to, because he would often jump in with a question or make an observation. I was sure that my work bored the living daylights out of him, but he genuinely cared, and that meant everything to me.

The server returned with the drinks, carefully placing a large wine glass in front of each of us.

"And how was your week?" I asked Spencer as I took a sip of the red wine. It was delicious, went down smoothly, and wasn't the least bit peppery. "Mmm, good call on the wine, by the way."

"Thanks. Yeah, my week was good," he began. He took a sip of wine and swirled it in his mouth before swallowing it. Ah yes, that's how you're meant to do it. We had taken a wine tasting class together last spring, but somehow, I'd forgotten pretty much everything we had learned. I guess that's what happens when you skipped over the *spit after every mouthful* part.

"Any news about the promotion?" I asked.

Spencer's eyebrows squished together. "No, not yet." I could hear the dejection in his voice.

"Hey." I reached across the table and squeezed his hand. "You'll get it. You've been doing brilliant work lately. The Japanese fusion restaurant-slash-jazz bar. This place. I mean, look around. It's totally packed. And it's all because of you."

"Well." Spencer tugged at the top of his shirt.

It was a tell. I knew all of his tells, and this one meant he was uncomfortable.

"You're doing that thing," I pointed out.

"What thing?"

"That shirt or collar-pulling thing you do whenever you're uncomfortable."

"I am not." He brought both arms down and pressed his palms firmly onto the table.

Spencer hated accepting compliments. "It was a team effort, Cass. We all worked hard on all of those campaigns."

"Sure," I agreed. "But you're the one leading the team. Spence, if you want that promotion, you need to sell yourself."

He let out another adorable *tee-hee-hee,* and when he uncovered his mouth, he said, "Are you really telling someone who works in marketing and public relations how they should be promoting themselves?"

I chuckled. "Okay, sorry. I know you know this. But"—I lifted my wine glass—"you're a nice guy, Spencey. And you know where nice guys finish."

He considered my words before deftly moving on to other work-related stuff. I must have zoned out for a minute because the next thing I knew, he was staring at me.

"What?" I blinked twice before looking him over. A wicked

look danced across his features. "You're up to something, Spence. I can tell. What is it?"

"What?" His voice lifted by an octave. His eyes widened all innocent-like, and he gave me his most earnest *I'm up to something but doing my best to hide it from you* face. I wasn't buying it.

"I know you, Spencer James Montgomery. I can tell there's something on your mind. You're not fooling anyone."

A rosy hue filled his cheeks.

I shook my head and let out a giggle. "Now spill, Mister."

3

SPENCER

That's the thing about knowing someone since you were six years old. There was no way to hide anything from them. Any off sideward glance, any movement that was ever so slightly out of the ordinary, was picked up on—and examined ruthlessly—in an instant. That could be both a good and a bad thing.

"Okay, then. You got me, Cass. I do have an ulterior motive for inviting you to dinner."

He smirked, narrowing his light brown eyes at me. "I knew it."

I brought the wine to my lips and took another sip, considering my approach. "You know how I've just finished working on that rebranding campaign for the hotel in Florida?"

Cassius nodded firmly. "Yeah. That was a huge project for you. One of your biggest so far, right?"

"Right. They did a huge refurbishment, overhauling the place completely. It was built in the 1980s, and it looked like, well—like it had been built in the 1980s."

Cassius' bottom lip curled up into a smile.

I continued. "Anyway, now the place looks amazing."

"Ooh, the slogan could be, 'Puts the *zing* in amazing.'"

I let out a small laugh, bringing my hand to cover my lips as I shook my head. Then I thought about it. "Actually, that's not the worst idea you've ever had."

"You are free to use it, my friend," Cassius said as he went for an over-the-top head bow. But he got a little too cocky for his own good, the accompanying hand gesture almost knocking his glass of wine off the table. He managed to catch it in the nick of time. Our elderly table neighbors shot us another unimpressed look. I was starting to tally them up in my head.

"Getting back to the campaign. It was..." I trailed off. I hated talking about myself or anything that resembled boasting or bragging, which, I know, I know, was weird for someone who worked in PR.

But what drew me to this career was not about selling a bunch of useless crap to people who didn't need it.

What I liked about my line of work was that it focused my energy on the good, putting a positive spin on things and helping people and businesses do better. It wasn't as altruistic and feel-good as what Cassius did, but in my own way, it made me feel like I was doing something positive. That was all I wanted—to do good. I didn't like talking myself up and ruthlessly climbing the corporate ladder, fucking people over along the way. That was not my thing at all.

Cassius, as always, picked up on my hesitation. "The campaign was a huge success. I know."

I scrunched up my eyebrows. "How do you know?"

"Uh, because of, like, the ten million views on YouTube that it got. I probably contributed about a million of them myself." He chuckled, drawing his tongue along his lower lip, which for some reason, I was unable to look away from.

"I am the target market, after all," he went on. "And hot dudes dancing in nothing but speedos...in slow motion..." Cassius cocked his head to the side, letting his tongue fall out of his mouth completely. I never realized how long his tongue was. My eyes stayed glued to it. "I couldn't remember what you were selling, Spencey, but I was buying it."

Another laugh escaped me, which I quickly tried to hide. Cassius was right, though—the video had been a huge viral hit. And while it may not have been the most highbrow campaign I ever came up with, it did what it was intended to do. It booked the resort solid through until the end of summer—two years from now.

"One spaghetti bolognese and one seafood marinara salad," the server announced as he placed our plates carefully on the table in front of us. "Would either one of you like some cracked pepper?"

I shook my head, but Cassius nodded. "Yes please." The server sprinkled some pepper over his spaghetti bolognese.

"That's great, thank you," he said.

The server shot us both a warm smile. "My pleasure. Let me know if I can get you anything else." And with that, he walked away.

"So," I continued. "The resort is called Elysian, and it's in Key West, Florida." I paused for a second and studied Cassius' face for any sign of recognition of that name. I got nothing. "Have you heard of it?"

He shook his head as he tried to tame a long strand of pasta around his fork. "No. Why? Should I have?"

"Yeah. It's only, like, the number one all-male luxury resort in the world."

Cassius gave an insouciant shrug as he accomplished his most important mission: successfully navigating food into his mouth. "If you say so."

"You don't sound too impressed," I observed. "You know all-male means gay, right? It's a resort for gay guys. I mean, everyone is welcome, of course, but it's a place where gay men can feel safe and comfortable and be themselves."

Cassius nodded and continued eating. I took a bite of my salad.

I knew Cassius hated labels, and I had my work cut out for me here. I understood why he thought labels were limiting and, in today's world, borderline redundant. I didn't think people should box themselves in either, but sometimes, for some people, labels could be useful.

People like me.

Cassius had no problem with being gay. And he had the most supportive mom and two great sisters who were there for him when he came out to them in the last year of high school. It's just that, for whatever reason, Cassius always seemed to shy away from gay bars, gay parties, heck, even other gay dudes.

His love life was almost as sad and pathetic as mine.

Almost.

I'd only ever slept with one girl. Cassius was a good-looking guy, so I was sure he got a lot more action in that department than I did. Not that he ever talked that much about it. Oddly, that was the only topic we never really broached in any significant detail.

We ate in silence for a while. He was staring down at his food, clearly avoiding me. The last thing I wanted was to make him feel bad or uncomfortable, but I also knew that I had to keep pressing if I wanted an answer. I needed this trip—and not just to get a better tan. It was my chance to tell him the truth.

My truth.

Okay, I had gotten him eating pasta. Now it was time to defuse the situation with some humor.

"You should be a little more impressed. From everything I've seen, this place now ranks up there as one of the best luxury resorts not just in the country, but in the world. It's totally...ritzy."

His head cranked up. Insults about my use of the word "ritzy" should start in approximately three...tw—

"Ritzy?"

Bingo!

He dropped his fork to his plate with a loud *clang*, earning us another eye scolding from the elderly couple next to us. "I don't think I've heard that word since the '90s."

"Yeah, well, I'm bringing it back."

I raised my hand and fished my cell phone out of my front pocket. I made it look like it was ringing and I absolutely had to answer it. I brought the phone to my ear, nodding earnestly a few times. I covered the phone with my hand. "Oh, hey, Cass. This just in: Montell Jordan approves."

Cassius looked around the restaurant, his eyes darting furiously, before he met my gaze square on and gave me the finger.

"Cass," I exclaimed, dipping my head low. I could feel myself starting to blush.

He sat back farther in his seat, looking mighty pleased with himself that he managed to get the rise out of me that he wanted. Like he always did.

"I assume there's a point to you telling me all about this all-male —which is secret code for gay—resort, Spence?"

I pushed some of the salad around my plate as I nodded. "There is. They were so impressed with the results of the campaign that they have very kindly gifted me a long weekend stay in their brand-new deluxe ocean villa. It's their way of saying 'thank you' for a job well done."

Cassius seemed genuinely happy for me. "Awww, that's great, Spence."

He lifted another forkful of spaghetti bolognese to his mouth, apparently oblivious to where I was going with this. Before I went for the big one, I needed a minor detour.

"How's the food?" I asked.

He chewed on it for a while longer with a faux-serious expression, like he was a chef on one of those TV cooking shows, analyzing the bite he was taking with an almost scientific precision. "Let's just say it's a step up from cereal and ice cream."

My lips lifted. "Good. I'm glad."

Okay, this was it. He had made fun of me, and he was liking the meal. The timing was perfect. I waited for a moment as he scooped up another too-large-for-his-fork mouthful and crammed the pasta into his mouth.

Time to strike.

"So, I've booked us in to visit next weekend."

His jaw stopped moving mid-chew. A few seconds later, his mouth flew open.

"Cass, that's gross. Close your mouth, man."

He snapped it shut as he furiously tried to wolf down his food. He reached for the napkin and wiped the corners of his mouth. "You did what now?"

"C'mon, Cass." I threw him my double *hopeful smile, wide-eye* combo look that sometimes worked on him. Hopefully, this time would be one of those times.

"It'll be fun," I went on. "You do remember that, don't you? Having fun?"

He shot me a pointed look but didn't say anything.

"When is the last time we"—I waved my hand between us—"did something fun?"

"Hey, I have fun all the time. I...gwerk."

I wasn't buying it, and I could tell that Cassius knew it. He tilted his head to the side, considering my question.

I did the same, trying to cast my mind back to the last time we actually did something fun. Something fun *out*, that was. Because every time we hung out together, we had a good time. I didn't mean lazy Sundays watching TV or me dragging Cass to my new favorite restaurant. I was trying to think of the last time we went out somewhere, let loose, got wasted, and had such a brilliant time that we couldn't remember any of it the next day. I honestly couldn't remember.

"We are officially the most boring twenty-three-year-olds in the world, Cass."

Cassius scratched the side of his face and shot me a look I couldn't recognize. "You're so cute when you get like this."

I sat up a little taller. "Like what?"

"You get so...earnest."

I didn't know what to do with that. So, I shrugged the comment off and continued with my argument—less earnestly this time. "Look, Cass, it will do us both a world of good to get away. Just you and me. They've given me an amazing suite, right on the ocean. It's got two huge rooms, each with a California king-sized bed. There's twenty-four-seven room service. A massive pool. You'll love it. It's, like, next-level ritzy."

Cassius smiled. His facade of resistance was cracking, but I still needed something to make it fully crumble.

"Two words," I said, lifting two fingers. "Swimup bar."

He looked at me quizzically. "That sounds like it should be three words...or at least be two hyphenated words."

"Don't be an asshat."

His lips hinted at a smile, which he looked like he was trying— and failing—to suppress.

"And what is a swimup bar, pray tell? Because it sounds like exercise, and you know how I feel about that."

"Exercise? No." I laughed into my drink. "How do you not know what a swimup bar is, Cass?"

"I don't know a lot of shit."

"Yeah, no kidding."

After I explained that a swimup bar was literally a bar in a swimming pool, where you could—as the name implied—literally swim up to order a drink without having to get out of the pool, Cassius nodded.

But he still hadn't given me what I was trying to pry from him: an answer.

Alrighty, time for the pièce de résistance to really seal the deal.

I took another sip of wine, savoring the rich flavor of the red, as well as my imminent victory. "Apparently, there's a great hiking trail near the resort."

His eyebrows twitched. Ever so slightly. To anyone else, they wouldn't have noticed a thing. But I did.

"That's...cool." He tried to sound casual.

"And"—I was on a roll now—"you don't have to worry about work."

"I don't?"

"Nope. I've spoken to Olivia, and she has rearranged your schedule, so you are free from appointments and meetings from next Thursday until Tuesday. So that means we can have a five-day getaway."

"It looks like you thought of everything, haven't you?"

I couldn't conceal my smile, so I didn't even bother. "Yes, I have—and you're welcome."

And that's when it happened. The moment when Cassius' Mr. Too Cool For School exterior finally collapsed. "Thank you, Spencer." His voice was soft, his tone genuine. "Thank you for this dinner, and thank you for this trip. It's so thoughtful of you. And you know what? You're right. We do need to have more fun. I think this weekend getaway is just what we both need."

His words sent a warm shiver up my spine. "That's awesome, Cass. I'm glad you're on board. Besides, maybe staying at an all-male resort might be the place for you to meet someone."

Cassius rolled his eyes. "Yeah, right. My love life is a complete fuckery wrapped in a shitshow surrounded by a catastrophe. You know that, Spence."

His words tugged at my heart. I couldn't figure out why Cassius had such bad luck with dudes. It certainly wasn't him. He was one of a kind amazing. Passionate. Goodhearted. A loyal friend. Funny (though sometimes less than he thought he was). The only negatives I could come up with were his appalling dance moves and questionable food choices, but they were hardly deal-breakers.

"You just haven't found the right guy yet, Cass. But you will. All the guys you've met so far have just been total asshats."

He giggled. "That's such a funny word, *asshat*. Like, why would an ass be wearing a hat?"

I cupped my hands over my mouth as the mental image of an

ass wearing a hat formed in my mind. "Oh my god. Now I can't stop picturing an ass wearing a hat."

The fun-hating couple looked at us again, directing a loud and unmissable disapproving "tsk" at us. I stopped laughing. I hated making people upset or uncomfortable. Even snooty, elderly asshats.

Cassius raised his glass. "To us."

"What about us?" I asked, raising my glass, too.

"This is going to be an awesome weekend. Plus, we've been friends for how long?"

"Since we were six," I said.

"Right." Cassius tipped his head up and squinted. "So, if we're twenty-three now, and we've known each other since we were six...that means..." He started reciting some numbers, but I knew this was going to fall flat. "Twenty-seven years?"

I chuckled. "Close. Try seventeen."

"Holy shit, that's still pretty impressive."

"More impressive than your math skills, yes."

Our glasses clinked—but not too loudly, I made sure of that. I didn't want any more disapproving stares or sounds directed at us.

"And you know what the really crazy thing is?" he added after taking a sip. "We haven't had a single fight in all of that time. Not a single big, proper fight in seventeen years. That's incredible, don't you think?"

I considered it for a moment and realized he was right. Sure, we'd had some petty, minor disagreements over the years, but we'd never had a major blowup or fight.

Ever.

"Yeah, that is incredible," I echoed, still reflecting on all the years we had known each other.

"And you know what else?" Cassius leaned in closer and lowered his voice. "We haven't fucked either. That's not a bad achievement for a gay guy and his straight best friend."

I raised my glass again. "To friendships with no fighting."

"And no fucking," Cassius added one more time for good measure, clinking our glasses together—loudly.

For just a tiny second, I stopped caring about what anyone else thought. Right there, in that moment, my heart was so full of happiness I thought it would burst.

I looked over at Cassius, my best friend of seventeen years. He made me feel like I was the luckiest guy alive. I wanted the feeling to last forever.

I hummed into my wine glass. But part of me knew that it wouldn't. What I wanted to tell Cassius would change things between us. Despite that, I knew I had to tell him.

And a weekend getaway was the perfect chance to do just that.

THURSDAY

4

CASSIUS

"Your boyfriend's here." Olivia's familiar taunt rang out loudly in the shoebox that also doubled as the center's administration office.

I breathed in sharply, preparing to shout my usual retort. "He's not my"—four steps (literally) took me from the desk in my sardine tin of an office into the waiting room—"boyfriend," I replied, ending much quieter than I began.

I ignored her teasing and smiled as I took Spencer in. He was standing by the door, wearing a white cashmere sweater, light blue jeans, and khaki-colored suede leather boat shoes. How was he always able to look so put together? Meanwhile, my internal clothes-picking conversation went something like this:

Good Cassius: *Let's do some laundry today so we have clean clothes to choose from.*
Bad Cassius: *Meh, this shirt only has visible stains if you squint reeeeally hard. Let's just wear it and hope for dim lighting.*

Nine times out of ten, Bad Cassius won out.

I walked over to Spencer and whispered in his ear. "I know I pinky-swore not to call you Fred, but come on, man."

Spencer pulled away and looked down at himself. His eyes widened as it hit him. He was dressed, literally, as Fred Jones from Scooby Doo. He let out a nervous giggle. "At least I didn't wear an orange ascot tie."

I wagged a finger in his face.

"Okay, I will burn this outfit the second we touch down in Florida. Promise."

My lips twitched. "Good. That's what we call teamwork."

Olivia cleared her throat. Loudly. Like she had a frog stuck in it or something. "Ooh, and he brought you flowers," she said in that mildly annoying singsong voice that only she could pull off successfully, keeping the annoyance level capped at mild.

Spencer blushed as he produced a beautiful bouquet of flowers he'd been hiding behind his back. He looked slightly unsure of himself.

"Flowers. Again?" I asked.

"Again?" Olivia quirked an eyebrow in my direction.

I looked back at Spencer. "What's the occasion this time?"

"Actually," Spencer began as a smile stretched across his face. "These aren't for you, Cass." He turned to face Olivia. "They're for you." He walked over and handed the flowers to her.

Olivia stood up from behind her desk. The woman loved color, and she wasn't afraid to rock a six-inch heel, either. Today, she was wearing a red-and-yellow polka dot dress with bright blue pumps.

The shoes didn't match her dress, but as she reached her hand out to take the flowers from Spencer, I noticed her bright blue fingernails. Ah, so if you didn't have a handbag, you could match your shoes with fingernails instead. Good to know.

"For me?" Olivia lifted the flowers to her face and whiffed in their scent. "They smell amazing. Thank you so much, Spencer. This is so thoughtful of you."

Spencer's cheeks were on a one-way track to Redsville. "Yeah, well, I wanted to thank you for giving Cass some time off."

"Oh, please," she said, waving her perfectly manicured hand in the air. "Feel free to take him off my hands more often." She was definitely the coolest manager I'd ever had. Also, the only manager I'd ever had, but I was pretty sure her coolness level was rare; so I appreciated it.

I smirked at her comment and once he was sans flowers, pulled Spencer in for a quick hug. I could feel the heat of Olivia's gaze on my skin. Friends hugged, right? There was nothing unusual about that. But, of course, like everyone else in the world, Olivia was under the misguided assumption that there was more between Spencer and me than just friendship.

"Oh, hey, Rocky," Jean said, sauntering in through the front door. Her eyes darted from Spencer to Olivia to me and then back to Olivia again.

"Rocky?" Spencer crinkled up his nose in confusion, shooting me a *what the hell* look.

I let out a deep sigh. "Uhhhh, it's nothing."

"Cassius encouraged us to kill birds on a hike a year ago by throwing rocks at them," Jean said with a smile in her voice.

"Cassius!" Spencer shot me an equally exasperated look to match his tone.

I raised my palms into the air. "I can assure everyone, no birds were injured, or harmed, or killed, during that hike."

"The kids wanted to call him bird killer, but we quickly shut that down since we couldn't allow language like that around people who have experienced trauma," Olivia chimed in. "Turns out that Cassius delivered a memorable Rocky-inspired speech on that same hike, so that's how he earned the nickname."

"We've been calling him Rocky ever since."

I really wished they wouldn't. Or, at least they'd get bored of it and move on to something else. I'd done plenty of embarrassing things since then.

The time I had hot dog mustard on my cheek and spent half the afternoon walking around with it on my face without realizing sprang to mind.

Or there was that time where I sat down on the old leather couch in the game room and it sounded like I'd let one rip.

Even the time I accidentally stapled my thumb to a piece of paper, and I cried—yes, as in *tears falling from my eyes* cried—because I was a baby with a pain threshold of zero-point-nothing.

Any one of those events could have warranted the creation of a new, better, funnier nickname, but for whatever reason, the kids liked Rocky, so I was stuck with it.

"Now, Jean"—I turned to the instigator of this maddening conversation as I spotted Spencer grinning like an idiot out of the corner of my eye—"I assume you came in here for something other than to make fun of me?"

"Uh, yeah." She looked over at Olivia, and I could have sworn they exchanged a funny look between them. "The shower is leaking again. It's pretty bad."

"Goddammit," I grumbled.

"Thank you for letting us know," Olivia said in a strangely stilted way as Jean turned around to leave. But not before casting a glance at Spencer, then me, then Olivia, then back at Spencer.

"How much time have we got before we need to get to the airport, Spence?"

"I've planned everything out so that we get there with thirty minutes to spare. Why, how much time do you need to fix the shower?"

"Half an hour should be fine," I replied.

"But that doesn't leave us with a window. What if there's traffic? What if the car breaks down? What if—"

"What if you help me so that I get it done in half the time?"

"Good thinking, Cassius." I felt Olivia's hand on my back, and I could have sworn she was giving me a gentle shove out of the

waiting room. "I'll keep an eye on your luggage while you boys fix
that pesky leaking shower."

"Great," I said, hooking my arm around Spencer's neck as he
dropped his backpack onto the floor in the corner of the room.
"Let's get this done, and then we can get our getaway on."

Less than five minutes later, we were back in the waiting room.

"That was weird," I said to Olivia, who was feverishly typing
away on the computer.

She looked up, pulling back a loose strand of hair around her
ear. "What's weird?"

"The shower's fine. It's not leaking at all."

"Oh." She turned her gaze back to the screen. "You know what
kids are like."

I looked over at Spencer and was met with a confused shrug.

"Anyway"—he glanced down at his watch—"at least this means
we'll get to the airport with twenty-five minutes to spare."

"Cool." I ducked into my office. "Let me just grab my bag."

"Bag? As in just the one?" he asked, picking up his backpack off
the floor and slugging it over his shoulder.

"Uh, yeah. Why? How many bags are you bringing?"

He shuffled his feet and looked down. "So...I've got this
backpack and then...four pieces of full-sized luggage in the car."

"Four!" Olivia and I exclaimed at the same time.

"Who are you? Diana Ross?" she joked.

I leaned over for a high five. "Nice one." It felt nice not being
the butt of a joke around here for once.

We both looked over at Spencer. He was tugging at the top of
his cashmere sweater, the way he always did whenever he was
unsure of himself. His face looked a little flushed, too. "What?" His
eyes flicked between Olivia and me. "I like having options, okay?"

"Hey, options are good." I gave him a friendly smile as I slung
my one and only bag over my shoulder.

"Options are great," Olivia said as her lips curled into a devilish
smirk. "Have a great weekend, you guys."

"We will." I waved back over my shoulder.

As we were being driven to the airport, I gazed out the window, thinking about the upcoming weekend. I still had some reservations about it, but I tried to put them out of my mind.

I wasn't good with change. It was never something that I liked or sought out—and that included changes to my carefully calibrated daily routine, like, say, my best friend swooping in to whisk me away for a weekend of fun in the sun.

Spencer knew that about me. And I was certain that he'd have every minute of the weekend planned out in a spreadsheet, and that made me feel better. Like I was being taken care of and looked after.

Going to an all-male resort was *waaaay* out of my comfort zone. Spencer knew that, too. I didn't know why, but I'd never been fully comfortable in the gay scene. It made no sense, since between my mom, sisters, and Spencer, I had the kind of love and support that any gay person could hope for. They didn't just accept me, they were also my biggest cheerleaders.

From the small glimpses I had gotten of the gay scene—by which I meant a few short visits to gay bars when I was in college—I was left with a feeling of being out of place.

Gay guys seemed so confident and polished. Meanwhile, I was a gwerking gwidiot.

Sure, I'd dated a little. And by dated, I meant had a series of semi-awkward dates that in most instances led to detached sex that felt mechanical. Almost robotic.

Maybe that was it. Maybe my problem was that I wasn't good at sex, which would be a deal-breaker for any typical red-blooded gay guy.

I hated short-term.

I hated casual.

I hated bad sex.

Despite the sputtering start my dating life had gotten off to, I actually did want full-on, long-term love.

Like, movie-level *falling in love on the beach with my special person while fireworks erupted in the background* kind of love.

Forever love.

As my mind ruminated on the list of things that could be wrong with me that prevented me from finding the right guy, a small smile broke through on my face. Even if I was bad at sex, at least I knew it couldn't have been my ace dance moves or the killer food combinations I came up with on a regular basis that were throwing guys off.

The cereal and ice cream creation was just the latest in a long line of concoctions I'd created. My previous favorite was a unique take on a kale smoothie. My twist? Replacing the kale with gin.

I leaned my head back against the seat. I knew the perfect guy was out there.

Somewhere.

I cast a glance over at Spencer. He was looking out the window. My chest tingled with appreciation for him.

For being such a wonderful friend.

For inviting me on what I knew would ultimately be an awesome getaway because he would have planned it to perfection.

For letting me be me and never judging me for what I secretly knew were terrible dance moves and godawful food combinations that would wreak havoc on any normal person's digestive system.

It *was* going to be a great weekend.

I nodded firmly, willing myself to believe it. I nudged Spencer's arm and his head jerked around toward me. "We're going to have the best time, Spencey. I can't wait. Thank you again for all of this."

His eyes met mine. For just a moment, they grew a little darker. Like I'd interrupted him in the middle of a serious thought. He shot me a closed-lip smile.

"Yeah, we will, Cass. We will. I can't wait, either."

5

SPENCER

Clink.

The sides of our glasses touched. Cassius' eyes sparkled like glitter. "And they just keep bringing the alcohol out? For the whole flight? For free?" His voice kept getting higher with each question, like he couldn't believe his good fortune.

I took a sip of the complimentary bubbly before answering with a nod.

"Wow." Cassius drained three quarters of his glass in one go.

It was his first time flying anything other than coach. I'd used my points and upgraded our tickets to business class. I liked doing nice things for Cassius. Seeing his reaction made it so worth it.

I leaned in toward him. "Just take it easy. Alcohol affects you differently in the air."

"I'll be fine. I can handle it." He waved his hand at me before finishing off the rest of the drink.

"Another drink, sir?" The attendant's timing was perfect.

Cassius leaned across me, holding his empty glass out. The scent of his shower gel wafted into my nostrils. "Why, thank you."

With his glass topped up, I couldn't help but let out a quiet chuckle. "I'm serious, Cass. Take it easy with those."

A few moments later, as the wheels lifted off the tarmac, I felt Cassius' head land on my shoulder. I looked across and saw his half-drunk glass perched perilously close to the edge of his fold-out tray.

As I reached over and grabbed his drink, I heard Cassius breathing heavily. A breath later, it had shifted into purring. Finally, Cassius' sleepy noises settled on a light humming sound, stopping (thankfully) before descending into snoring territory.

Yep, that was Cassius—the lightweight I knew and loved.

I held on to both of our drinks until the attendant collected them from me once we'd reached flying altitude. By that point, Cassius *was* snoring. But it was quiet and sounded almost...nice?

I shuffled in my seat, lowering my shoulder so that he would be more comfortable. It was a four-hour flight, and I didn't want him getting off the plane with a sore neck. That would not be an ideal start to our getaway.

I moved as slowly and carefully as I could to not disturb him and fished my phone out of my pants. Tapping away with one hand, I was able to bring up the spreadsheet of our itinerary that I had created. I was quietly confident that I had come up with the perfect combination of low-key, relaxing activities—such as hanging out by the pool, going for walks on the beach—with some more high energy experiences like hiking and a snorkeling boat trip.

I'd also—conveniently—peppered the weekend with multiple opportunities for "us" time, so that I could have the conversation I wanted to have with him. And yes, I realized the inherent contradiction in planning spontaneity, but that was just me. I had to do it. Telling him was already nerve-wracking enough as it was, I didn't want to add stressing about finding the right time to do it as well.

I peered down without moving my head and could see Cassius'

chest heaving with every breath he took. His warm body felt heavy against mine, and I liked it. I let out a breath through my nose.

God, how I hoped I wouldn't fuck everything up.

With a few taps on my phone screen, I closed my weekend itinerary and reopened the SoS spreadsheet. I tilted my phone slightly away from Cassius, just in case he were to wake up. I didn't need him seeing the notes I had been taking over the last six months.

It might have sounded pathetic and clinical—documenting all the information I could find online about sexuality—but I actually found it quite helpful. Until I had started looking into it, I was only aware of three sexual orientations: gay, straight, and bi. None of them felt right for me, which was why I started digging a little deeper.

The more I read, the more my mind opened. Over the past few months, I had discovered that there was a lot more to human sexuality than I had ever thought possible. At first, it was a little overwhelming.

Okay, a lot overwhelming.

Like, *holy shitballs, what rabbit hole have I fallen into?* overwhelming.

But that's where the organizational power of a spreadsheet came to the fore.

As I found information that felt right to me, I either recorded it in an existing tab or created a separate tab for it, as needed. Arranged alphabetically, of course, all the way from *A* to Z. Or in this case, *A* to *S*, as "straight" was the final tab.

My eyes flicked over the different headings.

Allosexual. Bicurious. Demiromantic. Graysexual. Omnisexual. Panromantic. Straight.

Looking at the terms, with my best friend's body pressed against mine, I let out another steady breath.

I didn't know which tab I belonged to. But there was one thing I did know for certain, I wasn't straight. At least not entirely.

And one way or another, I wanted to share that part of myself with Cassius.

I rested my phone on the tray table. My eyelids grew heavy and I closed my eyes, letting my mind drift off into the clouds.

The driver pulled into Elysian Resort, and boy oh boy, it looked amazing. I mean, I had spent months working on the campaign, so I'd seen hundreds of photos and videos of the place, but driving up the palm tree-lined cobblestone driveway was something else entirely.

My shoulders relaxed and I instantly felt a weight of worry lifting off me. There was nothing quite like the first few moments of a vacation—the excitement of being at a new place; the newness of the surroundings; everything feeling, smelling, looking so fresh and alive.

The car doors were opened for us, and as I got out, I was greeted by a light salty mist in the air as the tropical breeze brushed my skin. It felt divine.

"How good is this?" I asked, glancing over at Cassius. He stood by the side of the car with his eyes closed, taking a deep breath in. He looked to be enjoying the moment of arrival as much as I was.

"I feel like I've arrived in paradise. How nice is this weather?" he asked, slowly opening his eyes to take in our lush surroundings.

"Yes, I believe the local term for it is 'warm.'"

He let out a laugh, a typical Cassius bark that was always a few decibels too loud, often drawing the attention of people around him. Not that he cared, and, strangely, not that I minded, either. We were on vacation. It was time to loosen up a little.

I heard the car trunk shut, and I spun around. Two attendants were placing our luggage—okay, mostly my luggage and Cassius' one bag—onto a gold-colored cart. Once all the bags had been heaped on, one attendant pushed the cart toward the front door while the other attendant walked over to us.

"Welcome to the Elysian." He smiled warmly. "How was your flight?"

"It was great, thank you. We're pumped to be here," I replied.

"If you would like to follow me, let's get you gentlemen checked in so that your vacation can begin."

He turned and we trailed behind, still basking in the magnificent weather and excitement for the weekend stretching out ahead of us.

"Gentlemen?" Cassius mouthed, his eyebrows wagging excitedly. Being called a gentleman always drew a reaction out of him. And his predictable reaction always drew the same predictable response out of me: mild giggling and head shaking.

The first attendant who was pushing the cart with our luggage craned his head over his shoulder. "You guys sure did pack a lot."

"Yeah, well, Spencer here likes to have options, you see." Cassius patted my shoulder.

I nudged into him playfully. "Yeah, like the option of pushing you into that flowerbed over there."

The attendant smiled but didn't say anything else. We followed him through the automatic glass doors that opened to reveal the exquisite resort lobby. Again, something I'd seen in countless photos and videos, but in person it really was something else.

The floor-to-ceiling windows with views out to the ocean caught my eye immediately. The cloudless sky allowed the sun to stream in, filling the space with so much natural light; the amazing blues of the ocean danced in the distance; and the elegant, ivy-filled furniture gave the place a polished, luxe vibe.

Cassius elbowed me and motioned for me to look up. We were standing beneath a series of glittering chandelier columns. It was all very, *very* impressive. The refurbishment had clearly been worth every single cent.

The attendant led us to a sleek, all-white marble reception

desk. He turned to face us, flashing the same warm smile he had greeted us with.

"This is where I leave you, gentlemen. I hope you both have a wonderful stay with us."

"Thank you." I slipped a note of cash into his palm, and he smiled and walked away. I placed my forearms on the cold marble countertop, and with Cassius beside me doing the same, our eyes focused on the man behind the desk who was walking over to us.

"Good afternoon, gentlemen." The timbre of his voice was smooth and deep. He was an older guy, maybe in his early forties. He had an all-American look with big eyes and a strong jaw. "Welcome to Elysian. Can I have your booking name, please?"

"It's under Montgomery. Spencer Montgomery."

"Spencer!" His eyes lit up. "I'm Leo. We've emailed and spoken on the phone a million times."

Holy shit!

Leo Carter didn't just work behind the counter—he owned the place.

"Oh my gosh," I squawked an octave higher than intended. "What are you doing here? I mean, not here in the resort. You own it. I mean, here at reception."

He let out a low chuckle. "I'm very hands-on with this place. It's my baby. I bought it ten years ago when it was just a few beachside shacks and a run-down two-story building that barely met code."

I looked around the incredible foyer we were standing in and couldn't believe the transformation he had achieved with the place. I pressed my forearms onto the counter, leaning in toward him as I spoke. "Look, I can sell pretty much anything. It doesn't mean that it's actually any good. But this place, Leo, what you've done here really is beautiful. It's luxurious but relaxed. Upscale, yet personal."

Leo tipped his head graciously. "That's very kind of you to say, Spencer. You sound like a walking version of our website. I love it."

"Well, I did write most of it," I admitted, instantly feeling my cheeks burning up.

"And you did a great job with it. And not just the website—all of the marketing work you've done has been impeccable. The modern rebranding with the new logo, fonts, and colors; all the marketing collateral you developed; the press and media attention you garnered; the giveaway contest. Everything you touched turned to gold, Spencer."

Okay, now my cheeks were on fire. Damn the Floridian humidity.

"And that video, Spencer. Holy cow. We've never had anything go viral like that before."

I smiled, dipping my head slightly. "Thanks."

"It's all true, Spencer." Leo's eyes met mine. "I've sung your praises to your manager, too."

"You didn't have to do that." A familiar feeling of uncomfortableness brewed in my gut. It was the feeling I'd get whenever someone complimented me.

"I know I didn't have to. But I wanted to. If you'll pardon my French, you did a fan-fucking-tastic job, Spencer. And I'm a firm believer that good work deserves recognition and reward. Which is why I'm delighted that you and your"—Leo looked over at Cassius —"boyfriend are visiting us this weekend."

I smiled wryly. Cassius and I had been mistaken for boyfriends so many times it seemed comical at this point. It happened pretty much every time we went out in public together. Part of me didn't feel like correcting Leo. We were at an all-male gay resort, after all. What did it matter if people thought we were a couple?

"Oh, we're not together," Cassius chimed in. "We're best friends. Spencer's not even gay. I'm Cassius, by the way."

Leo met Cassius' outstretched hand with a firm shake.

I glanced sideways at Cassius, furrowing my brow. The words sounded strange coming out of his mouth. He was right, of course. We were just friends, but for some reason, I didn't like hearing him say that. The words sounded cold, and biting, and completely out of place in this warm, tropical paradise.

Besides, why did it even have to be said? In the twenty-first century, why did it even matter?

"Oh, I'm sorry. My mistake." Leo looked over at me apologetically.

"It's fine. Don't worry about it. Happens all the time." It was only as I spoke that I realized how tightly clenched my jaw had become.

What the hell was that about?

Leo turned his attention to the computer screen. "Ah, I see we have you here until Monday. Perfect. There are a few parties happening this weekend, as well as a number of sightseeing tours of the surrounding area. So, if you boys are up for fun, you will have your pick of things to see and do."

He slid two sheets of paper across the countertop. "Here is some information you might be interested in reading. It lists some of the good restaurants in downtown Key West, ways to get around, suggestions of good places for sightseeing, that sort of thing."

Cass leaned over to me and whisper-smiled, "Won't this interfere with your itinerary?"

He then straightened up and looked across at Leo. "Spencer is the king of spreadsheets. He has everything planned out, down to the last detail."

Leo shot me a knowing look.

"Actually, Cass, Leo and I have been in touch, and I've coordinated our weekend so that we can take part in some of these activities"—I lifted the sheets of paper and waved them in front of him—"while also having some quiet chill time, too."

That wiped the smugness right off his face.

"I'll organize your tickets to the White Party on Saturday night, as we discussed." Leo turned to me. "Everything else will be in your suite. Oh, and I've arranged for you both to have unlimited, complimentary drink vouchers for your entire stay."

"Wow, thank you so much, Leo. That's very kind of you." Cassius' words were laced with genuine appreciation. "Though I'm not much of a drinker."

I let out a sharp laugh, quickly covering my mouth. "He had a glass and a half of champagne on the flight down here and was out stone cold."

Leo smiled brightly. "In that case, I'll also throw in all your meals. How does that sound? Do you like to eat?"

"Do I?" Cassius' eyes grew so wide I thought they'd fall off his face. He looked like he'd just won the lottery, which for someone who could put away as much food as he could, I guessed he had. "Thanks, Leo."

"It's my pleasure." Leo reached across the counter and slid over two key cards. "Your suite is still being prepared, so why don't you boys head down to the pool? There's a meet and greet event being held there at the moment."

Cassius and I looked back at Leo with blank faces. Noticing this, he continued. "It happens every Thursday and Friday afternoon. We get a lot of new guests arriving for the weekend as well as previous guests returning. So everyone congregates by the pool area, catching up with old friends and making new ones. It's a way to get the weekend off to a great start."

Wow, what a genuinely lovely thing to do. I had never stayed at a hotel or resort before that did such a thing. It was a novel idea and great for people like Cassius and me, who didn't know anyone else here.

"What a cool idea," I said, and Leo beamed.

"You can leave your luggage here," he went on. "I'll arrange for an attendant to let you know once your suite is ready."

"That sounds great. Thank you so much for looking after us, Leo. I really appreciate it." I shot him a genuine smile to acknowledge his generosity.

"We both do," Cassius added as I felt his arm wrapping around my lower back.

"If there's anything you need during your stay here—anything at all—please don't hesitate to let me know. You did such a great job for us, Spencer. Now it's my turn to do everything I can to make sure you and Cassius enjoy yourselves and have a wonderful stay with us."

"Oh, we will." I gave a firm nod, leaning into Cassius' touch. "It's going to be the best weekend ever."

6

CASSIUS

We left the reception area and made our way to the poolside meet and greet, which Leo had told us was down a short path and couldn't be missed. As we stepped outside onto a pathway framed by lush, dense gardens, I felt the warmth of the sun hit my face.

This is going to be good, I told myself as I walked a couple of steps behind Spencer, who had an excited bounce in his step. I was here with my best friend. This place was amazing. I could relax.

Leo had seemed like a genuinely nice guy, and boy, was he taking care of us or what? I was starting to feel like royalty. First a business class flight down here and now this. Not that this sort of thing usually impressed me, but since I'd never experienced it before, I couldn't deny that it was nice.

And yes, the offer of free food had me salivating already. I wondered if there was a limit on it, though. Did Leo mean just the standard three meals a day? Because I was a brunch and pre-dinner snack guy, myself. Would those be included, too?

The gardens got denser and more fragrant as we made our way on the cobblestone trail from the resort's lobby to the pool area. There was bright green foliage all around the narrow path with vivid splashes of beautiful flowers I had never seen before. A sweet, almost tangy, fragrance filled the air.

Two middle-aged men—I assumed they were a couple, as they were holding hands—approached us on the narrow path. We all moved slightly to the edge of the path as we passed each other. The smell of coconut suntan lotion replaced the flower smell as they eyeballed us. We exchanged a friendly hello and a smile as we continued on our way.

See, this wouldn't be so bad. People were always the friendliest version of themselves on vacation. Maybe we would even make some new friends.

We reached the end of the path and the mini-forest of flowers and bushes cleared, revealing a massive diamond-shaped pool. Okay, now I saw why Leo had said it was unmissable.

"Holy shit," I exclaimed as Spencer and I took in the scene before us. The place was pumping. There were people everywhere, splashing in the pool or talking and laughing around the edges of it. Music was blaring from the speakers. The vibe was nothing short of electric.

I stole a quick glance at Spencer, studying his face. He was taking in the swarming mass of bodies in front of us like I was, and he didn't seem worried in the slightest. If anything, his eyes carried a curious gleam.

I had to give the guy credit. He was unflappable. Nothing ever got to him. Any other straight guy—no matter how progressive or open-minded—might have hesitated at the throng of semi-naked gay dudes swarming around him.

But not my Spencey.

It didn't seem to bother him at all. And his totally casual and *cool with it* reaction relaxed me as well.

I narrowed my eyes, soaking in the bevy of men I was seeing. They were fit, confident and looked like they had been here their whole lives. I knew I wasn't too bad when it came to fitness, thanks to my weekly hiking habit, but I was nowhere near the level these guys were. Their bodies were ripped, while my body ripped things.

Sounds of laughter, along with the occasional exuberant cheer, filtered through the air, above the beat-heavy sound I was hearing, which I believed kids these days referred to as "music."

It was quite the welcome.

"These guys look like they're all fit-fluencers," Spencer muttered to me.

I shot him a confused look. "Fit-fluencers? What the hell is a fit-fluencer?"

"Fitness influencers. I just made it up." His voice dripped with amusement. "You don't like it?"

I scrunched up my nose and shook my head.

"All right, then." He raised his fingers in front of his body, as if he were typing on an invisible, oversized computer. "I'm moving new expression into the trash bin. Pressing delete. Clicking *yes I'm sure I want to delete...* And ah, there we go. That expression has been banished from humanity forever."

He tossed me a wicked smile, and I burst out laughing. "You are such a nerd burger, Spencey."

I turned back to the scene in front of us. "What do you think?"

His eyes met mine, and he raised both eyebrows, waggling them excitedly. "This place is jammin'."

I cocked an eyebrow. "Jammin'? You taking me back to the '90s, Spence?"

He leaned over, his warm breath caressing my cheek. "If I had my way, Cass, the world would have never left the '90s." He smiled widely at me, his pearly white teeth sparkling in the sunlight.

"We should try and find a place to sit," I suggested, craning my neck as I scanned the rows of deck chairs scattered around the pool.

"Good idea." Spencer broke out into a confident stride heading toward the left side of the pool. As we made our way through the crowd, I could feel the heat from the looks that were being thrown our way.

Most passersby looked us up and down and smiled. I guess we were making an impression, since, by comparison to some of the skimpy swimming suits I was seeing, we were *waaaay* overdressed, given that we were still actually dressed.

I smiled back while sticking as close to Spencer as possible. *There, that's not so hard*, I thought to myself. Why was something so seemingly small and easy for everyone else to do—like smiling—so hard for me? I mean, I was a nice, friendly guy. I took a deep breath in and, as I exhaled, tried to expel some of my hang-ups...at least for the weekend.

"Over there." I tapped Spencer on the shoulder and pointed to the left.

He turned his head and followed my fingers. "Well spotted, Cass."

Getting to the deck chairs meant we had to navigate our way through a small yet dense cluster of men who had formed an impromptu dance floor between us and the empty recliners.

Spencer, as always, led the way fearlessly. I couldn't see his face, just the tops of his wide shoulders and the back of his thick head of golden hair, but he definitely wasn't shy about making his way through the crowd. With a series of polite "excuse mes" and "coming throughs," I could see his head bobbing from side to side.

I was curious to know what he was making of it all. We had only gone out to a few gay bars in college, but they were nothing like this place. Despite it being busy and loud, a sense of friendliness and relaxation permeated through it all.

The mass of heaving bodies around us got denser. Spencer reached his arm out behind him, and I grabbed onto it. Our steps were now reduced to shuffles as we made our way to the promised oasis of empty deck chairs. His palm felt reassuringly familiar wrapped around my hand.

After a lot longer than it should have taken to cross a relatively small distance, we finally reached our destination. But as we approached, I noticed a towel slung across the back of one of the chairs. It was a similar shade of blue to the deck chair, which was why I hadn't seen it from a distance. My heart sank in disappointment.

I squeezed Spencer's hand. "I don't think they're free." With my other hand, I pointed to the towel. He let go, and I turned my gaze downward to where our hands had been clasped together. It seemed silly, but I felt empty without his touch.

There were two speedo-clad men lying on the chairs next to the recliners I had thought were free. "Hey, guys," Spencer said cheerfully, sporting his widest, most irresistible grin.

The two men turned their heads at the same time. One was wearing a skimpy black speedo, the other an even skimpier blue speedo.

"Are these chairs free, by any chance?"

Blue speedo guy lowered his sunglasses down his nose, taking Spencer and me in, studying us carefully. The pause was long and heavy. I felt my pulse pounding in my neck, instantly transported to school days at the cafeteria, asking to sit with someone and praying with all my strength that they wouldn't offer me the ultimate humiliation: rejection.

Finally, *finally*, the guy wearing the skimpy blue speedo lying closest to us tipped his head. "Oh, gurrrl." The words practically purred out of his mouth. "Of course, of course, of course."

With a flurry of hand gesticulating, he leapt up and removed the towel covering one of the two empty chairs, throwing it onto his own chair. "I was just drying this thing off. Come. Join us. Please."

"Thanks. I'm Spencer." He extended his arm.

"Oooh, a handshake. How manly." He dragged the words out. "I'm Emry."

They shook hands.

Emry tilted his head over his shoulder. "And that's Hawk."

I looked over at Hawk. He was tanned, muscular, and had a solid square jaw. That was about all I could see of his face, given that the massive sunglasses he had on covered practically everything else.

"And this is Cassius." Spencer turned to me.

I was standing a few feet away and out of handshaking range, so I gave both guys a Spencer-style awkward wave before quickly sitting myself down on one of the two empty deck chairs.

Emry greeted me with a warm smile. Hawk simply tipped his head in my direction.

"So, you guys are a little overdressed," Emry observed once we both sat down.

"We've literally just arrived," Spencer explained as he began taking off his socks and shoes. "They're still preparing our suite, so Leo suggested we come down here to the meet and greet."

Emry flashed a toothy smile. "Then it's a good thing that clothes aren't needed here."

I looked past Spencer, cocking my head at Emry. "What do you mean?"

His eyes sparkled mischievously. "Uh, because it's a clothing-optional resort."

"Huh?" Spencer and I said at the same time, looking at each other, all confused.

"What—what does that mean, exactly?" I asked tentatively.

Hawk turned his head. "Clothes aren't mandatory. Take a look around."

Spencer and I jerked our heads over the crowd, and while most of the guys were wearing bathing suits of some sort, there were a few men who weren't wearing a stitch of fabric.

I could feel my heart thumping in my chest. "Oh."

"Are you okay, Cass?" Spencer leaned toward me.

"I guess," I replied, drawing my focus back to him and away from the naked guys I had been looking at in the crowd. "Are you?"

Our eyes met and he shrugged. "Yeah, it's just the human body, after all. No biggie."

No biggie? *No biggie?!*

Was that really what I'd heard him say? How was he staying so unflappable while I was flapping around like a bird with clipped wings?

"Besides," he added in a whisper. "It's just like your sketches, right?"

Uh, no. My sketches were figments of my imagination. This was real.

Very real.

"Don't worry, guys," Emry's head popped up over Spencer's shoulder. "First day you can keep your clothes on. Day two is usually when the fun starts."

I forced a smile, not wanting to appear rude. "Is there an option to keep clothes *on*?"

"Oh, of course." Emry stretched the words out and threw in a flamboyant hand gesture for good measure. "Honeyyy, you can do whatever you like around here. Be whoever you want to be. This is a safe space for everyone."

I kept smiling, nodding...and thinking.

Okay, so I already knew this weekend would be about getting out of my comfort zone. As it turned out, that meant I might also be getting out of my clothes. Or not. Either way, I could handle it.

I had a feeling Spencer and I would exercise option B and stay dressed. But based on what Emry said, that shouldn't be a problem. There was just no way I could see Spencer and me—

"Spence, what are you doing?" I asked as he stood up.

Instead of responding, he peeled off his white polo shirt, revealing his crazy-stupid-ripped abs. No, I meant like super-duper-crazy. Like, *someone call the cheese factory manager because I've just found the person who can grate all the cheese in the entire world* crazy-stupid-ripped.

My lips parted a little. Then they fell wide open as he unbuttoned his pants and turned around. He pulled his jeans down his legs, revealing a black boxer brief bathing suit hugging his two muscular butt cheeks. For some reason, my eyes drifted onto his round, supple ass. For some even stranger reason, my eyes stayed there.

Once his pants were pooled around his feet, he stepped out of them and turned around. Now I found myself staring at his front bulge. The speedo left *very* little to the imagination. I looked over at Emry and Hawk, who were each smiling with appreciation at Spencer's body-slash-*inspiration for every Greek sculpture ever made*. I guess that was the reward for a brutal exercise regime and a disciplined diet. No cereal and ice cream for this guy.

"Uh, Cassius. My eyes are up here, man."

I heard Emry let out a loud giggle. "Busted!"

I looked up at Spencer's face. As he stood there, barely a few feet away from me, I couldn't help but see him differently. In addition to having never fought—and never fucked—I honestly couldn't remember the last time I had seen Spencer shirtless. Or pantsless.

He was always so immaculately presented, wearing either some expensive, latest season business suit, or some equally expensive, latest season casual wear, that made him look like he had just stepped off a runway in Milan. Even his most casual sweatpants probably cost more than my fanciest shirt—the one with the buttons *and* the collar.

"What can I say? I came prepared." Spencer shrugged casually as he sat back down on the deck chair, stretching his legs out in front of him. That was so him. Typical Spencer. Always prepared and always thinking two steps ahead.

Emry and Hawk turned to me. "Looks like you're the odd man out, Cassius," Emry pointed out with a wink.

"Yeah," Hawk added as a smirk stretched the corners of his mouth. "What have you got underneath your pants?"

My mind drew a blank. I definitely wasn't anywhere as prepared—or as fit—as Spencer. I certainly wasn't hiding any abs under my shirt, that was for sure.

I also couldn't, for the life of me, remember what underwear I was wearing, probably because I wasn't expecting my choice of underwear to be a topic of conversation at any point during the day. I pulled the top of my pants away from my stomach and peeked down. My cheeks flushed with warmth as I looked back at the guys.

"I'm wearing Mickey Mouse boxer shorts."

I thought that if I said it quietly, the music blaring out of the speakers would go some way to cover my embarrassment. Maybe Emry and Hawk were the kind of people that would just politely nod their heads if they didn't hear something.

No. Such. Luck.

"Sorry. I missed that." Hawk leaned in closer, smirk still firmly in place. Emry scrunched in a little closer, too. In that moment, I realized how hard it was to force a smile while simultaneously shooting daggers at somebody with your eyes.

Spencer, who was sitting next to me, definitely heard me. I could tell because he had a wide, smart-ass grin spread across his face.

"I'm wearing Mickey Mouse boxer shorts," I repeated, this time loudly enough for the group to hear.

Spencer looked over at Hawk and Emry. "They're his favorites. He wears them all the time."

Did Florida ever get earthquakes? I asked myself. Because if it did, now would be a good time for one to hit and for the ground to swallow me whole, Mickey Mouse boxer shorts and all.

Hawk and Emry looked at each other, then at Spencer, and then finally, their gazes landed on me. There was another long pause, followed by a tsunami of laughter. Lots and lots of laughing.

"O to the M to the G. That is tooooo cute," Emry howled as the laughter started to subside. "I used to love Mickey Mouse...when I was a kid."

More laughter erupted from the group. Including Spencer.

"I'm glad I'm able to entertain you all." I flattened the front of my shirt, trying to maintain the slightest shred of dignity.

But inside, I was laughing right along with them. Even though we'd only just met, I could tell that Emry and Hawk were just ribbing me good-naturedly. There was no malice behind it. Still, it didn't stop my mind from filling with ways to enact my revenge on them at some point over the weekend.

"I might just keep these shorts on," I pouted, naively thinking that would be the end of it.

"No, no." Hawk gestured with his hands toward my pants. "Take them off, Cassius."

"Yeah, Cassius," Emry added teasingly. "Take them off."

"Take them off. Take them off. Take them off." Hawk and Emry started chanting in a low, deep tone before Spencer—my former best friend and current world's biggest traitor—joined in, too.

"Hey, Spencer," Hawk lifted his chin in my direction. "Looks like he doesn't want to cooperate. You might need to help your boyfriend take his pants off."

I was about to chime in with the usual "We're just friends, not boyfriends" line, but before I could, Spencer reached his hands toward my hips and started tugging at my pants.

"Come on, Cass." He looked up at me playfully. "Take them off and show the world what you—and Mickey Mouse—are working with."

What had gotten into him? Who was this person? Thirty minutes in a male-only, clothing-optional resort, and he was completely unrecognizable. What was happening here?

I shook my head from side to side as a fit of giggles overtook me. This. Was. Ridiculous.

Here I was, a fully grown man, about to take my pants off in public and let everyone see me in my Mickey Mouse boxer shorts. This was not how I expected our weekend getaway would begin.

"All right, all right." I gently slapped Spencer's hands away from my waistband. I shot a pointed look at Hawk and Emry, raising my index finger at them faux-sternly. "But don't say I didn't warn you."

And with that, I took off my clothes, revealing my Mickey Mouse boxers to them—and the world.

"Woot, woot," Hawk wolf-whistled.

"Are you guys happy now?" I asked, unable to conceal my grin. I stretched my legs out, letting my newly exposed skin soak up the rays.

"Your man has got quite the beefy body there." Hawke cast a look of approval at Spencer.

I turned to Spencer with my *I'll let you take care of this* expression. After all, I had corrected Leo when he'd assumed we were a couple, so it was now Spencer's turn to do the same with Emry and Hawk. Instead, he looked at me blankly and blinked a few times, leaving Hawk's comment unresponded to.

"Oh, yeah," Emry added. "Total bear realness."

There was that word again. *Bear*. Dammit, in all the countless hours I had spent on the internet finding cute cat memes and watching unboxing videos, why hadn't I looked up what being a bear meant? And how was I a bear? I hated hunting.

Spencer readjusted himself, getting comfortable on the recliner and pointing his face toward the sky.

I tried to brush it off, but something felt slightly weird with him. I'd picked up on it in the car ride to the airport, and here it was again. There was something on his mind. I knew him well enough that I could tell without him having to say a word; I just hoped it was nothing bad.

I tried to find the words to correct Hawk and let both him and Emry know that we weren't actually a couple, but somehow the words were playing hide and seek and I couldn't seem to find them.

I looked over at Spencer, who was soaking up the sun, so I figured I'd just relax and do the same.

Oh well, we had only just met these guys, so it really didn't matter what they assumed. And if we were going to hang out with them again over the weekend, we would be able to clarify things later.

There was no rush. After all, we were on vacation time.

The salty air.

The sounds of laughter.

The sun beaming down.

I took a deep breath, closed my eyes, and drifted into vacation mode.

7

SPENCER

After a few minutes of taking in the sun's rays, I nudged Cassius on the arm to stir him back to life. "Are you guys thirsty? I could really do with a drink."

"I was just thinking the exact same thing." Hawk reached under his deck chair and pulled something out. "This place does a mean cocktail. I've got the drink menu right here."

"Oooh, looksies please. Let me see what they got," Emry squealed excitedly, rubbing his hands together with glee.

I looked over at them both. It was funny they were friends given how different they seemed on the surface. Hawk was all cool, composed, and definitely had a tough-guy exterior thing going on. While Emry—from what I'd gathered so far, Emry was campy as fuck. And that was putting it mildly. I loved that they could both be who they were, so totally different from each other, and still be such good friends.

"A drink sounds great." I smiled, turning to Cass. His eyes were still closed, but his lips were slightly parted. Seriously? Could he have fallen asleep in just a few minutes? Then again, it was

Cassius, and the guy could sleep standing up. He was the best sleeper I knew.

I rubbed my hand up and down his forearm. His skin was so warm from the sun, and his arm hairs tingled the undersides of my fingertips. "Cass." I spoke a little louder and he stirred.

"Yeah?" He sounded like he'd just woken up from the deepest sleep, not an impromptu ten-minute siesta.

"We're ordering drinks. Would you like me to get you something?"

Cassius demonstrated his excellent multi-tasking skills by managing to both yawn and sit himself upright in his deck chair at the same time. "Sure. That'd be great."

"I'll have Two Cocks in My Ass, please," Emry said to Hawk.

Cassius and I snapped our heads toward Emry. "Huh?" we gasped in unison.

Emry let out a high-pitched giggle as he handed us the menu. "It'll make sense in a moment."

I took the menu from him and looked down. I didn't know what my face or eyes were doing, but it was enough for Cassius to reach over and grab the menu from me.

"Your face is being weird, Spence. You looked like you'd seen a —" He cast his gaze at the menu. "Holy crap."

"Right?" Emry's high-pitched giggle escalated into an uncontrollable cackle.

I took the menu off Cassius and scanned it again. All the drinks had been given an X-rated name-over. In addition to Emry's drink choice, I was also seeing things like a Cocksucking Cowboy, Masturbating Butterfly, Three-Legged Monkey, oh, and a Tie Me To The Bedpost. Ha!

"You should try the Rim My Freshly Shaven Hole," Hawk suggested. The words sounded especially funny given he'd managed to keep a straight face while saying them.

Cassius snatched the menu from me as Hawk and I stood up. "I think I might just stick to beer," I told him. "Cass, what would you like?"

"My Best Friend's 9-Incher," he replied, looking up and batting his eyelashes sweetly at me.

"Excuse me?" I sputtered.

"Make it a double." He handed the drink menu back to me.

Oh, right. It was a drink. For a minute there, I thought—never mind.

I cleared my throat. "Coming right up."

"We'll be back soon, guys," Hawk said. And with that, we set off toward the bar at the far side of the pool.

What should have been a short walk turned out to be a bit of a trek. The place was packed and pumping, meaning that like when Cassius and I had arrived at the pool area, we weren't walking so much as inching our way forward. At a snail's pace.

Despite being crowded, the place had a friendly vibe. Guys would smile at us as they made space for us to pass through, and the nods in our direction were accompanied by the odd backslap. And the occasional *lower down the back* slap, too. Funnily enough, it didn't bother me in the slightest.

Maybe it was escaping the cold or the fact that we'd finally arrived here, but I could already feel myself relaxing. There was something about being outside, feeling the warmth of the sun on skin that dissolved tension. Whoever bottled whatever that was would make a fortune.

Or maybe it had something to do with the fact that I was surrounded by a bevy of men as far as the eye could see. That thought brought a tightness to my throat, but as I walked behind Hawk, step in step with him, that tightness...eased a little. That was weird. Normally, a thought like that would send me spiraling. But for some reason, not this time.

It turned out we weren't the only ones feeling thirsty. When we finally reached the bar, the line was three people deep. "Looks like there might be a bit of a wait." Hawk turned to me, looking over his shoulder.

I found a spot beside him and wriggled my way into it. "I don't mind." We were standing shoulder to shoulder, but it was only then that I realized just how much wider his were than mine.

He had taken off his sunglasses, which meant I also got to see his face up close for the first time. He was strikingly good-looking. Big green eyes, a square jaw, and a set of perfect pearly white teeth. The latter I could tell because, for the first time, he was actually smiling. At me. I felt a buzz of...something shoot through me.

My thoughts were interrupted as I moved out of the way of a guy trying to carry—and not spill—the four drinks he was holding. Not an easy task when every step brought him into contact with someone who was either dancing or talking and not realizing he was trying to get through.

I moved out of his way, leaning over so that my upper back brushed against Hawk's huge chest. That gave the guy carrying the drinks a bit more room to maneuver. "Thanks," he said, looking up briefly to flash me an appreciative smile, before returning his gaze to the task-slash-drinks at hand.

"Have you guys been here before?" I asked Hawk once the guy had passed and I shuffled back to where I had been standing before.

"Yeah, I've been coming every year, sometimes twice a year since I turned twenty-one. What Leo has done with the place"—he turned to me, his face beaming with pride—"is truly extraordinary. It was great before, but this...this is something else."

I totally agreed. "So you know Leo?"

He nodded. "Yeah, we go way back."

Hawk started singing the praises of all the many aspects of the resort while I took the place in from where we were standing. I looked out over a sea of bodies and heard the joyous sounds of laughter and chatting mingling with the faint crashing of waves in the background. The unmissable beats emanated from a DJ booth closer to the center of the pool and blared out of speakers that lined the pool and bar areas.

After all of the research I did on the Elysian Resort for the marketing campaign, I knew just how special and important it was to the LGBTQIA+ community. It wasn't just the amazing location overlooking the Gulf of Mexico or the phenomenal parties and events that were held here. What it was most known and loved for was its truly outstanding hospitality.

Cassius and I had a brief taste of it when we'd checked in.

Leo Carter, the owner, was a legend in the hospitality world. His reputation was of being a truly nice guy. I could totally vouch for that, too. Of all the clients I had worked with in my career so far, he had been an absolute dream. Prompt. Professional. Polite. And with an understated humor that was right up my alley.

But it was how inclusive the place was that really stood out to me. As I read every single thing ever posted about the place online, I was struck—and sometimes moved almost to tears—by the testimonials and reviews of men who came here from countries where being gay was a crime, one sometimes punished in horrific, brutal ways. For those guests, this wasn't just a fun vacation resort. It represented a safety and freedom they couldn't experience back home.

"...total next-level luxury." Hawk finished his spiel and threw me another wide smile.

Shit, I'd missed most of what he'd said. I had been too preoccupied looking around and trying to imagine where these guys came from, what their stories were.

"That's my line, by the way," I informed him.

He shot me a quizzical look.

"I wrote that line, *next-level luxury.*" I explained to Hawk that I had led the PR and marketing efforts of the resort following its refurbishment.

He shot me an impressed look. "You did an amazing job with that. Emry and I were featured in the video that went viral."

Ah, yes. The infamous *slow motion, guys dancing in speedos* video that broke the internet.

"You're the one who did a good job. It's your junk that brought all these boys to the yard."

He laughed. It was a loud, wild laugh. Rough around the edges and untamed. It reminded me of Cassius'. "I can't take all the credit. I think there were at least a hundred close-ups of a hundred guys' packages."

"That is true." I grinned. The line cleared a little, and we stepped in closer toward the bar.

"Not a bad idea for a straight guy."

I froze. Wait, what did he just say?

"Sorry, I didn't mean to assume you were straight," Hawk quickly corrected himself, placing his hand on my shoulder. "Are you?"

Shit. Am I?

My brain—like my body, mouth and breathing—froze.

Hawk lifted his hand off me. "Are you okay, Spencer? Again, I apologize. I shouldn't have said anything. See, this is why I prefer to keep my mouth firmly shut."

I looked at him and could see the worry written across his face. He hadn't meant to offend me or send me down whatever fucked-up tunnel I was burying myself in.

I finally found my words again. "It's okay," I managed to get out. "It's not you. I'm just a little..." And just like that, my words were gone again.

Hawk leaned in closer. "It's okay, Spencer. I understand."

"You do?"

How did he understand when I had no idea myself?

He bit down on his lower lip. "Personally, I'm not a fan of labels. For many years, I struggled to find one that fit me."

"Oh." Okay, I could definitely relate to that. "So, did you find one? A label, that is."

He let out a deep breath. "Short answer: no. Long answer...we don't have time for that right now."

We reached the bar, but the bartenders hadn't looked over at us yet. Hawk placed his palms on the counter and fixed his gaze straight ahead. I could tell he was thinking about something...or maybe, someone?

"The bottom line is this." I was looking at him, but he just kept staring straight ahead. "If a label helps, great. Use it. That's what it's there for. But if you can't find a label..."

He twisted his head toward me and our eyes locked. I braced myself, planting my feet, because somehow I knew that the next words to come out of his mouth would knock me onto the ground.

"...then you have to create your own label. Even if it's not a word, just a feeling. Even if it's something that applies at one point in time, but then changes. Even if it's something that you'll never be able to explain or express to anyone else, you just have to create something for yourself. Something that's true for you."

Yep. I knew it.

I, Spencer James Montgomery, had officially been bowled over.

8

CASSIUS

Emry slid his sunglasses down until they dangled perilously close to the tip of his nose. His eyes shot up and down as we both watched Spencer and Hawk head off to the bar.

"Damn," he whistled once they were out of earshot. "Your man has got a seriously hot ass. That butt is bubblier than my last glass of champagne."

I smile-sighed. The smile was for the funny comment he had made. The sigh was because I knew it was time to clear things up.

Yet again.

I stood up and moved onto the recliner next to Emry. I lay down carefully, adjusting my boxer shorts to make sure I didn't accidentally expose myself. I didn't think that my cock peeking through Mickey Mouse's face would be a good look—for me *or* the mouse.

Emry's eyes were still following Spencer and Hawk. When the guys finally disappeared into the ocean of bodies, he cranked his head in my direction. His perfectly manicured eyebrows lifted as he shot me a devilish smile. "He's a mighty fine specimen."

I studied Emry for a moment. Even though we'd only just met, a few things were pretty obvious. He was fun. Campy. A little shocking. A lot out there. In some ways, he played into the old stereotypical image of an effeminate gay guy. So, in other words, the exact opposite of me.

And here's the thing, though—I freaking loved it.

Sure, I wasn't any of those things that he was. Most of the time, people were surprised when I told them I was gay. Which was so stupid. I mean, why did people still judge others—even if it was an unconscious thing they were doing without even realizing it—based purely on their appearance?

I was messy. I didn't wear tight-fitting clothes. I ate carbs. I didn't work out, except for hiking, but I refused to call that exercise. I shopped at Walmart, thrift stores, and the best department store in the entire world: Spencer's wardrobe. The range was extensive and the prices? Rock bottom. Besides an occasional faux grumpy-slash-surprised comment, I knew Spencer didn't mind me raiding his stuff. He was always buying the latest season's gear anyway. I was practically doing him a favor by clearing away his old clothes.

In fact, people usually only assumed I was gay was when I was with Spencer. And now I could add Emry to that long and continuously growing list.

He was flicking through a copy of *People* magazine. Every so often, he'd let out a short little comment about what he was seeing. His repertoire was peppered with "Ooh, girl" and "Bitch, please."

Not words that I would necessarily use, but again, something that I instantly loved about him. The reason I admired it was because he was simply being who he was. Which meant that he knew who he was. And he leaned into it—heck, he seemed to be embracing it with pure unadulterated enthusiasm.

Me, on the other hand, I was still figuring out who I was. As it turned out, I had a long way to go.

I inched in a little closer. "So here's the thing, Emry. Spencer and I, we aren't actually a couple."

Emry put the magazine down on his lap. "Oh?"

"Yeah, we're just friends. We've known each other since we were six years old."

"Uh-huh." Emry took his glasses off and pointed his face toward the sky. "See, I was sure I saw the two of you holding hands when you first came over here."

I shuffled uneasily in my recliner. Technically, he had a point, I guess. Time to bring out the big guns.

"Spencer is straight," I announced, hoping that would clear things up for him. "I'm gay, and he's straight. We're childhood best friends. That's it."

Emry turned and gave me a once-over. "Since when has that ever meant anything?"

His question left a tingling sensation in my chest. I had always been so careful with Spencer, so deliberate in having the boundaries we did. Up until just a few moments ago, I hadn't even seen him without a shirt for a good few years.

He was my best friend in the world, and there was no way in hell I would ever do anything to jeopardize that. It just wouldn't be worth it.

I'd be lying if I said that I'd never had a small, minuscule, fraction of a fraction divided by another fraction glimmer of hope that something more might have developed between us. But that was one fleeting moment during one hormonally fueled summer where puberty collided with the discovery that when rubbed the right way, my cock could produce a veritable feast of incredible sensations.

Thankfully, that moment of even remotely considering Spencer in a sexual way passed when I realized that said cock sensations didn't require the company of anyone else. Certainly not Spencer. Firstly, because he was straight, and secondly, because I didn't want anything to change between us.

What we had was the dictionary definition of a perfect friendship. I could be my weird-ass, gwerking, horrible-food-concocting self with him. And he could be his slightly neurotic, overly organized and *way too concerned with what others thought of him* self with me. It was a symbiosis that we had spent seventeen years crafting, refining, and mastering. I wasn't going to let anything destroy it.

"Trust me"—I cast Emry my most serious of serious looks—"if something was going to happen between us it would have happened by now. We really are just best friends."

Emry gave a casual shrug. "Okay, if you say so."

Eager to move to another topic, I asked, "So how do you and Hawk know each other?" I was deliberate with my choice of words. I didn't want to assume that just because they were lying next to each other at an all-male (clothing optional) resort, they were automatically boyfriends.

His bottom lip curled up into a smile. "We're dick twins."

"Huh?"

Seeing my reaction, his lips separated in a smirk. "Dick twins," he repeated, on the off chance I might have somehow missed it the first time. "What, you've never heard of it?" He made it sound like it was the most obvious thing in the world.

I shook my head. "Uh, that would be a big fat no."

Fuck. The list of gay-related terms and things I knew nothing about kept getting longer and longer.

"We met a few years ago," Emry began, crossing one leg over the other. "I can't even remember which of the hookup apps we were using at the time. It was meant to be a casual, one-time thing. You know?"

I didn't, but I nodded my head, anyway. I'd never used a hookup app before, but I didn't quite feel like letting him know that just yet. "So, what happened?"

"It turned out that we'd both"—he scrunched up his nose —"fudged the truth on our profiles. Just a little."

"Oh?"

Emry smiled at the memory. "Yeah. But funnily enough, we both told the same lie."

"What do you mean?"

A playful look landed on his face. He was clearly enjoying recounting this story. "We both said we were vers-tops. But, as it turned out, we were both just tops."

"So why were you both lying about it, then?"

Emry aimed a look my way that suggested I should have known the answer to that question. He was right. I probably should have. But I had no freaking idea.

"Let's just say you catch more bees with honey."

I lifted a finger into the air. "Actually, I think it's *flies*."

Emry cocked his head to the side. "Huh?"

"Flies," I repeated. "You attract more *flies* with honey. Why would bees be attracted to honey? They make the stuff."

Emry considered it for a moment before he burst out laughing. "Oh my god, all these years I've been saying *bees*." He slapped his palm against the side of his face. "I'm such an idiot."

I joined in the laughing, too. It felt good sharing a lighthearted moment with him. I liked the guy, and I could see us becoming friends.

"So, back to your story?" I prodded. He'd sucked me in, and now I was keen to know more.

"Right. Let's just say Philly was going through a bottom drought—"

"That's where you guys are from, Philadelphia?"

Emry nodded. "What about you guys?"

"Boston," I answered.

"Ah, nice. That's not too far. Anyway, we both had vers on our profiles in the hopes of attracting more guys. But, if you put it out there, then you have to back it up. In this case, literally."

My brain had clearly switched into vacation-mode because I was only now catching up to *bottom drought*. What the hell was that?

"Long story short, we decided that while there was some stuff we couldn't do, there was still some stuff we could. A blow and go, basically."

"Oh...okay. That sounds like a cocktail they'd have at this place."

Emry giggled sweetly before continuing with his story. "Anyway, when we got undressed, that's when we saw it."

I was leaning so far over the edge of my chair I was surprised I hadn't fallen over. "Saw what?"

"That we were dick twins. Our dicks are identical, Cassius. It's positively freaky. We have the exact same length and same width. We're both cut. No veins. The only difference between them is that Hawk has pubic hair and I don't."

"Good to know," I joked, my brain working double time to process all of that information.

"So, since then, we became fuck buddies. We hook up with other guys together. And we gave ourselves the name the Dick Twins. Along the way, we became friends. Hawk invited me to join him here at Elysian about two years ago, and we've been back three times since."

"Cool."

"Yeah." A smile lit up Emry's entire face as he looked around the pool. "It's a very good place to do some...dick twinning."

"I'm sure it is."

I let Emry's story sink in. *Hookup apps. Fuck buddies. Dick twins.* Something was stirring inside of me. What was it? I lay back on my recliner and closed my eyes for a moment. That's when it hit me. I recognized the feeling whirring around in my chest. I swallowed hard. It was jealousy.

Part of me wanted that. Not the actual specifics of what Emry had shared, but the fun-*ness* behind it. Going out, meeting people, getting into crazy adventures.

Spencer was right to press me when he asked the question at dinner at the Italian restaurant last week—when was the last time I'd had fun? The answer: never.

My life was good, but it was...small. I had my work, which I loved. I had my interests—hiking and sketching. I had a few good friends and an amazing mom and sisters. And of course, I had Spencer. But that was kinda it.

But what could a guy who didn't use dating apps and didn't like casual sex do that was exciting and fun?

Before I could answer that question, Hawk's deep voice boomed out. "Gentlemen, your drinks are served."

I looked up and saw Spencer standing next to Hawk, holding two drinks in his hands. He was still only wearing his bathing suit and the afternoon sun was reflecting off his smooth skin and highlighting his golden hair. It made me see him differently, somehow.

Suddenly, I felt something else stir within me. I didn't know what it was, though.

I reached for the drink as he handed it to me. "Do you want your chair back?" I asked.

"No, it's fine. You stay there."

"So"—Hawk looked around the group after he had given Emry his drink—"I know we've only just met each other, but I have a good feeling that the four of us are going to get along well."

We all looked at each other, nodding and smiling in agreement.

"Here's to a fantastic weekend and to the start of what will hopefully be a wonderful friendship."

We guided our drinks into the middle, clinking them loudly against each other.

"So..." Emry began with a teasing note in his tone. "How's your Best Friend's 9-Incher?"

I had just taken a sip of the naughtily named cocktail and it took all my effort to swallow it casually and look unaffected. "It's delicious." I smacked my lips together loudly. "A little sweet, a little salty. And it goes down nice and smooth."

Emry giggled. "That's just what you want. Let's drink to that."

My heart warmed...and it wasn't just because of the alcohol.

Emry and I clinked our glasses together again. He was a genuinely nice guy, and I liked him. He was easy to talk to and super funny.

Once I had settled back in my chair, Spencer furled his eyebrows at me. "So, did I miss anything? What did you guys talk about while we were gone?"

I took another sip of my drink before answering. Okay, *now* I was starting to feel the alcohol. I winked at Spencer.

"I'll tell you later."

9

CASSIUS

"But are you sure you're sure?" I asked Spencer for the fourth time as I nervously walked beside him. We were following the attendant, who was taking us to our suite for the first time.

I studied Spencer's profile. His razor-sharp cheekbones. His prominent nose with the pointed tip. That cute freckle on his right cheek. His lips. They looked fuller than normal. Pinker, too. It must have been the angle I was looking at them. Whoa, why the hell was I overanalyzing his lips?

I snapped myself out of the detour down Spencer Lip Lane. It must have been that second cocktail I'd had—and finished, without falling asleep or passing out which definitely progress.

Note to future self: one Best Friend's 9-Incher was enough. Two was too much.

I just really wanted to make sure Spencer was all right. Sure, we'd had a nice, albeit slightly boozier few rounds of drinks with our newest friends, Emry and Hawk. And yes, the place looked like a slice of heaven had been lowered to earth. But Spencer was still a straight guy at an all-male resort. How was he reacting to all of this?

Was he anxious? Nervous? Scared? I didn't mind what he was feeling, I just wanted to know what it was.

Sure, this whole trip was his idea, and he knew what he was getting into, *and* I'd seen him strip down at the pool without a moment's pause—but Spence's happiness was always going to be my top priority. Of course he was fine around me, but maybe there was a critical mass of gayness that he wouldn't be able to handle? My brain couldn't stop spinning long enough to figure out if that was a reasonable thought, so I just kept bugging the poor guy.

"Cassius." He stopped mid-step, folded his arms over his chest, and looked up at me through his light lashes. I stopped, too, anxious to hear his response. "I am perfectly alright. In fact, I'm more than all right. I love it here."

He waved his hand around us at the lush tropical garden surrounding the path we were walking on, the architecturally designed white building that we were approaching—this place really was paradise.

"I liked meeting Hawk and Emry. They seem like great guys. All the guys here seem nice." He patted me on the shoulder. His touch was reassuring. "I'm good, really. You can stop asking, and you can definitely stop worrying."

We started walking again, speeding to catch up with the attendant.

"Are *you* okay?" Spencer asked, lowering his voice.

I sent him a smile. "I'm good, too, Spence. And I agree with you. Everyone here seems really nice and friendly. And I loved spending time with Emry."

Spencer nudged into me playfully. "You never told me what you two were talking about."

I motioned for him to come closer as I whispered some of the most noteworthy highlights regarding our new dick twin friends into his ear.

Spencer did his hand-over-mouth laugh as his eyes widened. "There you go. You learn something new every day," Spencer whispered back, taking it all in his stride. Although I couldn't help but notice his cheeks were a slightly redder shade than before my story.

I shook my head. I had to give him credit, the way he was taking it all in. At some point during my story, his hand found a home in my lower back. I could feel him pressing his palm, resting it in the crook of my back.

"Here we are." The attendant turned to face us. "Your home for the next four nights, gentlemen."

I smiled involuntarily at hearing that word.

Spencer pulled his hand away as we walked up beside the attendant. My smile vanished as I felt the tiniest hint of longing, like I was missing his touch, which was beyond silly.

The attendant looked at the two of us and smiled. "Your luggage is already inside. We've placed it in the master bedroom."

Spencer pulled out a fifty-dollar bill from his wallet and handed it to him. "Thank you, my good man. We appreciate your help."

The attendant's eyes lit up. "Thank *you*, sir," he said and turned to leave.

I eyed Spencer. Maybe I was a little boozy, but that was such a sweet gesture.

He looked at me questioningly. "What?"

"Nothing, big spender," I teased.

"Hey, I can't help it. I feel guilty about how kind and generous Leo has been to us. Free oceanfront suite. Free drinks. Free food. Especially given how much you eat, I'm worried the guy will go bankrupt."

"Hey," I protested weakly.

Spencer's hand returned to my lower back. "The least I can do is tip well."

Right after he said that, my heart started beating a little faster. Shit. Heart palpitations at twenty-three, that was not a good sign. It couldn't have been because I was super touched at Spencer's kindness. Or the fact that his hand felt so right pressed against my body. No, it definitely wasn't that.

"Well, as someone who put himself through college waiting tables, I thank you."

Spencer shook his head, smiling. He swiped the access card and pushed the door open. "After you." He waved me in.

I scooched past him, so close I could smell the beer on his lips. Those weirdly plump, even more weirdly pink lips of his.

"Holy moly!" I exclaimed, stepping into the suite. My eyes were immediately drawn to the floor-to-ceiling windows. How could they not be? The view of the ocean, the waves, the cloudless sky, was beyond breathtaking.

Spencer stepped in behind me. "Wow." His warm breath tickled the back of my neck. "I knew we had the Ocean Suite, but this is mind-blowing."

"Uh-huh," I agreed, unable to move or look away from the view. "My mind is officially blown."

Spencer moved past me, and I finally managed to pull my eyes away from the beach. The suite itself was pretty spectacular, too. All-white, modern, sleek, and with amazing beach-themed artwork hanging on the walls.

There were two rooms, one on each side, coming off an open-plan kitchen, lounge, and dining area. I walked into the bedroom on the left. Spencer followed me in. My one bag and his four-piece luggage collection had been arranged neatly in the corner of the room.

"I guess Leo forgot to mention our situation to whoever brought our luggage in here."

Spencer just smiled. "You know, I think we should get some T-shirts printed up saying, *We're not together—we're just friends* written across them."

"That's a great idea." I clapped my hands together joyously. "You can wear that one, and I'll wear one that says, *No, we actually really mean it.*"

We both laughed. I thought back to Emry and the look on his face when I had told him that Spencer and I were just friends.

"You know, Cass," Spencer said as he sat down on what looked like a jumbo version of a California King bed. "This bed is huge. There's no reason why we can't just share it." A wide grin filled his face.

For a split second, I couldn't tell whether he was kidding or not.

I blinked a couple of times. He just sat there, grinning away to himself. I felt...perplexed. Sure, he had a point. The bed could comfortably sleep a football team, I thought. I didn't actually know how many players made up a football team since sports weren't really my thing. But did Spencer actually mean it, or were the four beers he'd downed finally catching up with him?

Before I could say anything, his stomach let out a loud growl. He looked down at it and patted his belly. "You hungry?" He flicked his blue eyes at me.

I stretched my hands out in front of me. "You know what the answer to that question is."

"Always," we said at the same time.

"They've got room service here, right?" I asked.

Spencer laid himself down on the bed. "Yeah, of course. This is five-star luxury, man."

"Ooooh, yeah," I sang out as I started doing my totally dorky happy dance. It was a bit like gwerking, but with fewer hip gyrations and a much stupider facial expression.

Spencer lifted his head. "What are you doing, doofus?" I could hear the smile in his voice, but nothing was going to stop my body from moving.

"This is my *we get to order room service and hang out together* happy dance," I informed him.

I could see his chest vibrating as he laughed quietly. After a few moments, he lifted himself up and sat cross-legged on the bed. "What are you gonna get, Cass? Let me guess. The usual?"

I added a nod to my room service happy dance. "You know it.

Two double cheeseburgers, large fries, and a strawberry milkshake."

Exasperation filled his eyes as he stared at me. "How can you eat so much crappy food and still look that good?"

"Dorky dancing burns calories. All these years you've been going to the gym and you didn't know that, Spence?" I could see him shaking his head out of the corner of my eye. "What are you going to get?"

"I'll just go for a chicken salad, with dressing on the side."

It was my turn to incorporate some head-shaking into my off-the-hook dance routine. I shimmied, shook and almost—but thankfully managed to recover in time not to—tripped over my own feet as I made my way to the phone on the nightstand by the bed.

As I sat down at the edge of the bed and reached for the phone, I felt the full force of a pillow hitting the side of my face. I turned to glare at the culprit. Spencer was on his hands and knees in the middle of the football field—I meant bed. He had a cheekiness written on his face. I knew that look, and it would only lead to trouble. The fun kind, of course.

I followed his gaze. He was eyeing the pillows resting at the top of the bed. I began to do some mental calculations. I was sitting closer to them, but I had to twist around to get them. Spencer could just lunge at them, possibly reaching them before I could. While I was considering a number of metrics, including velocity, speed, and body weight, Spencer's stomach grumbling filled the air between us...and the pillows.

I lifted my index finger and summoned my most authoritative look. "No. First, I order food. Then, and only then, do we engage in pillow warfare." I was pleasantly surprised at how commanding I sounded. *I* would have listened to me.

"Okay, okay." Spencer retreated toward the far corner of the bed, while pointing to the phone receiver I was holding in my hand. "Go on, then. Place the order."

I turned around and did just that. The very nanosecond the

receiver left my fingers, I was pummeled by Spencer, who had somehow leapt from one side of the bed to where I was sitting, bashing the silky pillow into my face over and over again.

"You asshat," I cried out. "You are going to pay."

I fumbled around behind me until my fingers clasped a pillow. I firmed my grip and aimed it precisely at Spencer's head. He rocked backward. Perfect. Just the opening I needed. I spun around and lunged at more pillows that were resting against the headboard.

I grabbed one in each hand and began pummeling Spencer's chest. But I had committed a fatal error: I hadn't secured the target. Spencer flung himself up, and the next thing I knew, not only was he retaliating—returning fire with his two pillows from earlier, whacking them into my face—he had somehow managed to maneuver himself into position beside me.

He gave me a sharp push that saw me landing on my side in the middle of the bed. God, he was so strong. He towered over me.

After copping more pillow-bashing to my face and the front of my body, Spencer was on top of me. Straddling me.

Holy crap, Spencer was straddling me.

And holier crappier, something was stirring in my pants...and it wasn't Mickey Mouse.

"I surrender, I surrender," I cried, raising my arms over my head.

Spencer looked down, and a strange expression crossed his face as he took in our current, er, position. I studied his face. He didn't look surprised, which surprised me, and then he did something that turned the surprise radar all the way into overdrive.

He straddled me harder, rubbing our bodies—specifically, his ass against my crotch—for just a second, before peeling himself off me.

There was nothing but a crackling silence between us, our haggard breathing and the faint hum of the ocean the only sounds in the room. I dragged my fingers through my hair. I needed to do something to unawkwardify this situation. Stat.

I went for my usual go-to. Humor.

I rolled over to the edge of the bed and got to my feet.

"I'm taking my bag, and I'm leaving. I'm leaving you forever," I cried out in mock indignation as I stomped across the room and picked up my sole piece of luggage.

"Awww, poor baby." I got the feeling Spencer sensed what I was doing, so he played it up, too, launching into full-on patronizing mode. He was smiling and looking all sorts of adorable with his messed-up hair and flushed cheeks. But behind it, something heavier lingered. What that was, I had no freaking clue.

"I'm going to have a quick shower before room service arrives," I informed him with a slight huffiness remaining in my voice, continuing along my escape route of lightheartedness. "After all, I like to look and smell good for the food I'm about to eat."

"How considerate of you," Spencer replied with a smirk. Then his grin faltered before it vanished altogether. "I'll do the same."

I closed the door to his room as I left. And then I pulled out my cell phone and waited. Putting all thoughts of weirdness and straddling aside, once sixty seconds had passed, I opened the door to his bedroom and barged into the bathroom.

"Cassius, what the hell?" Spencer jumped a few feet into the air. "What are you doing? I could have been having a shower."

"Pffft." I waved his words away dismissively.

"What if I was on the toilet?"

"Oh, please," I retorted. "You go to the bathroom exactly five minutes after you wake up every morning. Sometimes, after your second coffee." It was true. Like everything else in his life, Spencer's bowel movements were coordinated down to the very second.

"What are you doing in here? You scared the living shit out of me."

I looked over at the cabinet and saw exactly what I had come in here for. "Ah ha! I knew it. You were rearranging the bathroom supplies."

A look of guilt washed over his face.

Busted!

"Yeah, well, soaps and gels don't belong with hand cream and body lotion. It doesn't make any sense, Cass. I was just organizing things in a more logical way. That way, I can just chill out and relax for the weekend."

"That's all I needed to hear you say, Spencey. Okay, I'm done in here. You can go back to doing your thing now."

"Did you want me to do your bathroom once I'm done in here?"

I reached the doorway and turned around. "I'm all good. But thanks for the offer."

And just like that, the weirdness from before vanished. For good, I hoped.

I made my way to my bedroom, which was only a little smaller than Spence's and still super fancy. I threw my bag onto the bed and jumped into the shower, smiling as I thought of how well I knew Spencer.

I just knew he would be rearranging bathroom supplies. And if I showered for more than ten minutes, there'd be a good chance I'd walk out to find him doing the same thing in the kitchen. He was such a unique guy. It was one of the things I loved most about him.

Why couldn't I find a gay version of Spencer? Now, *that* would be my perfect guy, right there.

I heard a knock on the door as I was coming out of the shower. I dried off quickly and opened my bag, pulling out a whole bunch of clothes and throwing them across the bad. Why was it that the clothes you needed to wear first were always at the bottom of the luggage?

I grabbed my comfiest pair of gray sweatpants and my trusty *Go With the Flow* T-shirt and headed out toward the kitchen. Spencer had already answered the door and was carefully arranging the food on two plates. Even when he was doing something so simple, his face was full of concentration. Like he was trying to get every last detail just right.

I walked up to the counter and grabbed my burger, taking a massive bite into it. "Oh, this is good."

Spencer looked up and covered his face. "Gross, Cass. Don't talk with your mouth full. We've spoken about this."

I gave an innocent shrug. "What?" I asked with a mouthful of half-chewed burger. "I'm hungry." Classic line of defense.

"So am I." Spencer was fussing with his salad, barely drizzling any of the dressing over it. "But there's no reason why we can't eat at the table and use plates. Like normal people."

"Pffft," I blew out. "Who wants to be like normal people?"

After arranging my fries and burger on the plate, he carried the food over to the dining table, placing the plates next to each other so that we both had a view out to the beach.

We ate mostly in silence. The sound of me chewing and gulping down the burgers complemented the crashing waves of the ocean quite nicely, I thought. Spencer seemed to be drifting in and out of his own thoughts, too.

I always thought it was a sign of a healthy friendship when two people could comfortably share silence without it getting awkward or feeling like it needed to be filled with constant, mindless chatter.

After our meal, Spencer cleaned up, while I watched Spencer clean up. I liked this. Spending time with Spencer was always so easy. We didn't have to be doing anything exciting or crazy. Just chatting away while he did the dishes was fun. Or eating a meal while we quietly stared out at the ocean. Or sitting on my couch back home while I ate cereal and ice cream and he massaged my feet. It all just felt so...natural.

We decided to call it a night. It was still relatively early, but we had the entire weekend ahead of us. I had a feeling we needed to rest up for whatever he had planned for us.

We said our good nights and retreated to our separate rooms. I brushed my teeth, only to find myself fully awake. I reminded myself that I had taken a three-hour nap on the flight.

I quickly arranged the room, Cassius-style. That meant that all the clothes I had tossed onto the bed earlier, I now tossed onto the floor. Before throwing my bag into the corner, I reached in and pulled out my sketchpad along with my pencil set. Drawing always relaxed me. It might even make me sleepy, I hoped.

I stripped out of my sweatpants and shirt and jumped in under the covers. I stared out into the darkness. Although I could hear the thundering waves crashing outside my room, it was fully pitch black outside. Clouds must have been covering the stars and moon.

I still couldn't believe we were here; it felt a little surreal. My mind was beginning to leave the real world behind. I was enjoying this vacation too much to be thinking of everyday things like back-to-back work meetings and grocery shopping. I much preferred drinking cocktails by the pool, ordering room service, and impromptu pillow fights.

I opened my sketchpad and glanced at my drawings. Spencer always encouraged me to pursue my art, but as I scrolled through the half-done images, all I saw was the mistakes, the things I didn't like, leaping out at me.

I'd never had any real training in drawing. It was just something that I had always done, ever since I was a little kid. I just doodled or sketched. Probably as a way to distract myself. I didn't want to be the best at it, I simply found it was a way I could express myself without using words. There was something really cool about that.

I quickly flipped through the rest of the pad until I got to the final sketch. A pair of very familiar eyes stared back at me.

It was Spencer.

He was always the last drawing in all of the sketchpads I'd used over the years.

It didn't feel weird to draw him. I knew his face better than anyone else's. Although, as his display by the pool this afternoon had highlighted, it had been a very long time since I had seen the rest of his body. His very tightly defined and toned body. I never sketched his body because, well, I didn't know what it looked like. But now...I did.

I felt something stir within me. I looked down, and my eyes widened in surprise at the massive tent pole that had formed in my sheets. Holy shit. Thinking about Spencer had gotten me hard. Like, rock-hard.

How could that be?

I placed the sketchpad beside my body and kicked the bed covers down toward my feet. My rigid cock sprang out into the air, freed from the confines of the Egyptian cotton sheets. I looked down at it and hesitated. It throbbed, aching for release.

I should have turned the light off.

I should have just gone to sleep and thought nothing more of it.

I should have just put it down to the alcohol coursing through my body. A business class flight and an afternoon drinking session in the sun would have been enough to make anyone think silly things about their incredibly good-looking, speedo-clad best friend with the plump, cherry pink lips and the strong legs he used to straddle me during our pillow warfare.

This was crazy. I never thought of Spencer in this way.

But the next thing I knew, my hands were moving down my body. Involuntarily. My fingers slid across my stomach, my fingertips reaching the top of my pubic hair. My cock pulsed in anticipation.

Before I touched it, I ran my hands up and down the insides of my thighs. The friction of my palms against my hairy legs sent a pleasant tingle all the way up my spine to the back of my neck.

It took me back to Spencer's touch. Or, rather, touches. As in plural. Nudging my forearm as we made our way out of the car to the reception area, his hand on the small of my back as we were led to the suite, the heaviness of his body as he crashed into me with a pillow.

I closed my eyes and hungrily grabbed the base of my shaft. I began stroking it with a firm pressure. A pressure that had been bottled up within me for longer than I had realized.

My eyes shot open as a heavy dose of reality hit me smack bang in the middle of my chest.

I should have stopped right there.

I should have gotten up, maybe even had a cold shower to wash away whatever these feelings that had overtaken me were.

I should have...but I didn't.

I wrapped my fingers around my cock and formed a tight fist, jerking up and down the entire length. My movements were hard, quick, urgent. I closed my eyes and grabbed my left nipple between my index and middle finger. I squeezed it as I furiously sped up my stroking.

With one eye, I glanced down at the open sketchpad beside me. Spencer's face was staring back at me. Those baby blue eyes. His cute nose. Those pouty-as-fuck lips.

I closed my eyes, but it didn't shut Spencer out of my mind. All I could think about was him. The way he smiled. The way he was so attentive to my every need. The way I knew every single thing about him. And how he knew every single thing about me.

My cock got heavier in my hand. I increased the pace of my stroking. The hot flesh of my cock burned underneath my fingers.

And then I felt it. The rush tore through me so hard I thought it would split me in two. I threw my head back as my hips shot up off the bed. My ass clenched tightly while my whole body shuddered in the throes of the most intense orgasm I had experienced in a very long time.

I looked down at the creamy mess that had pooled in patches across my stomach. I was done. Drained. And thankfully, finally tired. I let out a loud yawn.

What the fuck had I just done?

FRIDAY

10

SPENCER

My eyes twitched. A few moments later, my eyelids fluttered. The worst part was that I had become aware of it happening, which meant that I was awake. Or at least, waking up.

Dammit.

I was on vacation time, but someone had clearly forgotten to tell my brain that. I squished my eyes together, hoping to will myself back into slumber. But it was futile. My senses were coming online, and there was nothing I could do to stop it.

I could feel the warmth of the new day peeking in through the slight crack in the curtain. At least sunlight was a sign that it wasn't too early. Begrudgingly, I cracked one eye open and groggily glanced over at the bedside clock.

6:32.

Okay, so it was too early. But still, back home, this would have been considered a sleep-in. I usually woke up at the crack of dawn, headed to the gym, came back home, and got ready for work, while sending off at least a dozen or so emails in order to get a jump-start on the day by the time I arrived at the office, usually just after seven.

I had been hoping to make up for some sleep deprivation this weekend, but since we'd called an early night, I wasn't feeling too bad about it. Maybe my mind needed more than just an afternoon of drinking by the pool and a quiet night in with Cassius to unwind.

Or maybe what my mind really needed was to unburden itself.

I glanced over at the clock again. The bright green digits now read 6:35. Way too early for these sorts of thoughts. Existential life crisis opening hours were from seven to seven. Everyone knew that.

I let out a loud yawn, pulling the sheet off me. On my next yawn, which followed shortly after, I got up and walked over to the wardrobe. After saying goodnight to Cassius last night, I had unpacked, sorted, and arranged all the contents of my luggage before going to bed. It was secretly one of the things I loved most about traveling.

Every hotel had a different wardrobe configuration. Some had plenty of hanging space but few dresser drawers. Others were tight and compact with barely any space for clothes, much less for storing suitcases. Some had the security safe tucked into the bottom corner, which severely restricted shoe storage space.

That was the joy of opening up the cupboard doors, seeing the hand you were dealt, and then coming up with a system that was organized, convenient, and looked good, too. *A place for everything and everything in its place.*

Okay, maybe that sounded a little more tragic than I had intended it to.

It's just that there was something about being neat and organized that I really enjoyed. It relaxed me knowing that things were where they were meant to be. It gave me the ability to switch my mind off because I didn't have to worry about the little stuff, leaving me more time and energy to, instead, stress about the big stuff.

And boy, did I have that in spades.

Nope, not going there again before 7 a.m.

I had sorted my gym clothes in the second drawer from the top. I pulled it open, grabbing a workout shirt, shorts, and socks. I scooped up my shoes from the floor of the wardrobe. If I was going to be up so early, I might as well make the most of it and squeeze a workout in.

I got dressed, splashed some water on my face, and brushed my teeth. I laced up my sneakers and headed out of my room. My head turned—no, was pulled, like a magnet being clipped onto a refrigerator door—to the amazing view outside of our suite. The ocean was a lot stiller than it had been yesterday. It looked like the tide was out, and the sky was imbued with delicate flourishes of light blue and orange.

Okay, being up so early might have sucked hairy balls, but a view like that sure made up for it. I looked across to the other side of the suite. The door to Cassius' room was shut. No surprise there. The only thing that could ever get the guy out of bed early was the promise of a hike. Otherwise, he'd sleep in until midday if I'd let him.

And, no, I wouldn't be letting him. We had an itinerary to stick to.

For some random reason, I thought about the different ways people reacted to stress. For me, it kept me up at night, killed my appetite (*that*, I wasn't complaining about), and drove me into an even more hyperbolic frenzy of organization and planning.

Cassius on the other hand...he could sleep through anything, eat like he hadn't been fed in a week, and manage to keep his cool, too. I had no idea how he did it, but I admired him for it.

Especially given all the stress his job placed on him. Me, I was worried about missing a deadline or a campaign not hitting some arbitrarily assigned benchmarks. In his work, he dealt with real tragedy, heartbreak, and loss. Every single day. Another thing I admired him for.

I tiptoed into the kitchen and gently pried the refrigerator door open. I grabbed a bottle of water as well as a room card that lay on the counter next to the fridge. I quietly closed the door as I left, careful not to wake Cassius up.

I made my way past the now deserted pool area. It looked a little eerie, being so still and empty, given how packed the place had been yesterday. All of the deck chairs had been turned onto their side, and the bar area was locked up. I looked around. Not a soul in sight. I figured everybody was still asleep. Like I wished I still was.

As I made my way past the pool and toward the gym, a shirtless guy cracked open a door, clutching his shirt and shoes in his hands, and quietly crept out. He reminded me of a mime artist, moving in slow motion, focused on closing the door without making a sound. Once the door was closed, he let out an audible sigh.

He began to put his shirt on when our eyes met. He looked guilty, like he'd been busted doing something naughty. I smiled brightly at him, not wanting to make him feel bad or as if he was being judged. That was the last thing I wanted him to think I was doing.

"Morning. Big night?" I asked the guy as he walked past me barefoot, his shoes still dangling in his hands.

"More like big mistake." He shook his head.

"I hope you have a good day."

He eyed me up and down. "Yeah, you too, man," he said as he continued along on his walk of shame.

I wished I could say I knew the feeling, but I didn't. I'd never had a one-night stand before. The only person I'd ever had sex with was Natalie.

Parts of being with her felt so right, but other parts...weren't so right. Not bad, necessarily. It was more like—I looked at my watch and breathed out a sigh of relief. It was still before seven, which granted me another reprieve from existential issues...for a few more minutes at least.

One thing I knew for certain about myself, though, was that I was a *sex in a relationship-only* kinda guy. It didn't bother me if my other friends chose to play around—again, no judgment—it's just that it wasn't what I wanted to do.

The thought of being with somebody for one night and then leaving them in the morning just didn't appeal to me. If I spent the night with a wom—person—it would be because I cared for them. I wouldn't want it to end after just one time.

I guess I could add that to my ever-growing list of weirdness, right alongside my exorbitantly high enjoyment of vacation unpacking. And my mother wondered why I was still single.

The thought of her made me shudder. Which was quickly joined by a heavy feeling of guilt for feeling that way about her. Which was then joined by an even heavier feeling of dread at the thought of having to see her tomorrow.

She lived in Florida with her latest husband, Steve Kornacki. (No, not *that* Steve Kornacki; the khaki-wearing NBC political journalist-slash-dreamboat who became known as "the map guy" after the 2020 election. Trust me, that would have been much cooler.) *This* Steve was third-generation wealthy, bald, had a beer gut, and apparently—as my mom had overshared with me last Thanksgiving—a low sex drive. So, in other words, her perfect match as she continued her gold-digging climb. Currently she was up to husband number four.

I reached the gym and swiped the access card to let myself in. The quietness I had experienced walking through the resort was the exact opposite of the scene inside the gym. I had been wrong in assuming everyone was still asleep. It looked like all the guys from the pool yesterday were here this morning.

I looked around for an empty machine but couldn't find one. Every single piece of equipment was in use. After doing a short walk-through, I gave up and decided to go for a walk on the beach instead. That view from the suite had been very inviting.

"Hey there," came a friendly voice from my left. It was Leo. A very sweaty Leo. He greeted me with a wide smile. "How are you this morning, Spencer?"

"I'm great, thanks. Cass and I had an early night last night, so I thought I'd sneak in a workout before breakfast." I cast my gaze around the busy gym. "I guess I wasn't the only one with that idea."

Leo laughed cheerfully. "You can't keep gay men away from the gym. It's like our second home."

I smiled as he continued. "Hey, listen. I've got your party tickets in my office. I can have them sent over to your suite at some point today, if you like?"

"Or I can pick them up now?" I suggested.

"What about your workout?"

"I think the universe is telling me to skip a day. Getting the tickets now sounds like a good idea, and so does coffee."

Leo flicked a smile at me. "We have an amazing on-site cafe. We get our beans from an ethical plantation in Costa Rica. It's the best, even if I do say so myself."

"Sounds good. What time does it open?"

"Seven," he replied. "So we can head up to my office. I'll give you the tickets, and then you can get your caffeine fix."

"Lead the way."

We stepped out of the gym and headed in the direction of the lobby where we had checked in yesterday. I took in all the amazing fragrances coming from the various colorful plants that lined the path and filled the gardens beautifully. Talking with Leo was easy; he kept the conversation light and friendly. We entered the lobby and walked past the front desk. Leo led me to a white door and turned to me before opening it. "I have to warn you, it's a little messy in here."

I waved his hands away. "I'm fine with a little mess."

I followed him into his office and holy shit. A little mess, I could have handled with some controlled breathing and calm counting-to-ten exercises I had memorized off YouTube, but this—*this*—was a whole ginormous craphouse of mess.

A little messy didn't even begin to describe the place. There was an Andes mountain range of papers stacked on the desk, boxes

stacked up six, seven, no, eight high and a whole bunch of other
random items—feather boas, water coolers, and a giant painting of
The Flintstones—littered all over the place.

Thankfully—and I didn't know how exactly—the place didn't
smell bad, at least. But that was literally the only thing it had going
for it.

My inner neat freak tapped my inner clean freak on the
shoulder and called an emergency meeting to determine the best
course of action here. Luckily for me, my inner *we need to play it
cool so this guy doesn't think we're a total nutjob* freak barged in,
took over the meeting, and promptly ordered everyone to disperse
peacefully.

"Now, where did I put your tickets?" Leo tapped his fingers
against his chin as he began shuffling piles of paper around on his
desk.

"So, uh, we met some nice guys at the meet and greet
yesterday." I had to say something to stave off the tide of panic
rising within me. Clearly, having so many things in a confined
space was fucking with the oxygen levels.

Leo stopped what he was doing and looked up at me.

"Oh, yeah. Who?"

"Hawk and Emry."

He gave an affirming nod. "They're good guys, those two. I
have a feeling you boys will all get along well. Especially you and
Hawk."

I could feel my eyebrows pinching together tightly. What did
he mean by that? I was about to ask, but Leo was back in search
mode, rapidly opening and shutting the drawers of his desk,
muttering something under his breath. I hazarded a guess it was
probably something to do with needing to tidy his office up.

I dodged what looked like a half-open box of streamers and
party supplies at my feet as I walked over to a beige wall. A
pinboard hung on it, displaying a series of black-and-white
photographs. They were of two men at the beach.

"Is this you?" I pointed to the board.

Leo looked up again and nodded. "Yeah. When I was younger." His voice carried a wistful undertone. "Much younger."

"And who's the other guy?"

A darkness swept across Leo's face. I noticed it straightaway. That, and the fact that he had bolted into an upright, frozen position, like he'd suddenly been called to stand at attention.

"Oh, sorry. I don't mean to pry."

"It's okay." His tone was calm but gave nothing away.

I stepped in closer, studying the array of snaps of the two guys. I could tell they were in love, enjoying a day at the beach. There were some other guys in the background. Friends, maybe?

Leo was a good-looking guy, but the other guy looked like a model. A South American one. Dark curly hair, an impressive build, a wide smile that lit up his whole face. I could practically see the joy radiating off both of them. It filled me with happiness just looking at the photos.

"You know"—I clasped my hands together, the seed of an idea beginning to germinate in my mind—"this would be great to use for some upcoming marketing, Leo. People love seeing this kind of history."

"It's not history. It's personal," Leo snapped back immediately.

Our eyes locked before his face softened. "I'm sorry, Spencer. I didn't mean to sound so aggressive. It's just"—he cast his gaze downward and took a deep breath—"Dante, my partner that you can see there with me, he died a week after those photos were taken."

Any remaining oxygen in the room got sucked up in that moment. "Oh my god. Leo, I am so sorry."

He kept looking down. "It's okay. It's still painful, that's all."

I glanced back at the photos, this time seeing them differently, through a filter of sadness. Life really was precious. One moment, you could be a beautiful young man happily in love, and then a week later, it could all be gone.

"Ah, found them."

I turned back and saw Leo holding up the tickets. He was forcing a half smile. I felt terrible for opening up a hornet's nest of memories for him.

"Here you go." He handed me the tickets. "I hope you and Cassius have a great time at the party tomorrow night."

"Thanks."

I took the tickets, but my mind was still stuck on the images I had just seen. It felt like they had been burned into my subconscious.

"I, uh, have some work I should probably get started on."

"Oh, of course," I muttered, making my way to the door. "I don't want to be in your way."

He opened his mouth as if he was about to say something, but then snapped it shut.

I wanted to say something, too. But what? Sometimes, there really were no words.

I settled for, "Thanks again, Leo. For everything. We're having a great time here."

Leo smiled. This time it was wider, warmer. "I'm glad to hear that. Have a great day, Spencer."

And with that, I let myself out of his office. I let out a heavy exhalation as soon as I had closed the door behind me.

I headed to the café, which was open by now, and ordered two coffees. And since it was after seven, my mind now had full permission to wade back into the existential issues plaguing me.

But after hearing Leo's story, my thoughts were different. It was as if his tragedy had changed my perspective on my own situation.

Life was short. Too short. So why waste even a second of it?

Five minutes later, I was walking back to our suite carrying two almond lattes in my hand and a newfound resolve in my heart.

11

CASSIUS

Knock, knock.

I grumbled as I heard Spencer enter my room. The smell of caffeine invaded my senses and, funnily enough, stopped my grumbling dead in its tracks. I scrubbed my palm over my face.

"What time is it?" I croaked.

"Rise and shine, sunshine. It's time to get up," Spencer replied with a smile. At least, I assumed he was smiling. His voice sounded smiley-esque.

The *OPEN* function on my eyelids hadn't activated yet. My eyes were glued together with sleepy, crusty bits everywhere. Luckily for me, Spencer had seen me in much worse states.

"How did you sleep?" he asked, handing me a coffee.

My primal survival instincts kicked in, and my arm reached for the coffee. I pulled myself into a semi-upright position and brought the brew to my lips.

Aah, that's better.

My eyes were free to fully open now.

"Like a baby." I took another sip. "Mmm, almond milk. You remembered, thank you."

"You've converted me. I've switched to almond milk, too." He raised his cup to his lips. Those stupidly cute lips of his.

Oh, shit!

The caffeine hit collided with the memory of the thing I did right before I fell asleep.

Jerking off wasn't bad.

Jerking off while fantasizing about my best friend? That was a whole world of wrong.

I raised my sheet slightly higher to cover my stomach. I was so exhausted after coming that I hadn't bothered to clean myself up. The last thing I needed was for Spencer to see the end result of my wildly inappropriate him-inspired wank.

"How about you?" I asked, keen to get my brain off *that* topic and onto...anything else, really.

"Awesomely." He smiled warmly as he sat at the foot of the bed. "I wish I'd slept in a little longer, but the bed is super comfortable."

I raised my eyebrows in agreement. "Mine, too."

After a few sips in silence, I asked, "So, what's the plan for today? Actually, what's the plan for this whole weekend? You've been guarding the schedule like it's some sort of top secret."

He threw a pointed look in my direction. "Cass, would you even remember if I *had* told you?"

He had a point there. I probably wouldn't have. Not because I didn't care but because I knew that Spencer would take care of it. That he'd have planned the most perfect weekend for us and every single last detail to go along with it.

So, since he had it all under control, why did I need to take up valuable brain space thinking about it when I could use that allocated mental capacity for other things, like coming up with more wild and exotic food combinations?

His eyes narrowed. "You did read that email I sent you, though, didn't you?" His voice carried a serious air to it.

Email? What email?

"Uh, sure," I replied, hoping to mask my lie under the cover of my coffee cup.

"Uh-huh." He didn't sound convinced.

Technically, it wasn't a lie. I had seen the email come in. I just hadn't read it, yet. Crap. Okay, so it was a lie, but just as soon as Spencer left my room, I would read it. Which lessened the outright lie into a half lie... Right?

I downed the rest of my coffee. "So, plans," I said energetically, buzzing with caffeine. "What do I need to get dressed for?"

A smile spread out across Spencer's face. "First, we'll have some breakfast because I'm assuming you're hungry."

I tipped my head. "You assume correctly, kind sir."

"And then after that, we're going hiking."

"Hiking? But I didn't bring my hiking gear."

"Oh, really?" Spencer clutched at his chest feigning shock. "Even after reading my email? You know, the one with the subject header 'URGENT—THINGS TO PACK FOR THE WEEKEND' in all caps? Followed a day later with the email 'CASS, I'M SERIOUS. PLEASE PACK THIS STUFF.' Also, in all caps."

I slapped the side of my face. "Oh, you meant *thooose* emails. Right, right, right...yeah, no, I didn't read any of them."

He got up off the bed and flashed me a knowing smile. "I figured...which is why I packed some stuff for you."

"Oh, Spencey. You're the best." I was genuinely touched. He really was the best friend a guy could hope for.

"It's all right," he shot back a little too gleefully. "That's my three good deeds for the day done."

"Three? Whoa, look at you go. Run me through them."

"Number one, I got you coffee."

"Thank you. It was delicious."

"The beans are from Costa Rica."

"I have no idea what that means, but it sounds impressive."

He let out a small laugh, but didn't quite catch covering it behind his hand.

"Number two, I packed your hiking boots."

"You did. And for that I am eternally grateful."

Then silence. Spencer's gaze traveled south of my face for some reason.

I cleared my throat. "And number three?"

Spencer got up and walked over to the door. He spun around to face me, an unusual gleam flickering in his eyes. "And my number three good deed for the day is telling my best friend that his chest is covered in dried cum."

My head dropped as I frantically searched my chest. Fuck. He was right. Patches of dried cum had collected in my chest hairs much farther up than I had realized. My whole body flushed with embarrassment as I yanked the sheet up over my chest right up to under my neck.

Spencer covered his mouth as he let out another of his signature *tee-hee-hee* laughs. "You are one of a kind, Cassius Draper."

He began to close the door. "Breakfast is in ten minutes. Let's not be late."

The door shut quietly behind him, before opening again. His face peeked around the edge. "And hey, I love you, man." With that, the door clicked shut.

I slid down into the bed, wishing it was a wormhole that would swallow me whole. The only thing worse than Spencer seeing me *in this state* was if he'd known how I had gotten myself *into* this state.

And it was right at that moment that I turned my head to the left and looked down at the floor. My sketchpad lay there. The last page, wide open. Spencer's illustrated face beaming back at me.

I slunk further down and pulled the sheet over me. I hoped against hope that Spencer hadn't seen it. This was not how I imagined my day starting.

At least the hike would be good. Nothing bad could ever happen when I was hiking.

12

SPENCER

Forty minutes later, and right on schedule, Cassius and I jumped into the open-top red Jeep I had rented for the weekend. That was, of course, after Cassius had taken full advantage of the all-you-can-eat buffet breakfast. Luckily, I had factored that into my timings for the day, too. He had gorged on three full plates, and I had lost count of how many pancakes. Meanwhile, yeah, I stuck with Greek yogurt and granola cereal, because calories, unfortunately, didn't take vacations.

We were on our way to the Sonny McCoy Indigenous Park. I wasn't much of a hiker myself.

Okay, I outright hated it.

I didn't like being outdoors with all the animals and trees and stuff. It just wasn't my thing. Plus, I didn't like getting my shoes dirty, which meant that I generally avoided any activities that got them dirty in the first place.

One of the reasons why I had chosen this park—and yes, I did compile a list of all possible hike locations in a spreadsheet to evaluate the pros and cons of each option—was that it had nice wide paved pathways.

The pros column also included that it was a short drive from the resort, it attracted a parade of wildlife including birds, freshwater turtles, and herds of non-native iguanas, which I thought Cassius would get a kick out of, and it offered something no other hiking trail in Key West did: a natural freshwater pond.

I cast a quick glance at the car's navigation system. We were on the right track and making good time. In retrospect, the open-top car wasn't the best choice as it made talking almost impossible. We had shouted a few things to each other when we first started driving, but given how hard it was to hear, we drove in silence.

Which, in a way, was a good thing. It gave me time to think. I'd planned a number of activities over the course of the weekend that gave Cassius and I some alone time. I planned on using that alone time to talk to him about my sexuality.

Another pro of the park was that it tended to not be too busy at this time of year. I figured since Cassius liked hiking so much, it could be a good, *private* environment to tell him that I was—hmm, what was I?

Okay, different tack. I could tell him what I knew I wasn't: straight. At least, not in the strictly technical, legal definition of the term. If a technical, legal definition of the term actually existed.

"You okay over there?" I yelled.

His brown hair flopped around like crazy in the wind, his mouth slightly open as he stared out the passenger side. For just a second, he reminded me of the golden retriever I'd had as a kid. Milly loved car rides so much. Cassius, like Milly, was always so happy, wherever he was.

He gave me two thumbs up, accompanied by a cheesy grin. I shook my head and smiled. The guy was such a goofball, and I loved him anyway.

A few minutes later, I pulled off Atlantic Boulevard and into the parking lot of the Key West Wildlife Center. I saw Cassius' eyes light up when he read the sign. "Ooh, I like this place already."

I cut the engine and faced him. "I'm glad to hear that, Cass."

To get to the park, we actually had to wander through the wildlife center before descending down a flight of stairs. The walking trail was to the right. I smiled at the wide, paved trail. My white Nike sneakers were the closest thing I had to hiking boots, and they would remain clean and protected on this pathway.

"So, this is nice," I observed as we entered the dense canopy.

Cassius' head was jerking around all over the place, taking it all in. I had done a few hikes with him before, but now that I thought about it, I couldn't remember the last time we had gone out together. Maybe when we were teenagers? Watching him was like looking at a kid in a candy store. He loved it so much.

"It's amazing, Spence."

He grabbed my hand, and we stopped walking. "Thank you for this. I know you're not much of an"—his grip on my hand tightened as he scanned around, looking for the right word—"outdoorsy person. So I really appreciate it."

"Hey, no problem." I gave his hand a squeeze right back. "What are friends for, right?"

We kept walking, Cassius seemingly enjoying it more with every step. Me, on the other hand...I was struggling with the realization that the farther in we got, the farther away we were from medical care should something happen to one of us.

No. Wait. That wasn't it. At least, not entirely.

The truth was that the more we walked, the more it dawned on me that we were approaching the moment.

The moment.

Was it a coming out moment? I honestly didn't have an answer to that.

I'd read a lot about people's coming out stories online. What struck me as a heartbreakingly common through line was the fear people felt of being rejected, abandoned, criticized, or hurt, sometimes even physically.

A swirl of emotions whirred throughout my body. I steadied my breathing, inhaling the tropical air deeply through my nose. What was *I* feeling?

I guess my biggest fear was that Cassius would freak out. I knew better than anyone else how much he hated any type of change. But how would this necessarily change things between us? It shouldn't, but at the same time, I wasn't confident that it wouldn't.

"Oh, look." He grabbed my forearm with one hand and pointed over to the right. "An iguana."

Sure enough, a green iguana was sunning itself at the edge of the trail. I scooted far over to the left, drawing a laugh out of Cassius.

"Relax, Spence. It won't hurt you."

"I know, I know. It's just...ew."

He threaded his arm through mine. "I'll protect you, Spencey. You're safe with me."

We continued walking, his words echoing in my head. Even though it often seemed that because I was the organized one, I somehow carried the load in our friendship, I often felt that it was actually the other way around.

Cassius' carefree and non-judgmental approach to things did something to me. It unwound me. It got me out of my own head...at least, for some of the time. And even though he had meant it in jest, I did feel safe with him. Truly safe. Which made telling him what was going on with me that much more difficult.

I heard a rustling to my left. There was a gap between the trees. I looked closer. In the small space, there was a pathway. A tiny one, barely room for one person to fit through and definitely not paved. I followed it for as far as I could see from where we were standing. I squinted, and in the distance, I could make out a person. A man.

I moved in closer. My eyes widened. I could see two men. They were naked. And...fucking.

"Hey, Cass. Come over here a sec." I waved him over.

Cassius came up beside me. I motioned my head at the two

men in the distance down the narrow pathway. He furrowed his brow, unsure of what I was wanting him to see. But I could tell the moment his eyes landed on the two men because his eyebrows lifted, almost touching his hairline, and he jumped a foot back in the air. "Whoa."

"Relax, Cass. It won't hurt you."

He shot me an *I see what you're doing there* look as he stepped back next to me. We watched in silence for a few moments as the two men continued fucking. Then I felt the heat of Cassius' gaze on me.

"Are you okay with this, Spence?"

"Yeah, I'm fine." I might have answered a bit too quickly, judging by the funny expression on Cassius' face. Sure, maybe we shouldn't have been looking. But if the guys wanted privacy, they wouldn't have been fucking in public.

I mean, it was just sex, after all.

For some reason, I couldn't take my eyes off them. They were good-looking guys. One looked about a decade older than the younger guy, who might have been close to our age. But I couldn't really be sure.

The sunlight streamed through the trees, lighting up parts of their exposed skin. The older guy sported a chest beset with a thick patch of dark hair. I noticed that, too. Apart from that, we were standing too far away from them to notice any other details.

Cassius took a few steps toward them, peering in to get a better view. "Oh my god," he exclaimed in a hushed whisper. "That's Toby."

I stood next to him. "Who's Toby?"

"A kid from the center. Well, he was at the center. Toby left a few months ago. I told you about him—his family died in a car crash, and then when he moved in with his biological father, he kicked him out when he found out Toby was gay."

"Oh, yeah," I said, jogging my memory. "I remember you telling me about him. Which one is he? The top or the bottom?"

Cassius whipped his head at me so fast I was surprised he didn't pull a muscle. "How—how do you know those words?"

I lifted my shoulder casually. "I know...stuff."

If only he knew how much I had been researching every single aspect of human sexuality for the past few months. My spreadsheet was full to the brim—no, overflowing—with terms, acronyms, sub-groupings, slang, you name it. If it had anything to do with sexual orientation, I was all over it, kinda like these two guys were all over each other.

Was now a good time to tell him? No, that was a stupid idea. Two guys fuck-bombing—which was like photo-bombing, but with, you know, fucking happening in the background instead—the conversation was not how I had imagined it unfolding.

"Toby's the guy on...the bottom." Cassius spoke the words so delicately. It sounded like the verbal equivalent of holding expensive porcelain glass in your hands. His words were fragile and his expression was completely unreadable. I would have loved to have known what was going on in that head of his.

I nodded. "Right. So, Toby isn't the one who looks like a bear?"

Cassius scratched the side of his face. "How the fuck do you know that word...and I don't?"

Uh-oh. Surely, straight people knew about bears, otters, cubs, wolves, pups, bulls, and whatever other animal kingdom-inspired slang had entered the gay male lexicon?

Or maybe not.

Cassius' eyes felt like they were burning into my soul. I tugged at the top of my shirt, suddenly feeling the heat of the Floridian sun in a way I hadn't been just a few moments earlier.

"Maybe we should head back?" I suggested. "You still want to check out the wildlife center?"

"Yeah, all right." He stretched his words out, and I could tell his mind was in overdrive.

We turned around and walked back, neither one of us saying a word. I peered over occasionally at Cassius, but all I noticed was the way he was walking, gripping his wrist with his other hand, his fingers gently stroking over the *DAD* tattoo he had there. His face remained blank, his eyes fixed forward.

Okay, so that hadn't gone exactly to plan. No biggie. I had come prepared. There were other opportunities for me to tell him.

Because one way or another, I *would* tell Cassius this weekend. And two dudes fucking in the woods wasn't going to stop me.

13

CASSIUS

Well, that was fucking weird, stacked on top of weird, with an extra side helping of—*you guessed it!*—weird.

Seeing Toby during the hike had been unexpected, to say the least. What was even more of a shock was to see Spencer's reaction to it. He didn't seem to mind...at all. While it was great that he was secure enough in his own sexuality to not be a dick (pun unintended) about gay stuff like, say, public gay sex, I couldn't help but feel like it was almost—*almost*—as if there was something more to it than that.

I might have just been imagining things, but it seemed as if he was enjoying watching Toby and the bear fucking. Not in a creepy *guy using binoculars to spy on his next-door neighbors who aren't aware of said creepy guy and his pervert-staring tendencies* kinda way. More in a—actually, I didn't know how to finish that thought.

Which brought me to my next *thing I never knew about my best friend of seventeen years* point. Since when did Spencer swallow the gay dictionary and start knowing all those terms? *I* didn't even know them, and *I* was the gay dude.

We drove back to the resort in an open-roof-induced silence.

We'd tried talking, but with the wind flapping around us so loudly, it made it impossible to bellow out more than a few words at a time.

By the time we got back and pulled up in the resort's parking lot, it had to be at least a hundred degrees, and I was parched. "Pool time?" I asked, getting out.

"Great idea," Spencer replied with a smile.

We strode through the resort lobby, making our way down the same path we had walked down yesterday after we arrived. The sight and scents of the vivid tropical plants felt familiar and instantly eased the tension I hadn't even realized I was carrying in my shoulders.

When we reached the pool, another familiar sight greeted us. It seemed that we weren't the only ones who had the bright idea of whiling away a few lazy hours. The scene in front of us was even busier than yesterday.

"Jammin' enough for ya?" I joked, placing my hand on Spencer's shoulder. I couldn't help but feel how tight it was, too. Maybe what we'd seen during the hike had affected him more than I thought?

He let out a smile. "I'm game if you are. The challenge is going to be finding somewhere to sit."

As we both surveyed the scene, searching for an empty spot, I quickly spotted one difference from yesterday—one key, unmissable difference. My mind wandered back to the conversation with Hawk and Emry about the whole clothing-optional thing.

They were right. On day two, the option *not* to wear clothes was on full display.

I turned my head and observed Spencer. It looked like he was having the exact same realization that I was. But again—just like how he had been on the hiking trail—he didn't seem bothered by it.

At all.

I mean, hanging out with gay dudes was one thing. But hanging out with a bunch of naked gay dudes? Surely that had to be setting something off inside him. If it was, he was doing a good job of hiding it.

"I've got a feeling we're not in Kansas anymore," he spoke as his mouth curved into a smile.

"Unless Kansas just got a whole lot sexier, I think you're right, Dorothy."

We both looked at each other and laughed. The weirdness was officially broken. For the time being, anyway.

"Heyyy ladies."

I yanked my head around and spotted Emry approaching us from behind. That drawl of his was something else. I loved it. "I've been looking out for you two. Where ya been hidin'?"

"We went for a hike," I replied. "And then we thought we'd lounge by the pool for a bit."

Emry gazed up at the sky, while my eyes traveled down from his face, to his chest, over his washboard abs...and yep, there they were.

Dangly bits.

"Perfect weather for it," he remarked, oblivious to where my gaze had wandered to.

My eyes bounced back up to his face at his words.

"It sure is," Spencer said with a grin plastered on his face. "Now we just need to find somewhere to sit. This place looks like it's even busier than it was yesterday."

"I was just thinking the same thing," I chimed in.

Emry nodded. "Not everyone can get away on a Thursday, so a lot of guys arrive on Friday." His eyes darted around us. "There'll probably be even more arrivals tomorrow. No one in their right mind wants to miss the White Party."

The White Party? What the heck's a White Party, and why didn't I know anything about it? I had a feeling it might have had something to do with the still unread emails Spencer had sent me.

"Yeah, I hear it's meant to be epic," Spencer concurred. I shot him a *how do you know about this and I don't?* befuddled look, but then I remembered, he probably had it all planned out well in advance. In a carefully organized, alphabetically arranged (I'm assuming with ninety-nine percent certainty) spreadsheet.

"Anyways...you boys are in luck. Someone—in addition to being super fab, cute, and gorggggg-eous—has saved you two seats."

Spencer's eyes lit up. "You did? Oh, wow. That's so nice of you, Emry. Thank you."

"Yeah, thank you," I joined in.

He smiled as he waved for us to follow him.

"What are new friends for, right?" he sang brightly over his shoulder.

We made our way to a row of deck chairs on the other side of the pool from where we were hanging out yesterday. Hawk was already lying down, and he too, was naked as could be.

Hmm, what was the etiquette here? I didn't want to be rude and not look at him, but I didn't want to stare, either. I went with a casual wave and was met with a head tilt in return from Hawk, as I pulled up onto the chair next to Emry.

We chatted casually for a few minutes, filling the guys in on our morning hike—minus the part about accidentally catching two guys having sex in the woods. Hawk had spent the morning in the gym and catching up with old friends, while Emry went into town and did some shopping. Spencer perked up at that and asked Emry for recommendations. Emry rattled off a number of store names that I'd never heard of.

Somehow, the conversation turned to food. Oh, yeah. I think it was some time right after I blurted out, "You guys, I am so fucking hungry that I think I'll die if I don't eat something in the next five minutes."

Once the guys stopped laughing, Spencer and Hawk offered to order food from the pool bar. Emry handed me a food menu. I was half expecting to be met with a slew of creatively worded options such as Beefy Big Ass Burgers and Frisky Fries, but no, all the food was normally named. I told Spencer what I would like while Emry placed his order with Hawk. The two guys set off, leaving me with Emry again.

I looked over at him—the upper half of his body—and said, "Hey, thanks again for saving these seats for us. That was really thoughtful of you."

Emry turned and took off his sunglasses, resting them on his head. "No problem." He sat up a little straighter. "Hey, can I tell you something, Cassius?"

"Sure." I settled back into my chair, stretching my legs out in front of me and getting a little more comfortable.

"I really like you—" He cut himself off as his eyes widened. "Not like that, though," he quickly clarified. "No, I mean, I really like you as a friend."

I gave him a warm smile. "I really like you, too, Emry. As a friend."

"Really?" He bit down on his lower lip, and for the first time, he looked...vulnerable. "You don't think I'm too loud, or too out there, or too...stereotypically offensively gay?"

I let out a nervous laugh. That was a very loaded question. "No, I don't think that at all. In fact, I think it's great that you are who you are. I wish—" I stopped myself from saying *I wish I knew who I was*.

Emry looked across as if he were measuring me with his gaze.

I changed tack slightly, going for a less personally revealing option. "I think it's important that people are who they are. As long as you're being real and authentic, that's what the world needs more of, right?"

I smiled as I paraphrased the words my dad would say to me each night when he would tuck me in as a kid. I guess the hike had made me think of him again. Like it always did.

A smile broke out across Emry's face. "I am *soooo* relieved to hear you say that. You have no idea how many guys have it in for femme dudes."

I wrinkled my nose. "Really?"

"Like you wouldn't believe." He let out a loud breath. "I have no gay friends, and the main reason I get laid is because of Hawk. He pulls guys with that whole strong, silent thing he's got going on, and then he makes it clear we're a package deal."

"And that works?"

Emry nodded slowly. "Most of the time, yeah."

"Oh." I didn't know what else to say.

"There's only one thing that most gay dudes like more than one big dick"—a smile flickered over Emry's lips—"and that's two big dicks."

"Well, I think you're really nice. And I don't give a shit about how big your dick is."

Emry clapped his hands together, shifting from mild melancholy to exuberant joyfulness in less than two-point-three seconds. "Thanks, Cass. Can I—can I call you Cass?"

I grinned. "Of course you can."

Only the people closest to me called me that—which was basically my family and Spencer—but I had a really good feeling about my newest friend.

The guys returned with two bottles of water. "They'll bring the food out to us," Spencer informed us after noticing the confused—and hungry—look on my face.

We fell into a casual group chat. Hawk was a lot more talkative today, pointing out some of the guys hanging out in and around the pool and telling us more about them.

I scanned the sea of people, looking for one person in particular: Toby. I knew it was a long shot, but maybe he was staying at the resort, too? If he was, it would be nice to catch up with him. I was keen to know how he was getting on since leaving the center.

"The hazelnut and feta salad?" the server asked as he made his way over to us.

"That's me." Spencer raised his hand, ever so politely.

I tried to make eye contact with him to shoot him an *I can't believe you're not splurging at least a little while we're on vacation* look, but he was deliberately avoiding looking at me. Damn, he knew me too well.

"Two double cheeseburgers, extra fries, extra sauce, with a strawberry milkshake?"

My stomach growled. "That would be me."

The server handed Emry and Hawk their food before leaving.

When I next looked up, I was met with two stunned expressions on Hawk and Emry's faces.

Emry gaped at me. "Are you seriously going to eat all of that food?"

"Uh, yeah, what else am I going to do with it?" I replied, plowing the first, delicious mouthful of burger into my mouth...as elegantly as I could, of course.

"I know. It's not fair," Spencer said, looking at them while picking at his salad like he hated it (which I secretly knew that he did).

"What's not fair?" I asked, cramming a fistful of fries into the tiny remaining empty space left in my mouth not currently occupied with burger. Getting the burger-to-fries mouthful ratio right was an art form I had spent many, many years perfecting.

Did it look sophisticated, or even like what a normal person with table manners would do? No.

But did it more than make up for that by being the bestest-tasting thing ever invented? You betcha!

"It's cruel and immoral that you can eat all that shit and still have a body like that," Emry exclaimed, not beating around the bush.

"Exactly," Spencer chimed in, as he braved his first bite of the salad.

"I intend on writing a strongly worded email to the food gods," Emry sighed while somehow managing to giggle at the same time.

"You might want to send that email off to the genetics gods," Hawk cut in. "That's what a lot of it comes down to."

"Nah, you guys don't know what you're talking about," I managed to get out during a very rare occurrence: a moment of time where food was resting on my plate and not in my mouth. "I'll let you guys in on a secret."

All three of them—yep, even Spencer—leaned in closer, hanging on my every word.

"I'm a firm believer in a guilt-free diet," I announced proudly.

"Sorry." Hawk leaned in even more. "Did you say gluten-free diet?"

I had just bitten into my burger and was about to answer Hawk's question while I chewed, when it dawned on me that we were in front of people. New people. This wasn't me eating like a slob on the couch by myself or in front of Spencer, who had seen it countless times over the years.

I raised my hand to indicate that I needed a moment to finish. I chewed the remaining mouthful as quickly as I could and grabbed a gulp of the milkshake to wash it down.

"No," I said once my mouth was finally empty. "I said *guilt-free* diet."

"What is that?" Hawk eyed me suspiciously.

"It's simple." I wiped the corners of my mouth with a napkin. "You can eat whatever you like. There's no 'good foods,' and there's no 'bad foods.'"

I could see Emry's eyes lighting up.

"So you can just eat whatever you like and as much of it as you want. And then"—I paused for dramatic effect—"when you're done eating...you don't feel guilty about it."

I was met with a smirk from Hawk and a blank expression on Emry's face, and I could see Spencer's lips begin to curl upward. He had heard my dubious, totally non-science-based food theory on more than one occasion.

"Riiiight." Hawk settled back into his seat, clearly not buying any of it.

"Guilt"—I lifted a few fries into my mouth—"is fattening. So no guilt equals no fat. It's a very simple scientifical fact, you guys."

I heard Spencer mutter "scientifical" under his breath, accompanied by a massive eye roll.

Emry practically squealed with excitement. "I fucking love that. I'm going to get that printed on a shirt."

I looked over at Spencer and poked my tongue out. "See, Emry thinks it's a good idea."

That managed to draw a chuckle out of him.

Once we had finished the meal, I fell into my usual post-food coma. I felt the sun beating down on me, and it was pure bliss. I closed my eyes and placed my hands behind my head, my body melting into the deck chair. Spencer lay beside me, doing the same.

"So"—Hawk's deep voice filled the silence—"it's day two, boys. So you know what that means?"

My eyes shot open. I stared at Hawk, then Spencer, before turning back to Hawk. He dropped his head down. "It's time for you guys to activate the *optional* part of clothing optional."

I swallowed hard. "Oh, I don't know about—"

"Sure." Spencer's voice rang out clear as day.

I jerked my head around to see him standing up. Before I knew what was happening, he took off his shirt. My eyes momentarily drifted down his chest, noticing how smooth and supple his skin looked, how his nipples were the same shade of cherry pink that his lips were. Fuck, he even found a way to color-coordinate *that*. I snapped myself out of it.

"Spencer." My tone was low, guarded. "What—what are you doing?"

"What does it look like I'm doing?" His eyes had become all wide and innocent-like. "I'm just following day two rules, Cass. I wouldn't want to be rude, now would I?"

No, he wouldn't. Spencer took people pleasing to a whole new stratosphere. But I still couldn't believe he was about to do...*this*.

He kicked off his white Nikes and socks.

I leaned in toward him and whispered in a hushed tone. "You don't have to do anything you don't want to, Spence."

"Oh, I know that," he said, slowly peeling his hiking shorts down his muscular legs. I could feel the heat from his gaze pinching my skin. What was happening here? Spencer was stripping off in front of me, and I was...liking it?

No. No. No. Get a grip. That couldn't be it...could it?

Spencer stepped out of his shorts. He was wearing a pair of white Calvin's. Of course he color-coordinated his shoes to his underwear. That was so Spencer of him. I started to turn away, thinking this was where this whole little strip show detour would end. He was just pulling my leg. He wouldn't go any further than this. No more clothing was coming off his perfectly toned, tanned, and tight body.

But nope, I was wrong.

He wasn't stopping.

In one fell swoop, he bent over and dragged his underwear down to his feet. He carefully stepped to the side and picked up his briefs in his hand, waving them around with his fingers, like he was showing off some prized possession.

My jaw landed on the ground. I couldn't believe it. Standing there in front of me was my best friend of seventeen years, completely and totally buck naked. My cheeks flushed, and suddenly, it was a lot warmer than it was a few moments ago.

I ventured a peek in his direction, holding up my hand to shield me from his, well, dangly bits.

"Geez, that's nice," Spencer joked, pretending to be offended. "It's just my dick, Cass. It's not roadkill."

It might not have been that, but for me, Spencer's dick was like the sun. I couldn't look directly at it.

"Margarita, anyone?" Emry offered.

"Yes!" I cried out.

Okay, maybe I shouldn't have yelled it with all of the urgency of a person undergoing a traumatic life experience, but in my own way, I kinda was. I'd have to check my health insurance policy, but I was pretty sure that seeing your best friend's cock qualified as something requiring medical care.

"We'll be right back."

Emry and Hawk got up, leaving Spencer and me alone.

In complete and utter silence.

And that was how we stayed, both lying on our deck chairs, soaking up the sun—without exchanging a single word to each other—until Emry's unmissable, campy voice rang out excitedly with a bouncy, "Here comes fun!"

And with that, margarita glasses landed in our hands.

"Cheers." I lifted my drink into the air.

Spencer, Emry, and Hawk did the same, our glasses making a loud *clink* sound. I took a big gulp of the icy cold drink. It cooled me down instantly. The day just kept getting hotter and hotter.

"So," Emry said, eyeing me off as he slunk down into his deck chair. "What's up with you, Mr. Pants?"

"What?" I replied, perhaps an octave too defensively. "It's clothing *optional*." I emphasized the last word deliberately. "So I'm choosing the option where I get to keep my clothes *on*."

A cheeky grin filled Emry's face. "I have a theory."

"Oh, do you now?" I matched his smile. "Care to fill me in? Because I am *dying* to hear it."

"Glad you said that. Okay, here it is. Take a look around, Cass. All the guys who are wearing swimwear or shorts? They all have small dicks."

I chuckled. "Oh, is that so?"

"Uh, yeah." He made it sound like it was the most obvious thing in the world. "I mean, if you've got it, you flaunt it, right? Especially at a place like this. So, that means if you're not flaunting it, it's because you ain't got it."

"Your theory sounds very scientific and fact-based." I was doing my best to hold back a smile. The zanier he got, the more I liked the guy. He was so out there and free. It was inspiring.

"For the record," Hawk added. "I completely agree with Emry on this one. And also, Cassius, I think that Emry's theory has more *scientific* credibility than your dubious dietary claims." His lips then curled into a subtle smirk while he proceeded to give me a very unsubtle once-over.

Exasperated, I turned to Spencer for backup. "Spence, what do you think about all of this?"

Not missing a beat, he answered, "I don't know much about the small dick theory, but I do think the human body is a wonderful thing. I mean, you sketch it all the time, and I love your sketches."

Emry grabbed my arm. "You sketch?"

I turned to face him. I wasn't used to talking about my sketches with anyone other than Spencer. "Yeah, just for fun. They're not that great."

"Not great?" Spencer made an exasperated choking sound over my shoulder. "They're fucking fantastic. Cassius is such a talented artist. Everyone in the world thinks so."

I brought the back of my hand to my mouth. "By 'everyone,' he means himself, you guys."

"Could I see them sometime?" Emry asked softly, looking up at me from under his lashes.

"Sure." I smiled, quirking an eyebrow at him. "Does that mean I can stay clothed?"

"No chance," Emry shot back. "We're going to start chanting if you don't."

"Worse"—Hawk added with a wink—"we'll all think you have a small dick."

"Oh my god," I chortled in disbelief. "I don't think I've had a conversation about the size of my dick since high school."

I looked at each of the guys. Their eyes were all on me, waiting expectantly. They weren't giving up. I blew out a noisy breath and got to my feet.

Fine, I'll show them.

I shrugged off my shirt and threw it onto the deck chair. I toed off my hiking boots and socks. And finally, I unzipped my shorts and pulled them—as well as my Bart Simpson boxer shorts—off.

I turned to Emry and Hawk, facing them front on. As in *full-frontal* front on.

"So have I debunked your theory, Emry?"

Both of their mouths hung open as their eyes roamed my body, freezing below my waist.

"Uh-huh." He spoke slowly, as if his brain had momentarily shut down. "I stand erected—I mean, corrected."

"Good. I'm glad. I've never had any complaints."

"Complaints about what?" Spencer's voice from behind me asked. Spencer had stood up, so as I turned around, I was face to face—or, rather, as was the case here, cock to cock—with my best friend.

"Holy shit!" He leaped into the air as if he'd just seen a spider, or an iguana. "You've got to be careful with that thing, man." His wide eyes remained firmly fixed on my below-the-belt area. "You could take someone's eye out with it."

"Wait. You mean you guys have never seen each other naked?" Emry asked, sounding surprised.

"No," I replied, returning to sit down on my recliner and grabbing a towel to cover myself. "For the millionth time, he really is straight, and we really are just friends."

"And I am really super fucking hot," Spencer said.

I jerked my head around to him, nodding involuntary in agreement.

Well, duh.

"I'm going to go for a dip."

Oh, that's what he meant. For some reason, my mind went to—never mind. All good.

Nothing to see here.

Just two best friends hanging out with each other, completely naked, with their two new friends, also naked, in a luxury all-male resort filled with guys who were all naked, too.

This getaway was getting more interesting by the minute.

Spencer grabbed his sunglasses off the recliner and placed them over his head. As he did, his eyes landed on me. "Hey, Cass," he whispered.

Reluctantly, I turned my head in his general vicinity, being super careful not to get blinded by his dangly bits.

"At least now you'll have a better idea of how to sketch me...all of me."

And with that, he ran his hand through my hair, messing it up before he turned around and marched his toned, hard ass toward the pool.

14

SPENCER

My lips remained steadfastly stretched all the way until I reached the pool. I guess that was why every guy I passed flashed me a wide smile back. I still couldn't get over how friendly and laid back everyone here was. I was really diggin' the place.

Yes, diggin'.

To go along with jammin'.

Spoiler alert: I might move on to chillin', next.

Yep. Again with the '90s vibes.

Again, no apologies. It really was the best decade for pop culture and music. And that wasn't just scientific...that was a factoid.

I reached the edge of the massive pool, stretching out for what felt like a mile. I dipped my toe into the water and a sigh escaped me. "Wow, that's perfect," I murmured, quickly snapping my mouth shut the instant I realized I was talking to myself. I looked around. Thankfully, no one seemed to have noticed.

I stepped into the sparkling water. It was only waist deep at this end, so I trudged through into the middle. The water began to slowly inch higher and higher up my chest. I was met with more friendly smiles and glances. The pool was packed, but there was enough room to move around comfortably, although swimming laps was out of the question. Not that I minded.

As I looked around, I noticed that most of the guys were talking to someone or hanging around in small groups. I was one of the few people flying solo. Back home, that would have freaked me out some and made me feel self-conscious. But for some reason, here, I was okay with it. Everyone was just doing their own thing. There wasn't even the slightest trace of judgment from anyone. It felt...kinda liberating, actually.

I found myself in an empty patch, the clear blue water reaching just under shoulder level. I lifted my feet off the bottom of the tiled floor and floated weightlessly on my back. I closed my eyes, enjoying the sensation of gently bobbing about in the water.

My thoughts drifted back to the hike—and to seeing Toby and the bear fucking. And more precisely, to Cassius' reaction to me seeing Toby and the bear fucking. I knew he knew something was up with me, even though he hadn't said anything. The open-air Jeep granted me a reprieve from talking, and the packed poolside did, too. For the time being, at least.

But I didn't want to keep putting it off, either. The more time I spent here, the more I felt like the tightly wound coils of my mind were starting to unravel. I wasn't sure if they had loosened to the point where I had the right words to express what I was feeling, but it was bubbling just under the surface of my skin, so tantalizingly close to the tip of my tongue I could almost taste it.

I had organized a dinner tonight at Elysian's fine dining restaurant, booking us in to experience the eight-course dégustation menu. Just us. I would tell him then. Yeah, that could work. Well, food first, then tell him. Talking to Cassius when he was hungry was not an enjoyable experience for anyone involved.

I still had no idea what to say or even how to bring it up in the first place. My conversation with Hawk as we stood in line at the bar yesterday had been playing on my mind a lot. He'd said that if I couldn't find an existing label that worked for me, I could always create my own. I liked that idea. Something about it resonated with me.

I had a spreadsheet with at least ten tabs, each one packed with information and links to what felt like the entire spectrum of LGBTQIA+ information available online. And yet, even in that swarming sea of content, I still felt like I couldn't find the right word—the term, the tribe, the label—that fit me.

So where did that leave things?

Exactly where I had started. Right back at the beginning, with no idea what to say to Cassius, only knowing that I had to at least have the conversation with him.

"Excuse me, sir?"

I stopped floating, my feet touching the pool floor again. A guy was standing behind me. "I think these might be yours." He stretched his hand out. I looked down, and he was holding my sunglasses. I tapped the top of my head where I had placed them.

"Thanks," I said a little sheepishly. "They must have fallen off without me realizing."

He handed them back to me. "No problem. I'm Ian."

"Spencer. Nice to meet you."

"Nice to meet you, too."

I placed the wet glasses on top of my equally wet head and made a mental note to remember I had them on there.

"Can I... Do you... I mean..." Ian was stammering, and I wasn't sure why. He was an older guy, maybe in his forties. He was thin and had a long face and friendly eyes underneath his thick framed glasses.

"What is it, Ian?"

He looked down into the water.

"I'm here by myself, and I feel a little like a..."

"Fish out of water?" I offered, after his voice trailed off.

He let out a small smile. "Exactly. Everyone here has friends. They're all so young. And they're all so muscly and good-looking. Just like...you."

I felt bad for the guy. He seemed like a nice person. And yeah, I could totally relate to what he was saying. I felt intimidated at the parade of ridiculously hot-looking men that were staying here, too. I could imagine it might have been a lot harder for a slightly older guy like him.

I mean, if a comet collided into the resort and wiped us all out, it would singlehandedly destroy the male modeling industry for years to come. Some of the guys here were so ridiculously out-of-this-world attractive, I found myself having to do a double take.

"I'm here by myself in the pool, too. And I'm happy to have some company, if you are?"

His smile widened. He had an amicable manner about him. We swam over to the edge of the pool and sat down against a series of jets that lined up along our backs, squirting out enough pressure to feel nice and relaxing.

Ian was easy to chat with. I learned that he was from New York, and it was his first time at Elysian. He asked a few questions—what I did for work, how old I was, that sort of thing. It was the usual sort of getting-to-know-you chitchat, minus any awkwardness that sometimes accompanied talking to someone you had only just met.

"So, do you have a partner?" I asked.

"No."

His tone made it clear that I had inadvertently struck a raw nerve. I didn't know what to do, so I said nothing, waiting for him to speak—or not. The ball was in his court. After a lengthy pause, he did speak again. "I only came out at the start of the year."

"This year?" I clarified.

He nodded. "I'm forty-six, in case you're wondering, and for forty-five years of my life, I've been trying to run away from myself, who I really was."

"Oh, Ian, I'm sorry to hear that." I really was. It was terrible to think that there were people who still felt the need to hide who they were.

People like me.

"What—what made you decide to come out? If you don't mind me asking."

"My mother died," he replied with a shake of his head. "She wouldn't have accepted me. And I loved her too much to make her unhappy, especially given how unwell she had been toward the end of her life. I didn't want to put her through anything that would upset her. I wanted her to have a nice ending."

I chewed on my lip, considering his words. What a tough position to be in. My mother was a lot of things, but I was pretty sure she'd be okay if I was...not straight.

"I regret it." His words matched his tone.

"Why?" I probed gently, hoping that I wasn't overstepping the mark.

"Because I've missed out on all of this." He waved his arm around in front of his body.

We both looked out at the bevy of men in the pool.

"I'll never be in my twenties again. Young. Carefree. Appealing. Having the sort of fun these guys are."

"But you are here," I pointed out. "And you can still have fun, Ian. There's no age limit on that, last time I checked."

He turned and gave me one of those *you'll understand some day when you're my age* looks. "It's not the same, though. I'm old. I'm not in good shape. I'm going bald. I'm...invisible."

He looked away from me, as if he had shared too much. He might have felt a little overexposed. I looked down at the turquoise water, glittering brightly as it reflected the rays of the sun.

He turned back to face me. "Always follow your heart, Spencer." He looked crestfallen. "I really wish I had. Now, it's too late."

"Hey." I rested my hand on his shoulder. "I think you're a great guy. And I am sure that one day, you'll meet Mr. Right. You never know. He might even be here, or he might be back in New York. But everyone deserves love, Ian. *Everyone.*"

His lips curled up into a genuine smile. "Thank you, Spencer. I really needed to hear that."

15

CASSIUS

I must have dozed off for a bit, because when I opened my eyes, Emry was gone. I glanced past his empty deck chair at Hawk, who was engrossed in a book.

"Where's Emry?"

Hawk stopped reading and turned to me. "He's gone for a massage and a facial treatment. He loves all that beauty and pampering stuff."

"You don't?" I asked, letting out a loud yawn.

Hawk rested the book over his...dangly bits...and held his palms up. Even with an empty recliner between us, I could see how heavily callused they were. "Does it look like I do?"

I smiled at him. "No." I turned to the other side, and the deck chair was still empty. No Spencer.

"Looks like your boyf—Spencer—has made a new friend," Hawk said in his deep voice, motioning his head toward the pool.

I followed his gaze until my eyes finally settled on Spencer. He was sitting at the end of the pool. A ray of light was beaming down on him, covering him in an angelic glow.

My eyes shifted and I noticed he was talking to someone. I

squinted to get a better look at who. It was an older man, probably in his forties. He was definitely talking to Spencer because there was no one else around the two of them.

I leaned forward in my seat, my eye zeroing in on the two of them. I didn't like the feeling brewing in my gut. And no, this time, it wasn't hunger. It was something else. And it was about as welcome as being covered by a thick blanket on a hot summer's night.

"Are you okay, Cassius?" Hawk asked.

I didn't move my head. Heck, I didn't even know if I was still blinking at this point.

"I'm fine."

It came out stilted, but it did the job. Out of the corner of my eye, I spied Hawk getting back to his book.

A sense of relief swept through me. I was glad he didn't want to talk about it, especially since I had no idea what was happening myself. Why was it bothering me so much that Spencer was talking to that older guy?

And why did it leave me with such a heaviness in my chest that made it hard to breathe?

Part of me wanted to march right on over to them and interrupt their happy little time.

Whoa... *What. Was. That?*

I shook my head. The part of me that didn't want to make a fool out of myself—appearing like some deranged ex-boyfriend—managed to overrule the crazy thoughts racing in my mind.

It was no big deal.

Spencer was just talking to a guy.

Spencer was straight.

And my best friend.

It occurred to me that I had been needing to remind myself of that a lot more recently. All of a sudden, it felt like an arrow had struck me right between the eyes. Before I could dive headfirst into the murky clusterfuck pond of whatever the fuck this was, Emry came back and saved me.

He was carrying three jumbo margaritas, and his face had a fresh glow. "Here comes more fun, gurrrlfriendssss."

I smiled as he announced his arrival in his typical, low-key way.

He handed the drinks out and preened in my direction.

"You look very...summery," I praised him. Given that it was fall, I thought that would be an appropriate compliment.

"Why, thank you," Emry beamed. "You should definitely get a treatment at some stage over the weekend, Cass. Andre is the best. His hands are di-viiiiine."

"Yeah, okay," I muttered, lacking any real enthusiasm.

"Are you okay?" Emry asked, sitting himself down next to me.

"I'm fine." Again, it came out in a way that made it pretty clear that I was anything but fine. Unlike Hawk, though, Emry picked up on it straightaway.

He shuffled a little closer to me. "What's wrong, Cass?"

I rubbed the back of my neck. "Nothing. I'm just... It's just"—here's hoping for third time lucky—"Spencer's in the pool talking to some guy."

Oh. My. God.

That's when I heard it. The whininess, the petulance in my voice. Sounding like a child speaking their last words before launching into the world's biggest tantrum in front of their exasperated mom in the grocery aisle. I felt like a world-class idiot.

"Hey." Emry's fingers grazed my forearm. "It's okay. Whatever you're feeling is perfectly all right."

I turned to him, my heart pounding in my chest. "But I don't know what I'm feeling, Emry."

His eyes softened around the edges. "And that's okay, too, Cassius. Be okay with uncertainty."

I arched an eyebrow. "That's very deep, Emry. Are you a philosopher now or something?" I teased.

"No. I saw it where I get all of my life advice from."

"Instagram?" Hawk offered, and Emry nodded with an impish grin.

I blew out a laugh, easing some of the tension that had been building...everywhere in my body. Maybe I should book myself in for a treatment. I was as stiff as a badger's ass.

"Hey, guys."

I turned around and came face to face with Spencer's head. No, not his face-head, his cockhead. My jaw clenched at the proximity between my mouth and the slightly rosy tip of his—I bolted up out of my chair.

Nope, not going to even go there.

Seeing Spencer naked was a massive shock. I guess we'd been friends for so many years that I just grew accustomed to his attractiveness. I stopped noticing it. When you saw someone so often, it's easy to become blinded to the things that new people might see in them.

And when you saw someone that you knew so well in a new light—like *without a shred of clothing on their bodies* kinda light—all of a sudden, it completely changed the way you saw them.

"What's—what's going on?" I stammered.

"I'm going into the jacuzzi with Ian," he replied.

"Who's Ian?" I could hear the agitation in my voice, but I couldn't explain why it was there.

"I've made a new friend. He's a really nice guy." Spencer batted his eyelashes—completely innocently, totally unaware of the raging storm brewing inside of me—before peering over at Hawk and Emry. "Do you guys want to join us?"

"I'm happy here," Hawk answered.

"Yeah, me too. But thanks." Emry added.

"Okay, cool. How 'bout you, Cass?"

I cleared my throat. "No. Thank you." My reply was slow and deliberate. "I don't like to jacuzzi with people I don't know."

A low laugh escaped Spencer's lips before he could catch it. "I'm not familiar with your jacuzzi etiquette, your royal highness, but suit yourself. Oh, and I'm going to go out and do some shopping this afternoon, so you have a few hours to yourself, Cass."

"Great," I muttered through gritted teeth.

"I'll catch you guys later," he said, giving his customary *arm by the side of the body* wave to Hawk and Emry.

I slunk back down into the recliner, my eyes glued to his perfect little butt cheeks as he bounced away. I was scowling, and breathing heavily, and the worst part? I had no fucking idea why.

"Are you okay, Cassius?" Emry asked with a worried look in his eyes. "I think I can see a vein popping out on the side of your head."

I took a deep breath and closed my eyes. "I am fine, Emry. Just fine."

I was a lot of things, but I was not fucking fine. Not by a long shot.

I stomped loudly back and forth in the suite, only looking up every few steps to catch a glimpse of the ocean, before rinsing and repeating.

Angry. Angry. Angry. Angry. Ahhh, beautiful calming ocean. Angry. Angry. Angry. Angry. Ahh, beautiful calming ocean.

Not even slipping into a pair of *Jetsons* boxer shorts and my beloved *Go With The Flow* T-shirt—slightly ironic given my current state—had managed to settle my frazzled nerves. I felt low-level agitated and high-level confused as fuck.

What the hell was going on with Spencer?

He had been acting so strange lately. I first picked up on it during the car ride to the airport. His expression was tight, almost pained. But since he didn't say anything, I assumed it might have been some last, lingering work-related thought or a miscellaneous entry to be filed under *he'll put it out of his mind once we're on vacation.*

But then we got here, and, well, he was fine with the clothing optional bit, and he was just as fine exercising the clothing optional option. But how, and why, wasn't any of this registering, I don't know, *anything at all* on his radar?

He also seemed to have no problem watching two dudes have sex. Not only that, he could barely turn his head away to face me because he was so intrigued by what he was seeing.

And now, the cherry on top of the confused-as-fuck sundae was that he seemed to be merrily acquiring new friends—while completely naked—and going on jacuzzi dates with said new, *naked* friend.

I came to a thundering halt, mid-stomp.

Shit.

Now that I thought about it, none of those things were really that unreasonable. Not really. At least, not on their own.

The car ride thing? That was probably me making a mountain out of a molehill. Whatever a molehill was.

The *watching the two guys banging in the woods* thing? Okay, that was a tad curious. But if I stumbled upon two people—of the male and female variety, for instance—going at it while I was hiking, would I stop and stare? Hmm, I probably would have. Watching people having sex didn't necessarily mean anything, even if they had a different sexual orientation. I was ascribing meaning to something that didn't warrant it.

And the new friend thing? Of course, Spencer would make new friends easily. Geez, I knew better than anyone that he was hands down the bestest of best people in the entire history of bestest people. Spencer made friends easily because he was approachable, smart, funny, and an all-round nice guy. There was nothing more to it than that.

I let out a disheartened breath. Suddenly, the twelve-hundred square foot suite seemed cramped and airless. I marched myself over to the sliding door and stepped out on the ocean-facing balcony. A gust of salty wind assaulted my senses, blowing my hair about wildly, messing it up even more than Spencer had earlier by the pool.

It was just what I needed. Fresh air and, hopefully, a fresh outlook on things.

I leaned against the handrail and took in the magnificent view. The thunderous roar of the waves crashing against the shore, seagulls flying overhead squawking out random high-pitched *caaaa-caaaas*. I looked up and got lost in that deep blue Floridian sky. Why was the sky in Boston never that color? It was the same sky in the same country, after all.

After a few moments, it hit me—not about the sky, but about my mini Spencer freak-out. Maybe I had been trying to find an answer to the wrong question. Instead of trying to figure out what the hell was wrong with Spencer, perhaps I should have been examining what the hell was wrong with me?

I was overreacting, overthinking, and definitely overanalyzing.

All of that *over*-ing, and I wasn't even doing the only type of *over*-ing I really liked doing: overeating. Speaking of which...

I turned around and trudged over into the kitchen. The more appropriate name for it was probably a kitchenette, but since it was pretty much the same size as my actual kitchen back home, I was fine to call it that.

I opened up the shelves above the microwave and peered inside. Hotel kitchens were a game of roulette—some were well-stocked, while others looked like they were the end result of someone who had decided to wing it at the grocery store and ended up buying a random assortment of items they thought guests would like. Elysian, for all of its otherwise awesomeness, fell into column B on the food-in-kitchen front.

Nevertheless, I fumbled around with what was in front of me in the cupboard. I pulled out a packet of cookies (gluten-free, *ewww!*) and dropped them onto the counter, rubbing the grossness off my fingertips as if I had been contaminated just by holding the packet.

My fingers wandered over some tea and coffee supplies. I spied a few granola bars and pushed them to the back. I might have been hungry, but I wasn't desperate. That was about as fruitful as my shelving forage went. It had been a so-so start.

I stepped over to the freezer, silently praying as I opened it that a tub of ice cream would appear before me. I could picture it so clearly. I'd open the door, the white, almost angelic light would brighten my face, and angels would sing in the background as my eyes would gaze upon a tub of unopened Ben & Jerry's or, if I was really pushing my luck, some strawberry cheesecake Häagen-Dazs.

To my great dismay, no angelic choir—and worse than that, no ice cream, either. All I was met with was shelves stocked with brightly colored cans of every single soda known to humankind and a top drawer stacked with an assortment of apples, pears, pineapples, and one single cantaloupe.

Hmm.

It would be a challenge to make this work. Even for a genius-level food-hybridizer like me. I flicked my eyes back over onto the countertop near the microwave, then back into the fridge. I knew it wouldn't be easy, but I was determined to find a way to create my latest masterpiece food concoction.

Ten minutes later, I was happily munching away from an oversized white porcelain bowl, my feet dangling off the balcony handrail, my sketchpad resting on my lap. I had connected my phone to the built-in speaker system and was enjoying the random shuffle of a mid-'90s groove playlist.

The sweetness of the fruit combined nicely with the crunchiness of the cookies, the sounds crackling loudly in my ears. Oh, and the soda that combined all the ingredients into what should henceforth be known as Fruit Cookie Soup—now *that* was a touch of mastery. *Thank you, thank you, there's really no need to applaud. Please, take your seats.*

I actually started to feel better with each mouthful of my latest culinary triumph. The exquisite tastes swirling around in my mouth, combined with the spectacular view of the beach, made me realize that I had been a little on edge since arriving.

In the understatement of the decade, I wasn't great at dealing with change. And being here was pushing me out of my comfort zone. But I had made a commitment to being open, and I was determined to see it through.

I glanced down at my *Go With The Flow* T-shirt. Funny how it was my all-time favorite. I'd picked it up at a bargain bin at one of the big box retailers—I couldn't remember the exact one—back when I was in college. It always fit right, and I loved the way it felt on me.

I wasn't rocking an eight-pack set of abs like Spencer (or Emry, or Hawk, or ninety-nine percent of the guys at this resort). I was a little squishy in the middle, but this shirt made me feel good wearing it, quickly becoming more than just a piece of material. It made me feel...protected.

Maybe I should take its advice and go with the flow a bit more myself?

Just as I opened my mouth to take another bite, I was interrupted by a loud knock on the door.

16

SPENCER

I leaped out of the car before the tires had screeched to a complete stop out the front of the Elysian lobby. The resort attendants had only taken their first steps toward it, presumably to open the door for me, but I was already flying past them, headed for our suite.

Technically, I wasn't late, since I hadn't told Cassius when I'd be back from my shopping excursion. I'd said I'd be gone for a few hours. And even if I had said I'd be back by five on the dot, I knew that he wouldn't remember that, much less care.

But my spreadsheet cared. And it knew that I had exactly thirty minutes to get back, get ready, and get going to what would be a life-changing dinner. And I wasn't talking about the food.

More importantly, was that I also only had thirty minutes to get Cassius ready. I was pretty sure that the state of preparedness that I would be met with when I arrived in our suite would fall somewhere between *wasn't even dressed* to *oh shit, that's right, we had plans tonight.*

I ducked and weaved through the heaving crowd that clung to the outside rim of the pool. I marveled at how busy the place was. It never let up. I guess with weather this good, what else would people rather do than soak it up?

I accidentally bumped into a few people or, rather, the oversized shopping bags I was carrying did. I always made sure to turn around and apologize, interspersing "sorry" with "excuse me" as I slowly made my way through.

Finally free of the crowd, I broke out into a light jog as I approached the door to the suite. Now, where did I put my room card? I patted down all the usual spots: pants pockets, front and back. Nope. I reached the door and placed the bags on the ground. I fished out my wallet and thumbed through the notes. Maybe it had slipped in there? Nope. Nothing.

Shit.

I sighed out an impatient breath. Oh well, Cassius was inside. He'd let me in. I knocked on the door and waited.

After a few moments, the door swung wide open, and I was hit by a massive sense of déjà vu. There he was, my best friend in the whole world, holding a giant bowl in one hand, a spoon hanging out of his mouth, and wearing his favorite white *Go With The Flow* T-shirt and a pair of *Jetsons* boxer shorts. His very well-worn boxer shorts. So well-worn that the elasticity on the waistband was starting to give, meaning they hung lower on his hips, meaning—I shot my eyes back up to his face.

For a second, I thought I noticed something flicker in his eyes. A curious look. But when I blinked again, it was gone and replaced with his signature wide and welcoming smile. No matter how many times I had seen it, that fucking smile always did something nice to my insides. At the same time, my breathing slowed and my face softened. Cassius was standing in front of me, which meant one thing: I was home.

"Spencey," he said, taking the spoon out of his mouth.

"Cass." I smiled back, picking up the bags and walking past him as he held the door open for me. "How have you been?" I placed the bags on the countertop in the small kitchenette. I couldn't help but notice how messy it had become, eyeing a half-open pack of cookies and a cutting board with the discarded remnants of fruit.

He walked up beside me.

"Did you miss me?" I asked, playfully nudging into him.

Cassius placed the bowl down next to the bags. His face grew serious, and he clutched a hand over his chest. I felt my pulse quicken. Was something wrong? With the other hand, he raised his index finger into the air, before turning that hand into a microphone, bringing it to his lips and singing (badly, it needs to be mentioned—very, very badly): "How do I live without you? I want to know... How do I—"

I clasped my hand over his mouth to prevent any more butchering of a mid-'90s Leanne Rimes classic. I had been so worked up about running late that I hadn't noticed the music playing in the suite.

He wriggled away from me, spluttering about exaggeratedly. "Hey, I was just getting started," he protested.

"No, you were done. Let's leave the Leanne-ing to the professionals, shall we?" I shot back as one of the most perfect pop ballads of all time continued in the background.

"How do you know I wasn't channeling the Trisha Yearwood version of that song?"

I slapped my palms onto the countertop. "Cassius Draper. The sheer blasphemy." I sent a withering look his way. "We may have been best friends for seventeen years, but this friendship will end right now"—I slapped my hands on the countertop again for added emphasis—"if I receive any indication that you were Trisha Yearwood-ing it, so help me god."

He barked out a loud laugh. His usual, the one that made his whole body shake.

Was it wrong that I loved this so much? *This*. These goofy, little moments that Cassius and I always seemed to find ourselves. These silly, inconsequential instances that we shared and if I ever told anyone else about, they'd look at me as if there was something seriously wrong with me.

Because despite how it might have appeared to the outside world, this was my idea of heaven. Every single second I spent with Cassius was the definition of perfect. Even if he had managed to create a huge mess in the kitchen in the short time I'd been gone.

"What's all of this?" I waved my hand over a bowl of what looked like another one of Cassius' misguided forays into what he called food making.

"What's all of *this*?" He mimicked my hand movement—channeling his inner-Emry and adding some unneeded sass to it—as he peeked into one of the bags, prying it open with his fingers.

I playfully slapped his hand away. "I bought you clothes. For dinner."

He turned to face me, blinking a few times through his dark lashes. "You did?" He sounded genuinely touched.

"Uh, yeah." I tugged at my shirt collar. "I planned for it when I was packing for you and noticed you didn't really own anything suitable to wear to a super fancy restaurant."

Cassius dipped his head and stretched the fabric out in front of him. "You mean, *this* won't do?"

I laughed. Loudly. Way too loudly. I covered my mouth as Cassius' puppy dog eyes gleamed at me. How was he able to do that? Getting me so relaxed instantly. Everything else in the world just faded away, and it was just him.

And me.

And us.

I shot him a pointed look. "We have T-minus twenty..." I squinted at my watch, "...four and a half minutes to get ready."

I picked up the three bags of clothes I had bought for Cassius and pushed them into his chest, giving him a gentle shove toward his bedroom.

"I picked out a couple of shirts I thought you'd look good—I thought that would fit you. I also got you some pants, a pair of shoes, and socks."

He crumpled his face at me. "You didn't think I'd bring socks with me?"

"Did you?"

"Uh..."

I smiled as his warm breath lingered between us. I kept my hands firmly gripped into the flesh of his wide shoulder, reluctantly pushing him closer and closer to his room. "You have plenty of options, Cass. I'm sure you'll find something you like to wear."

He wrestled free of my grip as we reached the bedroom door. His eyes had a fiery glint to them. "You know how much I like having *options*, Spence."

His gaze collided with mine, and my cheeks heated. "And you know," I somehow managed to get out, "how much I hate being late. Now, scoot!"

Exactly thirty-one and a half minutes later, we were being seated by a friendly server at a table right by the window, facing out to the water.

It took us the whole twenty-five minutes I had allocated to get ready. Cassius, for some reason, insisted on trying all three linen shirts I had bought—the black, the white, and the forest-green. If I didn't know any better, I would have sworn I was picking up on some vibes from him. Vibes of what, that I didn't know.

But it was definitely out of character for Cassius to give a shit about something as trivial as his appearance. And my joke about it not mattering what he wore since I'd already seen him naked that day went down like a lead balloon. Also not like him at all.

Then he'd raided my hair supplies, completely messing up how I had neatly arranged them—no, not by size, but by order in which I used them: spritz, gel and then spray. Cassius never did anything with his mane. His idea of grooming involved brushing his hand through his hair. That was as far as it went.

Anyhow, twenty-five stress-inducing minutes later, I was pushing Cassius out the door, ignoring his protests that he needed to check his hair "one last time." I'd allocated what I thought was a generous five minutes for the walk from our suite through the resort to arrive at the restaurant.

I had also planned a one-minute buffer for us to take in the breathtaking view as we arrived at the restaurant. It was right at the water's edge, and my Google Map investigating revealed that it was a spot that deserved to be stopped at and the spectacular view admired. For up to sixty seconds.

Now that we were here, seated, and with menus in hand, I was feeling...hmm, I didn't quite know how I was feeling.

This would be it, the night I told him. I only knew that. Everything else was up in the air.

I cast him a quick glance and was met with a look of confusion.

"I'm confused," he announced.

I smiled knowingly. "What's up, Cass?"

He leaned in over the table. "What the hell is a dégustation menu? Isn't that what my mom has?"

I suppressed a tiny laugh, covering my mouth with the menu. "That's indigestion, doofus."

Cassius leaned back and slapped the side of his head. "Duh, you're right. Dégustation is the way our bodies process foods." He bolted upright in his seat. "Wait...that can't be right. If that's what it is, then what the hell is this whole menu about?"

I couldn't hold it in any longer. My cheeks were *this close* to exploding. I started laughing loudly—by my standards, anyway— as Cassius eyed me quizzically. When I had regained my composure, I explained, "Dégustation is a tasting menu. This one is an eight-course meal"—his eyes sparkled at that—"and each course is a small sampling that we share between the two of us."

Cassius gave a little shoulder shimmy. "Sounds so fancy. I feel...French."

I grinned as I swiveled slightly to admire the view. The sun was setting, filling the sky with bright splashes of tangerine and light purple. The sea was restless, and it looked like the tide was going out.

"Gentlemen." I turned to see a smiling server carefully placing a plate in the middle of our table.

Cassius' eyes sparkled the way they always did every time someone used the g-word around us. We exchanged a knowing look but said nothing.

The server went on. "For your first entrée this evening, I present you with a myrtle-cured ocean trout with avocado, wasabi, cucumber, and citrus ponzu."

He was putting on that slightly haughty voice that servers at fancy restaurants often used. A tone that I knew Cassius would be mocking as soon as the server was out of range, which should be happening in about three, two—

"I don't know about you, old chap, but I think I might start with the ponzo." Cassius' attempt at a British accent was woefully funny. It sounded like David Attenborough with a bad case of the flu, due to having swallowed a Muppet that, unfortunately, remained lodged in his throat.

I started giggling. Cassius unfolded his napkin and tucked it into the front of his shirt—he'd gone with the black one. I told him it made him look striking. But if I thought he was done making fun of the meal, I was about to be proven wrong. Cassius was a long way from being done.

"One does have to wonder, though"—he ignored my groans as he carried on— "if by eating a citrus ponzo, does one, indeed, become a ponzo himself?"

I continued giggling, unable to help myself. My napkin, which was already occupied covering my mouth, was officially placed on standby to capture the tears welling in my eyes.

"Cass, stop," I whisper-pleaded. "I don't think I can take much more."

He took a deep breath in. "A cowboy, a priest, and a ponzo walk into a bar..."

That was it. I was gone. The napkin was forced to pull double duty, hiding my uncontrollable laughter while dabbing at the tears spilling out of my eyes. Cassius' raucous laughter erupted around me, filling my insides with pure happiness.

Finally, *finally*, he was done.

Although, interestingly, I hadn't looked around once to see whether anyone was casting disapproving glances our way or whether anyone had even noticed the two naughty kids giggling uncontrollably by the window.

We brought our forks to the plate and shared the first course. Then the second, and third, all the way up to the last round: dessert. A dark chocolate, mandarin, coconut, and lime torte.

"I am stuffed," I announced, picking up my spoon and skirting it around the edge of the cake. I normally never ate dessert, but a small bite couldn't hurt. Surely, I had pre-burnt some calories during our morning hike. "You have the rest." I pushed the plate away after tasting one small but incredibly dense mouthful.

Cassius' face lit up like a Christmas tree. "You don't have to tell me twice." He grabbed the small bowl and made quick work of the bite-sized dessert.

The meal had been exquisite. The company and conversation, first-rate. It couldn't have gone more smoothly even if I had planned it. Which, of course, I had. Down to the very minute. And post-food—once Cassius was fed and happy, but before he fell into a food coma—was the moment I would tell him.

I took a sip of the sparkling water, suddenly wishing the bubbles were of the alcoholic variety. I still had absolutely zero freaking idea how to begin this. A million possible suggestions were whirring about in my brain—

So, Cass, funny thing, I think I might be... Nope. Dead end.

Hey, Cass, did you ever in your wildest dreams expect me to be... Bah-bow. Another dead end.

Come on, Cass, do you believe in love? 'Cause I've got something to say about it, and it goes something like this... Whoops, that was the start of a Madonna jam.

Listen up, Cass, I've got something to tell you...

Hmm. Seemed like I'd just found a winner.

He squinted his eyes at me. "You look like you've got something to say, Spence."

I nodded, wiping the corners of my mouth with the napkin. I placed it on my lap, my fingers fidgeting nervously with it. "I do, actually."

This was it. This was the moment I was going to tell him my truth. I took one deep, final breath and opened my mouth to speak—

"Hey, Cass."

I cranked my head around and saw Hawk and Emry standing just behind me.

"Hey, Spencer," Emry said warmly.

"Oh, er, hi, guys." I choked on the words as I said them.

"How was your meal?" Hawk asked, and I managed to get a nod out.

"It was delicious," Cassius answered. He was still able to use words. Lucky guy.

"Hey, listen, guysss," Emry drawled. "There's an impromptu bonfire happening about a quarter of a mile down on the beach. We're gonna go check it out. Do you want to join us?"

Cassius flashed a toothy grin. "That all depends on this guy right here." He dipped his forehead toward me. "Spence, is there room in your spreadsheet to accept this invite?"

I reached for the glass of water, nodding like a madman, as I downed the whole thing.

"Great," Cassius replied, getting up from the table, thankfully oblivious to my heart drowning in a pool of its own pity.

Fuck.

I came *this close* to telling him. I was right there on the verge. I got up, too, letting out an almighty exhale.

Hawk patted me on the shoulder. "You all right there? You sound like my grandpa when he gets up off a chair."

I smiled. "Big meal, that's all," I said as we headed toward the exit. I couldn't be mad at Hawk and Emry. It wasn't their fault they showed up when they did. Besides, they had no way of knowing what I was about to say.

"How was your meal?" the maître d' asked as we left.

"It couldn't have been better."

I pressed my lips together. The food had been exquisite. If only the conversation hadn't ended so abruptly.

As we walked along the beach, I reasoned with myself. It was only Friday night. We weren't leaving until Monday morning. I still had two full days to sit down and talk to Cassius. This might have been a missed opportunity, but I knew I'd have more occasions to broach the topic coming up.

I'd consider tonight a practice run, a dress rehearsal of sorts. And hey, at least I now knew how to start the conversation. That was something. Progress, of sorts.

Okay, it was pretty weak reasoning. But I didn't want to be a total party pooper, so it was the best I could come up with on such short—and unexpected—notice.

I reached Cassius and threaded my arm through his. He looked at me and smiled, the moonlight bouncing off his face.

"You know, you really do look striking in that shirt," I told him softly.

He squeezed my arm closer into his body. "That's because I have the best friend in the world who bought it for me. Thanks again, Spencey. I love you."

That's when it happened.

The instant, the exact moment when my entire world got flipped, fucked, and folded all at once.

Right there. Walking arm in arm along the beach with Cassius.

Months of questioning, researching, spreadsheeting, all boiled down to that one precise moment and those last three words he had just uttered.

I pulled my arm away, jamming my hands into my pockets.

How could I have been so blind?

All these years...

The closeness that I felt...

The connection that we had...

I put it down to friendship. That having a best friend since you were six years old *felt* like this, *was* like this. Comfortable. Familiar. Filled with a myriad of silly little moments that colored my day. That were, most of the time, the highlight of my week. The thing that I looked forward to with all the anticipation of a kid opening their presents on their birthday.

And all of it—every single little last thing with him—always feeling so effortless. So...natural.

I peered over at Cassius, his eyes gazing out into the distance. His thick hair was flapping in the wind, carrying the scent of the resort's shampoo and all of my hair products he had used, over to me.

I breathed it in.

I breathed him in.

The smell filled my entire body, reaching into every pore, every part of me.

When I breathed out again, the scent diminished, but the essence of him stayed with me. In me. All around me.

It was intoxicating.

The sand was uneven under my feet. I tripped slightly.

Cassius reached his arm out. "Are you okay, Spence?"

No, I wasn't.

I couldn't walk.

Every breath I took reminded me of him.

That was the exact opposite of okay.

I didn't care about the walking. I just wanted to keep inhaling him.

"I'm all good."

It wasn't the truth, but it was dark. So as long as the moon didn't conspire against me, I would hopefully get away with it. I'd increase my daily good deed quota to five tomorrow if it meant that Cassius couldn't hear the lie in my voice or see the love in my eyes as I looked at him.

I looked at Emry and Hawk. They were walking ahead of us. I kept my eyes fixed on their backs, using it as a steadying anchor while I was thrashing about in the sea of holy fucked-ness.

How?

How, after seventeen years of friendship, was I only just grasping this now? How could it not have dawned on me earlier?

I, Spencer James Montgomery, finally learned something about who I was.

I was in love with the most amazing person who ever existed.

17

CASSIUS

The next time Spencer decided to poke fun at me for living a boring life because I wasn't great with change or surprises, I'd point to the last twenty-four hours as proof of the exact opposite.

In that time, I'd jerked off to him, stumbled upon two guys having sex while hiking, and stripped down naked by the pool in front of a resort full of strangers. So, when approached by our two newest friends (making new friends—another recent accomplishment, yay!) and asked if we wanted to join them at a beachside bonfire, I decided to ride the *I'm outta my comfort zone* train for one more stop and agree to it.

Okay, so a couple of those points weren't my finest moments— and definitely not things I would ever share with Spencer for fear of freaking him out completely—but at least they proved I was willing to take chances.

Which meant that now that I'd had my fill of out-there adventures, I was very much looking forward to waving goodbye to the craziness of the last day and a half and saying a warm hello to the rest of our getaway. Which I was hoping would be the relaxing, rejuvenating trip I was sure Spencer had planned to the very last detail in his spreadsheet.

All I wanted was one simple thing: no more fucking surprises.

So this was how the rest of the night would play out. We'd go and check out this bonfire. I'd start yawning within ten minutes. Spencer would notice and suggest we leave. We'd make a gracious exit, and my head would be on my pillow before midnight. Just like a gay, twenty-first century Cinderella... With better dance moves.

Yes. Crazy Town was growing smaller in the rear view mirror.

Next stop was Normalville.

We reached the fire. Small groups of people were huddled around it sitting on blankets. Some were drinking out of red plastic cups, and others were laughing, while a few simply enjoyed the flickering flames in silence. I smiled, liking the laid-back vibe.

"Hey, I think we see someone we know." Emry tapped me on the arm. "We might go say hello. Are you guys okay by yourselves?"

"Of course. Go. Have fun," I responded.

I watched Hawk and Emry walking over to a guy and—*hello*—I certainly hoped they knew him because all of their tongues just got very intimately acquainted. First Emry, and then Hawk, gave the guy the kind of kiss you'd see in movies. Deep. Passionate. And very tongue-y.

Spencer saw the whole thing, turned to me, and smiled. "After what we saw this morning, that seems kinda mild, don't ya think?"

I grinned. "Yeah, I guess it does."

Spencer pointed to a clearing a little bit away from the fire. "Wanna go sit up over there?"

I gave a nod and followed him up the slight embankment. When we reached the spot, he tugged at my arm. "I didn't bring a blanket."

The panic in his voice made it sound like he had just remembered he had left the oven on back home. But knowing Spencer like I did, I knew it mattered to him.

"I don't want to get my clothes all sandy." He didn't need to explain. I already knew that was the reason for the mini-panic I could tell was bubbling inside of him.

"In that case..."

His eyes widened. "Cass, what are you doing?"

"What does it look like I'm doing? I'm taking off my shirt so that you can sit down and not get your clothes sandy."

"You don't have to—"

"Too late." I proudly held up the shirt in front of him. I flapped it open before kneeling down and placing it on an even patch of sand. I looked up at him, standing over me, his face frozen in disbelief. At least I thought it was. He was kind of blocking the moonlight a bit.

"Sir," I said, bringing back my British accent from dinner. I didn't mean to blow my own horn, but it was a dead ringer for Hugh Grant, maybe even Sean Connery. Actually, I didn't really know. They all sounded the same to me. "If you would be so kind as to graciously lower your...ponzo."

He let out a sweet *tee-hee-hee* as he sat down gingerly at the edge of the makeshift blanket. "There's room for you, too."

I plonked my ass down on the sand beside him. "Nah, you enjoy it. I'm good here."

"Thank you, Cass."

I looked over at him and matched his smile. A few moments later—and right on cue, as predicted—my eyelids grew heavy and I yawned. Loudly. Then another yawn followed shortly after.

I leaned my head on Spencer's shoulder, looking out at the fire burning brightly and the dark ocean behind it. I felt his arm cradle me.

"Are you cold?" he asked, rubbing up and down my upper arm. "I feel bad you had to lose your shirt, just for me."

I didn't move. "I'm good, Spencey. I'm happy right here."

"I am, too."

As much as I was enjoying the moment, I eventually had to lift my head up if I didn't want to suffer from a sore neck the next day.

As I adjusted myself to get more comfortable, I felt Spencer's eyes on me. Our faces were close to each other. The glow from the moon was beaming down on us so brightly I could clearly see the freckle on Spencer's right cheek.

I suddenly remembered that Spencer was about to tell me something back at the restaurant, right before Emry and Hawk showed up at our table. I wanted to find out what was on his mind. He seemed kinda serious.

Now that I thought about it, he'd been awfully quiet on the walk over here after dinner, too. But before I could ask Spencer what he wanted to talk about, I felt his fingers caressing the side of my face.

Uh... Okay, that was new.

The backs of his fingers ran across my cheekbone and then dipped down, dragging lightly across my jaw. What was he doing? And why was it causing my body to heat instantly, like I was back by the pool in the middle of the day?

Our eyes met, and his warm gaze gusted over me. I studied his face. He sucked his lower lip in between his teeth. That full, pouty lip. For some reason, I wanted to know what it tasted like. What *he* tasted like. His lips. His teeth. His whole fucking mouth.

Whoa, whoa, whoa.

We hadn't even had anything to drink, so I had no excuse for these kinds of irrational thoughts that were racing through my mind at the speed of light.

So I cast the blame on Spencer's fingers. Yeah, that was it. What were they doing on my face in the first place, exploring my skin with a tenderness that tapped into a reservoir of longing I had somehow managed to convince myself didn't even exist?

But it did.

I swallowed and could feel my Adam's apple banging against the front of my throat. It felt like I was free falling, feeling things I knew I shouldn't be but that I was powerless to stop. Unwilling to stop.

I needed to be held.

I wanted to be kissed. Desired. Wanted. Adored... Loved.

I wanted someone to see me. All of me. And when they did, I wanted them to tell me that I was okay.

"Is this all right?" Spencer dipped his voice low in a way I hadn't heard before. His index finger ran along the bridge of my nose. I tried to follow it, going cross-eyed in the process, drawing out another cute *tee-hee-hee* from him.

From Spencer.

My friend.

My best friend.

My best friend whose fingers felt so good tracing the ridges of my face. Who I could joke around with, banter with like it was the easiest thing in the world, sing terribly at, dance even worse at, and share my latest gourmet food creations with.

That Spencer.

That Spencer whose blue eyes had fallen dark as the night ocean. Whose gaze on me was making my heart beat faster—and louder—than the 60 *Minutes* stopwatch.

I struggled to find words. "Uh-huh," I managed to breathe back.

I was confused, as if I'd woken up from a vivid dream and was still half in dreamland and half in reality. Unsure of what was real and what wasn't. But this was real, wasn't it? This was happening.

His fingertips lightly traced my bottom lip.

Yep, that answered that question. This was definitely not a dream. The silence between us whistled in my ears. I looked at his lips again. I'd never really seen them this close up before and for this long. A fire had been lit in me.

Was this stupid? I didn't want to do anything that would change things between us. Our friendship was the one thing in the world I'd fight to the death for.

"Are *you* okay?" I needed to know what was going on behind his soulful eyes, but asking the question left me feeling exposed.

Vulnerable in a way I hadn't expected. I didn't know why. It was a pretty simple three-word question.

Maybe it had something to do with the fact that it meant that my mind was awake. Alert. It was here, processing this. I couldn't fall back on the *it felt like a surreal dream* excuse to justify or walk any of this back when the light of day finally shone down on what we were doing.

What was happening here between us was as real as the sand beneath me and the stars above me. I would never be able to deny that or excuse it away.

"Cassius."

My name on his pretty pink lips created a ripple of desire that traveled across my skin. His eyes went glossy. I felt warm flesh on the back of my neck. It was his hand. It was pulling me toward him.

He closed his eyes. I closed mine, too.

And then...

Silence and fireworks.

The brightest of explosions and the deepest depths of darkness.

Everything and nothing. All happening at once.

Our lips met for the very first time.

The wind danced around our faces, pushing us together. I leaned closer, resting my hand on his knee. Our lips parted slightly. I felt his tongue—warm, sweet, scared, and inviting—touch the underside of my top lip.

I shivered delightfully. My fingers spread, covering his whole knee. His grip around my neck got firmer. He pulled me in closer. His tongue danced its way into my mouth. I could feel every movement, every gentle flick, so graceful and beautiful. I'd never been kissed like this before. I felt weightless.

Spencer opened my mouth wider with his tongue. The tips of our noses met. My eyelids fluttered as Spencer's tongue explored me with a surging confidence. Like he knew what he was doing. Like he meant what he was doing.

We'd reached the point of no return.

"Spencey." His name vibrated in my throat. It felt so good. So unbelievably good.

I let go. I surrendered to the kiss. My hand lifted off his knee and landed on his chest. I grabbed at his shirt, collecting some of his warm flesh underneath my fingers. I pulled him in closer.

I wanted this.

I kissed him back. My hunger rising, my inhibitions falling.

He wanted me, too. I felt his hand dragging through the back of my hair, lightly scratching my scalp. It sent a cascade of electricity through my body, right down to my toes.

He sucked in a breath as he pulled our mouths apart, just slightly.

"Cassius."

"Spencer."

Our noses met. I lifted my finger and grazed the tip of his nose. He hated it, the slight protrusion, but I loved it. I'd never touched it before.

"Cass."

"Spence."

His lips curved up. Instantly, I knew what he was doing: playing a spur-of-the-moment word game. Well, bring it on. I was up for anything—

"Ca..."

"Sp..."

Our lips collided again.

—including spending more time inside my best friend's mouth.

SATURDAY

18

SPENCER

I hadn't slept a wink, so it was no surprise that I looked like total shit. I wiped the fog created by the hot shower I had just taken and stared at myself in the bathroom mirror. Dark circles under my eyes, puffy cheeks. Just great. And of all the days to look like crap, of course it had to be the day I was going to see my mother.

My eyes fell to my lips. The same lips I had kissed Cassius with last night.

I ran my fingers over them. The same fingers that had traced Cassius' soft, moonlit face.

And here I was, back to thinking about the thing that had kept me tossing and turning all night: Cassius and that kiss. That fucking amazing—no, wait, out-of-this-world—no, scratch that, out-of-this-goddamn-universe—kiss.

I didn't regret it for a millisecond.

In fact, it might have been the single best thing I had ever done in my whole life.

I stepped out into the bedroom with a wide smile on my face. I glanced through my neatly arranged clothes, looking for something mom-appropriate to wear, settling on a pair of dark jeans and a black dress shirt. We were meeting for a late breakfast, as it was the only time she could squeeze me in during the five days we were in Florida.

I got dressed quickly, hesitating briefly before opening the bedroom door. It was too early for Cassius to be awake...unless he hadn't slept a wink, either.

I cracked the door open and snuck my head around. Yep, the coast was clear. I found a pen and a pad of paper by the phone and scribbled a note for Cassius. I had told him I'd be out this morning on the way back from the bonfire, but despite being pretty much the only words we'd exchanged on the walk back to the resort, there was still a high probability he wouldn't remember it.

I placed the note on the kitchen countertop and tiptoed out of the suite, closing the door behind me as quietly as I could. I spun around and walked smack bang straight into Leo's massive chest.

"You know, Spencer"—I looked up to see a massive smile stretching his lips—"normally, most people don't do the walk of shame out of their own room. They do it as they walk back from wherever they spent the night."

I scratched the side of my face. "I wasn't sneaking out. I mean, yeah, it could have looked like I was. But really..." What was I actually doing? Why did I creep out of there like that? It was to not wake Cassius up. Yeah, that was it.

Leo let out a warm chuckle. "Looks like someone's in need of their morning caffeine fix. Want to join me?"

"Sure. That'd be nice."

It was way too early to meet Mom, and having a coffee with Leo was infinitely more appealing than my original plan: sitting in my car until nine-thirty and then driving the twenty minutes to the restaurant to meet Mom at ten. Yes, I'd be getting there nice and early. I didn't need to get chided for my punctuality...again.

Leo filled me in on a couple of marketing ideas he was keen to try out, and I provided him with some initial feedback.

I had run a couple of giveaways in the past as a way of

drumming up publicity for the resort, including a radio contest called *Happily Ever After*. Callers would ring in and share their worst dating experience. The person with the most tragic, terrible story won a weekend at the resort and hopefully, while here, might find their own happily ever after.

We'd run that contest about six months ago in the California market, and suffice to say, it lived up to its name beautifully. The winner, Mitchell, was truly lovely and, once at the resort, met another equally lovely guy named Cayman, and together, they both found their perfect ending.

Leo was considering repeating the campaign in a few other states, which I agreed was a good idea. We arrived at the cafe and placed our orders. "It's on me," he said when it came time to pay.

"No, Leo. I insist. You've already been more than generous."

He let out a low laugh. "You do realize that as the owner, I don't actually have to pay for the coffee around here."

I slapped the side of my face. "Oh, of course." I felt my cheeks heating up. "I guess my brain is still in pre-caffeine mode."

"How about we grab these coffees to go? Are you up for a walk on the beach?"

"Sure," I replied enthusiastically. "That sounds wonderful."

A few minutes later, we were strolling along the soft sand, taking in whiffs of the sea as the sun rose slowly into the clear, cloudless sky.

"So what's on the spreadsheet—I mean, agenda today?" Leo peppered his question with a cheeky smile.

I grinned back. I enjoyed his company. He was so relaxed and laid back. I found it easy talking to him. Then the grin vanished from my face as I told him, "My day is starting off with brunch with my mom."

"Why do I get the feeling that you're not bursting at the seams with excitement?"

I covered my mouth. "Was I that obvious?"

He gave an affirming nod.

"It's"—I looked out into the undulating surf—"complicated."

Leo took a sip of his coffee. "Ah, I see. Family stuff can be tricky."

"Are you close to your family?"

His eyes softened. "I am. Very. Both my parents are alive and still together, which is kind of a miracle these days. And I've got two older brothers and one younger sister. We all live in different parts of the country, but we talk weekly."

"Oh, wow. That's really...nice."

I tried to smile, but a heavy pang of disappointment pooled in my belly. Why couldn't things be like that with my mom? Dad and I talked frequently—maybe not every week, but often enough.

But Mom, she was a...challenge. And about as warm as an igloo. My two half-brothers from her two subsequent marriages after my dad were equally challenging and icy.

"Family is important," Leo continued. "But don't let it stop you from doing what you want. Remember, at the end of the day—if you'll pardon my Portuguese—it's your fucking life."

I wasn't sure what he was referring to specifically, but I noticed his jaw tightening. I wasn't going to pry, though. If he wanted to talk, I would listen. But I wasn't going to be nosy and ask him for any more details.

He took another sip of his drink. "Dante, my partner who you saw in the photos in my office, let's just say his parents were very conservative. They were Brazilian and Catholic and, unfortunately, very anti-homosexuality."

"I'm sorry. That must have made things difficult."

Leo bowed his head. "When Dante was killed, they wouldn't even let me attend his funeral."

I glanced at him before focusing my eyes straight ahead. I hadn't seen that one coming, and I sure as hell didn't want to make Leo feel any worse by staring at him. I had to say something, though.

"I'm so sorry, Leo. That sounds awful."

He looked back and forced a half smile. "That's why you have to live your life for you. No one else, Spencer. Yes, parental approval is important, but don't let it hold you back from doing what you want."

I considered his words. It was good advice. And he had no idea how close to home it struck for me. Despite my two half-brothers being complete losers—one was on a never-ending backpacking trek around Europe, while the other one was in juvie—somehow, I was the black sheep of the family.

I felt like I was my mother's biggest disappointment, and no matter what I did, it was never good enough for her. She'd ride even my smallest faults—like being late that *one time*—like it was the worst thing I could have possibly done.

She said it was tough love, that she only wanted the best for me. But I didn't buy it. I hadn't turned out so bad. I had a good, steady job with the promise of a promotion. A great apartment. I was self-sufficient. Tried to be kind and held doors open for people. I recycled. Donated to charity. Aimed for three good deeds a day (okay, today it would be five to make up for my little white lie last night). All in all, I was a pretty decent guy.

Why couldn't I just have the *love* without the *tough*?

"Thanks, Leo." He motioned for us to turn around and head back toward the resort. "That was just what I needed. Coffee and a good chat."

He smiled warmly. "I'm glad to be of service. I hope your time with your mom goes well."

I blew out a heavy breath. "Me, too, Leo."

19

CASSIUS

I slept like a baby—which, in my defense, I always did—but it was a (pleasant?) surprise that when I first opened my eyes, I thought for one second, it had all been a dream. One delicious, sexy-as-fuck dream. Me and Spencer, talking near a bonfire, sitting under a sky full of stars. And that kiss.

Fuck.

I sprang upright in the bed. Memories of that kiss flooded back to me. Okay, that was not a dream. That was a very, *very* real shitstorm.

Just as real as the hard-on pressing against my bedsheets. Not again. I palmed my dick down, hoping to deflate it. I was not—repeat, was not—going to jack off to Spencer...for a second time.

That would only add to the sky-high levels of confusion coursing through my veins. To recap our getaway so far: I had jerked off thinking about Spencer on our first night here, and then last night, we had shared a kiss.

And it wasn't just *any* kiss. It made every other kiss I'd ever had in my life up until that point pale into a sheet-white oblivion. In fact, it was fair to say that I didn't really know what a kiss truly was until...*that* kiss.

I looked down my body and grumbled noisily to myself. My cock was granite hard and leaking, my precum no match for the Egyptian cotton. I looked at the small wet patch I had created. It was a reminder of Spencer...urgh, and that kiss.

Okay, that was it. I had to get up. I couldn't keep stewing in my precum-inducing memories of last night. I needed coffee. Stat. Maybe my knight in caffeinated armor had gone to get me a cup? I slipped on the nearest boxer shorts I could find and padded out into the living area.

Spencer wasn't there, but the door to his bedroom was ajar. I knocked—which was strange because normally I would have just barged in—and waited. Met with no response, I stepped in. His bed was made—even though we had daily maid service. I peered into the bathroom. Empty, too.

Hmm, I walked back into the living area. Where could Spencer be? Maybe he was getting me my coffee? I spied a loose strand of paper on the countertop. It was a note from Spencer. I read it and remembered him mentioning something about visiting his mom last night, too.

But he'd told me after that kiss, so there was no way in hell I could have been expected to remember it.

I tapped my fingers along the counter and looked down at the tent pole that had stayed stubbornly in place in my boxers. I wasn't going to let my cock dictate the terms of the morning, I was grabbing the reins and taking charge. The first order of business: insert coffee into mouth hole.

I turned toward the most scary-looking steel coffee machine ever invented, squinting as my eyes ran over the unpronounceable European name, and said in my most menacing voice, "Okay, I don't like you. And you don't like me. But if we work together, we can create some magic."

Five minutes later, the promise of magic remained just that: a promise. I had managed to find the *ON* switch, but that was about it. Why did Europeans have to make coffee so complicated? I pulled open the top drawer and found the instructions accompanying the world's most uncooperative coffee maker.

The irony of a coffee machine requiring people to follow instructions before they had consumed the first cup of coffee wasn't lost on me. My throat let out a grumpy rattle as I tried to follow the steps outlined in the manual.

Grab a pod. Got it.

Insert pod into pod dispenser. Did that.

Fill up water container with water. Where the hell was the water container on this thing? I flipped to the back of the manual—because, yes, this thing was so freaking long that it had an appendix—looked at the diagram, found the water container, represented by the letter *E* in the diagram—because, yes, this thing was so complicated it required visuals to understand it—and then traced my fingers along until I found the matching part on the machine itself.

I sighed, somehow more tired now than before I had started. I managed to find and fill the water container, muddling my way through the rest of the instructions. I pressed the *Start* button, which made the light at the front of the console blink blue. The machine revved to life, letting out a loud percolating purr.

Two minutes—which in my caffeine-depleted state dragged on and felt more like two hours—and I was taking my first sip.

Aah, that was better.

I took the brew and sat out on the balcony overlooking the ocean, grabbing my sketchpad from the side of the couch where I had left it. Spencer wrote he'd be back in time for our midday appointment. *Appointment for what?* Dammit, why didn't I pay more attention to details? Oh, that's right. Because I had Spencer to do that for us.

I meant, Spencer was a friend who looked after the details side of things. I didn't mean I had him as in I *had* him. Sure, I had tasted his lips last night. And the insides of his yummy warm mouth. And that sweet, delicate, polite yet tantalizingly assertive tongue of his.

I scratched the back of my head, grumbling as I tried to ignore the incessant hardness in my briefs that just wouldn't quit. I rested the coffee on the side table, stood up, and scrubbed my face with my palms.

How was I going to get that kiss out of my head? It was burned into my memory. It had even drifted into my dreams. And now, even with caffeine doing its thing and waking my body up, cell by cell, the grip of Spencer's pretty lips was wrapped around me so tight. So snug. So...fucking...nicely.

Grrrrr. No, no, no, no.

I swigged the rest of the coffee, scalding the insides of my mouth in the process. I marched back inside and changed into a pair of swimming shorts. I grabbed a towel, the swipe card to the suite, some sunglasses...and where the hell were my flip-flops?

My eyes darted around my room, which looked like it had been devastated by a hurricane. Oh, what the hell, I'd go barefoot. I didn't need shoes to go for a swim. A dip in the cool water would wash away the remnants of last night.

At least, that's what I hoped.

I reached the pool, and since it was before ten, it was still pretty quiet. There were a few people around and the staff were opening up the bar area, but I wasn't here to socialize or sip cocktails.

I threw my stuff absentmindedly onto the nearest empty deck chair and dove into the pool. The water was colder than I expected, but it was just what I needed. The refreshing zing tore through my body as I held my breath, swimming breaststroke alongside the dark blue tiles of the pool floor.

I eventually made my way back to the surface. I caught my breath and flipped onto my back, letting the sun's early rays catch my face as I floated aimlessly in the middle of the pool, arms and legs stretched wide.

After a good amount of time had passed, I flipped onto my

stomach and freestyled to the edge of the pool. As I got out, I was greeted with a familiar, "Hey, honnnaaayyy."

"Hey, Emry." I smiled at the sight of him.

It was funny, I'd spent a good chunk of time with the guy, and most of it had been naked. Heck, I'd shared more time in the nude with Emry and Hawk than I had with some of the guys I'd actually had sex with. I almost didn't recognize him with clothes on. But there was no way I could miss his perfectly coiffed hair and the dazzling white smile he was flashing.

His outfit was a bit of a head-turner, too. He wore a bright pink shirt splashed with a purple sequined *YASS* across the front and tight black denim hipster jeans. A pair of gold glitter high boots capped off the stylish outfit.

Meanwhile, I looked as wet as a fish. My hair was stuck to the sides of my face in clumps, and the swim trunks Spencer had bought me three summers ago had faded so much you could barely make out the tiny pineapples that adorned them.

"Wanna be my breakfast date?" Emry asked kindly, seemingly unperturbed by my frazzled appearance. So much so that he was willing to be seen in public with me. What a cool guy.

I smacked the side of my face. "Ah, of course. Food."

I had been so caught up in that thing that I was trying to not think about—that *last night kiss with my best friend* thing that was quite possibly the coolest-slash-craziest thing I had ever done—that I'd completely forgotten about breakfast. Me. Cassius Draper, missing a meal? That had never, ever happened before, and I sure as heck wasn't going to let it start now.

"I just need a quick shower. Can I meet you in, say, ten minutes?"

"Of course. You get ready. I'll get us a table."

"Thanks, Emry. That sounds great."

I gathered my things and headed back to the suite as Emry's high-pitched "Byeee" faded into the background.

"Hey, baby boy!" Emry stood up and shouted—yes *shouted*, as in at full volume, as in causing half the packed cafeteria to turn around to see who was doing said shouting—as he spotted me walking in.

I made my way over to him, amidst a sea of heads all turning in my direction. It didn't bother me in the slightest. I never cared what other people thought anyway, and personally, I loved how loud and proud Emry was. The world needed more people like him.

"Hello, again." I smiled warmly. As I approached the table he was seated at, my belly let out a loud rumble.

Emry looked down at my stomach and laughed. "You go get your food first, Cass. I'll wait for you to get back, and then I'll go get mine."

"Are you sure?" I didn't want to appear rude. "You've been holding the table while I went back and showered. I'm happy for you to go first, if you like."

"It sounds like you need food more than I do. Now, go!"

I wasn't going to argue. At the buffet, I scooped up what I considered a hearty plateful, although judging by some of the sidelong glances I was attracting, maybe a stack of twelve pancakes was *sliiiightly* too much. I carefully balanced the plate as I walked back to the table, and then Emry got up to get his breakfast.

I waited for him to return before we both started to eat. His healthy meal choice was eerily similar—and equally as unappealing to me—as Spencer's.

"So"—Emry dangled a yogurt-and-granola-covered spoon in the air—"how did you and Spencer enjoy the bonfire last night?"

I suspended the forkful of pancake I was just about to inhale in midair, before dropping it down to the plate. "It was, uh, yeah, nice. Thanks again for the invite."

Emry arched one of his perfectly manicured eyebrows. "Uh-huh. Anything interesting happen?"

Our eyes met. His were sparkling as brightly as the *YASS* logo on his shirt. Mine dropped down to the uneaten pancakes hanging off my fork.

"So, you saw?"

There was no point in beating around the bush with him. I had a feeling he wouldn't have let me get away with it, even if I had tried to deny it.

"I did." His voice was surprisingly soft. I had been expecting something a little sassier than the earnestness I felt radiating off him.

I looked up. He smiled at me—genuinely—his eyes crinkling in the corners. "How are you feeling about it?"

I raised my index finger in the air. "Can you gimme a sec?"

Emry nodded while I piled forkful after forkful into my mouth. Yes, I knew I was in public. Yes, I knew I was sharing a meal with someone I had only met a few days ago. But goddammit, I was going to need carbs to get through this conversation. What could I say? The belly wanted what the belly wanted.

"Feel better?" Emry asked with a giggle and, happily, without the faintest hint of disgust at my display after I had finished gorging myself like a madman.

"Yes," I replied, washing down the syrupy pancakes with some water. "Now, where were we?"

"*You* were just about to tell me how you felt about kissing your best friend. Your *straight* best friend."

Oh, right. That.

At first, I couldn't find the words. I blamed the pancakes that were dégustation-ing their way through my system. I finally cleared my throat and spoke up. "I am feeling...fine-ish."

"Oh, okay." His tone suggested he seemed a little surprised by that.

"And a little confused-ish," I continued. "With some happy-ish...ness thrown in there, too."

"Wow, that's a very creative take on Engl-ish," he observed with a wry smile.

I took the napkin off the table and placed it on my lap, wrapping it nervously around my fingers. The truth was, I didn't know how I was feeling or what I should have been feeling. Both because Spencer was my best friend and my straight best friend. On their own, each of those two things would have been a lot to deal with. Combined, they were a clusterfuck of epic proportions.

"I just don't want things to change."

The truth of my words surprised me. But there they were, and the more I thought about it, the more I was convinced that those seven words were the crux of the matter.

"Why's that?" Emry's voice was soft, supportive. There wasn't any hint of judgment or even prying. It was as if he was sensing my mood and matching his tone to give me the comfort I needed.

I let out a shaky breath. "Because when things change, I always fuck them up. That's why I like my life just as it is. I have my work. My sketches. I go hiking. I love my family. And I've got..."

"Spencer." We said his name together.

"I like things the way they are." I sounded deflated.

"Sometimes, change is good," Emry offered. "It can make things better."

"Sometimes, it's bad," I countered. "And it can turn a good thing into a bad thing."

Emry nodded thoughtfully. "True. But sometimes in life, we don't have a choice. Things change, whether we want them to or not. And the best thing to do in that situation is to go with the flow."

I perked up at the inadvertent reminder of the catchphrase written across my favorite T-shirt.

He peered at me for a few seconds, the words on his lips, but not coming out for some reason. Finally, he bit the bullet and spoke. "Can I ask you something?"

I nodded. "Sure, go ahead."

"What if the kiss didn't change anything?"

I swallowed the remainder of what I was chewing and sat up a little taller in my chair. "What do you mean, Emry?"

He shot me a pensive glance. "Permission to speak freely?"

I chuckled. "Of course." I felt safe with him and was curious to get his take on things.

"Like you just mentioned, you're the kind of guy who likes things to say the same, right?"

I cleared my throat and gave a hesitant nod.

"And that's not in any way a bad thing," Emry said with an urgency in his voice, indicating that he must have picked up on whatever my face was doing. "Not at all."

Our eyes met and he let out a warm, reassuring smile. "It just means that when something—like this—happens, you might benefit from taking a different approach to thinking about it."

He was going to have to spell it out for me because I still wasn't getting it. "Rather than seeing you kissing Spencer as a change— which you probably associate as being something bad or scary and to be feared—why not see it as something else?"

"Like what?"

Emry looked around. "I don't know, like a...continuation. You guys have been best friends for so long. Think of this as just another experience you guys have shared together. Don't put too much on it, making it out to be this huge, colossal thing, when it doesn't need to be any more complicated than two guys sharing a kiss."

His words swirled around in my head, feeling both comforting and confusing at the same time. The idea of not getting freaked out about what had happened certainly appealed to me. And looking at it as a continuation, rather than a change, helped calm the nerves fraying underneath the surface of my skin.

"Thanks, Emry. That's really good advice. I'm going to think about what you said. I promise."

He cracked a smile. "Any time. I'm here for you, Cass. Now,

what do you say we go get our tan on?" He looked down at his arms. "I am still looking pasty as fuck."

I grinned. "Sure, but let's finish up here, okay? I'm only on my first breakfast plate. And that means I am a *long* way from being done."

20

SPENCER

It was a twenty minute drive from the resort to where I was meeting Mom. I had swapped out the open-top Jeep for a more appropriate—specifically, more Mom-appropriate—midsize car. The last thing I needed was to add questionable rental choices and messed-up hair to Mom's ever-growing *reasons why I'm disappointed in Spencer* list. If she wanted to keep adding to it, fine, but I wasn't going to make it easy for her.

I pulled up out the front of Deesha Indian Curry House—her choice, not mine—at ten to ten and cut the engine. Don't get me wrong, I loved Indian food. The Indian joint around the block from my apartment was one of my favorite go-tos. Chicken tikka masala? Yes, please. Lamb samosas? Stop it, I'm drooling. But at this time in the morning? It was an interesting choice to say the least. But it was Mom's call, so I didn't dare question it.

With a full ten minutes to spare, I caught my reflection in the rearview mirror. The bags under my eyes had lightened a bit. I looked okay. Decent. Ready for this. I blew out a deep breath and repeated my pre-Mom visit mantra to myself in a low whisper,

"Strength. Resilience. No stress. No carbs. Strength. Resilience. No stress. No carbs."

All right, let's do this.

I got out of the car and spotted my mom turning the corner, walking toward me. She was looking every bit the Floridian power wife wearing a brightly colored, stylish blue, green, and yellow blouse, white linen three-quarter pants, and wedges.

"Spencer, darling."

She stretched her arms out while I leaned in for a sorta hug. I always thought it took two people to hug. As in, when you hugged a person, they tended to hug you back. But Mom kept her arms weirdly wide while I wrapped mine around her back.

I pulled away, straightening myself out a little. She glanced down at her watch. I tried not to grimace as I braced myself for what I knew was coming.

"Oh, and look. You're right on time for a change."

I should've placed a bet. An odds-on favorite that those would have been among the first words out of her mouth.

"Hi, Mom. It's good to see you. And"—don't say it, don't say it, *go high not low*, don't say it... Nope, I'm gonna say it—"I'm actually five minutes early."

Damn, I'd need to keep working on channeling my inner Michelle Obama.

Not that Mom bothered to respond to my comment. She didn't even look like she'd heard it. Her lips remained unmoved, a thin hard line. Her eyes flicked over to the rental car.

"Is this yours?" she asked, lowering her bright red sunglasses as she tipped her head to look at it.

"Yeah," I replied, suddenly feeling like I was a kid who had done something wrong, but didn't quite know what, exactly. "I originally got an open-top Jeep, but you know." I patted my hair down, aiming for at least a mild response from an admittedly pretty weak joke.

I got nothing from her. A tiny wrinkle formed on her forehead.

It disappeared just as quickly as she spoke. "And they didn't have anything better than a BMW?"

Wait, I thought BMW was a good brand. Was she expecting me to show up in a Ferrari or something?

"It's fine." She clasped my arm, her long fingernails impaling through my dress shirt. "We'll say our goodbyes inside. That way people won't see us"—she meant to say, "won't see *me*"—"near it. Being the deputy sheriff's wife means I have a standing, a reputation I need to nurture and protect."

Of course my mom would be more interested in nurturing and protecting her image than, say, I don't know, the feelings of her eldest child. Priorities.

I held the door open for her and followed her inside, silently repeating my Mom-mantra at double speed in my head.

Once we were seated and left to look over the menu, I leaned in and asked, "So, what made you choose this place, Mom?"

"It was featured last week in *Florida Today*."

"Uh-huh." Of course, if a place was in a newspaper or magazine, Mom had to be there, too.

I turned my head, taking in the entirely empty restaurant. Yep, we were the only people crazy enough to be eating Indian at ten in the morning. I was surprised the place was even open. Oh well, at least we wouldn't have to worry about people eavesdropping.

"I need to get my reading glasses," she huffed, her tone irritated. "The writing on the menu is too small."

It was kinda small, I guess.

"So, Mom, have you had Indian before?"

"No, why?" She looked up at me briefly before returning to browse through the menu.

"No reason. It's just that, Indian is usually more of a lunch or dinner kinda food."

She shrugged dismissively. "I'm sure it will be fine, Spencer. I see you're still as rigid and uptight as ever."

I bristled and literally bit down on my tongue to stop myself from taking the low road again. We perused the menu in silence, although food was the last thing on my mind. My thoughts were invaded by Cassius.

Last night.

Kissing him.

How good and right it felt.

The only thing that was freaking me out was how little it was freaking me out. I mean, I should have been in mid-existential crisis mode. I'd kissed my best friend. A guy I'd known since the first day of school. Who I'd grown up with and who felt more like family than a friend. Oh, and that little nugget of me being kinda-sorta but definitely *not* straight anymore.

And yet...I was feeling all right about the thing. The whole thing.

Hmm. What did that mean?

I glanced across the table. Maybe having brunch with Mom at a deserted Indian restaurant was exactly what I needed right now to take my mind off things. Maybe all my nerves were occupied, preparing for whatever assault the woman was about to throw at me. Kissing Cassius felt like a pleasant dream by comparison.

"Are you ready to order?" the server asked when she returned.

"You go first, darling," Mom said without looking up.

"Okay, I'll have the chicken tikka masala please, and a cheese naan. Oh, and a mango lassi, too."

Mom tore her eyes away from the menu and looked at the server. "I'll have the prawn red curry, please. But can I have the sauce on the side?"

The server and I glanced at each other. She smiled politely as she told my mother, "The curry is the sauce, ma'am."

Mom nodded and smiled that wide, patronizing smile of hers that was the warm-up act to an equally patronizing grand finale verbal spray. "Yes, I know that, dear. So, I'd like the curry sauce"— she said the word *sauce* louder and slower this time, as if somehow that's what was needed here—"on the side, please."

The server looked at me pleadingly.

"Mom, you can't separate the curry sauce from the dish. It *is* the dish."

Mom glared at me for a moment or two before glancing up and smiling at the server. "Fine. I'll have it the traditional way, in that case."

Relieved, the server quickly confirmed our order and spun around so fast I could practically hear the soles of her shoes squeaking against the tiled floor.

Mom rested her elbows on the edge of the table, interlacing her fingers. "So, darling, tell me what's been happening with you? Have you heard anything about the promotion?"

I shuffled uncomfortably in my seat. "Uh, no. Not yet. But Cass and I are down here because the owner of the resort is really impressed with the work my team and I did on his campaign. It was a huge success. He said he'd put in a good word for me."

Mom's sigh was laced heavily with disappointment. "You need to be more assertive, Spencer." She took a sip of water. I guess criticizing your firstborn and making them feel like all they wanted to do was crawl under the table was thirsty work.

"How is Cassius?" Her tone was dripping with dislike.

Over the years, Mom had gone from casual disdain to all-out contempt for my best friend, dropping any pretense of kindness towards Cass. He wasn't ambitious enough. He didn't live in the right part of town or socialize with the right kind of people. Basically, she looked down her nose at him and his family. Meanwhile, I would have swapped places with him in a heartbeat. *His* mom loved him unconditionally.

"He's doing well."

"Is he still living in that rat-infested apartment in"—she lowered her voice even though there was no one around us —"Mattapan?"

"Yes, he is, and he's loving it. It's a nice apartment." Okay, that was a half-truth. But Cassius had made the inside of his place feel homey, even if the outside, and yes, the neighborhood, left a lot to be desired.

Mom looked as if she could see right through me, probably because she could.

"I've never understood what you liked about that boy. Your friendship makes no sense to me."

Mom only stopped talking when the server returned with our food. When she had left, Mom leaned in and said, "This. This is a curry?"

I took a bite of chicken and nodded. "Uh-huh."

She didn't look impressed but began to gingerly pick at the food with her fork. "As I was saying..."

Great, here we go again.

"...that boy is beneath you. You're a hard worker. You're ambitious. One day, you'll even be successful."

Wow. Even when she was trying to pay me a compliment, she still managed to find a way to have a dig.

One day I'll be successful?

I was twenty-three and already working on—no, wait, *leading*— massive, multi-million dollar marketing campaigns. I had a great apartment and my own car. I was totally self-sufficient and light years ahead of my two deadbeat half-brothers.

As much as I wanted to say something about them, I decided not to. I silently repeated my Mom-mantra and, instead, listened to her as she droned on and on about all the things that weren't up to her standard about Cassius, until she wrapped up with, "You're just too good for him, darling."

I dropped my fork onto my plate. The loud *clank* caught her attention. She shifted in her seat. Her eyes narrowed in on me, dark and curious.

"Stop it, Mom."

My tone might have been measured, but my pulse was racing in my ears. I'd had enough. If she wanted to criticize me under the guise of tough love, then fine. There wasn't much I could do about that. But I was sick of hearing her piling on about Cassius.

The guy who had been there for every single major moment in my life.

The guy who made time, people, and the rest of the world disappear whenever we were together.

The guy who knew every single one of my faults and didn't judge me for any of them.

The guy who could make me smile with a single, stupid dance move.

The guy who I loved and who I knew loved me back in a way that Mom couldn't...or wouldn't. Unconditionally.

The guy who...

That's when it happened. The moment the truth slammed into me at a hundred miles an hour.

And I knew—*I just fucking knew* with a level of certainty I had never experienced before.

The jigsaw pieces of my life snapped magically into place in that moment.

I had always assumed that people had life-changing revelations at major points in their lives. Like on their deathbeds or after reaching the peak of Everest, stuff like that. I didn't think it would ever happen while having brunch in a deserted Indian restaurant with my mom.

"What? Why are you looking at me like that?" Mom asked, interrupting my thoughts and looking at me like she was genuinely surprised and more than mildly pissed off. "I'm just telling you the truth, Spencer. I can't help it if you have trouble dealing with it."

I slammed my palms onto the table. "The truth. Is that what we're doing? Telling each other the truth, is it?"

She tugged at the top of her blouse. Ah, so that's where I got it from. I winced at the unavoidable reminder that we were, indeed, related.

"I'm not sure I like your tone, Spencer."

My jaw twitched, and yet, I felt a steady, steely calmness wash over me as I said, "The truth is, Mom, that Cassius is the best person I know. Cassius is the only person in the world who loves me unconditionally, and Cassius is the man I am in love with and going to spend the rest of my life with."

Mom's mouth hung open in an undignified and out-of-character way. She quickly rectified that situation, drawing the napkin to her lips and dabbing around the edges of her mouth.

Sure, what I'd said was a lot to take in. I couldn't be entirely certain which part of it she was reacting to—the under-the-surface assertion that my own mother didn't love me in the way I needed her to or my very overt and plain-to-see announcement that I had more than just friendship feelings for Cassius.

And then Mom continued her foray down Undignified Lane by doing something I'd never seen her do in private, much less in public. Tears welled in her eyes and she started crying.

"I do love you, Spencer. More than—more than you'll ever know."

I handed her my unused napkin. "Then why don't you tell me so that I do know?"

She took the napkin from me and used it to gently brush away the tears from her cheeks.

"Alright, then." She sat upright and looked me straight in the eye. The tears had stopped, but my internal alarm bells didn't.

"Are we still doing this whole truth thing? Fine, here it is." She took a deep breath in, before the words gushed out of her.

"Your younger brother, Matthew, isn't just backpacking around eastern Europe with his girlfriend. He's backpacking around with his girlfriend...and their illegitimate child. Your other brother, Gavin, just got his sentence extended after getting caught smuggling narcotics into the detention center."

My breath caught in my throat. For all her many, many, *many* faults, I still hated seeing my mom so upset.

"And ever since 'Steve Kornacki' became a thing after the

election"—she did air-quotes when she said "Steve Kornacki" and the lower edges of her lips curled in disgust—"it seems that my Steve has been fucking any legally-aged blond 'thing'"—air-quotes, again—"under the age of twenty-five and with a pulse in the greater Key West area. Oh, and our maid, Sylvia, too, who I think might actually be pregnant, seeing as she spends most of the mornings in the bathroom but doesn't clean it."

"Oh, Mom." I reached for her hand. She went to pull it away, but then stopped herself, allowing me to hold her.

Her lower lip trembled. "You and your father are the only two good men I have ever known and loved."

Great, now *I* was crying into my chicken tikka masala. "Why didn't you tell me any of this before?"

"Why didn't you tell me about you and Cassius?"

"It's all kinda new, to be honest. I didn't realize any of this until we came here."

She dropped her head down. "Do you really love Cassius?"

"I do. With everything I have in me."

Mom slid her hand out from beneath mine and placed hers on top. "Then go for it, darling."

"What about all that stuff you said about him just before? You made him out to be the biggest loser in the world."

She pulled her hand away. "I thought your father was the biggest loser in the world because he didn't have money, and he lacked the ambition to get it. So I left him for men who did have money and ambition, only to realize they weren't even half the man he is. Your father is a kind, generous, and loving person. And"—she blew out a heavy breath, her face loosening slightly— "so is Cassius."

She raised her fork in the air. "When you find a good man— and, more importantly, when you fall in love with a good man— never let him go, Spencer." Her eyes had turned dark and serious. "Never."

I sat back in my chair, completely blown away.

Wow, okay, I was expecting the weirdest thing about this morning to have been eating Indian before noon. Never in a million years did I think I'd be having this conversation with my mom. At all. Ever.

It was...a lot.

I glanced down at my watch. "Shoot," I grumbled in between clenched teeth.

"Have you got somewhere you need to be?" Mom asked, and I nodded.

Her face softened even more, revealing the kindness in her blue eyes. "And you still hate being late, don't you?"

More nodding from me.

"You're so much like your father sometimes."

The truth was, I was a bit like both of my parents. And for the first time in my life, that didn't feel altogether bad.

"Come on, let's go, then. I'll settle the bill so that you can head off."

"But what about your food?" I pointed to her barely touched meal.

She waved a hand. "It's too...saucy."

We stared at each for a moment, before bursting out laughing. It was nice to see her smiling and to share a moment like that with her.

Once she'd paid—ignoring my insistent pleas that she let me cover the meal—we walked out to the front door together.

I jammed my hands into my pockets. "I guess we should say goodbye here." I motioned with my head toward the rental car.

"Don't be silly." She threaded her arms through mine and walked me to the car. Once we reached it, she grabbed me by the shoulders and looked me straight in the eye. "Thank you, Spencer. It was good to see you."

"It was good to see you, too, Mom."

And with that, she pulled me in for a hug.

This time, her arms wrapped tightly around me.

21

CASSIUS

Tap, tap, tap.

My non-freak-out about last night's kiss was gone. Over. Way behind me now.

I looked down at my fingers drumming against the front counter, tapping away as fast as my thoughts were racing around in my head.

So, if all I wanted was for things to stay the same between Spencer and I—a continuation, as Emry had put it so well—then all I had to do was keep things normal. We'd been doing "normal" for the past seventeen years, so it wasn't like one kiss could completely derail that. I just had to act natural and not weird. Super easy.

"And where is your boyfriend?" the attendant, Patrick, asked, glancing up at me from behind the front counter of the day spa.

My fingers froze. "Uh, he's not my boyfriend," I responded reflexively.

Patrick arched a brow, before looking back at the computer screen in front of him. "But you are getting a couples massage. Is that correct?"

"Uh, yeah. I—I guess so..." Great. Now I was stammering.

In my defense, I had no idea what I was showing up for. The note Spencer had left this morning only mentioned to show up at the resort spa at midday on the dot. It hadn't mentioned what the treatment was going to be, and it certainly never mentioned anything about a—

"What exactly is a couples massage?" I leaned forward, sinking my body weight against the counter, suddenly feeling slightly lightheaded. "Because if we have to massage each other, I need to point out that I suck at giving massages. But Spencer? Oh my god, his hands are divine."

Yeah, almost as divine as his lips.

Shit! Focus, Cass, focus.

Patrick was about to say something, but of course, I had to keep rambling. "I mean, he gives the best shoulder massages ever, don't get me wrong. Oh, and his foot rubs. Oh my goodness. They're just —" Shit, my knees actually buckled. I was suffering from an acute case of leg bucklage.

"Divine?" Patrick suggested, finishing my longwinded thought.

"Actually, yeah." Now I was smiling so hard my cheeks started to hurt. What was going on with me? I felt like I was a piece of clothing in a washing machine, being spun, twisted, and thrown about like crazy.

I stood up a little taller, trying to steady myself on my stubbornly uncooperative feet. "So, you see, Patrick, it would be totally unfair if we had to massage each other because I suck at massages. In fact, I don't think I've ever—"

"Let me interrupt you right there..."

Oh, thank fuck.

"A couples massage," Patrick explained, somehow managing to keep both his voice and face serene, "simply means that the couple, or friends, are each getting a massage from a qualified therapist at the same time and in the same room."

"Oh, I see. And what's so good about that?" Oh, shit. I probably should have thought that question, not asked it aloud. Now, my brain was experiencing signs of bucklage, too.

Hold up, hold up, hold up—was bucklage even a word?

Geez, you shared one kiss with your childhood best friend, and suddenly, you felt like you're an alien experiencing his first day on this weird planet called Earth. A planet that believed in people being massaged together in the same room, it seemed.

Patrick smiled and, luckily for me, didn't seem offended. "Well, you get to experience a relaxing massage, which is great on its own, but by sharing it with someone, it can make the whole experience even more special."

I nodded. "Okay. That makes sense, I guess."

At least my brain was reacquainting itself with the English language and starting to do a better job of understanding how these pesky word thingies worked.

"Once your friend gets here, we'll take you both in together. In the meantime, please feel free to take a seat."

"Great. Thanks, Patrick."

I flung myself down into an empty chair in the small waiting area. There was a couple sitting across from me, holding hands and looking super loved-up, and another guy sitting in the corner, flicking through a magazine.

I reached for my phone and looked at the time. It was two minutes past twelve. I blinked twice and checked again. Yep, I wasn't mistaken.

Spencer was late.

Spencer was *never* late.

And the even scarier thing: what the hell was I doing noticing things like punctuality? I never did that.

I let out a sharp breath through my nose. Okay, *think normal thoughts, think normal thoughts.* I couldn't help but worry that brunch with his mom hadn't gone well. The woman was a lot to deal with. I hoped Spencer had survived. I had to give due credit to his impeccable planning skills. If he was ever going to need a massage, it was right after seeing his mom.

Just as I had that thought, I spotted Spencer scurrying in through the front door. He looked disheveled, his face flushed, his lips slightly parted. Mmm...those lips.

Naughty, Cassius! Focus.

Spencer even had a few hairs out of place. God, how badly had brunch gone?

He'd also probably been freaking out about being late. He tugged at the top of his shirt, before spotting me. His face relaxed a little, and he did his customary—and suddenly, cute as fuck —*straight arm by the side of the body wave* before coming over and sitting down next to me.

I smiled at the first sign of normalcy.

"Hey," he whisper-breathed.

"Hey." I studied him with the same seriousness I applied to examining baked goods before a purchase. "You okay?"

He nodded, tugging at his shirt collar again. He wasn't okay. And suddenly, I felt a sinking heaviness in my gut. Maybe he wasn't freaking out about seeing his mom, maybe he was freaking out about seeing...me?

I leaned over toward him. "Hey, listen, Spence. About last—"

"Spencer and Cassius?" Patrick's voice called out.

Spencer whipped his head over to him and stood up, motioning for me to do the same. Dammit, I really wanted to talk to him.

As if he could sense what I was thinking, he placed his hand into the small of my back as we made our way to the treatment room and said, "We'll talk later, okay?"

I stared into his eyes. They were unsettled.

So was I.

Fuck. Maybe having a massage would unwind us both a bit?

"You promise?"

"I do." His reply provided me with instant relief.

We entered a dimly lit room. Candles were burning, I could

hear soothing music in the background, and the room smelled all nice and incense-y.

"All right. Now, please strip and lie down on the table once you're ready. Your therapists will be with you in just a few minutes."

Fantastic. Nothing weird about this at all. Just getting naked in a confined, dimly lit room with my best friend.

Spencer looked at me and smiled awkwardly as he began to unbutton his shirt. He may have kept smiling, or he may have stopped. I had no idea. My eyes were glued to his fingers as they traveled lower and lower down his dress shirt. He finally unbuttoned it. As he took it off, I was transfixed by the glow of his smooth chest in the candlelight.

Slightly flustered, I pulled my T-shirt up and over my head. When I next looked at Spencer, his eyes were on me. But not on my face. Now he was the one gazing at my chest. A look of something hot and dangerous skittered across his eyes.

A charged energy crackled between our bodies. We stepped out of our pants at the same time, but instead of lying down on the table, Spencer walked over to me. Now his eyes were on my face. Mine on his. He looked at me differently—a strange, heady combination of confident and completely unsure of himself at the same time.

With his eyes still pinned to my face, he broke the silence between us. "Why are you looking at me like that?"

I guess I must have been looking at him differently, too.

My throat tickled; it was dry. I opened my mouth to speak but stopped myself when I realized I had no idea what I wanted to say.

Spencer's hand settled softly on the back of my neck, in the same spot it had nestled into last night on the beach. He stepped closer, and his breath sizzled across my cheek. Heat rushed up my neck, pooling in the skin underneath his fingertips.

"What—what are you doing?"

He heard my scratchy voice and stroked the back of my neck.

Like always, he knew exactly what I needed: reassurance. And as his presence always did, it calmed me down.

He swooped a little lower and grazed my jawline with his tongue. My head fell back, a moan tumbling out of my mouth. His hand reached around to the front of my neck, gliding over my Adam's apple, before descending lower, roaming across the top of my chest.

Our mouths melded together. I didn't know who initiated the kiss, if it was him or me, but I didn't care. I tasted the same softness of his lips, the same warm and inviting sweetness of the inside of his mouth, and I felt like I had arrived home.

I was just about to let him inside my mouth again when the door swung open, and Spencer and I both jumped into the air.

Two male therapists entered the room.

"I'm Andre," the taller one spoke first.

"And I'm Julian."

"If you would both like to lie down on your tables, we can get started," Andre said once Spencer and I had introduced ourselves to them, too.

I took one last look at Spencer before lying down on the table and squishing my face into the round hole at the top. I squirmed a little as I got myself comfortable.

"Are you ready, Cassius?" I heard Andre ask me.

I gave him a backward thumbs-up, which was met with a, "Good. Let's get started then."

I felt some lightly heated oil landing on my skin and then the firm pressure of some heavenly strokes running up my back and across my shoulders. The only massages I had ever received were from Spencer—and they were brilliant, don't get me wrong—but holy crap, a professional massage was, like, the best thing ever.

Andre's fingers found spots, especially around my neck and shoulders, that were painfully tight, but somehow, he was able to knead and stroke his way to make them feel a hundred times better. The tension was literally melting off me.

"Can you lift your head please, Cassius?" Andre asked softly. I raised my head, and he placed a lavender-scented pillow under it. He gently guided my head back down. I was facing right and looking straight at Spencer. Julian had placed Spencer's head on a pillow and oriented him toward me. Thankfully, Spencer had kept his eyes closed.

There was nowhere else for me to look but at Spencer. His face was smooshed into the pillow like I'm sure mine was, too. He looked funny. Adorable. Tender.

There was a sparkle there between us. A familiar kindness, yet also a thrill-seeking heat.

For the first time in my life, it occurred to me that what we had was more than just friendship. That maybe this road of continuation that we were on—that had started with the kiss last night and continued with another one right before the massage— maybe it wasn't a dead-end road. Maybe it was more like an interstate...toward our future?

Don't be stupid, I chided myself. This was Spencer, after all. My one hundred percent heterosexual best friend, Spencer. He was probably just vacation-horny. And I was probably just his safest option at an all-male gay resort. A way to blow off some steam until he got back to Boston and could do whatever he wanted with whoever he wanted...of the female kind. For some reason, my stomach churned at the thought.

Julian repositioned Spencer's head back into the head hole and began massaging deeply into his neck. It looked like he was tight in that area. I wondered if he was as sore around there as I was.

I wanted to know what was going on with Spencer, what he was feeling and thinking, and I didn't mean about just the massage.

He had kissed me again.

Or maybe I had let him?

Either way, it had happened. Our kiss count was now up to two. Not bad for less than twenty-four hours. But did that mean it was...good?

Without a doubt, this was a new and not entirely unwelcome development.

But still, confusing as all fuck.

Julian repositioned Spencer's head again, and this time, our eyes were locked on each other like missile targets. His lips ticked upward at me and my cheeks heated. Thank god for dim lighting.

I blew out a shaky breath, unable to stop my brain from asking if this was just a vacation thing. Were we acting like this because we were on a short break from the real world and our real lives back home?

Once we were back in Boston in a few days, would we just forget about it and never speak of it again? That thought sent a cold shiver down my spine, and I must have shuddered because I saw Spencer's eyebrows twitch.

He mouthed, "Are you okay?"

"Yes," I mouthed back.

That was a half lie, and I think we both knew it.

But as Spencer had said, we'd talk later. That's all we needed to do. Sit down, talk, and figure it out.

In seventeen years of friendship, we hadn't had a single fight. Why? Because we knew how to communicate.

And even though the whole kissing thing was something we'd never done before, I was sure we'd find a way to discuss it so that we could...move past it? Resolve it? Find a way to keep doing it again and again and again? Hmm, I was liking that last option.

I closed my eyes, surrendering to Andre's magic touch as he continued to rub, stroke, and knead all of the knots and tightness out of me.

Two hours later, allegedly—and I say allegedly because there was no way time could have gone that fast—the massage ended. Julian informed us there would be water and tea waiting for us out the front once we got dressed. He brightened the lights slightly so that we could see better as he and Andre left the room.

I heard the door click shut behind them, but I wasn't moving anywhere. At least not yet. Happily, Spencer wasn't getting up either. We both just lay there, our eyes drinking each other in.

"How do you feel, Cass?" His voice sounded sleepy and soft and so, so tender.

"Like I'm floating," I replied dreamily. "That was so good."

He smiled. The whiteness of his teeth gleamed in the soft light.

"This is the best getaway ever, Spence. Your planning is top-notch. Normally, I'd give you a thumbs up at this point, but that would involve, you know, moving."

"You don't want to do that."

"I don't," I agreed. "I could lie here forever..." *Looking at you.* The words were right at the tip of my tongue, but I managed to catch them just in time.

"I suppose we should get up." Spencer pulled himself off the table, grabbed the towel, and wrapped it around his waist.

My eyes lingered on his body, watching as he stepped over to me. He grabbed my hand and helped me sit upright. I was feeling a little woozy, and I didn't know how much of that was due to the massage and how much of it was down to the fact that Spencer was holding my hand, looking at me like I was the most important thing in the world.

"Thanks," I croaked, getting up.

We started getting dressed, facing away from each other.

"Once we get outta here," Spence began. "We can just chill in the suite, if you like. Maybe order some room service?"

"That sounds good. It's amazing how lying by the pool all morning can really work up a boy's hunger."

"But you had breakfast, right?"

"Only three plates," I shot back, quickly adding, "And that was a good five hours ago."

His sweet-sounding *tee-hee-hee* danced in the air between us.

"Oh, hey." I glanced over my shoulder. "I was talking to Emry about the party tonight. The one that we're all going to."

"Uh-huh."

"I hope you don't mind, but I invited Emry and Hawk to our suite for some pre-party drinks."

Spencer was putting on his shoes as I turned around. "That sounds great. I love those guys."

"Great."

I was floating from the massage. I had the promise of more food on the not-too-distant horizon, as well as our new friends to hang out with later. And in the meantime, I had a few hours coming up with my best friend in the world.

This really was the best getaway ever.

22

SPENCER

The massage was heavenly...but I couldn't enjoy it.

The room service we had ordered was as delicious as always—and thanks to Cassius' order, could have fed a small village—but I didn't really taste it.

The White Party we would be going to later that night would be incredible...but I wasn't looking forward to it.

Everything that was going on around me was blunted like a knife that needed sharpening by the fact that, despite having had multiple opportunities to sit down and talk with Cassius, an actual real conversation had evaded us. Until now anyway.

Now, I didn't care if aliens came down and abducted us. I'd find a way to tell Cassius as we were being light-beamed onto their spacecraft, and definitely before they conducted any of their anal probing experiments on us.

I had to tell him.

I had to get this thing out of me.

The longer it stayed inside, the more I felt like I was suffocating. Worse, it was sucking all the enjoyment out of what was otherwise a brilliant time I could have been having.

We were sitting out on the balcony, our feet resting on the railing as we both took in the sounds and salty smells of the beach in front of us. We had just finished our room service meal, and Cassius' face was doing that post-meal happy thing it did where his jaw got looser, his lips parted ever so slightly, and his eyes became a little unfocused. I'd seen him like this a million times before, and I loved it every single time.

"You feeling good?" I asked with a smile.

He looked like turning to face me was a struggle. "Soooo much food. Soooo yummy."

Yep, he was in his post-food coma all right. I'd give him a minute or two to enjoy it.

It suddenly hit me that this could potentially be the last time I looked at Cassius as just a friend. Because our conversation would change things. Not in a bad way, necessarily—or at least, I hoped with everything in me that it wouldn't—but things would be different.

A large part of our friendship dynamic was built upon two piers: he was gay, and I was straight. It wasn't the defining quality of our friendship. Heck, it really didn't even matter to either one of us. But it was there nevertheless, an unspoken understanding that brought with it a set of boundaries that we'd always stuck to.

Like, say, I don't know...no kissing.

But fuck me if kissing Cassius wasn't the most wonderful feeling in the world. And an experience that I wanted to repeat again and again and again.

I'd been having more lightbulb moments over the past few days than there were light switches in one of Oprah's mansions. Part of it was being here, in a place like this, where the weather was warm and everyone was so chill and friendly. I felt safe and could lower my guard a little.

But it was more than that, too. It was the culmination of months of my methodical research and scrupulous self-examination that had gotten me to this point. So, when Hawk mentioned that if you couldn't find a label, create your own, that idea resonated with me because I had gone into labeling overdrive, only to discover that there wasn't a label that I could conveniently slap onto myself.

And with that, I unhooked my feet from the railing and plonked them down onto the tiled balcony floor, glanced across at Cassius, and began a conversation that would change things between me and my best friend forever. "Cass, can we talk?"

His eyes had been fluttering, half-open and half-lidded as his body *dégustationed* the insane amount of calories he had inhaled. But as soon as he heard my question, he bolted upright, his feet landing next to mine.

"About the kiss?"

"Yeah, about that. But also...there's something about me that I want to share with you."

"Okay."

This was it. The moment had finally arrived. My heart was beating a little faster, but apart from that, I didn't feel the torrent of heightened emotions I had been expecting—fear of rejection, nerves, anxiety. Nope, nothing. If they were there, they were lying dormant. I took that as a good sign.

"Cass"—I looked him directly in the eye—"I'm not straight."

His light brown eyes went slightly wider, but otherwise, he didn't move a muscle. "Okay."

There was a pause, and okay, now—*now*—I was feeling skittish. A thousand butterflies flittered in my stomach.

I studied him, wishing there was some way I could get inside his brain and find out what was going on. I just had to give him a minute. I'd taken a very direct approach, not gradually building up to it or giving him any warning, really. He looked to be deep in thought. Cassius needed to process this, and I had to give him the time he needed to do that.

After what felt like an eternity and a half, Cassius finally spoke in a measured and surprisingly steady tone.

"Do you want to tell me about it? You don't have to," he added quickly. "Please only say whatever you feel comfortable sharing."

Relief flooded through me as I settled back into the seat. Okay, we were off to a good start. He hadn't freaked out or had a meltdown.

I considered his question, and the next thing I knew, my mouth took off, finding the right words without me even realizing it. "I guess it's something that's always been inside of me, but I didn't really start to explore it until after Natalie dumped me."

"What was coming up for you?" Cassius' voice was soft, caring.

"That's a good question."

I stood up and walked over to the railing, gazing out into the horizon. "It's not that there was anything wrong or off, necessarily. I guess it just always felt like something was...missing. And it's taken me a while to recognize that as a valid feeling. I just thought it was normal, that everyone felt that way, you know?"

Cassius nodded. "I do."

"At first I thought that it was Natalie. Maybe she wasn't the right one. But that wasn't it. So then I turned my focus onto me, thinking there was something wrong or broken about me."

"Oh, Spencey." Cassius' face twisted in pain at my words.

"It's okay, Cass. I don't feel that way anymore. It's just that I always thought there were only three options when it came to sexuality: gay, straight, or bi. Over the last few months, I've realized *that* was the wrong thought. There are more sexual orientations than you can point a stick at."

Cassius nodded, gently encouraging me to keep going, and I noticed that the more I talked, the better I felt. This conversation wasn't anywhere near as scary as I thought it would be.

"I know this will sound so cliché, but, this 'journey'"—I used my fingers to mark out quotation marks, accompanied by a slight eye roll— "that I've been on has actually been really good for me. And I'm finding that it's not just about my sexuality. It's impacting other areas of my life, too."

Cassius sat up a little taller. "Like what?"

"Well," I went on, "I'm feeling more confident about things that previously I hadn't, and I'm starting to give less—"

"Fucks." We said the word in unison, smiling brightly at each other, sharing another one of the countless little moments we created every time we were together.

"I mean, I stripped down naked in front of the entire resort. In front of...you."

Cassius stifled a giggle, but it was accompanied by a flare in his eyes, too.

I shrugged happily. "See, that's what I mean. Old Spence would have never strutted around a resort buck naked and oblivious to what anyone thought of him."

"That's very true," Cassius concurred.

"Or even at dinner last night. We were laughing away like crazy, and I didn't look around even once to see whether anyone was paying any attention to us. That's not like me at all."

A playful smile drew Cassius' lips upward. "I liked Old Spence, but I think I might like New Spence even more."

Cassius got to his feet and stood next to me, our shoulders gently touching as the salty breeze gusted around us. His face fell serious, and my breath hitched in my throat.

"I'm genuinely next-level happy for you, Spencer. It takes courage and bravery to go on the type of 'journey'"—yep, he did the air quotes thing too, as well as a cheeky little eye roll—"you're on. I want you to know that wherever this path leads you, I want to be with you, supporting you, every single step of the way. I've got your back, like you've always had mine."

I exhaled a lifetime of suppressed breaths. "Oh, Cass."

I leaned into him for a hug. My body melted into his. I always knew that telling him was the right thing to do because he was my best friend and deserved for me to be as honest and open with him as he had always been with me.

What I wasn't prepared for was how good it would make me

feel. The burden had lifted, and I could already feel the difference in my body, my mind, my soul.

And his reaction. Holy fuck, it was beyond brilliant. Not that I should have been surprised. He was my best friend for a reason, after all.

As Cassius rubbed his hands across my back, the warmth of his body nestled against mine, it dawned on me that I was feeling something for the very first time in my life: freedom. I was truly and completely free and unburdened.

I closed my eyes, sinking deeper into Cassius' touch as an endorphin rush washed through my body. I felt lighter than air, like I was floating. My skin was tingling, and I knew that there was no turning back.

I had told Cassius the truth. My truth. And while there was still one more thing I had to tell him, for now, I just wanted to enjoy this blissful bath I was soaking in.

23

SPENCER

I looked down at the note in my hand, as if staring at it would somehow make it make more sense. It hadn't worked since the moment I'd noticed it when I first unpacked, and it didn't make any more sense now.

I picked up the tiny white mesh thong (G-string? jockstrap?—I wasn't super knowledgeable when it came to skimpy types of underwear, being more of a Calvin guy myself). Then I looked over at the accompanying white wings. From what I could make of it, they'd go over each shoulder, completing the whole quote-unquote look.

My eyes flitted over the words again. By this point, I had them committed to memory.

Options are good, and you'll look good in this option for the party.

The fact that wearing a skimpy, practically see-through pair of the tiniest underwear ever invented wasn't the craziest part of this weekend was really saying something. But hey, I was open to new things and not giving a fuck about what other people thought, right? I shrugged as I put them on, sliding them up my legs.

That's when the impracticality of the almost invisible piece of material sank in. I reached my hand down over my junk and tried stuffing it in, but it only just worked. I glanced up nervously at the reflection in the mirror. Okay, I was in. Barely, but in. I looked up and silently prayed to the wardrobe malfunction gods to look down on me with kindness and spare me from a truly embarrassing episode tonight.

I spun around and admired the sun lowering in the sky outside my room; the sea was rough, with the waves pounding against the shoreline.

It had been quite the day.

Brunch with Mom had taken more than one unexpected turn, but overall, it proved to me that she did care for me. Sure, it was in her own unique way, but deep, deep, *deep* down, it was there. She would always be my mother, and I would always love her.

In all my years, I'd never seen her break down and open up like that. It was real, and her words really struck a chord in me. I knew it already, but having her confirm that you couldn't buy love made me realize that I did, in fact, love Cassius with all of my heart.

And while I may not have worked up the courage to tell him that, I had opened up to him about my sexuality. I could feel the lingering effects of that still buzzing about excitedly in my body several hours later. I would tell him the rest—about my feelings for him and that I wanted to spend the rest of my life with him. I would. But right now, I had a party to get ready for.

I heard a loud knock on the suite door. "I'll get it!" Cassius cried out.

That'd be Hawk and Emry, and shit, I was unprepared and late...again. That made it twice in one day. A new record for me, but it didn't fill me with the usual dread and shame that it normally would have.

I grabbed the white wings and placed my arms through them. I adjusted them on my shoulders and checked myself in the mirror again. I was wearing quite possibly the most revealing outfit ever worn by a person who wasn't Lil' Kim.

Underwear and wings, that was it. The entire outfit. But we were at a clothing-optional resort, so it kinda didn't matter. And on the plus side, getting out of it would be a breeze at the end of the night.

To sleep. By myself. That was what I meant.

I took a deep breath as I opened the door to my room and made my way out onto the balcony where Cassius had taken Hawk and Emry. As I approached, first I saw Hawk's head spin around, his eyes blowing out like balloons at the sight of me.

Then Emry twisted his body, and his mouth fell wide open.

I was starting to feel like Bridget Jones in that scene where she got dressed up in costume for a party—only to realize it wasn't a costume party, and everyone else was dressed normally.

My heartbeat ticked up a notch. Hawk's and Emry's eyes were stuck on me like superglue. By the time I stepped out onto the balcony, a stunned silence permeated the air.

That was until Cassius saw me and cried out, "Holy motherfucking shitballs! Spencer James Montgomery, what on earth are you wearing?"

"Oh, you mean this?" I waved my hand in front of my body just in case it wasn't clear to anyone that I did, in fact, have some fabric on my body.

I eyed Hawk and Emry in their white tank tops and white pants. Even Cassius was dressed on time—and, far more impressively, on theme—in a white V-neck shirt and matching white shorts. Okay, I was definitely the odd man out.

Emphasis on *odd*.

"Where is the rest of your outfit?" Cassius' eyes kept roaming up and down the length of my body, which, for some reason, ignited my insides. "You're literally just wearing underwear...if you could even call it that." There was shock in his voice, and also an element of something else too. Something I couldn't quite decipher. The poor guy. So many changes and revelations all in the one day.

"I like it." Hawk flicked an approving thumbs-up and a wry smile my way. "You'll be a very popular man tonight, Spencer."

"Well, good." I tried to muster up a little self-confidence, which wasn't an easy thing to do when your ass cheeks were exposed for the world to see. "I like being popular."

Cassius cocked his head to the side, his eyes gleaming at me. He gave a crooked nod. Okay, we were doing it. Sure, I was clearly underdressed and had a string riding up my crack, but priorities, people. We had a line to deliver.

We said it at the same time, in the same well-practiced, monotone voice we always did. "Being popular is the most important thing in the world."

"What. Was. That?" Emry asked, pausing for what seemed like forever in between each word.

Cassius and I laughed. "It's a line from *The Simpsons*," I answered. "You know, Homer's dubious parental advice to Bart?"

Nope. We weren't getting anything out of Hawk and Emry. I guess, as always, Cassius and I were out on our own weird little limb with this silly inside joke of ours.

"So, your outfit, then?" Cassius looked at me expectantly after a few moments, drawing the focus back to arguably a much more pressing matter.

"Wait. So didn't you get this for me?"

Cassius' eyebrows scrunched together in curiosity. "Uh, that would be a hard hell to the no."

He stood up, inspecting me thoroughly from top to toe. Something about him doing that made my skin feel tingly. "What makes you think I got this for you?"

"The note," I explained, trying to remain cool, calm, and collected as it was dawning on me that something was up here. "You know, the one in my luggage."

Cassius raised his palms up to his shoulders. "I have no idea what you're talking about, Spence." Then his eyes dipped down. "But, hey, if some magical note gets you into that outfit, then I'm all for it."

I heard a stifled giggle escape from Emry's general vicinity.

"Will you excuse us for a moment?" I asked the guys.

"Sure." Hawk answered, exchanging a bemused look with Emry.

"Great."

I yanked on Cassius' hand and marched him into my bedroom, closing the door behind us. I walked over to the bed—suddenly very aware that, with him behind me, his eyes were probably on my ass —and handed him the note. His face was a little flushed as he read it.

"That's not me." He handed the note back to me. "You know my writing isn't that neat."

I studied the note again. Of course. It was actually legible. It couldn't have been Cassius who wrote it. His writing was so bad it was his excuse for not writing grocery lists. He'd get to the store and spend half of his time squinting at what he'd written, unable to make any sense of it.

"Besides," he added. "I haven't written in cursive since, like, the third grade."

I looked up at him. "So who did this?"

He met my gaze, our eyes dancing with each other as we considered it. Then, at the exact same time, we both exclaimed, "Olivia!"

"That whole bullshit about there being a leak in the shower that she made us go and check out before we left. That was all a ruse"—yes, he stopped and smiled at his own usage of the word *ruse*...as did I—"just to get us out of the room so that she could plant this outfit in your luggage."

"But why?" I threw myself onto the bed.

Cassius joined me, sitting down so close to me our knees knocked. "You know she's always wanted to see us together."

I felt something brushing against my thigh. I looked down and it was Cassius' hand. "Maybe she thought this outfit would be the thing that made me realize how hot you are and make me fall head over heels in love with you?"

His fingers kept stroking, and it felt like fire. I placed my hand over his, and the movement stopped. Our eyes met.

"And did Olivia's plan work?"

I had no idea what made me ask that question. A momentary lapse in judgement. Maybe the tight underwear was cutting off circulation to my...cock? No, wait, that didn't make any sense. None of this was making any sense. Was it even really happening?

Yes, that was it. This wasn't real. It was all just a dream. A crazy, surreal dream where I was wearing a skimpy G-string and angelic wings, my best friend's hand was grazing my thigh, and I just asked him whether he was falling in love with me.

Okay, time to wake up, Spencer... Come on, now...

WAKE.

UP.

"What are you doing, Spence?" Cassius shot me a *you're acting like you've lost your mind* look.

"Nothing," I said, looking down at the red mark I was leaving on my arm from pinching myself. "I just wanted to make sure this wasn't a—"

"Dream?"

Fuck, he knew me so well.

He wriggled his hand from underneath mine. It went north, up my leg, over the tiny band of my underwear and then gently across my lower stomach.

My heart raced, slamming mercilessly against my ribs.

"Is this okay?" His fingers were now moving up the front of my stomach.

"Yep," I breathed.

"You've got nice abs, Spencey."

"Thanks."

"They're so firm. Hard."

They weren't the only thing that was firm and hard. And since my underwear was offering me about as much protection as holding up a piece of paper in a thunderstorm, I knew that Cassius knew.

And I knew that he knew that I knew.

Eep!

"We, uh, we should get back to Awk and Hemry. I mean...Hawk and Emry."

"I don't think you're in any state to be leaving this room, Spencer."

Yep, there it was. The confirmation I didn't need to have. He knew I was hard, and he knew that he was the reason that I was hard. Which felt so. Fucking. Hot.

I blew out a deep breath. His fingers were still exploring my stomach, so I took his hand in mine again and placed it delicately onto the bed beside us. If he kept touching me, I'd remain in a *not suitable for public consumption* state for a lot longer.

Would that have been such a bad thing? No.

But we had guests, and I didn't want to be rude.

"We, uh, need to talk some more, Cass. Maybe at the party?"

He looked at me for a while without saying anything. I couldn't tell what he was thinking, which was a worrying feeling. Normally, I knew exactly what was on his mind and could predict with pinpoint accuracy what he would say and do next. But right now, I didn't have the faintest idea what that would be.

"Okay," he said, finally getting up. "Let's talk some more at the party."

24

CASSIUS

Okay. So I'd never been to a circuit party like the White Party before.

Full disclosure, I'd never even heard of circuit parties until Emry had filled me in about them at the pool earlier in the day.

Apparently, circuit parties were the LGBT equivalent of dance festivals, and color-themed parties, such as White, Black, and Red parties, had been a mainstay of the gay scene for the last few decades.

Who knew? Definitely not me. Like I'd always freely admitted, I was a bad gay when it came to this sort of stuff. I mean, I still wasn't entirely sure what a bear was.

The party was being held in the resort's massive nightclub area, which was located right above the main lobby. Being up so high meant that there was a great view overlooking the entire resort, as well as the beach. Since it was night, we couldn't actually see the ocean, and since the music was pumping so loudly, we couldn't hear it, either.

"This place is amazing," Spencer yelled loudly enough for the four of us to hear.

We had just cleared the entrance line, showing the door people our tickets. In front of us was a wonderland of white clothes, tanned men, muscles, and glitter. The walls were stripped back, all exposed brick and industrial-like. Green laser lights sprang out from the DJ booth, which overlooked the packed dance floor.

"Look at the lights," I shouted into Spencer's ear while pointing toward the flickering beams.

Spencer's eyes followed my fingers. "Very cool."

"I feel like I'm in a JLo video."

Spencer laughed, but with the music blaring, I couldn't hear it. He didn't bother covering his mouth, which made me feel happy for some reason. Anyone else in this situation would have shot me a *what the fuck* stare? But not my Spencey.

His eyes met mine. "Which one?"

"Huh?"

"Which JLo video does this remind you of?" he clarified.

"*Waiting for Tonight*," I yelled back, unable to wipe the stupid smile off my face, surrendering to the silly dreaminess of our totally ridiculous conversation topic. "It was an early song of hers. She was in a rainforest, then on a river looking all sparkly, and then in a nightclub that had lighting just like this."

See, anyone else would have left the conversation there without saying another word. Clearly, Spencer and I were not just "anyone else."

Spencer rested his palm against the base of my back, drawing me in closer to him. "I don't think she was using the moniker JLo until her second album. You know, the one she called *JLo*."

I elbowed him, still grinning like an idiot. We really did live in our own little world, Spencer and me.

And I fucking loved it.

Especially if that world involved more kisses on the beach. More of Spencer not giving a crap about unimportant things. More of Spencer giving a crap about me. Oh, and more complimentary room service. Yes, lots more of that, please.

"What do you guys want to do?" Hawk asked the group.

Spencer and I remained transfixed by the lights—or maybe each other?—so Emry stepped in and shouted. "Hawk and I might go around and do our usual whore lap."

I must have looked baffled because he drew me in closer to him to explain. "We go around and just have a look at what...treats are on offer tonight. You know, get a feel to see if there's any interest in the dick twins."

"Right. Got it." I patted him on the shoulder. "You guys go have fun, and I'm sure we'll catch up with you later." With a wave, they were off.

That left Spencer and I standing together. Although, as I was quickly noticing, I might as well have ingested an invisibility pill, given that absolutely zero guys were looking at me. They were all too busy leering at Spencer. I mean, in that outfit, it was kinda hard to miss him.

And yes, the guy had the kind of lean swimmer's build that would make anyone drool. Especially when the only fabric covering it was a flimsy piece of material and a couple of wings attached to his broad, tanned shoulders. I checked the corners of my mouth to make sure *I* wasn't drooling.

There was no denying it. My best friend was gorgeous. I could see that, and I could see other guys seeing that, too. And that felt a little...funny. Not *ha ha* funny, but *get your eyes off my man* funny. *Uh-oh...*

I wrapped my arm around his narrow waist protectively. "What do you want to do, Spencey?"

I could see him looking a little unsure of himself. It was one thing to be wearing an outfit like that in the privacy of our suite and only in front of Hawk, Emry, and me. It was another thing entirely to be at a party surrounded by hundreds of people who weren't shy about checking him out.

I gave him a little squeeze. "If you're uncomfortable, we can always go back to the room," I suggested.

He shot me a look to let me know that wasn't even an option. "Are you kidding me, Cass? This is amazing. Look at all these guys. Everyone here is having fun. We should, too!"

I bit down on my lip. "Okay, as long as you're sure. And if you change your mind, just tell me, okay? I don't mind what we do..." *As long as we're together.* Part of me wanted to say that out loud, too. But it was noisy and busy, and it wasn't the right time.

"Let's do a whore lap, just without the whoring. I'd like to check this place out, Cass."

I nodded. Spencer threaded his fingers into mine and led the way. The entrance spilled out onto the biggest dance floor I had ever seen. It took up pretty much most of the open space. And it was packed. Guys were dancing and grinding up on each other, laughing, talking, and having a great time. I really liked the atmosphere. I even found my head involuntarily bopping somewhat in time to the music.

"I'm totally diggin' this vibe," Spencer said joyfully over his shoulder.

"Diggin'?" I couldn't resist pointing out another of his totally dorky '90s-esque references. I saw his lips curling upward. He didn't say anything else, but it felt like he was holding on to my hand tighter than before.

"Will you be gwerking tonight, Cass?"

I blushed. It felt a little strange hearing him say that word, in public, with all of these people around. That was our word, our private *just between him and me* word.

But ever since Emry had spotted Spencer and me kissing at the bonfire, the lines between private and public were starting to blur. And maybe, just maybe, that wasn't such a bad thing?

We veered toward the right side of the space. Booths and couches lined the wall. The music was less blarey, and there were fewer people around, too.

"I feel like I can breathe now," I yelled way too loudly.

Spencer laughed. "You might like to try controlling the volume of your voice."

I nudged into him playfully. "Sorry. I seem to be having trouble controlling what my mouth is doing at the moment."

I hadn't meant for it to come out like that, but now that it had—and Spencer had shot me a look letting me know he got the double meaning—I was glad I'd said it.

It was true. I was in some sort of vacation dreamland, acting in ways I would have never done back home.

I couldn't deny it, though. Over the last couple of days, I'd been seeing Spencer in a whole new light. Maybe it was the fact that we were having such a great time together. Or that we'd seen each other naked. Or that we'd kissed...twice. Or that he was wearing an outfit that made me want to reach down and caress his exposed, peach-perfect ass cheeks. With my tongue.

"Hey, Cass. My eyes are up here, man." Even through all the din of the noise around us, his *tee-hee-hee* laugh filled my ears and warmed me up inside. Thank god *that* hadn't changed.

"Hey, wanna go outside and get some fresh air?" He motioned toward a doorway that led out to an open-air balcony.

"Sure, I might just get us some drinks first. What would you like?"

"Okay. I'll just have water, please. I'll find us a nice spot and meet you out there. Maybe we can talk?"

I nodded. "I'd like that."

He let go of my hand and stepped in to face me. We were inches apart from each other. He shot me a fierce look while my eyes lap danced the entire length of his body. A fire crackled between us.

I'd never experienced this sort of sexual tension with anyone else, much less Spencer. And for the first time since I'd jacked off thinking about him, there wasn't an ounce of guilt or bad feeling attached to it. Just desire. Wanting. Hunger. And...love.

"I'll be right back."

As I headed to the bar, I scanned the scene. The dance floor was impossibly packed, even busier than before. How people could move, much less dance, was beyond me. I needed an entire living room to do justice to my gwerking routine.

As I took it all in, my gaze settled on Hawk and Emry. They were right in the middle of the dance floor, and it seemed they had acquired a target. A very attractive, well-built one who had some killer dance moves. All three of them did, actually. They may or may not have put my gwerking to shame.

I moved out of the way so that people could still walk past me as I studied them for a moment from the edge of the dance floor. The sexual chemistry between the three of them was unmissable. It felt wild. Freeing. Primal.

All things that, up until this point in my life, I had avoided. But ever since Spencer and I had kissed, I realized that not only were those things absent from my life, I missed not having the chance to experience them.

I wanted to share a deep connection with someone. I wanted to be desired by a person who had eyes only for me. A guy that would make me feel like I was the most beautiful creature in the world.

Which was exactly how Spencer made me feel.

I scampered over to the bar, got two bottles of water, and headed toward the balcony.

Yes, Spencer and I had to talk. And for some inexplicable reason, I wasn't scared.

I was so proud of him for opening up to me about the exploration he was undertaking of his sexuality. God, that sounded so formal, but it was true. Spencer had taken a very Spencer approach to things, one that worked for him. Yes, it involved a spreadsheet and carefully mapping out the myriad different options, but good for him.

Realizing you're not straight could produce an overwhelming torrent of emotions. He didn't deny it, suppress it, or try to ignore it. No, he dealt with it. Head on. And that took real strength.

And yes, a part of me couldn't help but want to know just exactly what "not straight" entailed. What he was looking for. Could it be...me?

In spite of the few unexpected turns our friendship had experienced this weekend, nothing could shake the foundation of stability and familiarity that we had. We'd been best friends for too long to let anything jeopardize what we had.

Or so I thought until I stepped out on the balcony, the salty night air spritzing my face.

I looked around for Spencer. I smiled as I spied him standing by the railing, looking out into the dark ocean. As I got closer, though, I realized that Spencer wasn't alone. Standing beside him was his jacuzzi-going friend he'd met the day before. Robert, Sam, Ian—or whatever his name was.

My throat got real dry real fast. My fingers pressed into the bottles of water I was holding. I noticed my breathing had gotten heavier, too, firing out of my nostrils in angry spurts. Spencer and the guy whose name I couldn't remember were talking and laughing.

A switch in my mind flipped, and I had the thought, *I should be the one talking and laughing with Spencer. He's mine.*

Holy shit.

That wasn't good.

I wasn't normally like this.

And then I remembered why I liked stability and familiarity so much. It was because when things changed, *I* changed. And not always in a good way. I would say and do stupid things. I could be impulsive, and I didn't like that about myself. So keeping things the same was both my security blanket, as well as my insurance policy against acting like a dick.

I liked being good ol' boring Cassius. The guy who gwerked, hiked, and only got experimental when it came to combining foods. Not when it came to dealing with icky things like feelings and other people.

But—just like you could see a car accident before it happened and be powerless to stop it—I was now that car about to careen into a wall...and totally unable to do anything about it.

My jaw clamped shut tightly as I screwed the bottle of water roughly into Spencer's back. He spun around and smiled. "Hey, Cass. You're here."

"You sound surprised," I shot back.

Uh-oh. This wasn't going to end well. I could already tell I was speeding down I'm About To Be A Dick Avenue at full speed with no brakes.

Spencer shuffled out of the way, giving me a better view of what's-his-face. "I'd like you to meet—"

"I don't want to meet anyone." My gut tightened with shock at how rude I was being. No, no, no. This wasn't like me at all. Why couldn't I just shut up and stop? Why couldn't I be normal, say hello to Spencer's new friend, and not make a complete idiot out of myself?

Why? Why? Why?

"I thought we were going to talk." My voice was shaky and low.

Spencer's eyes darted around my face. He looked over at the guy and threw him a pensive, probably apologetic, smile.

He then leaned in closer to me and whispered in a hushed tone, "We will talk. Just later, okay? I thought we could hang out with Ian. He's a really nice guy and—"

"I'm sure you're a lovely guy, Ian," I interrupted, looking over at the man who seemed about as comfortable as a patient waiting for a colonoscopy. "But I have a terrible headache all of a sudden. Must be all of this fresh air. I'm going back to the room. Have a good night."

I spun around to leave. I felt Spencer's hand on my shoulder, but I broke free of his grip and continued walking.

Even before I had taken more than a few steps, I regretted acting like such an idiot. I even considered stopping, turning around, and apologizing...but I couldn't. I just couldn't. My veins were coursing with such raw emotion that I knew the best thing to do was to leave.

I'd have to deal with the consequences of my bad behavior in the morning.

As it turned out, Spencer had other ideas.

25

SPENCER

"Cass, wait up. Come on, Cass. Please. Stop."

For someone who had an allergic reaction to hearing the word *exercise*, Cassius was surprisingly fast as he navigated the packed nightclub, heading for the nearest exit.

Admittedly, he had gotten a head start.

After his mini-outburst, I turned to Ian with tears in my eyes. I felt a rising tide of emotions flooding my chest, but I wasn't able to coherently identify even one of them. What had just happened? Why was Cassius so upset with me? And why was it killing me that I had made him feel so bad?

"Go after him, Spencer."

Ian's words managed to make the spinning in my head stop a little. At least enough to acknowledge that he was right.

I nodded my head. "Okay. I will. I'm sorry. Thank you."

Ian responded with a kind smile and a knowing nod. "Go!"

I turned around and rushed after Cassius. Yelling out after him in a noisy nightclub was—unsurprisingly—completely ineffective.

I hadn't imagined the pain in his eyes or the tremble in his voice when he saw me talking with Ian. But what did that mean? I had no idea, but a surge of determination tore through me as I chased Cassius down the cobblestone pathway, past the deserted pool area, and onto the beach, my feet squeaking in the sand as I flicked sheets of it up onto my calves.

Finally, his shape got closer, and his loud, haggard breathing filled my ears. I closed the distance between us, reaching my hand out and grabbing his arm. He didn't pull away. Instead, he stopped and turned to face me, his face smeared with tears and sweat that glistened in the moonlight.

The roar of the waves thundered in my chest right next to my racing heart. It took me a few gulps of inhaling the salty air to catch my breath. I looked down at our touching hands and swallowed hard before speaking.

"Please don't make us do this." My words came out jittery, insecure, because that's exactly how I was feeling.

"Do what?" Cassius' voice carried more alarm than anything else.

I lifted my gaze and met the most beautiful set of eyes staring back at me. "This bullshit, cliché thing where two dudes have a misunderstanding and don't talk to each other."

Cassius' fingers grazed the back of my hand softly. "We're not a cliché, Spence."

My heart hummed with relief for the fact that he was talking, but even more than that, that he was standing here and touching me. He had no idea how much I needed that right now.

"So, let's do it," I said, mustering all the courage and strength I could find in me. "Let's talk about everything. What's on our mind, what's in our hearts. All of it."

His eyes went dark, and he pulled away from me, my fingers left cold, dangling lifelessly by the side of my body. "What are you doing, Cass?"

Without saying a word, he peeled off his shirt and laid it down on the sand in front of us. Before I could tell him that it wasn't necessary, he was patting it down, silently encouraging me to sit on it. My heart clenched at the thoughtfulness of his gesture. Getting sand in my butt crack would not have been enjoyable.

We both sat down and settled into a silence that stretched out as far as the ocean before us. I guess we both wanted to talk, but neither one of us wanted to be the one to speak *first*.

For some completely unknown reason—and one that I was sure I'd be psychoanalyzing with a therapist for years to come—thoughts of brunch with my mom invaded my mind.

Seeing her so unguarded, and listening to her talk about her life in such a real, brutally honest way, was a wakeup call. So was hearing her talking about love, and how if you found it, you had to hold on to it. Those words crystallized what was going on for me and my feelings for Cassius.

Blurting out that I loved him and wanted to spend the rest of my life with him came as much of a surprise to me as it did to her. But the second the words were out, I felt like a gold miner who had just struck gold. It was the most luminous moment of clarity I'd ever had in my life.

Having shared not one, but two kisses with Cassius helped to loosen me up, too. It helped allay any fears I had that this was a one-sided thing. I was picking up on something more than just friendship feels from him. I saw the way his eyes dragged up and down my body when I stepped out onto the balcony looking like a male version of a Victoria's Secret angel. It made my skin prickle with a kind of uncontained heat that felt exhilarating.

And just wearing this crazy outfit did something to me, too. Sure, when we first arrived at the party, I felt overwhelmed. I was definitely one of the least dressed people there and attracting a lot of attention. But after a while, I got used to it. It didn't feel like I was being judged by anyone. People were simply looking. If anything, I felt supported, like they were saying "good for you" for having the balls (pun intended) to wear something like that.

All of these things took me to the place where I was ready—one hundred percent soul-level ready—to tell my best friend in the world my truth. I wanted nothing more than to lay it all out in the open. The truth about my feelings for him, not my balls.

My mouth opened and closed like a goldfish in a tank a few times. I cleared my throat and squared my shoulders. *Just take it easy. You can do this.*

"So, Cass, you know how we talked earlier, and I told you that I wasn't straight?"

Something skittered across his face, drawing his jaw in tightly. "Uh-huh." He scratched the side of his face nervously. "What— what does that mean, exactly?"

"That, I don't know yet," I started somewhat guardedly. "I have a spreadsheet, and I've been narrowing down all of the applicable choices. For a while there, I'd gotten it down to about five or six options. Words, labels, that resonated here." I placed my hand over my heart.

He gave one single nod. "Okay," he muttered. Then he went back to being eerily still. "And how many options have you narrowed it down to now?"

I swallowed around the lump that had lodged itself in my throat. "One."

He went a little pink around the ears, shimmering in the moonlight. "Oh. And what—what is it?"

I didn't hesitate. "You. It's you, Cassius. You're my option. My only option." I leaped to my feet, electrified by the sudden burst of energy that was thundering through my veins.

I started pacing in circles in front of him as I continued speaking. Okay, possibly rambling and shooting specks of sand into the air around me as I moved. But I was excited, lit up inside and alive in a way I'd never been in my entire life. "I know that it probably doesn't make much sense to you. Believe me, it's been freaking me out for the past few months..."

Cassius' eyes were following me as I stomped around like a madman.

"Heck, maybe it's been there the whole time. I don't know,

really. And I thought that the answer was out there..." I waved my hands around madly, indicating that *out there* meant somewhere in the outside world.

I looked at him and let out a deep sigh. "But really, the whole time, the answer has been right here."

I dropped to my knees in front of him. "The best thing in my life has been right in front of me the whole time, and I never even knew it. Well, I did, of course, but I never thought it could be like this."

His eyes welled with tears as I cupped his face in my hands. "I'm in love with you, Cassius. So fucking much that it hurts."

26

CASSIUS

Spencer's words whirred around in my head, making me feel dizzy and disoriented. Had he really just said it? That he was in love with me? That I was the person he wanted to be with?

I lifted my chin to meet his gaze, his eyes swollen with so much affection I thought my heart would burst at the sight of it. The sweeping realization ran through my entire being, from head to toe.

"I love you, too, Spencer. With all of my heart." I didn't have to think to say the words. I just let them flow from my heart.

I smoothed my hands down his chest, and when I glanced back up at his face again, his eyes flared wide. There was a blistering heat behind them. A short silence followed before...

Spencer jumped on top of me, sending me flying backward into the soft sand. A blur of heat, lips, skin, fingers, and the softest, sweetest-sounding moaning emanating from his mouth enveloped around us. We were in our very own little bubble.

I was feeling every single sensation with such clarity. It was as if my whole life up until that point was in black and white, and now it had transformed into high-definition color.

The light of the moon shining down on us, the deafening

sounds of the waves crashing on the shore, the powdery sand against my back, as Spencer guided me to lie down, while he pulled down my shorts around my ankles.

Oh—*oh!*

My brain snapped back to reality. Spencer had just pulled my shorts down. That could only mean—shit.

"Spencer."

His eyes shot up to meet mine. "Are you okay?" There was a huskiness to his voice I hadn't heard before.

I gave a half nod. He pulled himself up, his face hovering over my heaving chest.

"What—what are you about to do?" I managed to get the words out somehow. My mouth had suddenly transformed into the Sahara Desert.

His hand palmed an erection that I hadn't even realized I'd had. "I think you, Cass." Then his eyebrows pinched together adorably as he asked, "Is that okay with you?"

I gulped but nodded my head sharply. "Yes. Yes. Yes."

I smiled as I spoke, and he did, too.

Oh my god, this was actually happening. My best friend of seventeen years was about to go down on me.

In one firm yet gentle movement, I felt his fingers hook into the waistband of my briefs. Seconds later, they were joining my shorts, down around my ankles. I kicked my way out of them as Spencer's warm hands landed on the insides of my thighs.

The salty breeze rushed over my exposed and hard-as-a-steel-post cock, before Spencer wrapped his fingers around it with an iron grip. He lowered his head, but instead of going for my dick, I felt his tongue joining his fingers on the insides of my legs, swirling it around gently. It tickled a little but felt amazingly good a whole lot more.

His eyes flashed up to meet mine. I couldn't turn away. The sight of him, huddled slightly awkwardly over me, was out of this world.

And then he did it. He focused his eyes on my cock, stuck his tongue out, and reached toward it, tasting just the tip. I traced my fingers across his face. "You can stop whenever you like, Spencey."

He craned his face upward, fear rolling in his eyes. "Why? Am I doing something wrong?"

"No, no, no."

Shit, that wasn't what I was saying. "I just mean, if you ever want to stop at any time, you just tell me, and we'll—"

He took my cock in his mouth and holy. Mother. Fuck! It felt amazingly good. It had the added bonus of shutting me up, too.

I flung my head back, taking in the sparkling stars in the sky while Spencer took more and more of me into his mouth. I'd need to have a look at that spreadsheet of his because whatever notes he'd taken for giving head were beyond on point.

His fingers cupped my balls, rolling them gently between his fingers like dice, while he continued to bob up and down on my dick, flicking his tongue on the underside of my sensitive head whenever he got there. How did he know that was my secret spot? I'd never told him that. I'd never told *anyone* that, and yet, somehow, he just knew.

I ran my fingers through his silky hair, my arms moving up and down in time with the tempo his mouth was setting. He was, like, next-level good, deep-throating me right down to the base before expertly pulling all the way up along my length and swooping back down again. The sounds his mouth was making as he slurped at my saliva-slicked cock smacked out into the salty air occasionally, creating even more heat around our bodies. It felt so dangerous and exciting. So much for thinking I was a prude.

I closed my eyes, and the loss of sight ignited my other senses immediately. From the wind gently whirling around us, to the slight dampness of the sand against the backs of my legs, to the insane warmth and wetness Spencer was producing with his mouth, driving me higher and higher, until I heard the unmissable drawl of a "Hey guuuurl," pierce the night air.

Wait. What?

My eyes burst open to see Spencer diving over my exposed dick in an attempt to protect whatever was left of my modesty.

"Did you hear that?" His voice was raspy, his lips swollen.

"Of course I heard that," I replied urgently, putting the instance of raspy swollen sexiness out of my mind, but making a mental note to definitely return to it later.

"Over here, you guys. Don't worry. We've covered our eyes so we're not looking." That was Hawk's voice.

Great. They were both here to witness this.

Spencer spotted them and motioned to the right. I looked over and saw Emry and Hawk, facing away from us. It looked like they had, indeed, covered their eyes in addition to turning around in the opposite direction. At least that was something.

Spencer helped me tug my shorts back up my legs. He even found time to give my cock a frisky fondle before squeezing my erection into my shorts.

Once we were done and I was decent, he looked at me, asking me with his eyes if I was okay. I nodded in agreement.

He called out to Hawk and Emry. "Okay, you guys, you can turn around now."

They came over and stood a few feet away from us. "We were just going out on an innocent nighttime walk, when we stumbled upon those two savages going hell for leather on the beach," Emry said, doing his best Southern belle impersonation.

"Look at you boys," Hawk added, his smirk reflecting brightly in the moonlight. "Just friends, hey?"

We all chuckled.

"I guess the jig is up," Spencer conceded, getting up and stretching his hand out, helping me to stand up, too.

"I'm happy for you boys," Hawk continued. "I could see it from the moment we met that you two had something special. If it was friendship, great. But hey, isn't this better?"

I smiled goofily. "It totally is."

"We really didn't mean to interrupt you guys," Emry said, ditching the accent and returning to his normal voice.

"That's all right. We, uh, probably should be getting back, anyway."

The raspy undertone that persisted in Spencer's voice made me smile and feel all gooey on the inside. That, and the fact that he had captured my hand, caressing it into his as we said our goodbyes to the guys and walked back to the resort. His grip was firm, possessive even. I liked it.

And the best bit? The night wasn't over yet.

27

SPENCER

The second the door to our suite snapped shut, it was on like Donkey Kong.

Cassius was on me, over me, all around me, and I loved it. He really was the most beautiful person I'd ever seen.

And I knew one thing with utmost certainty: I only had eyes for him.

I didn't quite know what tab that placed me in when it came to my spreadsheet, but fuck it, I'd start a new tab, one called *Cassius*. Because of all the terms and labels I had pored over, desperate to find one that fit me, that right there was the one that felt most right.

I managed to wrestle my lips away from his for a nanosecond to ask, "Your bedroom or mine?"

"Mine," he replied in between peppering me with a series of delightful smaller kisses. "Your room is too neat. It gives me anxiety."

My giggle was interrupted by a series of longer, deeper kisses. I didn't mind at all. Cassius' lips could have stayed on me forever, and I would have been the happiest guy alive.

We strip-fumbled our way into his room, somehow managing to

avoid falling over as I wrestled the clothes off his body as if they were a mortal enemy. They were. Anything that stood between me and Cassius' glorious flesh was prime enemy number one as far as I was concerned.

My outfit was, as expected, a lot easier to peel off. I was naked, hard, and dripping wet in no time. Holy shit, I looked down at the drop of precum that glistened on the tip of my cock. It had been a while—a long while—since I was this turned on that I was leaking like a faucet.

Now that I'd seen him naked at the resort, going back to a life where clothing optional wasn't a choice was going to be hard. But I'd think about that later. Right now, I was feasting on the incredible view—and I didn't mean the ocean.

Cassius was lying on the bed, fully naked.

I paused for a moment, my eyes soaking in the splendor that was his body, from top to toe. His messy hair with strands flying around in every direction, his eyes that told me everything I needed to know about him without saying a word, his chest that was broader and fuller than mine, the dark hairs that covered his belly that led down to his cock, jutting out of his body like a pier into the ocean. Down his meaty legs, thick from all the hiking he did, all the way down to those feet that I'd spent hours rubbing. Fuck, I wanted to taste those toes in my mouth.

The thought of all the new ways I could explore and experience Cassius' body was like rocket fuel. I was excited in a way that I'd never been before. I was more than ready to do this. I had to do this. Like breathing, like my heart beating, it wasn't a choice. It was an involuntary pull that I needed to surrender to, let it take me over.

I crawled on top of him and began kissing him, starting just above his knees. His leg hairs tickled my nose a bit, so I stuck my tongue out and began tracing a pattern around them, just like I'd done on the beach earlier. I spread his legs open slightly, my tongue swirling around his inner thigh. I could taste myself on his skin from earlier, but it didn't feel strange. It felt amazing, that the flavors of our bodies had combined. We were joining together in a way we'd never done before.

A series of heavy moans left him. I was only just getting started, but already, I couldn't wait until all I heard was groaning, sighing, and more sexy sounds coming from Cassius. My fingers joined my tongue, kneading into his thighs, pressing into his warm flesh.

"That feels so good, Spence."

I smiled and looked up, but I couldn't see his face. My view was obstructed by a certain... pier.

It was thicker and veinier than my cock, but fuck, I had never wanted something more in my life. I lunged at it, greedily swallowing it down into the depths of my throat.

I honestly had no idea how I'd feel about sucking cock.

Sure, I'd researched the fuck out of it and might have been the only man on the face of the planet who could say—and honestly mean it—that he'd been watching porn for research purposes only, but doing the thing? When it came down to it, I knew there'd only be one way to really tell—and that was by doing it.

And with a mouthful of cock crammed into my throat and Cassius' pubes lightly brushing against my nose, let me tell ya, it was the best feeling in the world. I felt his fingers digging into my scalp. The touch was light, but I wanted more.

I was in completely uncharted territory here, so I was acting on instinct and instinct alone. And my gut was telling me something I'd never heard it say before.

I wanted to surrender. To him. Only him.

I reached for the back of my head and placed my hands over his, pushing down on them, indicating that I wanted him to take control of my head...however he wanted to. I let go of his palm, and he let go, too.

"Spence, are you saying what I think you're saying?"

I scooped my head up, my mouth filled with his cock, and nodded at him. I guess I'd need to spell it out for him.

"Fuck my face, Cass."

His eyes went wide with surprise, before he burst into the happiest smile I had seen on him in years.

"All right," he said as his hands landed in my hair again.

With a steady, firm, but still reserved pressure, he forced my face onto his cock, controlling the movement completely. How far down I'd go, when I'd come back up. I was there just to please him, and god, that was all I wanted to do. I'd never felt more alive, more sexy, more free in my life.

I'd spent so long wondering what sex stuff might be like with a guy. Would it feel weird? Would I freak about it? Or would I like it? The answers, as I was discovering while bobbing up and down on Cassius' cock, were no, no, and holy fuck yes to the power of a million.

Because, for me, it wasn't about the act as much as it was the person I was doing the act with. Being at the mercy of Cassius' hands, having his cock stretching the insides of my mouth, was beyond any pleasure I thought was possible. It was electrifying.

"Harmpffder," I spluttered.

Okay, so trying to talk with a mouthful of dick wasn't a great idea. Rookie mistake.

Cassius gently pulled my head back, allowing me to release his cock from my mouth. "What did you say? Is something wrong? Was I going too hard? Did you want to stop?"

It filled my chest with such contentment to hear his concern for me. I cherished it so much, but the last thing I wanted was to stop.

"Actually"—I peered up at his perspiring, pleasure-soaked face through my own sweat-drenched lashes—"I was saying harder. Don't hold back, Cass. I am loving this so much."

"You are?" His voice was soft, vulnerable.

"Like you wouldn't believe. I've never felt like this before."

He beamed. "Good. Me, too."

And with that, he grabbed me by the sides of my face and gave it to me harder...and faster...with just the right amount of roughness that I needed. That I craved on some deeper, instinctual level that I only realized because it was him...and me...and us.

I closed my eyes and surrendered, trusting him to guide the movements and allowing myself to experience the blissful frenetic energy of the moment.

It was wild.

And crazy.

And hot.

And so beautifully, sacredly intimate.

And sooooo fucking good.

And I wasn't the only one who thought so. I heard Cassius cry out, "Oh, fuck. I'm getting close. Spence. Oh, fuck. I'm gonna come, I'm gonna—"

And with that, he filled my mouth up with something warm, liquidy, and a little gluggy. Once I could feel his dick starting to soften, I released it carefully and swallowed down his cum in one big gulp. It didn't have much of a taste, more of a gooey, slightly warm consistency than anything else. I had a part of him inside of me forever.

I kissed my way up from his belly to his neck. His face was flushed. His forehead and upper lip were beaded with sweat. He looked so radiant, so alive. It was like I was looking at him for the first time because, in a way, I guess I was.

"How was that?" I asked as I kissed my way along his jaw.

"Ohhh myfghunikhswq."

I nibbled on his ear lobe. "So, good, then?" I wasn't an expert at these things, but I figured making someone unable to enunciate was a sign you'd satisfied them.

"How did you—how...?"

His voice trailed off, although I distinctly heard him whispering something about needing to see that spreadsheet of mine.

SUNDAY

28

SPENCER

I rolled onto my side and groaned.

Dammit.

Despite it being our third morning here, my body clock was still stubbornly set to anything but vacation time. I let out a big yawn and peeked over at the green display of the bedside clock.

7:05.

Okay, so I had at least slept in until seven, but 7 a.m. was still criminally too early to be awake for a Sunday morning. What to do now?

I could go to the gym, but that was about as appealing as, well, as it sounded, really.

A walk on the beach was slightly more tempting, but still, not something that was getting me to jump out of bed all excited and ready to take on the day-like.

I sighed as I propped myself up onto my elbows. I looked over at the empty side of my bed, wishing it was filled with a certain somebody. But after our adventures in Cassius' room last night, which ended with him drifting off to sleep in my arms, I snuck away to my room, figuring he would need some space in the light of day to process everything that had happened between us.

My heart was burning with an almost insatiable urge to creep back into his bed, slide under the covers, and wrap him up in my arms. But again, knowing Cassius as well as I did meant that I had to give him what I assumed he was needing now more than ever: space.

Closely followed by caffeine. So I jumped out of bed, got dressed quickly, and made my way down to the café.

With two large almond lattes in hand, I returned to our suite—armed and ready to check in on him. It was still only twenty past seven by the time I got to Cassius' bedroom door, but with caffeine in hand, I calculated that the threat to my life was reduced immeasurably. The risk of a few minutes of Cassius' irateness was a price I'd have to pay.

Knock, knock, knock.

I waited a moment. Nothing. I was about to ask if he was decent, but considering I'd lost count of how many times we'd seen each other naked this weekend—as well as the fact that I'd had him in my mouth last night—I decided it wasn't altogether necessary.

Instead, I went for, "Rise and shine, Sleeping Beauty," as I let myself in. Cassius had forgotten to draw the curtains, so the room was brightly lit. Yet, in spite of the sunlight streaming through, he was still, somehow, sleeping like a zombie.

I approached the bed and smiled. When Cassius slept, he slept. Hurricanes, tornadoes, alien invasions...yep, he'd sleep through it all, wake up the next morning, and it wouldn't even dawn on him that a catastrophe had befallen humanity until after his third bowl of cereal. Ice cream optional.

He was lying face down on his front, his head turned to the side. Thick strands of hair covered most of his forehead and splayed out messily onto the pillow. His lips were smooshed together, and as I placed the cups of coffee down on the bedside table, I could hear the faintest sound of...let's just call it purring because it was the cutest little snore I had ever heard. Well, the cutest little snore since the one I'd heard emanating from him on the plane down here.

I stopped and looked at him for a moment, catching myself and what I was doing. The last thing I wanted was to creep him out by watching him sleep. He was already likely to be on edge and frazzled by all the changes swirling around us. The last thing I wanted to do was freak him out even more.

"Cassius." I thought I'd said it pretty loudly, but judging by his total lack of a response, I guessed not.

I cleared my throat and tried again, mustering a little more volume than before.

"Cassius."

Nothing.

I nudged him on the shoulder.

Not a thing.

Seriously? There was deep sleep—and then there was this.

"Cassius!"

I bellowed it out so loudly people walking on the beach would have heard it.

Finally, he stirred. Then, something between a groan, a yawn, and a heavy breath escaped from his lips.

Movement and sound. It may have taken a solid few minutes, but hey, I was making progress.

His eyelids fluttered, and then, *finally*, we had lift-off. Or, in this case, eye contact.

"Spence," he uttered groggily. "What—what are you doing here?"

I reached for the cup of coffee and ran it under his nose.

His ears pricked up. Then a hand reached to brush away the hair that had fallen over his eyes. And then he propped himself up onto his elbows and sat upright, the sheet bunching around the base of his belly.

"Thank you," he said as he took the cup from me and brought it straight to his lips, keeping it there for a long time. A suspiciously long time. As if he was using it as a diversion to not have to, you know, speak to me.

Shit.

He was freaked out. Maybe more than I had expected. Dammit, I knew all of this would be too much for him.

"Look, Cass—"

He raised his hand, and I stopped talking mid-sentence.

"Please, Spence, can I say something first?"

I nodded. "Sure, go ahead."

He took another sip of coffee before placing it onto the bedside table. He folded his legs up and wrapped his arms around his knees. "I owe you an apology. I acted like a—"

His eyes drifted around the room, searching for the right word. A small smile curled the edges of his lips upward. "I'm sorry for acting like such an asshat last night. I don't know what got into me, and I'm sorry. And..."

He scratched the side of his face. "...I owe Ian an apology, too. I was rude to him, and he did nothing to deserve it."

Cassius' head was hanging low.

I leaned over and hooked my index finger under his chin. Our eyes met, and I smiled. "Thank you, Cass. That's big of you. I was actually worried and thought you might have been weirded out by, you know, the stuff we did last night."

"What? No. Are you crazy?"

He reached for my arm. My hand was still holding his chin up. It must have looked like a weird sight, the two of us holding on to each other somewhat awkwardly, but I certainly didn't want to let go of him, and as his fingers wrapped tighter and tighter around my forearm, I got the feeling he didn't want to let go of me, either.

"I just feel like such a douchebag for the way I acted toward Ian. It was out of line, but when I saw you guys talking... I don't know, something just exploded inside of me."

I felt relief flooding every pore and cell in my body. God, he was such a good person. So concerned about the way he made someone else feel and, just as importantly, seeming to handle the latest developments between us incredibly well.

He looked like he had more to say as he took a deep breath. "Even earlier in the evening, when we first got to the party... Everyone was staring at you because you looked absolutely amazing in that outfit, and I hate to admit it out loud, but I felt...jealous."

My gaze narrowed at him. "Jealous?"

He nodded sheepishly. "Yeah, like some creepy, possessive boyfriend or something."

Hmm, that didn't sound so bad. I meant the *boyfriend* bit, not the *creepy, possessive* part.

He was scratching the back of his neck, but I had momentarily tuned out, hypnotized by the way his bicep was bulging beside his face. When did he get such strong arms? And why had I never noticed them before?

His eyes widened in recognition as he saw the object of my staring. He moved his arm. Now he was rubbing his chest with his palm. My head followed every single movement he was making.

"Spencer!"

Whoops!

I got busted.

"What is going on with you? With...us?"

I managed to break my gaze from his meaty chest and looked up, studying his face like I was committing it to memory. I guess a part of me was.

Last night had been incredible. Telling him I loved him, being intimate with him. I didn't want it to be a one-time thing. I wanted more, a certain assurance that this would continue post-getaway when we returned to our normal lives back home.

Cassius was doing well with everything so far. So I decided to bite the bullet and just go for it. But first, I handed him his coffee. "When we get home, Cass, I want this to continue. This isn't a one-time vacation fling for me. It's not an experiment or a phase that

I'm going through. I meant what I said last night. I love you. So..." I exhaled sharply. "When we get back to Boston, I'd like for you to be my...boyfriend."

Holy shit.

Saying it, actually saying the word *boyfriend,* made it so real...and so fucking fantastic. Why had I waited so long to get to this moment?

I took Cassius in. He was blinking and breathing, but that was about it. The rest of his face was blank, and his hand was suspended, holding the coffee cup in midair. I knew this was a lot to put onto him, especially given how much I knew he hated any sort of change, but at the same time, I'd meant the other thing I had said last night, too. I didn't want us to be walking clichés, getting lost in a maze of miscommunication and unspoken confusion.

"Cass, say something. Please." I carefully edged myself up on the bed, getting closer to him but leaving him with enough breathing room, too. "What are you thinking? Feeling? Tell me, please."

"Boyfriends?" His tone was flat, serious.

I nodded and smiled, lit up by a fire of hope that had been burning inside of me since our first kiss. "Yeah, boyfriends."

His mouth had gaped open a little. He clamped it shut and ran his fingers through his hair. His stillness was replaced by restlessness. It looked like he was squirming, uncomfortable.

"Hey, I know this is a lot—"

"Yeah, it is," he agreed, licking his dry lips. "I might—I might need some time to, uh, process everything."

Oh shit.

Had I gone too far? Was he freaking out? Of course, he was freaking out. He was just doing his best to try and hide it from me. I looked down at his coffee cup, and his arm—his whole freaking arm —was shaking.

I didn't like the feeling brewing in my gut—the thought of

making Cassius feel bad was the worst feeling in the world and the last thing I had meant to do.

I leaped up off the bed. "Let me give you some time to process this, Cass. Okay?"

I saw him give a noncommittal head nod as I headed toward the door. That was what he needed. Space and time to think it all over.

Damn.

I should have eased him into this differently. After seventeen years, I should have known better. I was mentally punching myself when I turned around at the door. I bit down anxiously on my lip.

"We're going to be all right, aren't we, Cassius?"

He looked up and forced a smile before dropping his head down. "Of course we will be, Spencer."

I closed the door behind me, and, for some reason, doubt overtook my desire to believe him.

The question entered my mind like an unwanted guest: had I just screwed up the best thing in my life?

29

CASSIUS

I stared blankly at the TV screen. I'd flicked it on a few seconds after Spencer had left my room, desperate for my mind to think about something, anything else. I didn't care what. Which was how I'd ended up watching this...fighting sports thing. Boxing, I think they called it.

The two boxing dudes—seriously, I don't know any sporting terms at all—were brutal. I mean, they were really pummeling each other. How—*why?*—did people watch this for entertainment? I kept covering my eyes and turning away every time things got too violent. Like right now for instance, when one of the boxing dudes fired off a round of brutal head knocks that downed his opponent to the ground.

"And there you have it, ladies and gentlemen," I heard one of the commentators commentate—because that's what sports commentators did, they commentated, right? "The killer one-two punch combination that is a signature Brock MacKenzie move."

I let out an exasperated sigh. I'd recently experienced a one-two combination myself. At least mine didn't end up with me on the floor, bruised and bleeding.

I scrubbed the remaining sleep out of my eyes. Spencer and I had been doing an awful lot of talking lately, as well as other things with our mouths, too. It was a lot to process, but in all honesty, I wasn't freaking out too much about it. I just genuinely needed a second—okay, maybe a few seconds—to just think things over in my mind.

Okay, let's review here.

Spencer wasn't straight. Yep, I was a cucumber with that, as in, *cool as a...* No issue there, whatsoever.

I was gay. Old news, terrible in love, even worse with gay terms and words, but still, old news. No change on that front.

Spencer loved me. Yeah, I knew that, too. And the feeling was more than mutual. I loved Spencer more than anything or anyone else in the world.

Spencer wanted us to be boyfriends.

Ah, there we go. Cue mild nausea forming in back of throat, unsteady breathing and involuntary body shaking.

The *B* word.

Boyfriends.

As in him and I being...together-together. It might have only been a four-letter difference, but the space between best friends and boyfriends was, like, a solar system. Or a galaxy. Or a Milky Way. Whichever one was the biggest.

A creeping sense of guilt was coiling itself around all of my major organs and flooding me with shame as I remembered the look on Spencer's face as he left the room barely a few moments ago, but already, it felt like I'd been without him for an eternity.

I didn't actually want him to leave, but he got up so quickly, mumbling something about giving me space, and my mind was so foggy and dopey and dazed, not having had the effects of the caffeine kick in yet, that I stupidly just sat there and let him go.

Fuck, why hadn't I said something to stop him from going away?

I knew what he was doing. He was being the amazingly kind

and considerate man I knew him to be, allowing me the time and space he thought I needed to let me deal with this in my own way.

But if I had just been able to speak up, I would have told him that I didn't want him to leave. And I especially didn't want him going away thinking that I was upset with him.

Confused as all fuck? Yes, just a tad more than slightly.

Angry or pissed at him? Hell to the no.

I grumbled to myself as I turned the TV off. I pushed the sheet off me and jumped into some boxer shorts and my *Go With The Flow* shirt, making my way out to the living room and kitchen.

There was no sign of Spencer. I noticed a note he'd left on the countertop. It was a reminder note (as usual) about our boat trip at one. I wandered over to his bedroom and knocked on the door.

No answer.

"Spence. Are you in there?"

No answer.

I guess he had gone out, giving me the space I needed but didn't want at all. I wanted to be with him. Even though I had spent so much time with him this weekend already. I missed him. A lot. Like, way more than usual.

I spent the rest of the morning sitting on the balcony, with my legs stretched out against the railing, absently sketching whatever came into my mind. It looked more like the doodlings of a bored six-year-old, but at least it was relaxing me a little.

I waited until noon, and when he hadn't shown up, I ordered room service. For two. When he didn't show up by twelve-thirty, I ate his meal, too.

At ten minutes to one, I showed up at the pier. On time, heck, early, and looking forward to spending the afternoon on a boat with Spencer. It was just what we needed, an activity we could do together. Casual enough so that the conversation would likely remain light, but close enough so that it felt good, like it always did whenever my best friend was sitting right beside me.

I jerked my head around the crowd of maybe a dozen or so

guys, but no sign of Spencer. He'd be here soon. Spencer hated being late, after all.

The tour guide greeted the group and invited us to step onboard. I glanced around and still couldn't see him. *Oh well, I'll get on the boat and save a seat next to me,* I thought.

As I sat down, a hand landed on my shoulder. "Cassius?"

I turned around. "Oh my gosh... Toby!"

"Hey, man." He greeted me with an unexpected hug, so my arms kinda flung around the sides of my body like octopus tentacles.

"How are you?" he asked when we pulled apart.

"I'm good," I replied, still a little surprised to be talking to him and becoming increasingly concerned about Spencer still not being here.

"Are you staying at the resort?" Toby asked.

"Yep. How about you?"

He nodded. "And... I've found myself a bear."

I smiled politely but avoided telling him that not only did I know that, but that I had stumbled upon that little nugget of information by seeing him fucking with said bear in the woods. I didn't want to embarrass the guy.

"We've been having the best time here."

As I observed his face close up, I could see him radiating a positive glow. He had filled out a bit in the few months since he'd left the center, and it suited him. Stubble lined his jawline, and his hair was longer, too.

Toby leaned in a little closer and covered his mouth to whisper. "We have been fucking everywhere. The gym sauna. The beach. We even went on a hike—"

"Uh-huh." God, I hoped I wasn't blushing.

Here he was, boasting about his sexual adventures, and yet I was the one getting embarrassed. Why, I didn't even know. He was owning his sexuality, and I definitely wasn't judging him for it.

"And"—he nudged his arm against mine—"I have you to thank for it."

I scrunched my entire face up. "Me? For what?" I squeaked.

"For helping me get to a place where I can be so free, Cassius. I am who I am...and I'm good with that."

"That's great, Toby. I'm glad you feel that way, but I'm not sure what I have to do with it."

He studied me for a moment. "Do you remember that story you told me on one of the weekly hikes? The one about your dad?"

I dipped my head. "Yeah, I remember."

"That story changed my life. How you said that he would always tell you that he loved you—the *real* you. And you told me to go out into the world and be the real version of me. I thought about what you said, and the next day, I wrote down 'Be The Real Me' on a piece of paper and stuck it on my bathroom mirror, and it changed my life."

Pride burst from my chest. I was genuinely touched. I had always hoped that my work made a small difference in the kid's lives, but hearing this from Toby made me see that for him, I'd actually made a pretty damn big difference.

"You have no idea how happy I am to hear that, Toby."

He continued. "I'm out, and I'm proud. And I don't care what anyone thinks of me. I do what I want. Say what I want. And fuck where I want. And if anyone thinks that it makes me a bad person, or a slut, or whatever insult they want to hurl at me, do you know how many fucks I give, Cassius?"

I smiled, forming a zero with my fingers and raising it between us.

"Bingo," he said, and we both laughed.

"And how about you? What have you been up to in the last few months?"

Unsurprisingly, the answer was very little had changed in my life since he'd left the center. Same job. Same apartment. Same weekly hikes. Same sketching. And yet, while all of those things were great, it didn't fill me with the usual sense of contentment it usually did.

"Oh, you know, not much," I responded, hoping he wouldn't ask any follow-up questions.

"Look, I have some friends I'm sitting with. I should go. It was great seeing you, Cassius."

"It was great to see you, too, Toby. I'm so glad you're in a good place. You deserve it."

He smiled as he sauntered over to sit with his friends, while my pathetic response to his question ricocheted in my head. My life had stayed exactly the same, like it had always been. So, why did it feel...bad?

And when did *same* equate to *bad*? I thought *same* was what I wanted, what I clung to.

"Two minutes until we leave," the guide called out.

I twisted my head around, looking back down the pier. Where was Spencer? He was cutting it mighty fine. And then it hit me. Like a boat anchor being dropped into the water, the heaviness dropped in my belly.

Spencer wasn't coming.

I'd stuffed things up supremely this morning, and he wasn't going to be here.

Fuck!

I dragged my fingers through my hair roughly, angry at myself for reacting like such an idiot. I bolted onto my feet and rushed over to the side of the boat, which was still moored to the pier.

The tour guide smiled as he saw me approaching. "We're just about to depart. Is everything all right?"

"I have to go," I yelped. I flailed my hand toward the shore. "Spencer. Mistake. Talk. Change."

The guide shot me a quizzical look. "Are you all right, sir?"

"Yes, I'm fine." My brain snapped into gear and out of *can't form a coherent sentence* mode. "I just have to get off this boat. I'm sorry."

"Uh...okay, then."

The guide stepped out of my way, and I climbed the few steps onto the pier.

"Thank you and sorry," I yelled before taking off.

I started running down the pier toward the beach. God, I hated running. I was a mess of dripping sweat and haggard breathing after barely a few strides, but I didn't care. Even if it killed me, I was going to make things up to Spencer.

My lungs were burning by the time I stumble-jogged back into the resort. I headed for the pool, figuring it might be where Spencer would be hanging out-slash-avoiding-me-slash-giving-me-space.

Space.

I gritted my teeth. That was now officially my most hated word of all time, replacing both *moist* and *bunion*, the previous holders of that dubious honor.

"Cassius?"

I spun around and saw Emry, Hawk, and another guy chilling out on some deck chairs. I didn't even register that they were all naked. By now, I would have been more shocked if they weren't.

"Spencer." I puffed out. "Have you..." More heavy breathing. God, there was a reason why I liked hiking—it wasn't running.

"Have you guys seen Spencer?"

Emry bolted up and stood next to me. "No, we haven't." He dipped his head beneath mine, concern etched across his face. "Are you okay?"

"I'm fine, I'm fine," I said, breathing heavily like an *anything but fine* madman. "I just need to see Spencer. I've fucked things up with him, and now I need to un-fuck them."

I snapped my fingers. "He might be in our suite. I'll try there. Gotta go."

I gave Emry a sweaty pat on the shoulder and shot off again, using what little remaining strength I had to race over to our suite. Once inside, I saw Spencer's bedroom door was open. I wobbled my way over to it, my lungs on fire.

He was there, sitting on the edge of his bed, staring out into the ocean. He spun around and flew over to me, propping me up, because, yes, by now, I was needing support just to stay upright.

"Oh my God, Cassius. What happened?"

I leaned into him. He smelled so clean, like he'd just stepped out of the shower. Meanwhile, I was dripping my gross sweat all over him.

He reached around my waist and guided me to a chair in the corner of the room. "You look like you've just run a marathon. And your hand is shaking."

My hand wasn't shaking, I was making the international signal for *get me a glass of water please*...but yeah, maybe in my current state, it looked more like shaking.

"Water," I gasped, replacing the shaking movement with patting my throat.

"Right."

Spencer bound out of the room and returned almost immediately with a tall glass of water. I downed it in one go. His eyes remained fixed on me as slowly, my breathing returned to normal and I started to feel like a human again.

Until of course, I spoke.

Or rather, blubbered.

"Spencer, I'm so sorry for my reaction earlier. I didn't want you to leave. I don't want space. I only want you. And god, I'm just hearing myself say these words out loud right now and I know I must sound crazy, but I'm not. Okay, maybe a little. And also, you should probably know that I jerked off about you. And also, just because I think it bears repeating. I'm not crazy... I just... I just..."

I had finally run out of puff—*thank God!*

Out of nowhere, Spencer's lips landed on mine. They felt so soft. And fuck, they tasted good. He spread my lips with his tongue, pushing inside of me.

He didn't know it—no wait, of course he did, this was Spencer —but he was giving me exactly what I needed.

Him.

The fact that he was in my mouth, well, that was just an added bonus.

He ran his fingers through my hair. My messy, gross, drenched-in-sweat hair.

I reached around and pulled his hand away. "Spencer, I'm all sweaty and gross."

He gave me the most beautiful smile, and I couldn't help but match it. "You're not gross to me, Cass."

He brushed a sticky strand of hair that had fallen onto my equally sticky cheek. "I love you, Cassius."

"I love you, too, Spencer," I replied without the slightest hesitation.

Out of nowhere, a single tear streamed down my cheek.

God, he loved me—the real, gross, sweaty, messy me.

He delicately brushed the tear away, but he was doing more than that. He was brushing away a lifetime of fears and doubts and insecurities that I had. The reasons why I clung to keeping things the same were being swept away because I knew that if things stayed the same, we'd never have *this*.

We had a connection, and it was deeper than just best friendship.

He pulled away from me, his blue eyes sparkling as he arched an eyebrow. "Wait, you jerked off about me?"

Fuck, why did I say that out loud? I didn't mean to. It just fell out of my mouth. "Uh, yeah, kinda?"

"Cass, I have a spreadsheet that lists pretty much every single sexual activity ever invented. I must have missed a kinda-jerk off."

I blushed. I blushed so fucking hard that if I died right now, my ghost wouldn't be white, it'd be a bright shade of red.

"You know..."

A smile lifted the corner of his mouth. "I think we need to keep talking."

"Uh-huh, but first," I dug my fingers into the back of his neck. "I want to kiss the lips off your face."

Wait, did that even make sense? Who cared?

Tee-hee—

Before he could cover his mouth, I swooped in and gave Spencer James Montgomery the most passionate kiss of my life.

30

SPENCER

Boy, oh, boy was I happy Cassius showed up when he did. The day had dragged on forever without him, but I was determined to stay away from him—no matter how hard that was—to give him time and space to work through things in his own mind.

I thought I'd ruined things between us, so I lurched around the resort with one massive, immovable lump permanently lodged in my stomach all day. Not because I wanted to. If I had my way, I would have superglued myself to Cassius' side so we'd spend every moment together. (Yes, this imaginary superglue had an "un-glue" function to allow for bathroom breaks...it was *magical* superglue, after all.)

No. I was doing it for him. Taking myself out of the picture and giving him the time he needed to help make what I'd said to him become a distant memory. One that, hopefully, it wouldn't be too late for us to forget about and move on from as if it had never happened.

My sexuality stuff I knew he would support me with. Always. But the Cassius stuff, well, we could put it down to a crazy weekend away, intoxicated by the beauty of the place and the headiness of being a million miles away from our real lives in the real world. A *what happens at Elysian stays at Elysian* type situation.

His lips ravishing me was a million times better, though.

"Wait." I grabbed his shoulders and stared him straight in the eye. "We really do need to talk... Beer?"

He nodded with a wide grin, following me out into the kitchen. I swiped two beers from the fridge, opened the caps, and handed him one. I motioned to the couch, and we padded over to it in silence.

"Cheers," I said, lifting the bottle into the air.

"What are we cheers-ing to?" he asked, keeping his tone light.

I let out a giggle as I thought of the perfect response. "To having options."

We exchanged a spirited look. "To having options."

Clink.

"So," I spoke, breaking the silence.

"So," he said, echoing the uncertainty in my own voice.

I took a swig of beer, hoping the cold bubbling liquid would dissolve the tightness that had formed in my throat.

I stretched forward and placed the bottle down on the coffee table, on a coaster, of course. I tapped my thighs. "Come on," I said, looking down his legs.

His eyebrows twitched, but he shuffled around and brought his feet up, placing them gently in my lap. I began doing what I'd done a million times before, giving him a foot rub and smiling as his face did what it had done a million times before: softening under my touch.

Only this time, while his face softened, something of mine, er...hardened.

But I was determined to ignore that.

First, we needed to continue our real talking because for everything we had said, a lot of things still remained up in the air.

We both started to speak at the same time.

"You first," he said.

"No, you first," I insisted.

He took a deep breath. "Okay, I guess I want to start by repeating my apologies. I feel like all I've been doing lately is saying *I'm sorry*, but I guess that's what I get for acting like such an asshat."

I grinned. "You haven't been that bad."

"But I haven't been that good, either. And I am truly sorry, Spence. I don't know what's gotten into me."

Me. I want to get into you. All the way into you.

God, what was wrong with me? Talk about inappropriate timing. Down, brain, down.

Cassius continued. "I mean, I still feel so bad about last night. I don't even know what Ian must think about me. He probably hates me, and I wouldn't blame him, honestly."

I shook my head. "Nope, that's where you're wrong. In a funny way, I think he saw what was happening between us before we even did."

"I'd still like to apologize to him before we leave."

My heart swelled. Cassius was such a good person. And decency, according to both me and my cock, was sexy as fuck.

"I'm sure we'll see him before we check out, Cass."

"Good. Wait, how do you think he knew about this, us, before we did?"

I shrugged. "Hasn't the whole world known forever?"

His laughter crackled loudly between us. "Yeah, I guess so. Geez, how could we have been so blind all this time? Although, in my defense, I have to say I was operating under the assumption that you were straight."

"Hey, so was I."

This time, we both laughed.

"So..." He shot a quick glance at me.

"So..."

He gulped down his beer while I dug in deeper into his foot with my thumb and index fingers.

"Fuck, that feels so good." His head fell back as he moaned, and again...my dirty mind went to a dirty place with that. I wanted to hear those words—and sounds—from him again, but in a much more *dirty* setting.

Also, his sexy-as-fuck toes had a new destination they needed to be in—my mouth.

He exhaled, and as his eyes drifted open, they landed on me.

"You were saying?" I said with a smirk.

"I was about to say, we have to talk about...us."

I focused in on the spot just above his heel that was always so tight, massaging it with a firm, even pressure.

"What about us?" I asked, somewhat coyly.

I really wanted to hear what he wanted first before I said anything. I needed to know that it was coming from him and not affected, or in response, to what I was feeling.

He thought about it for a minute. The timbre of his voice deepened. "Boyfriends."

The word hung in the air between us, while I tried to figure out whether it was a question or a statement.

I slowly began to nod my head, timing it with the movements I was making on his foot. "Boyfriends."

I didn't know if I had just responded with an answer or a confirmation.

I kept kneading his foot, the flesh warm and tight under my fingers. The physical connection felt more intimate than it had ever been in the million times I'd rubbed his feet before.

A beam of light streamed in and lit up Cassius' light brown eyes, making them sparkle like glitter. He looked so beautiful. I mean, he'd always been beautiful, but now I was seeing it in a different light.

A boyfriend light.

His jaw twitched. "I've never had a boyfriend before."

"If it helps, neither have I."

He looked down, and when he looked back up, something had shifted in him. His eyes contained the tiniest glimmer of...hope?

"You really want me to be your boyfriend?"

My chest heated, and I could feel my heart thundering in my ears. I'd never thought he looked more striking, more handsome than he did right now.

"I do." My voice was low, steady, oddly calm.

My hand settled softly on his calf, stroking his dark leg hairs. "You know what might be good? A walk on the beach."

Cassius' face lightened. "You know what would be even better?"

I shook my head.

"A walk on the beach...with ice cream."

"Just ice cream? No cereal this time?" I teased.

Cassius shared the most exquisite smile in the world with me.

"Just ice cream...and my boyfriend."

31

CASSIUS

Fifteen minutes later, Spencer and I were licking away at our ice creams—I went for three scoops of chocolate. He chose one scoop of low-fat, low-dairy, and very low-flavor vanilla. Light shards of golden sand flicked up behind us as we strolled away from the resort. Despite it being late in the afternoon, it was still hot, so we had taken our shirts off and tucked them into the backs of our shorts.

The energy between us was shifting.

I could feel it in every little thing. The way he'd glance over at me and smile. Yes, he'd looked and smiled at me countless times over the past seventeen years, but this time, there was something different about it. I didn't know what it was that made it better, but it sure as hell made me feel all gooey inside.

I wanted to feel gooey forever.

Spencer peeked over at me. "Good ice cream?"

I nodded. "Yep. Yours?"

"The best."

We kept walking.

The silence that filtered through in between sporadic bursts of conversation was an intricate balancing act.

On the one hand, there was a lifetime of stuff to say. I wanted to know everything about his sexuality, what he was thinking and feeling. I meant it when I said I'd support him every step of the way. I couldn't wait to return some of the love and encouragement he had given me for so many years.

I also couldn't deny that I wanted to know when he figured out that he had feelings for me. Was it when we first kissed or sometime before then? Had my gwerking sealed the deal, or was it some other aspect of my sparkling personality that got him hooked?

On the other hand, opening up any line of questioning at this point felt like it would only splinter the conversation into a million never-ending pieces. The thought of that was more than just a little overwhelming.

As was the thought that in less than twenty-four hours, we'd be back in frigid Boston, freezing our asses off.

"Penny for your thoughts?" Spencer's words stirred me back to life. To this very moment. Here, walking on the beach, ice cream in hand, with him. My...*boyfriend.*

"I was thinking about home, actually," I said, cramming the last remaining piece of the cone into my mouth.

"Cass!"

Spencer covered his eyes and looked away. But he was smiling. Like he always did whenever I did something totally gross, which was code for normal by my standards. There was something snugly familiar in his response.

"What will it be like when we get back?" I stopped walking and turned to face him.

He finished off the last remaining piece of his cone—in a much more civilized fashion, obviously—and grabbed both of my hands.

"It will be perfect."

He lifted each hand to his mouth and placed a gentle kiss on each. "You and I have an amazing friendship. That's the best foundation for any relationship. We're gonna be amazing together."

My heart was doing backflips in my chest. All my life, I wanted to hear those words. I wanted to have someone say those words to me and really mean them.

And now, here I was, standing in front of my best friend, the guy who knew me since the first day of school, who had seen me through the best and worst times in my life, who not only saw, but actually loved, the me—*the real me*—saying them.

It was everything, all at once, and I shivered.

"I believe you," I said. And I did. Despite not knowing any of the details, I knew that he was right. We would be amazing.

The narrowed-eye look Spencer sent my way pierced into my soul. He knew me so well we could talk without saying a word. He was looking to see if I really meant it, that I really did believe him.

When he let out a small smile, I knew he knew that what I had said was true. I believed him. I trusted him.

In that moment, I didn't think I could love him any more.

"Hey, Cass," he breathed into my ear. "Let's go back to the suite. I'd like to make love to my boyfriend."

Okay, *now* I couldn't love him any more.

Another fifteen minutes later, we were back in the suite and hurricaning our way back to my room, with arms, elbows, and legs flying out everywhere. The only thing holding us together was our lips, which were engaged in a supreme tussle for mouth dominance.

"Wait, wait, wait."

I mustered up every ounce of dormant responsibility cells I had stored in me from years of ignoring their very existence and pulled away from Spencer. "Wait, we should talk, Spence. About sex. Specifically about gay sex."

Spencer's lips parted slightly. "Sure. What would you like to know, Cass?"

I threw a playful punch that landed on his upper arm. "I meant you, doofus."

He shrugged. "I'm fine. I've been taking notes, remember? I have a spreadsheet packed with all sorts of useful information. Plus, I also have an imagination and, you know...a dick."

That word sounded so sexy coming from him.

"So I think I'm kind of okay with everything."

"But you've never...been with a guy before, right?"

The corners of his mouth twitched slightly. "Are you asking me if I've been saving myself for you, Cass?"

I guess I was. But now that he'd asked me, it felt silly to be admitting it. But I couldn't lie to him, either. I could, however, mutter incoherently for an impressively long time.

"Well, uh, I mean, you know—"

He placed his index finger against my lips—thank God, I could have kept going but it wouldn't have been pleasant for either one of us—and he made the sweetest-sounding shushing sound. His balmy breath ignited my cheeks.

"Are *you* okay with sex?" He stared at me so earnestly. It was cuter than the cutest cat video I'd ever seen. "Specifically, are you okay with having sex with me?"

I saw what he did there, and I was unable to resist grinning at him doing the whole *I'm going to twist your words around and use them against you in such a roundabout, yet charming way while actually asking you if you want to have sex with me* thing.

"I know that you love me, Spence. I do. But it's just..." My voice trailed off, but I had to find it in me to tell him. I'd always been honest with him. I wasn't about to start lying to him now. Even if this was going to be one of the most awkward things I'd ever said to him.

"You're hot. Like, Scandinavian supermodel hot. Are you sure you want...me?" I dropped my head. "I'm not as attractive as you are. I'm gross and messy. I often walk around with flakes of food stuck to my face for a really long time before realizing it. You know how I feel about showering, as well as my policy on only wearing clean clothes, which I think is discriminatory against stained clothes."

I then slid my hand over my belly. I saw Spencer's eyes fall and follow my fingers. "And I don't have sculpted muscles and rock-hard abs like you. I'm a little...soft in the middle."

Spencer squeezed my cock through my shorts and smirked wickedly. "You're hard where it counts."

I dipped my voice. "I'm serious, Spence. You might love me, but that doesn't automatically mean you find me physically appealing or sexually attractive."

We exchanged a contemplative look, and then a long silence fell between us.

"Is there anything else you want to say?" His voice was low and gravelly. "I want to make sure you've said everything you want to say before I respond to it."

He sounded so formal. Was it wrong that it kinda turned me on?

I nodded.

"Good. Because I want you to listen to me, Cass." He brushed a loose strand of hair behind my ear. "I don't have eyes for anyone else. I don't see anyone else—but you. We're staying here, at a freaking clothing-optional resort. I'm surrounded by hundreds of guys. Attractive guys. Naked guys. Sure, I can recognize that they're good-looking, and yes, sometimes I do that guy thing of, you know, peering down and comparing."

I smiled. Yeah, it was true. Guys really did do that. And there was a word for those who said they didn't: liar.

"But there's no sexual fire there for me. It doesn't do anything for me. But, when I've been looking at you lately, I feel this"—he looked around, his free arm shaking as if he were trying to summon the right words to perfectly describe what he was trying to say

—"this heat building inside of me. This indescribable passion. This intense sort of attraction that makes me literally shake. I want you so fucking much, Cassius Draper."

He trailed his finger down my arm. "Every time I've kissed you, it's been the best kiss of my entire life. Last night, I loved having your taste in my mouth. I love being so close to you. This feels like nothing I've ever known before."

His words were making my skin tingle. "But that's no longer enough for me, Cass. I need you. All of you. And I want you to have all of me, too. Tonight. Right here. Right now."

I was lost in his eyes. His words lifted me, and I felt like I was floating above the clouds. That was the power he had over me, making me forget all of my silly doubts and insecurities. In that moment, for the first time in my life, I felt what it was like to be truly wanted by someone else.

"I want you, too, Spence. More than anything else in the world."

A deep longing settled in his eyes. It suited him. I stroked along his jawline. "Will you make love to me, Spencer James Montgomery?"

His lips looped upward at the edges. "I thought you'd never ask, baby."

32

SPENCER

I could have stayed lost in Cassius' eyes forever. And believe me, nothing would have made me happier. Oh, actually, wait, scratch that. There was one thing that could have taken that mantle—making love and being inside of him.

So far, all of our intimate experiences had been flurries of passion and heated rush. This time—*our first time*—I wanted to take it slow.

I was having the most amazing time with Cassius this weekend, and along with that, I had this indescribable feeling percolating within me. It was like I was shedding layers and layers of dead skin and, at the same time, discovering a series of revelations that felt light, right, and oh so fucking good.

It might have had something to do with spending so much time naked with Cassius, and it definitely had a whole lot to do with the pleading in his voice when he'd asked me to make love to him.

Make love.

It struck me in that moment that I'd never done that before. Sex? Sure. But actually making love, showing love, feeling love...*being* loved. That was totally next-level shit. But I was ready for it. More than ready for it.

Our bodies moved closer until I wrapped my arms around Cassius' broad shoulders and nibbled at his lips with a series of tender kisses. They stretched out even further as he smiled, which was good. It gave me more surface area to cover with my tongue, licking along his lower lip, before turning my attention to his full, top lip. His sweat, tears, and *Cass-ness* melded into the most delicious taste I'd ever had.

We kissed for a long time, the tempo, rhythm, and intensity of our mouths rising and falling like the waves outside the windows, crashing onto the shore.

"How did I not know you were such a good kisser?" Cassius murmured into my mouth.

"You never asked," I replied, and he released a hearty laugh.

Our lips crashed into each other again, and this time, as the intensity rose between us, so did my hunger. We were still sitting on the edge of the bed, our bodies pressed as close together as they could be, but it wasn't enough for me.

I crawled up onto the bed, and Cassius followed, landing on top of me. The heavy warmth of his body over mine felt so right. I was struck by the thought that for all the countless hours we had spent together, I'd never seen him from this angle. I was seeing him differently. He was still familiar and still very Cass, but also brand new at the same time, too. It was...intoxicating.

The way his hair fell over his forehead, threatening to hide his beautiful eyes. The underside of his mouth, jaw, and chin that looked so tempting, inviting me to reach out and stroke, touch and lick them. And the unmissable hardness of his cock that was pressed against mine, making me ache so hard for him.

God, I wanted to be inside of him so bad and do all sorts of sexy, delicious—

Oh, crap!

My mouth popped open.

"What is it, Spence? Cassius asked softly.

"I want us to make love, but I didn't bring..."

He squished his eyebrows together. "Bring what?"

"You know...protection."

The edges of his lips rose slightly as he cranked his head in the direction of the bedside table. "Open the top drawer."

He lifted his arm to allow me to wriggle from underneath him. I crawled over and opened the drawer, pulling out a box of condoms and a giant bottle of lube. I was confused. "You brought this with you?"

He shook his head, grinning like the adorable goofball he was. "No, not me."

I matched his grin.

"Olivia," we said in unison.

"We gotta give her credit," I said. "*This* was a much better present than her outfit for me."

"Oh, I don't know about that." Cassius flipped over onto his front. "You looked pretty damn good in that outfit."

"Not as good as you're looking now," I replied.

Cassius had positioned himself on his hands and knees in front of me. His lower back arched, his ass in the air. It was all the invitation I needed.

I tore open one of the condom wrappers with my teeth and slid it over my cock. I opened the tube and lubed up my dick with a few solid strokes. The wet gliding sensation felt so good. I was already so turned on. I hoped I'd be able to last.

Cassius wiggled down the bed, wrapping the tops of his feet over the edge. I stood up to walk behind him, spreading my feet far enough apart to be able to line up my cock with his hole.

Holy hell, this was the first time I was seeing it. Another new side of the guy I knew so well. And man, it was a thing of beauty. Bright pink, smooth, and slightly puckered. As much as I wanted to be inside of him—right this fucking minute—I'd read in my research that preparation was key. I knew I had to go slow.

So I greased up my left index finger. I grabbed Cassius' ass with my right hand as I slowly slid my finger in. I could see Cassius drop his head down.

"Are you okay?"

I heard him blow out a deep breath. "All good," he replied. "Just take your time, okay? I'm a—I'm a little out of practice with this."

For him, I'd take all the time in the world.

Besides, my solitary left finger was having a jammin' time exploring the warm insides of Cassius' body. It was only the second time I'd fingered an ass, the first one being my own. Hey, I needed the practice.

After a few minutes, once I could feel Cassius loosening up, I added another well-lubed finger. His breathing regulated into deep inhales followed by breathy exhalations. "Would you like one more finger, baby?"

"Yes. Please."

His voice was barely more than a whimper, and it unleashed a surge of protectiveness within me. I knew that what we were about to do was something special. But I was starting to get the feeling it would be even more than that. It would be sacred, cementing our bond in a way that took me by surprise...in the best way possible.

Once I had worked up a decent three-fingered tempo and Cassius' ring of muscles had relaxed, I could tell that he was ready for me. I was ready, too. But, something was missing. It took me a few beats to figure out what it was.

Then it hit me. I couldn't see him, or his face, at least. In that moment, for whatever reason, I needed his eyes on me, his lips pressed against mine.

Sensing something was happening with me, Cassius twisted his head over his shoulder. I could read the concern in his profile. "You okay back there, Spence?"

"Can we change positions?" I felt strangely nervous for some reason. "I—I want to see your face."

His lips stretched and he gave a slight nod. "I was just thinking the same thing."

I slowly pulled all three fingers out of him, and as Cassius turned over, he reached up, planting a soft kiss on my lips.

He lay back down and hooked his hands under his knees, exposing his freshly fingered and slightly gaping hole. "Better?"

"Fuck, yes, baby..." I leaned over him, our foreheads pressing as my cock lined up perfectly against his glistening hole.

Yes, I needed this, to see the beautiful face of the man I loved as I made love to him for the very first time.

I reached my hand down, gripping my dick and pressing the head against his entrance. As I stared into a set of eyes I knew almost as well as my own, I entered him. Slowly at first, just the tip. Then inch by inch, he took me inside of him, encasing me in his warmth.

I studied him as I bottomed out, observing how he responded to the fact that I was all the way inside of him. We were closer than we'd ever been in seventeen years. I started thrusting, happy to begin with a slow but steady pace.

I loved noticing all the small details and subtle shifts he was going through. How his eyes were darker than they normally were. How his jaw clenched and loosened. How he'd lick his lips and open his mouth to produce the sultriest sounds I'd ever heard.

Another protective surge tore through me. "How are you feeling, Cassius?"

Cassius hated any type of change, and having his best friend on top of him and fucking him would probably be up there with one of the most monumental changes of his life.

"I'm...good."

His tone conveyed he was genuine, and I believed him. He then looked me up and down, as my body rocked against his, my pace increasing, the sound of my balls slapping against his ass filling the air around us. There was a hunger in his eyes, a lust that crackled between us that told me this was the most right, most perfect thing we had ever done.

But still, I had to make sure. I stopped thrusting, the stillness feeling surprisingly good. I peered at him seriously. "So you're not weirded out by this?"

He shook his head. "No." There was a steely certainty in his voice. He was telling the truth. I knew it.

A sense of relief washed over me.

"What about now?" I pulled a silly face, sticking my tongue out, squinting my left eye shut and bugging my right eye wide open.

He let out a deep, rumbling laugh that made his whole body shake, and the first place I felt the vibration was in my cock. It felt good. And surprisingly soothing, too.

"You're such a doofus," he said, rubbing his palms down my chest.

"Doofus in love with you."

Wait, that didn't make any sense, did it? But who cared? I knew Cassius would get it.

"Yeah, well, I'm a doofus who's in love with you, too."

His whole being, not just his face, but his entire body lit up in a beautiful glow, and we shared the most beautiful smile.

I leaned down, and we kissed, softly, tenderly.

He clawed his fingers into the back of my head, pulling my head ever lower. He whispered into my ear, "And now I want you to fuck me like I fucked your face."

So I did, replacing the stillness with urgent, thrashing thrusts as our bodies rocked and bucked wildly against each other. Cassius grabbed his cock and began to jerk it furiously. I peeled myself off his body, my hands finding the backs of his thighs and throwing them onto my shoulders.

There was just one more thing I wanted to try.

I reached for Cassius' left foot, dipped my head, and began to lick his toes. He arched his back off the bed, letting out a series of cries as he came hard and heavy all over his stomach and chest.

I took his toes into my mouth, flicking my tongue around them hungrily as my balls tightened and I came, too. The intensity of my orgasm washed away all of my strength, as his foot fell out of my mouth and I came crashing down on top of him, our sweaty foreheads touching again.

Cassius' sweet panting filled my nostrils as I looked at him with more love than I ever thought was humanly possible to feel.

"That was..." My brain couldn't produce any more words.

"The best thing ever?" Cassius gulped the words out.

"Yes," I managed. "Very that."

MONDAY

33

CASSIUS

I could have slept forever, but instead, I set my alarm for seven thirty. I silenced it before the vibrating buzz had the chance to wake Spencer up. I carefully lifted his arm off me and peeled myself from his warm, solid body, trying my best to keep the bed still and not make any noise.

I stood up and stepped into the nearest pair of briefs and shorts I could find, my insides responding to the movement of my legs. I smiled. I'd be feeling the effects of last night all day...and I couldn't have been happier.

Last night was...well, there weren't any words for it. At least, not any words that I knew. Anything that my still partly discombobulated brain could come up with was woefully inadequate. Brilliant. Amazing. Wonderful. Incredible. Nah, they didn't even begin to scrape the surface of what last night had been.

It was the most intensely passionate, sensual, and downright filthy sex I'd ever had. The way Spencer took his time and knew what he was doing blew me away. He prepped me with such tender care that I thought I'd melt right there and then, turning into a pile of mush on the bed before he even got a chance to fuck me.

Which thank god for me I didn't. Otherwise, I would have missed out on his incredible lovemaking skills.

And oh my god, the look on Spencer's face when he had my foot in his mouth. It was nothing short of a delicious, delirious ecstasy that I needed to see again and again and again. Who knew my Spencey would be so uninhibited in the sack?

It was another new thing I was learning about him, and it only made me love him even more.

I turned and smiled as I took in Spencer's peaceful face, his droopy lips and his ruffled-up hair. He looked like an angel, which only flooded my mind—and my cock—with that heavenly outfit he'd worn to the White Party.

I so badly wanted to kiss him, or at least touch him, but I managed to resist. He'd been waking up early every day. It was ironic that he finally managed to sleep in on the day we were leaving. He needed his rest after last night, and he'd be needing his energy for what I hoped would be a repeat performance once we got back home tonight.

I shrugged on a shirt that had only a mildly offensive odor and tiptoed out of the room, closing the door gently behind me.

I scratched the side of my face as I looked around the kitchen countertop for the swipe card to get back into the room. I didn't want to be doing this right now. I would have been perfectly happy not moving from that bed, staying snugly wrapped up in my boyfriend's—God, how I loved how that word sounded—body. But there was a chance that if I didn't do it early, I could miss the opportunity entirely.

I marched myself over to the resort lobby. Leo was standing behind the counter, looking way too spritely for this early in the morning.

He greeted me with his usual warmth. "Morning, Cassius. How are you this fine Monday?"

I tried to contain it, but I couldn't help letting out a pained wince. "Not too good, actually."

He dipped his eyes. "What's wrong? What can I do for you?"

"I made a mistake, and I need your help to fix it."

I told him my situation. He listened patiently, and thankfully, I felt like he wasn't judging me. I was glad. That only would have made me feel worse.

He gave me what I needed. Armed with it, I thanked him and headed off to do what needed to be done.

Knock, knock, knock.

I stepped back from the door. A few moments later, it opened. I was met with a bewildered look. Hey, it could have been worse. At least it wasn't a punch to the face.

"Hi, Ian. I hope I'm not interrupting you."

He leaned against the door. "Actually, your timing is pretty uncanny. I was just about to leave. I've got an early flight back to New York."

I looked down and blew out a breath. "Then it's lucky I caught you."

I looked back up and gushed, "Look, Ian, I owe you an apology for how I acted the other night. I'm so sorry for being rude to you. I don't normally act like that, and I just want you to know that I feel real bad about it."

He studied me for a moment before smiling warmly, his eyes crinkling around the edges. "Thank you, Cassius. I appreciate your effort in coming to see me, and I accept your apology."

I let out an audible breath. "Oh, that's so good. I thought you hated me, and I wouldn't have blamed you if you did."

He chuckled. "I could never hate someone who was just following their heart, even if it was a tad misguided."

Ian paused for a beat. "How are you and Spencer?"

A wave of happiness rolled from my belly and broke out as a massive smile across my face. "We're doing good. We're, um, together now. We're boyfriends."

Yep, I wasn't going to be getting sick of using that word anytime within the next decade or so.

His eyes gleamed. "That's wonderful news. I don't know either of you that well, but from what I've seen, the two of you belong together."

"Thank you. Look, I should get going. We're checking out today."

"Same here. I should get packing. Thank you again, Cassius, for stopping by. You've made my morning. You're a good man."

"No problem. Have a safe flight back home."

"You, too."

And with that, I felt like a ginormous weight had been lifted off my shoulders. I strode over to the cafeteria and ordered a large almond flat white for me and...my boyfriend.

I slipped back quietly into my room. Spencer was still sound asleep. I felt bad for having to wake him up, but we still had to have breakfast, pack, and say goodbye to Emry and Hawk. I had a sneaking suspicion we were already behind today's planned schedule, so unfortunately, I had to bite the bullet and just to do it.

And okay, maybe there was a *teeeny* part of me that couldn't wait for him to wake up, too. I mean, how could I not want to look into those baby blue eyes of his?

"Rise and shine, sunshine." I put on my brightest and most annoying voice, mimicking the way he'd woken me up countless times over the years. "It's time to wake up."

Spencer let out a yawn and rolled over onto his back. He glanced up at the time on the bedside clock and bolted upright. "Holy shit, we're behind schedule."

"Relax." I handed him the cup of coffee. "We're making good time on the caffeine consumption, at least."

He smiled at me before shaking his head. "Thanks, Cass. You're the best."

I sat down beside him. "How are you feeling after last night?"

He was about to take a sip of coffee but stopped. "Amazing. Brilliant. Incredible. Hang on." He lifted a finger into the air and took a sip of caffeine. "Now that I can think a little better...

Wonderful. Magnificent. Like I want to run around the world naked yelling at the top of my lungs how I'm the luckiest guy in the world to have you. Do you want me to keep going?"

I rubbed my hand down his leg. "You don't want me getting a big head now, do you?"

He covered his mouth. *Tee-hee-hee.*

His gaze traveled south. "No, I think your head is plenty big already."

I grinned and looked over at the time. "Look, we probably do need to get going. How about we have a quick shower, get dressed, and go get some breakfast?"

He unfurled the sheet off himself, nodding as he sipped the coffee. "Sounds good. We've got some time to make up, so quick showers only, okay?"

I cocked my head to the side. "Spence, you know that's my favorite type of shower."

"Doofus," he muttered as I watched his tight butt disappear out of my room.

34

CASSIUS

Twenty-ish minutes later, I plunged my fork into a big chunk of sausage. I picked it up, chewing it from both sides until I had nibbled away at most of it.

A smile broke out across Spencer's face. "What?" I asked, still chewing the sausage around in my mouth.

"You eat like a pig...and for some reason, I love it."

I shrugged. "You're only human."

Another sweet *tee-hee-hee*. Another equally cute hand movement to cover his mouth.

I loved how we noticed the little things about each other, but more than that, I loved how we loved the little things about each other. Even if I was considering altering my eating habits a little bit and becoming a little more well-mannered. At least, when we were out in public.

The restaurant was busy. The line up to the buffet bar had been nightmarish, which was why I'd heaped everything—and lots of it—onto my plate to save myself from having to go back again. Okay, maybe I'd go back one more time. It'd be rude not to. I wouldn't want to offend the breakfast buffet gods.

We fell into a comfortable silence, apart from my noisy chewing. But we were holding hands, and I was happy. Spencer didn't look quite as happy, but that was probably due to his breakfast choice: granola and yogurt was enough to wipe the post-sex glow off anyone's face.

"Well, well, well..." Emry's unmissable voice rang out between us. "...What do we have here?"

I looked up to see Emry and Hawk standing at our table, their eyes coruscating at the sight of our touching hands. Emry was practically bursting with excitement, excitedly tapping his fingers together in front of his chest.

"I think the humane thing to do would be to put him out of his misery," Spencer said to me with a grin.

I put my remaining sausage onto my plate. "All right, I guess we can say it's official. Spencer and I are...boyfriends."

Emry started jumping up and down like a game show contestant who had just won the main prize. "I knew it! I knew it!" He turned to Hawk and nudged their shoulders together. "I told you they'd end up together. You owe me fifty bucks."

Hawk blushed while the rest of us laughed.

"You guys should join us." I motioned to the two empty seats at our table. We hadn't seen the guys since the White Party, so it would be good to catch up before we all left for our lives back home.

Hawk's eyes widened as he sat down and saw my plate. My admittedly very overflowing plate. "Looks like somebody worked up a big appetite last night," he joked.

"Oh no," Spencer replied straight away. "That's just how he eats all the time."

I picked up my sausage and devoured the rest of it. Hey, I had a big appetite. Nothing to be ashamed of.

"So, you know," I said to the group once Hawk and Emry had returned from getting their food from the buffet. "It's been awesome meeting you guys and hanging out with you."

Emry grabbed my arm and gave it a gentle rub. "We've loved meeting you guys, too."

"But, and I can't believe I'm saying this, even though we've all seen each other naked, I still have no idea what you guys do for a living."

Spencer waved his yogurt-coated spoon in front of him. "Yeah, come to think of it, that's true, actually."

Hawk went first. "I'm in construction, as you can probably tell by my hands." He lifted his thick, callused palms for us to inspect.

"I know Spencer does PR and marketing," he went on. "How about you, Cassius?"

I did something I had never done before answering a question during a meal—I finished chewing. "I'm a social worker at a homeless shelter for LGBTQIA youths."

Emry clutched at his chest. "Oh my god, Cass. That's amazing." He sounded genuinely touched, like it meant something more to him.

"How about you, Emry?" I asked. "What do you do for work?"

A bemused expression fell over his face. "I'm a pianist."

Spencer smiled. "Oh, wow. That's so cool. I love classical music. Where did you train?"

"Oh, nowhere," Emry replied airily.

Spencer and I exchanged surprised looks. "Huh?" we said in unison.

"What do you mean, you didn't train? How else did you learn to play the piano?" Spencer's eyes gently narrowed at the corners.

Hawk chuckled to himself, like he'd been witness to a similar conversation before. "It's neurological," he offered, which only confused Spencer and me even more.

"It's a long story," Emry added.

I grabbed his forearm. "So give us the short version." There was no way he could leave us hanging like this. I had to know.

"So the short version is I got struck by lightning a month before graduating high school, and when I recovered, I could play the piano perfectly despite never having touched the instrument before in my life."

I didn't know what my mouth was doing, but Spencer's was gaped wide open. "Are you serious?"

Emry nodded, and judging by his serious expression, he wasn't pulling our leg.

"Now I definitely want to know the long version." I looked over at Spencer, who was nodding his head furiously.

"I do, too. But we are a little behind schedule. It might have to be a story for another time?"

I began scoffing down the rest of my food. It sounded like a return visit to the buffet wasn't on the cards, so I was at least going to consume everything I had on my plate.

"Do we have time for a quick catch-up after breakfast?" Emry asked Spencer, looking at him with a pleading stare.

"Uh, yeah, sure," Spencer answered.

"Phew." Emry brushed the back of his hand against his forehead and let out a theatrical sigh. "It won't take long. I've just got a little gift I want to give to Cass before we leave."

"Funny you should mention that," I said with way too much food in my mouth. Hey, I was operating under a strict timeframe, and this was my best effort at multitasking. "I've got a present for you, too."

"Okay. I'll swing by right after breakfast."

"Sounds good."

And with that, Hawk and Spencer said their goodbyes, pulling each other in for a bear hug. It warmed my heart to see that they had developed a special connection, kinda like how Emry and I had.

∼

A few minutes after we returned to our suite. Poor Spencer was in a total panic. He'd never packed on the actual day of a flight before, he had always been ready with at least twenty-four-hours to spare.

I heard a gentle tapping on the door. Knowing it would be Emry, I scooped up my sketchpad from the floor and yelled out, "I'll get it," as I raced to the door.

He smiled as I opened it. "Hey."

"Hey, Emry." I looked down and could see a folded piece of material in his hands. He eyed the sketchpad I was holding.

"I know we don't have a lot of time, so I'll keep this short," he said, before lowering his gaze. "I've really enjoyed meeting you, Cass. I find it hard to make friends, but spending time with you has felt so easy."

"I feel the same. I've loved spending time with you, too, Emry."

He looked up, his face softening a little. "I made you this. It's nothing much, but I hope you like it."

I placed the sketchpad onto the small table by the door and unfolded the fabric he'd handed me. It was the YASS shirt I'd seen him wearing a few days ago, but he'd replaced the Y to a C, so it read... "Cass."

He peered up at me through his eyelashes. "Do you—do you like it?"

I brought it into my chest and flung my arms around his shoulders, giving him a tight hug. "Of course I do. I love it. Thank you, Emry. It's officially my new favorite shirt."

We pulled apart. I reached around for my sketchbook and carefully tore out two pieces of paper. I handed them to Emry.

He looked down, and his eyebrows shot up to his hairline. "Wow, Cass, these are amazing."

I beamed with pride. "You like them?"

He held both pieces of paper out in front of him, his eyes darting between them. "I do. You're super talented."

I had sketched him and Hawk. I had considered drawing both of them on the one piece of paper, but that might've unintentionally made it look too couple-y. And I didn't want to draw any conclusions about what *their* future held. Hope? Sure. But assumptions, no.

I blushed as we said goodbye again, promising to keep in touch. Emry suggested a joint vacation back at Elysian, which I thought sounded like a great idea and promised to run it by Spencer.

My heart warmed at the thought of seeing Emry and Hawk again, especially at the place where I had fallen in love with my best friend, who was now also my—spoiler alert: I'm going to use the word again—*boyfriend*.

35

SPENCER

Panic packing was so totally not my jam.

I mean, who in their right mind actually left it until the day of the flight? That's sheer lunacy and a sure-fire recipe for heart palpitations and uncontrollable sweating—two conditions I was currently suffering through.

In all the commotion of the last, well, the *whole* weekend, I'd completely forgotten to begin my pre-packing ritual, which consisted of folding dirty clothes away in the laundry bag and adding any toiletries I wouldn't be using again into the extra toiletries case I had brought so that I was reducing the packing burden when it did come time to pack—which normally would have been a good twenty-four-hours before the flight.

But this had not been a normal weekend by any measure, and as I was madly trying to brush my stubbornly uncooperative hair down into something at least semi-neat and presentable, I paused for a moment and smiled. This had been, by far, the best few days of my life. And if last-minute packing without the assistance of a pre-drafted spreadsheet checklist was the worst thing that came out of it, I was fine with that.

More than fine, actually.

This getaway had changed my life in more ways than one. And even though it was coming to an end—and I was sad about that—in so many other ways, it marked the beginning of a whole new chapter for me and Cassius. And I was so freaking excited about it.

Okay, enough with the self-staring in the mirror, I still had a quarter of a suitcase to pack, as well as two other items to tick off the imaginary spreadsheet I had begun drafting in my head over breakfast with Cassius and the guys.

With Emry coming over to exchange gifts with Cassius, I decided to make a dash for it myself. There was someone I wanted to speak with, too.

It struck me as I was jog-walking through the empty pool area how lucky I had been over the past few days. Obviously, with everything that had happened between me and Cassius, but also for the three bonus and unexpected friendships I had struck up.

Firstly, Ian.

He was a really nice guy, and although I hadn't seen much of him, we'd exchanged numbers and texted each other a few times during the weekend. He had met a few fellow New Yorkers, done some sightseeing in the area, and discovered what he called the best Italian restaurant in America in downtown Key West.

I was glad he'd found his feet and enjoyed his stay here. I knew he had an early flight, so we'd said our goodbyes over text the day before and promised to keep in touch. His advice to follow my heart had become my mantra for the weekend, and I'd be eternally grateful to him for his wise words—as well as the surprise he was helping me plan for Cassius.

Then there was Hawk.

Sure, the guy had the whole tough-guy exterior thing going on, but from the moment Cassius and I met him and Emry at the meet and greet on the day we arrived, I felt like he'd taken a shine to me.

The way he had opened up when we were lining up at the bar to get drinks had stayed with me all weekend. The idea that if you couldn't find a label that fit, you could create your own changed something deep inside of me. It might have even given me the push I needed to realize my feelings for Cassius. My real feelings.

It was sad to say goodbye to him over breakfast, but when we hugged, he pulled me in extra close and whispered into my ear, "I'm here if you ever need me." That told me everything I needed to know about him. He was a genuinely good and decent man. And with Philadelphia not being that far from Boston, I knew we'd see them both again.

And then there was...

"Good morning, Spencer."

Leo.

Friendly. Professional. A great listener and an even better advice-giver.

"Hi." I pulled up to the front counter and shot him a warm smile.

"You boys all packed?"

"Barely," I muttered, giving an overexaggerated eye roll.

He chuckled. "What can I help you with?"

"I know you're busy"—I eyed all the people milling about in the reception area, all part of the mass Monday exodus that was well underway—"but I just wanted to say thank you. Leo, you have no idea how much this weekend has changed my life."

He fixed his gaze on me. "Just *your* life?"

I let out a tiny giggle, quickly covering my mouth. "Okay. You got me. *Our* lives... Was it that obvious?"

He placed his palms onto the counter, his whole body inclining forward. "I knew it the second I saw the two of you walk in here."

My eyebrows pinched together. "Really?"

He nodded, his face beaming. "When two people are in love, Spencer, you can see it. You can"—he shifted back, rubbing his fingertips together—"feel it. And I could instantly tell that you two boys were very much in love."

"I wish someone had told me that years ago."

Leo's face turned serious. "Don't say that, Spencer. What you guys have now, and will have into the future, is because of the past you've had. That solid friendship that you've developed over the years is your foundation, and it may very well be the reason why you guys stay together. Forever."

I weighed his words, like they were pieces of gold. The guy was good. "Ever considered a career change into relationship counseling? You'd make a killing."

He let out a deep snicker. "I'll stick with part-time psychoanalyzing from the sidelines."

I looked down at my watch. God, we were *soooo* behind schedule. Wait, we didn't even have a schedule. We were just late. At this rate, we'd just scrape through to the airport the recommended sixty minutes before departure time. That was cutting it way too fine for my liking. But I had wanted to do this, and I was glad that I had.

"Thank you again, Leo." We shook hands and smiled at each other. "And I hope you find happiness, too."

He steadied his smile. "Thank you, Spencer."

I left the reception and hightailed it back to my suite. As I opened the door, I wondered what state I'd find Cassius in. Lying on the couch watching Netflix? Half-dressed, unshowered, and unbothered? In the kitchen, bowl in hand, a combination of ingredients in said bowl that I didn't want to know about, but would undoubtedly be too curious, buckle, and inevitably ask about?

What met me was none of those things.

"We're late, Spencer."

He stood in the small entryway, arms folded across his chest, his feet—dressed in shoes, already—tapping against the tiled floor. All four pieces of my luggage were stacked neatly beside him, and he had his backpack slung over his shoulder.

"You—you packed for me?"

He tapped his fingers against his arm, staying in his faux commando character. I was totally fucking digging it.

"Just don't expect any of your clothes to be folded, bundled correctly, or neatly packed. But it's all in there. Toiletries, shoes, angel wings, everything you came with."

I leaned over, running my finger down his nose. "All I really need to take home with me is the one thing I didn't come here with. My boyfriend."

The corners of his lips twitched. His steely resolve was melting. I could feel it. "Is—is that so?"

I pressed my lips to his cheeks. "Thank you for doing this, Cassius."

And just like that, his lips broke into the wide smile of his. The one that flooded my insides, oozing like lava and making me feel all sorts of loving, tender things.

"Anything for you, Spencey. I didn't want you to be worried. Especially since..." He hung his head low.

I wanted to touch him, to gently raise his face so that I could look into his eyes and immediately know what was going on without having to wait for words. But I didn't. I held back, out of respect. Somehow, I knew there was something on his mind, something he needed to say...in his own time.

"Especially since this is the official first full day that we're...boyfriends. The sixteenth of October."

That warm feeling seeped inside every part of me until I felt like I was overflowing with so much love for him that I wouldn't be able to take it.

I jumped into his arms. "God, I love you."

He strengthened his grip around my waist, and I loved how safe that made me feel. "I love you, too, Spencer."

I wanted to stay in his arms forever...but I also wanted to catch our flight on time. And we had one last unexpected pit stop to go before we reached the airport.

36

SPENCER

"Are you sure you don't mind?" I asked, cutting the engine off.

"For the ninety-seven-thousandth time, no, I don't. But only if you want to. I'm more than happy if you want to do this on your own."

"No. I want you to be there." I stepped out of the car.

"I'll be there. Right by your side," Cassius said with a reassuring smile as he shut the car door.

We walked up to the front door, hand in hand. I blew out a heavy breath. This was going to be a lot, and it could go any number of ways, but I also knew I wanted to do it.

I turned to him, chewing down hard on my lower lip. "This is it."

He squeezed my hand. "I got you."

Ding dong.

"How traditional," Cassius joked, and I quickly covered my mouth.

The door opened, and Mom almost jumped back in fright. "Spencer, darling!"

She took a beat to regain her composure. "What are you...boys doing here?"

She eyed Cassius. Then her gaze dropped to our hands. Our joint hands.

I studied her face. If I picked up on any signs of judgment or anything negative in the slightest, I would turn around and leave.

"Darling, I'm so happy for you." She pulled me in for a hug so tight it gave Hawk a run for his money. Her hair filled my face. I closed my eyes and savored the moment. This was good—it was better than good, actually. Her positive reaction meant the world to me. Because despite being an adult, I did still want her to love and approve of me.

I stepped back. She looked at Cassius again. There was a slight hesitation there, but then she pulled him in for a big hug, too. I could see her hands running up and down his back.

She stepped back and looked at both of us. "I am very happy for you... For both of you."

"Thanks, Mom." I looked over at Cassius, and he gave me a slight, almost indiscernible nod. "Actually, I came here to tell you something."

"You don't need to tell me, darling. I think it's pretty obvious." Her eyes were shifting between Cassius and me.

"I don't mean us. I wanted to say something I haven't said to you in a very long time."

She leaned against the door, her forehead wrinkled. "Yes?"

"I—I love you, Mom."

Her eyes widened, then narrowed, then unleashed a waterfall of tears. I could feel them running onto my shoulder as she pulled me in for another hug, her body shaking against mine. Holy shit, she wasn't just crying. She was sobbing.

We stayed like that for what felt like a really long time. I didn't mind. She needed it—and I guess I did, too.

Out of the corner of my eye, I could see that Cassius had

stepped back away from us, giving us—well, mainly her—some privacy. I appreciated the thoughtful gesture.

"I love you, too, baby," she breathed into my ear, her hand stroking the back of my head.

After a few more moments, we said goodbye, hugging for the third time, and left.

We got into the car, and I exhaled for what felt like the first time since we'd pulled up to her place.

"How are you feeling?"

I started the engine and reached for my seatbelt. "I feel good. I think I needed to do that."

"You're a good son, Spence." Cassius' hand landed in my lap. "And you're an even better boyfriend."

And with that, we made our way to the airport to begin our new life together.

ONE MONTH LATER

37

CASSIUS

"Your boyfriend's here." Olivia's familiar taunt rang out loudly in the shoebox that also doubled as the center's administration office one Thursday afternoon.

I began to shout back my usual retort. "He's not my—" before stopping. Because, wait, now he actually was. I guess it was going to take a little longer than four weeks to wind back a lifetime of reflexive corrections.

I took the four steps from my broom closet of an office to step out into the reception area. And as always, the sight of my —*boyfriend*—sent fireflies of electricity running through my body. It could have been the dark gray three-piece suit he was wearing. He had just come straight from the office, and I knew he had a major pitch today to a potential new client, but it was most likely the flood of memories of what he looked like without the suit (in fact, without a stitch of clothing on) that really got me.

For seventeen years, Spencer James Montgomery had been the *best* best friend a guy could have. And I didn't know what I had done to deserve it, but now I got the chance to experience him as the best boyfriend in the world as well.

We kissed modestly on the lips, both very keen of Olivia's gaze not leaving us for even a microsecond. I looked down and suppressed a smile. He looked so adorable whenever he tried to hide something.

"What's behind your back, Spencey?" I asked, loudly enough for Olivia to hear without having to crane her neck...any more than she already was.

"These are"—Spencer pulled out a massive bouquet of bright flowers—"for the most wonderful, kind, and patient...boss in the world."

A squeal escaped Olivia's lips as she ran up from her desk to collect her prize. I mean, the flowers.

"What did I do to deserve these?" she asked, excitedly eyeing the colorful arrangement.

Spencer raised an eyebrow in amusement. "Two things. One, your little additions to our luggage when we went down to Elysian last month."

"Oh, that." Olivia smiled, waving away the words dismissively with her brightly painted red nails. "That was nothing."

"No, it was everything." Spencer stepped in and dipped his head to meet her gaze straight on. "Thank you, Olivia. For giving us that little extra push that you clearly knew we needed."

"You didn't need me," Olivia pointed out. "You guys would have found a way to each other with or without me."

Spencer mulled her words over for a moment. "True, but let's just say that you, uh, helped."

He was talking about the condoms and lube bit, but too adorably modest to say it. I could tell by the way the tips of his ears had turned a rosy pink hue.

"Yeah, and"—I stepped in, wrapping an arm around Spencer's shoulder—"that angel outfit you gave Spencer is burned in my memory forever. He was the sexiest angel in history."

Olivia giggled. "I'm sure he was. Too bad you didn't take photos."

I heard a throat being cleared. "Look, I don't mean to get all Spencer-like on you, but we do have a plane to catch, baby."

"Feel free to get all Spencer-like on me anytime you want," I replied with a grin, turning around to grab my backpack from my office.

"And that's the number two thing I'm thankful to you for, Olivia." I heard Spencer say behind me. "That you've given Cass another day off. I really appreciate it."

"I do, too." I'd returned, backpack slung over shoulder and ready to go...wherever it was that Spencer was taking me. I had no idea. It was all a big surprise.

"My pleasure, you guys. I hope you have fun wherever it is you end up going. Oh, and if there are any fancy outfits involved, please remember to take photos this time."

We laughed and left the building. I was keen to get this mystery adventure weekend underway.

All I knew so far was that we were going away somewhere, hence the need to pack. "How many bags of luggage did you bring with you this time?" I teased Spencer as we drove to what I assumed would be the airport.

"The usual four." He said it so unapologetically, and I loved it. I could have pulled him in for a kiss right there and then if he wasn't, you know, behind the wheel and driving.

"I know you won't tell me anything about where we're going—"

"That's right. I won't." He glanced over and flashed me a way too sexy smile.

I'd resorted to bribing him during the week with a blowjob for information. It hadn't worked. I did give him a blowjob, but the only thing exchanged was fluids, no weekend getaway details.

If there was one thing I knew about Spencer, it was that the guy was a vault. The best secret keeper in the world. Normally, a very admirable quality, unless it was me that he was keeping the secret from.

"Can you just give me one tiny clue, please?" I pleaded as I noticed that Spencer had taken a weird turn that wasn't in the right direction of the airport.

"I can let you know that wherever we are going to, we're not flying."

"Yeah, I just figured that one out myself, Einstein." I folded my arms across my chest. I may or may not have added a sulky pout, too.

Spencer took one look at me. *Tee-hee-hee.*

"All right, I'll take pity on you." He held up three fingers.

"You want to insert three fingers inside of me? Is that the clue?"

More *tee-hee-heeing.* "What? Cass, no. There are three big things that will happen this weekend."

"That's it? That's my clue?"

"Uh-huh." He looked way too happy with himself.

"That's like saying, 'This weekend you will breathe.' It's not very helpful," I protested. "I already knew there would be surprises. I'd like to know what they will be."

"Then it wouldn't be a surprise now, would it?"

Spencer's smirk stayed on his lips as we pulled into the parking lot of the Boston Back Bay Station. Ah ha, so we were catching a train to somewhere.

I immediately thought of Emry and Hawk. "Are we going to Philly to see the guys?"

"No, we are not." Spencer pulled into an empty spot in the reserved section of the lot. Because of course he had pre-booked parking. "If we were going to Philadelphia, we'd be flying. I think the train takes over six hours. That's a bit too long for me."

He cut the engine and turned to me. "We're going to New York."

I clapped my hands in front of me, channeling my inner-Emry. "Ooh, is that one of the three surprises?"

"No," Spencer said as a naughty grin returned to his lips. "But what we're going to do on the train is."

I hadn't been on a train in forever, and of course, Spencer, being Spencer, had chosen the fanciest train we could take. We were sitting in a private first-class car. There was plenty of room, comfortable leather-bound fold-out seating, and, as I was about to discover, a whole world of privacy.

Once the train started moving, Spencer got up and locked the door to the cart, drawing the curtains at the same time. When he turned around, in one smooth move, he peeled off his navy blue polo, standing there shirtless in front of me.

"What—what are you doing?" Somehow I managed to get the words out, as my eyes roamed up and down the breathtaking—I mean that literally, since breathing had just been relegated to a *nice to have* but *hard to do* bodily system function—combination of muscles and flesh of his tanned torso.

"What does it look like I'm doing?" He started to unzip his pants.

"Spencer!" I exclaimed. "We're on a train."

He shrugged like it was no big deal. "We're in a private car. We have a three-hour journey. Just think of this as a hotel room...on tracks. You're not a...prude, are you, Cass?"

I reached out and hooked my fingers around his waistband, pulling him in close. The train suddenly jolted, causing Spencer to crash down on top of me.

"Oh, shit, are you okay, Cass?" He pushed himself off me.

"Just like a hotel room?" I smiled as I rubbed my head where he had landed.

He slid into the seat next to me. "Let me make it up to you." He gave me a kiss, slow and tender. "There, is that better?"

I batted my eyelashes. "A little, but nowhere near enough."

Another taste of his lips on mine. God, how I loved kissing Spencer. His lips were everything lips should be. Soft, sweet, and backed up by a tongue that could go from gentlemanly to filthy in a matter of a few swirls.

Which was kinda a little how we were as a couple. We looked super cute and innocent on the outside, but then get us on a train from Boston to New York, and we turned into two guys that couldn't keep our hands off each other. There was nothing innocent about what we were doing...or about to do.

And the best bit was I got to do it with the man I loved more than anything or anyone else in the world.

Somehow, Spencer managed to get both of us stripped down to our boxers without his lips ever leaving mine for more than the few seconds it took to rip my shirt off me. I loved how he was able to do that.

Up until him, sex had always felt so mechanical and robotic for me, a series of awkward moves—yes, even more awkward than my attempts at dancing—that led to an okay, but nothing to shout home about, climax. And even though I knew I wouldn't be able to yell at the top of my lungs since we were, you know, on a train, I had no doubt about the ending, or the fun we'd have getting there.

Spencer pulled away from me, his lips bright pink, smudged with a faint trace of me like mine were of him. He opened a backpack and pulled out the required supplies. The lube tube Olivia had given us was long gone. We were now up to our third bottle.

Spencer motioned for me to stand up so I did. With his ocean blue eyes locked on mine, he slid our briefs down our legs, the tips of our cocks touching. I looked down at the sight. Spencer's smooth cock jutted out from his flat, rock-hard body. Mine was extended out from a slightly hairier, slightly softer body. But somehow, they looked perfect together.

Like they belonged together.

Because they did.

Spencer formed a fist, one end encasing my dick, the other end his. He slowly jerked his fist, barely more than an inch or two, keeping us connected. The pressure and the slow, steady movement rocked through my body.

My knees were weak with wanting. Him kissing me. Him inside me. Him loving me. It all blurred and blended into everything I had always hoped for...and so much more.

He leaned in and kissed me. "I got us a car on the left side of the carriage." His warm breath danced across my jaw.

"Why did you do that?"

"Apparently, it's a nicer view. And I thought you'd enjoy it"—he pulled back a touch, his eyes gleaming with mischief—"while I'm fucking you from behind."

There it was. That heady combination of nice and naughty. Familiar and new. Because even though we'd known each other as friends for most of our lives, we were only on the tip of the iceberg when it came to getting to know each other as boyfriends. Partners. Lovers.

And I was more than all right with that.

I turned to face the window, bending over to give Spencer a good view of his own to enjoy—my meaty ass.

I heard the condom wrapper being torn open, and his warm hand gently grazed my left cheek. "Oh, Cass. You're so beautiful."

A lump formed in my throat, like it did every time he said that. And he told me that every single time before we made love. I never realized how much I needed to hear that.

I had been so closed off for so long and never let anyone get close enough to me, but with Spencer, all my walls were down. That was the difference. I'd lowered my guard with him, and because I had, it opened up a whole world of connection, and discovery, and passion that I never knew existed.

Yes, it was a risk. There was a chance that everything could blow up in our faces. But with each passing day, with each moment we spent with each other—as boyfriends, *and* best friends—that risk was getting smaller and smaller.

I felt his wet finger playing with my hole.

I turned over my shoulder and sent him a searing look. "I want you, Spence. Inside of me."

Hey, if I was going to get fucked on a train, I was going to lean into it with everything I had.

His finger explored me like it always did. Patiently. Respectfully. But having fun at the same time, too. Spencer had done his research—of course he had—and knew that anal sex required a little time to prep and get the body loose, relaxed, and open.

But I was hungry. My need was rising within me like the mercury on a thermometer in the middle of summer. The movement of the train gently caused us to move and buck unexpectedly, only adding to the thrill.

"Now. Please," I whisper-begged. I couldn't wait any more. I had to have him now.

Spencer obliged. I felt his hands pulling up against my shoulders. I arched my lower back, giving him the right angle, and then, I felt him.

Slowly at first, but fuck, it was still a feeling of fullness that I could never find words for. His grip on my shoulders increased as he dug his fingers in, while he pushed deeper inside of me.

Everything else that was going on—the fact that we were on a train, the view whizzing past me outside the window, any other random thoughts running through my mind—all screeched to a halt as the feeling of Spencer's cock being inside of me overtook every cell in my body, every particle of my being.

"Are you okay, Cass?" he asked as he bottomed out.

I gulped, sucking down on air like I hadn't been breathing. Because, somewhere along the line, I had stopped. "Yeah, just gimme a sec."

"Of course." He changed hand position, moving his fingers toward my neck and beginning to massage me.

I let out a not-too-loud moan, sinking myself deeper under his magical fingers. "Oh, that feels good." His kneading of my neck spread a warmth through my entire body, and then it happened. The magical moment where the pain and resistance melted away. The sky cleared, and all I could feel was lightness, love, and Spencer starting to move inside of me, pulling out and pushing in with a gentle yet powerful consistency.

I dropped my face, leaning my forehead against the window as Spencer sped up, each thrust finding new parts of me, reaching deeper, taking what was his.

Me.

All of me.

And I was taking him, letting him inside me and touching parts of me that I guess I had been saving for him all along without even realizing it.

Despite being on a speeding train, our movements were seamless, flowing naturally as he kept fucking me, our bodies rocking together, his hands dancing across my back and igniting my skin.

"I'm getting close," he whispered urgently.

I twisted my neck, my eyes meeting his. I could see tiny beads of sweat dripping down his forehead. I wanted to be able to reach around and lick them off.

"No." I shook my head. "This ride still has over two hours to go. And Spencey, I ain't just talking about the train."

His face contorted in a half smile, half look of *how am I going to be able to keep this up for another two hours?*

I initiated a position change with just hand movements, no words.

The general gist was:

You—lie down.

Me—get on top.

Spencer lay down on his back on the carriage floor. I lowered myself onto Spencer's cock, spreading my knees out wide beside his body. His fingers found the fleshy groove just below my hips and above my thigh. Once I had all of him inside of me again, I slowly started to rock, bounce, and swivel my way on his cock.

His eyes rolled into the back of his head, and he let out a deep, guttural moan. It was the filthiest sound I'd ever heard come out of his mouth...and I loved it.

I grabbed onto the seat on my left and the wall on my right as I sped up, using the grip to bounce up and down on Spencer harder and with more intensity.

"How does this feel?" I asked.

"So fucking good," Spencer murmured, his eyes flitting, opening and closing involuntarily.

My sexy angel.

His fingers dug into me, so I sped up even more.

"No, wait," he cried out urgently. "I'm too close. I'm too close. I don't want to come yet."

I didn't want him to, either.

So I stopped. Coming to complete stillness, pressing down firmly, encasing his entire length inside of me.

"We can, just, you know, hang out like this for a while," I suggested playfully...innocently...and not at all sounding like someone who was stuffed to the brim with a massive, rock-hard cock in their ass.

He grinned, his eyes opening fully. "That'd be nice."

"So, uh"—I looked around the car—"you come here often?"

His grin widened. "Doofus."

"What's a nice-looking boy like you doing in a place like this?"

And that's when the most magical thing happened.

With Spencer balls-deep inside of me on the floor of a carriage on a train to New York, for the first time ever, Spencer let out his beautiful-sounding *tee-hee-hee* laugh...and this time, he didn't cover his mouth. Or even try to.

My insides exploded, bursting with love and happiness and joy at the sight of him. He wasn't hiding his beautiful rows of teeth, or the crooked part of the tip of his nose, or the freckle on his right cheek.

Instead, I could see it all.

All of him.

The *real* him, laughing beneath me, inside me and all around me. I had never experienced elation like it before.

"Come for me. Now." I dipped low and kissed his mouth with all the strength I had in me as I thrust up and down on his cock.

"Oh god, oh god, oh god." His words kissed into me as his body buckled beneath me, his torso twisting and his face producing veins on his temples that looked like they were about to burst.

I fisted my cock and began to jerk it off in rhythm to my body bobbing up and down, my release spilling out of me at the same time as his filled me up.

Once our breathing had returned to normal, I moved off him as carefully as I could, lying down on the floor next to him, wiping the beads of sweat off his forehead with my thumb.

His eyes sparkled as he looked at me, clearly still spent over what looked like a pretty fan-fucking-tastic orgasm.

I smiled, leaning in toward his ear. "I love you, Spencey."

"I love you—" His head suddenly jerked back, and it looked like it was consuming a lot of energy just for him to speak.

His eyelids were growing heavy... "too..."

He let out a tiny yawn... "baby."

38

SPENCER

"Spencey... Spencey."

Cassius' warm hand brushed across my cheek, stirring me back to life. I opened my eyes, letting out a massive yawn. For a moment, as I breathed Cassius in, I wondered if it had all been a dream.

"Looks like someone got a little sleepy after"—he leaned in closer as his lips swerved into the start of a smile—"giving me the best fucking of my life."

Okay, nope. It wasn't a dream. It had really happened.

Another yawn escaped me. Cassius was looking around our car as I suddenly realized we weren't moving. "Why aren't we moving? Has something happened?"

He let out a laugh. "Yeah, something's happened. We've arrived in New York."

I scrambled up to a seated position, somehow letting out another yawn in the process. "God, you've drained me of all my energy," I said as I tugged at Cassius' waist, just because I wanted to touch him again.

He perked up. "That's not all I drained you of."

He bent over, his delicate kissing helping to wake me out of the unexpected deep sleep I had fallen into. "I liked my first surprise, thank you. I can't wait for the next two."

Good thing for him he wouldn't have to wait too long. We were only in New York Friday through to Sunday. And I planned on taking Cassius to surprise number two right after we checked into our hotel.

And in a sign of how much I had changed in just the past four weeks, I had only spreadsheeted the events of today. The rest of the weekend had been left blank. I thought it might be good to just see where life took us when we didn't make plans. That approach seemed to be working well for me.

"You know, this is super dangerous," Cassius informed me.

"Uh, we just had sex on a train. I can't help it if I'm feeling kinda adventurous," I replied with a smile I knew he couldn't see.

"Yeah, but one of us wasn't blindfolded during said train sex."

He had a point, but we were literally only a few steps away from our destination. Although I had forgotten just how busy New York was compared to Boston and severely underestimated how many stares me guiding my blindfolded boyfriend down a busy SoHo street would generate.

This was meant to be New York City, the world capital of anything goes. Maybe not so much anymore.

"We're almost there," I hedged as I spied my destination. Ian was already there and had spotted me. I didn't have a spare hand to wave, so I gave him a warm smile.

He mouthed out, "Are you okay?" and I replied with a sharp nod.

Less than a minute later, I was carefully guiding Cassius through the front door. Ian closed it behind us, and the din of the city fell by a few decibels, dropping to a nice background hum.

"Where are we?" Cassius stuck his nose up into the air and

started sniffing around like a dog searching for a bone. "I don't smell food." He sounded a little disappointed.

"That's because we're not at a restaurant."

"You know very well, Spencer, that if food doesn't enter my system regularly—and by that I mean at least once every two hours—I suffer from a very rare medical condition that means I could die."

I rolled my eyes at Ian, who was smiling quietly at us.

"Unless..." Cassius' voice dropped an octave. "You're planning a follow-up to our train ride with another—"

I clasped my palm over his mouth.

"Stop talking, Cassius."

I lifted my fingers off his lips. "Why, you got something else you'd rather be doing with my mouth?"

I clasped my hand back over them. "Cass," I hummed into his ear. "We might not be alone."

Slowly—*very* slowly—I peeled my fingers off his mouth, hoping he'd get the hint and stay quiet. No such luck.

"As you have recently discovered for yourself, I ain't no prude, Spence. An audience might be kinda ho—"

Okay, I was going to have to keep my hand permanently fixed to him.

We took a few more steps inside, and thankfully, Cassius stayed quiet the whole time. I knew he'd appreciate it later. He'd be just as embarrassed as I currently was when he found out our audience was Ian, and he'd inadvertently given him a glimpse into our—admittedly scorching hot—sex life.

I brought Cassius into a spot right in the middle of the room. I looked over expectantly at Ian, and he gave me a slight nod. This was it.

The right spot.

The right moment.

And, I prayed, the right reaction from Cassius.

I let go of Cassius' shoulders. "I'm just going to take the

blindfold off," I informed him as I untied the knot at the back of his head. "Keep your eyes—and your mouth—closed, please."

I took his silence and slight nod as a tacit sign of agreement. I slipped the blindfold off and threw it down onto the ground beside us. Cassius was holding up his end of the agreement. His eyes were firmly shut. As was his mouth.

"Okay, you can open your eyes now."

He did, and when he did, they instantly flew wide open. So did his mouth, along with the words, "Oh my fucking god."

For a few heart-attack-inducing seconds, I couldn't get a firm read on whether it was a happy *oh my god* or a shocked, cruel, and twisted one. The tears welling in his eyes only added to my paralysis.

Ian stepped forward, and that's when Cassius saw him for the first time, jumping back in shock.

"Ian," he exclaimed. "What are you doing here?"

"I'm glad to see you both again. And welcome to my gallery." He waved his hand around the space, the brightly lit walls displaying some of the most beautiful sketches I had ever laid my eyes on.

Cassius looked at me, as if he was silently asking me for permission to look at them. Instinctively, I nodded. "Go on, have a closer look."

Cassius paced carefully toward the wall on our left. His steps were measured, like he was trying to avoid any deliberate movements. He was more than just a little shell-shocked. I couldn't blame him, really.

He stopped a few feet away from the sketches and craned his neck out as he examined them.

He turned around to Ian and me. "I don't—I don't understand. How...?" His voice trailed off as he moved over to the next wall.

Ian and I stayed silent. I was enjoying watching Cassius' reaction too much to say anything. I got the feeling he was leaning toward happy and was simply letting it all sink in. When he reached the fourth and final wall, I walked up beside him. "So, what do you think?"

He opened and shut his mouth a few times before managing to get actual words out. "How is this possible?"

I took his hand in mine, kissing the back of it. "This is Ian's gallery. We've been in touch since we got back from Florida, and he mentioned he was keen to see some of your sketches. So, I took a few photos of the stuff you had up on your walls, and he loved it."

"I *really* loved it." Ian joined us and smiled warmly at Cassius. "You're incredibly talented. I honestly can't believe you haven't had any training."

"I taught myself," Cassius responded. "I've never taken an art class in my life."

"So"—I went on—"Ian loved your work so much that he kept asking to see more. So, I've been scanning your sketches and emailing them to him."

"And then I printed them out and put them onto this stretch canvas, which I hung up on these walls that you're looking at right now. And if it's all right with you, Cassius, I'd like to set up a showing."

Cassius turned to me, his eyes as big as two footballs. "As in show them...to people?"

Ian let out a low chuckle. "That's usually how a showing works, yes."

"It's totally up to you, Cass." I gave his hand a solid squeeze. "You don't have to do anything you don't want to do. From here on in, it's your call. All I wanted to do was to show you how amazing your work really is. I wanted you to see it how I see it."

"Agreed," Ian added. "If you decide you don't want anything further to happen, that's fine. There's absolutely no pressure."

"Thank you," Cassius said as he stepped away from us, casting his gaze around the space. I could tell it was a lot for him to process. He'd always played his talent down, dismissing his sketches as silly doodles that he did in his spare time.

But I knew that he had talent, and I also knew that he wouldn't believe me if I kept saying it like I had been for all of these years.

If nothing else, I just wanted him to experience what it felt like to see his pieces hanging in a gallery. Maybe that would shift something and make him see the pieces the way that I, Ian, and, I was sure, the rest of the world would see them, too.

He spun around to face us. "Thank you both so much. This is amazing." His voice was a little shaky. "And if you really think that they're worth showing"—he cast his gaze to Ian—"then yeah, let's do it. Let's have a showing."

Our bodies moved closer, and we embraced. I ran my fingers through Cassius' thick hair as he kept whispering, "Thank you, thank you, thank you" over and over into my ear. I never wanted to let him go. Nothing made me happier than seeing him like this.

Even though so much had changed between us in the last month, that was the one thing that remained constant: All I wanted was to make Cassius the happiest guy on earth.

39

CASSIUS

Was there a word for when life felt so good that you honestly thought that you were dreaming because you never thought it would even be humanly possible you could feel this way? If there wasn't, someone needed to invent one because I was floating on air as we stepped out of Ian's gallery and straight into the hustle and bustle of SoHo.

But I didn't notice the sounds, the smells, or even the people around us. All I felt was Spencer's hand clasped in mine and the overwhelming feelings of happiness, gratitude, and love that were swirling through my body.

What had I done to deserve him?

First, the train ride to New York. We definitely put the *ass* into first class on that trip.

Then his beyond thoughtful gesture, working with Ian to display my work in his gallery. It was beyond surreal to see it blown up and hanging from clean, well-lit walls, and not in my own dingy apartment. It somehow made me see them differently, and while I still saw all the little imperfections in the sketches, I also noticed way more things that I liked about them.

Were they the best in the world? No. But were they okay to show and maybe get some people to like them, maybe even buy them? There was only one way to find out.

In the same way that I was learning that taking chances was a good thing with Spencer, maybe it would be a good thing with my art, too? Who knew? The lesson was, if you didn't try, you'd never know. And there wasn't a day that had gone by in the last month where I wasn't grateful I'd broken through my carefully guarded barriers to let Spencer in.

I beamed as I eyed him, looking all handsome in his white cashmere sweater—I looked down—and his faded blue jeans. I rubbed the back of my hand against his chest. "You did it again."

He arched an eyebrow. "I did what again?"

"You're wearing your Fred Jones Scooby Doo outfit again."

His eyes gleamed. *Tee-hee-hee.* Again, no hand covering his mouth, and it made my skin warm with joy.

"What can I say? I like this outfit. And besides, I hardly think Fred could afford it. This is real cashmere, baby."

I grabbed a piece of it from his bicep, running the material between my fingers. "You look perfect."

"You do, too, Cass."

"So where are we going?" I asked, realizing Spencer wasn't hailing a cab to take us back to the hotel.

"There's one more surprise, remember?"

How could I forget?

"Is it very far?" I didn't want to sound like I was whining, but at the same time, I did need to gently remind Spencer that, at some point, I needed to consume a burger...or three.

"Because, it's just, that, if you don't count the snacks I ate on the train after you fell asleep, I'm pretty sure my daily caloric intake is well below the recommended lev—"

"We're here," Spencer announced, cutting me off mid-not-whine.

I looked up at the nondescript white wood-paneled building we had come to. A brown *JIMMY* sign framed the top of a back door. "What is this place?" I asked, regretting it immediately as I knew what Spencer's response would be.

"It's a surprise," I mouthed the words as he said them.

We stepped into a small entryway. The waiting elevator shot us up onto the eighteenth floor, which was also the top floor. We stepped out into an impressive, but not stuffy or pretentious in the slightest, cocktail lounge. Jazzy music played in the background, and the place was busy, but not packed.

I took a few steps forward and gasped. "Holy shit, the view."

"It's pretty impressive, right?" Spencer pulled up next to me, admiring the Manhattan skyline just as much as I was. "You like it here?"

I nodded. "It's amazing."

And so was the table Spencer had booked for us, right by the massive windows. We had front-row tickets to the best view in New York.

And the food? Spencer knew I loved a good burger, and the all-American beef patty with a classic mint julep was mouthwateringly delicious. So good, I had to have two, and even after my second helping, I still had no freaking idea what a julep was.

I was just about to raise this earth-shatteringly important observation when I noticed him tugging at his collar. I hadn't seen that signature tell of his, since we'd started dating.

I wiped the sauce from around my mouth with a napkin and not the back of my hand or sleeve—bending forward to take a bow, *thank you, thank you, thank you.*

"Spencey, what's wrong?"

I saw him give a nod to the server, who deftly approached us and placed two glasses of champagne on the table.

"Thank you," we both said to him in unison.

"Are you full?" Spencer reached for the flute.

I nodded. "Sure. I mean, I wouldn't want to be rude and say no if you suggest we peruse the dessert menu, but that doesn't have to happen right this minute."

Spencer smiled, but it didn't reach his eyes. He patted down his shirt collar and I realized he had ignored my question, asking if something was the matter.

"Well, then, we should toast."

I quirked an eyebrow. "To the fact that I'm full?"

He giggled nervously. "That is quite an accomplishment, isn't it?"

"Spencer, what's wrong? You're acting funny."

He put his drink back down on the table and let out a noisy breath. "I'm nervous."

"I don't understand. Why are you nerv—"

"Will you marry me?" He winced. "Shit, sorry. I'm meant to be down on my knee." He pushed his chair away from the table and dropped to one bended knee in front of me. From somewhere, he had produced a dark blue jewelry box and opened it. I blinked through the tears that had formed but not yet fallen in my eyes, staring down at a beautiful, elegant, refined white gold band.

"I prepared a whole speech"—Spencer tipped his head up, his eyes just as glossy as mine—"but I can't remember a word. I kinda freaked out about it a few moments ago. That's probably what you picked up on." The words were gushing out of him.

"I just love you so much, Cass, and I want to spend every day of the rest of my life with you. I don't care where we are or what we're doing as long...as long as we're together."

Our eyes met. "Will you marry me, Cassius Draper?"

My name had only barely left his lips when I cried out a delighted, "Yes!"

It delighted everyone around us, too. I hadn't even noticed that the entire restaurant had frozen with everyone looking at us, but a roar of cheering erupted all around us as people clapped and whistled.

Spencer slipped the band on my finger. It fit perfectly, and we hugged. His warm body and breath felt so good against me.

I closed my eyes, determined to let the feeling sink in so deep that I would never forget it for as long as I lived.

My best friend.

My boyfriend.

Now, my fiancé.

And soon, my husband.

EPILOGUE - CASSIUS

TEN YEARS LATER...

"No. No kissing. Naughty." I wagged my finger and was met with a doey, loveable, brown-eyed stare. And a few blinks. Why was it always the blinks that made me waver?

Be strong, Cassius. Be strong.

"Okay, you can kiss me a little bit."

It's funny what Great Danes can understand. "Down, boy" and "drop it" was selective, yet "Yes to kisses" was somehow always understood.

Scooby went wild, licking up and down the side of my face before turning his attention—and his tongue—to my fingers, getting them all slobbery wet.

"I don't know why you like licking so much, but you're just too cute to say no to." I rubbed his head between my wet hands, giving him a few scratches in the spot under his neck, just the way he liked.

Yes, we'd bought a dog.

Yes, he was a brown, two-hundred pound thing just like the cartoon version.

And of course, we had to name him Scooby.

I wish I could have blamed his eagerness to lick anything and everything in front of him on the fact that he was a young, untrained pup going through that annoying licks-anything, chews-anything phase that all puppies went through. Scooby had gone through that stage, too...eight years ago when he was actually a pup.

The difference with him was that he'd never come out of the other side of that phase. He was almost nine years old, and he definitely knew better. He only pretended that he didn't.

After Scooby had finally decided he'd had enough of wetting me, he walked over to his massive bed in the corner of the kitchen and plonked himself down on it. I grabbed a napkin from the kitchen table and dried myself off a little before returning my focus back to the spreadsheet that was open in front of me on my laptop.

Paid the bills and conducted my annual review of our house and car insurances? Check.

Ordered our weekly groceries for home delivery, remembering to get Spencer's favorite brand of mac and cheese? Check.

Done my thirty-minute calisthenics workout, followed by a ten-minute guided meditation session? Check.

I sat back in the chair and hummed in self-satisfied approval. I was on top of things today. As I had been every day for the last few years.

I didn't quite know when it had started exactly. I mean, it wasn't like I woke up one morning and decided I needed to work out, start eating clean, and develop a spreadsheet to schedule and document every aspect of our busy lives, but somehow along the way, Spencer and I had *Freaky Fridayed* our way to this current situation.

They said that some couples started to morph and meld into each after being together for a long time. As in they started to talk the same way, think the same way. Heck, sometimes they even began to look like each other.

But not Spencer and me. Nope.

We seemed to have—over time and imperceptibly at first—swapped characteristics. It's like we switched personalities without even realizing it. Which meant that I was now the responsible one who watched what I ate, while Spencer stuffed himself with carbs like they were going out of style. Don't worry, I hadn't completely converted to the diet dark side. I did still, on occasion, indulge in my crazy food concocting passion.

I had become the kind of guy who did things like *exercising* for reasons like it was *good for bone density* (yep, I'd become one of *those* people) while Spencer's gym membership had lapsed years ago.

I had also morphed into the *responsible and organized one*, who did responsible and organized things like paying the bills on time. Spencer, on the other hand, I didn't think he even knew any of our online banking passwords.

The funny thing was, this felt right.

Natural.

Sure, it might have sounded silly, and maybe it was, but in some ways, the person I was today felt like the person I was always meant to become. *The real me.* Which was not to say that I wasn't the real me back in the day, but people changed, right? So I was just doing the version of me that felt right for right now.

I eyed the time in the top right-hand corner of the screen as I took a sip of freshly brewed coffee. Five minutes and it would be go-time. Scooby was happily busily destroying the latest chew toy I had bought for him on his bed, while I was determined to stay dry and enjoy the last remaining moments of peace while it lasted.

I looked out the kitchen window and into the back garden filled with all sorts of bright and colorful flowers. None of them were native to Massachusetts, and it was a miracle that they had survived the move, but ever since Leo had driven them up—yes, *that* Leo—

all the way from Florida and given us his grandpa's secret fertilizer recipe, somehow the assortment of tropical plants had managed to survive Boston's mild summers and frigid winters.

It meant that whenever I stepped out there, the fragrances from the flowers took me back in time.

To Florida.

To that weekend getaway that transformed my life forever. No wonder then that the backyard was my favorite place to be in our home.

So, yes, in addition to buying a dog, Spencer and I had also bought a house. And a beautiful one at that. It was nestled in a quiet cul-de-sac in Brookline, a suburb known equally for its offering of great bars, restaurants, and coffee shops as it was for its beautiful green parks and highly rated public schools.

Actually, Spencer and I didn't buy the house together. I mean, yes, technically and legally, we did—it was in both of our names; I made sure of that—but it was in fact, me, who had paid for it. As in outright. As in with cold hard cash, baby.

The reason I could afford to buy an almost two-million dollar swanky home like this in the suburbs wasn't because social workers had suddenly become valued for the tremendous work they did and got remunerated accordingly—although as an eternal optimist, I hoped that they would be one day—it was the fact that I was now making ninety-nine percent of my income from my side hustle. Something that had started as a silly pastime, a way to relax, unwind, and escape. Something that I never in my wildest dreams would have even thought about pursuing professionally.

My sketches.

Or as *Apollo Magazine*, one of the world's most respected art magazines, put it, "*A masterful understanding of the dynamics of shade and light and translating them into powerfully detailed pencil drawings.*" Apparently, my adoption of pastel colors was both "*revolutionary*" and "*ushered in a new era in hyper-realism.*"

Yeah, I still had to rely on Google to translate a lot of the art-speak my pieces generated. I just sketched because I liked to sketch. Now I got to enjoy sketching while cashing massive checks and building up a stockpile of cash. Not too shabby for a kid from Boston who never attended a single art class.

But did you want to know one of the best things about having money? It wasn't buying a house—it was what buying a house represented. Safety. Security. Love. And family.

I paid off my mom's mortgage and paid for my younger sisters' college tuition and their first cars. I also got to take care of Spencer and me financially, too.

Spencer didn't get that promotion he was gunning for when we got back from Florida. And he didn't get the one he applied for after that. Or the one after that.

Why? It had nothing to do with talent or ambition because he had both in spades. He was just too nice of a guy to pursue opportunities if it meant being ruthless to others. He just couldn't bring himself to fuck anyone else over in order to advance his position at the company.

Until one day, about four years ago, we were having breakfast. He was scoffing down waffles, while I had found a really good brand of homemade granola (the secret was that they soaked the almonds overnight to activate the enzymes...okay, yeah, now I hear it—I am so definitely one of *those* people).

Anyway, as I was listening to Spencer complaining about being overlooked for another promotion yet again, I slammed my fists on the table and made him an offer he couldn't refuse: quit and start your own business.

He was reluctant to accept at first. But as someone who had once seen something in an insecure guy who didn't think that his drawings were all that great and said, "You have to believe in yourself," I used that occasion to echo his own words back to him.

Spencer was now the President and CEO of Do Good LLC. A public relations and marketing firm that only took on projects that, as the name implied, did good things. That included non-profits, schools, local community organizations, or new businesses just getting off the ground and who wouldn't otherwise be able to afford a professional marketing firm.

The company was thriving, and his client roster was getting longer and more impressive every year. I'd never seen Spencer looking so happy.

A noise at the doorway distracted me. I swiveled around and smiled.

It was Spencer.

My Spencer.

He was wearing his—which was formerly my—favorite *Go With The Flow* shirt. His long, dark blond hair stuck out in every direction, as if he'd just woken up.

And he was looking very, very *unhappy*.

"You woke me up," he grumbled, right before letting out a massive yawn. His mouth-covering days were over. That went for yawning, laughing, and definitely for crying out in the throes of an explosive orgasm.

I sat up a little straighter and smiled sweetly at him. "You know today is a very important day, Spencey." I tapped the top of my laptop screen. "We have a schedule to follow, and I had to make sure you got up on time."

"But four alarm clocks, Cass? That's just cruel."

"Hey, I had to make sure you actually got up. We almost missed our flight to Paris last year when I only set two, remember? I was almost late to my own exhibition opening. That would have been terrible. I would have looked like such an..."

"Asshat," we said at the same time.

I slunk into my chair and smirked, watching him as he trudged over, bleary-eyed, to the microwave, opening the door to take out his cup of morning coffee. The one I had already made him and kept warm for him every morning.

"We have to leave the house in thirty minutes." My tone was sharp, but fair. "I'm ready, which just leaves you and—"

"Already on it," Spencer declared. He took a sip of joe and padded over to me, planting a kiss on my forehead. His blue eyes were slowly starting to show signs of cognizant intelligence.

He pulled a chair out and sat down next to me. "How are you feeling about the day?"

"I'm good. I'm good," I replied in a tone that revealed I was actually more like, "Freaking out, freaking out."

He took another sip of coffee and cupped his palm over my hand. "Relax, Cass." He gave me the kind of smile that could melt an iceberg. He dipped his head, his eyes drifting over his shirt. "Just, you know, go with the flow."

I chuckled. "Yeah, how exactly did that shirt end up on your side of the wardrobe?"

His eyes went wide like saucers. "No idea," he whispered into his mug.

I shook my head, unable to resist his cheekiness. Or his puppy dog eyes. Or the way he had totally mellowed out. Or...well, anything and everything about him, really.

I stood up and put on my most *I'm trying to be stern with you, but you're just too goddamn cute for your own good* tone. "Twenty minutes. We have to leave in twenty minutes. And not one minute later. I've got this whole thing timed down to the second."

"Yeah, yeah," Spencer waved his hand in the air. "Relax, Cass. Just—"

I wagged a finger at him. "Don't say it."

"Go with the flow," he sang out playfully as I chased him out of the kitchen.

Exactly nineteen and a half minutes later, I was pulling our SUV out of the driveway.

Exactly thirty-nine minutes later, we were still in the car, stuck in traffic because a burst water main had ground traffic in both directions to a complete halt.

I tapped my fingers nervously on the steering wheel. "We're going to be late," I muttered impatiently to Spencer.

His hand found my lap, and as always, the touch reassured me. "Just breathe. We can't do anything about the traffic. Can we, James?"

I looked into the rearview mirror, at our son, James Draper. (Spencer's middle name, my last name. For some reason, my mom didn't give me or my sisters middle names.)

Our son's bright blue eyes met mine, and he waved into the reflection, his excitement written all over his face. The first day of school was a big deal. Which was exactly why I didn't want us to be late for it.

"Being a little late isn't the worst thing in the world." That was Spencer, who now said things like that, or, "Don't worry about the dishes. We can do them in the morning," or, "Let's just use what we have in the refrigerator and see what meal we can make out of it." Yep, total Freaky Friday shit.

But he was right.

And if anyone knew that being late on your first day and taking the last available desk next to someone wasn't the worst thing in the world, it was us. Being late on his first day was the start of our beautiful friendship, one that was still going stronger than ever.

It wasn't lost on either one of us that this wasn't just James's first day at school. It was the twenty-seventh anniversary of the day Spencer and I met.

But still, I had to hold my shit together. I promised myself, and James, too, on multiple occasions, that I wouldn't embarrass him by crying at school. I'd save the tears for the car ride home. If we ever reached the damn school.

Thankfully, after a few more minutes that seemed to drag on for an eternity, the burst pipe was fixed, at least temporarily, and traffic began to flow again.

We were however, late, arriving at Pierce Elementary School ten minutes after the bell had rung.

"We're going to have to take him into the office." I sighed heavily as I pulled into an empty spot in the parking lot.

Spencer turned around and smiled. "You ready to race me, little man?"

James let out an excited, "Yeahhh," as we rushed from the car, to the administration office, to the door of James' classroom, 1C.

This was it. Our little boy was going to start his first day at school.

We both crouched down next to him, peppering him with hugs and kisses. Don't worry, the classroom door was closed, and the hallway was empty. The only person Spencer and I were scarring for life was our son.

"Are you ready to go in, James?" I asked, biting my lower lip.

James nodded his head enthusiastically, before stopping and reaching for Spencer's hand. "Will you come in with me, Dad?"

"Of course I will."

"Love you, Papa." James rolled into me, and I squeezed him tight just one more time.

"I love you, too. You're going to have a great first day. We'll be here to pick you up this afternoon."

And with that, James placed his hand into Spencer's.

I blew out a deep breath as Spencer knocked on the door and stepped into the room. I watched from the glass partition in the door as the teacher introduced James to the class. He did that *straight arm by the body Spencer-esque wave* that he had obviously picked up from his dad.

And I smiled as Spencer guided him to a spot in the second back row. I saw Spencer exchanging a few words with the student sitting next to the empty desk.

My heart swelled, and I was fighting back against the tide of memories that were threatening to come flooding back. So much of what was playing out in front of me reminded me of the way Spencer and I had met that day twenty-seven years ago.

And technically, if I started crying now, I wouldn't be breaking my promise of not crying in front of James.

But, no, I exhaled heavily again and held it together as best I could.

James settled into his seat and began talking to the girl sitting next to him. She was a pretty girl with a friendly face, a big smile, and her dark brown hair adorably tied into two braids, one on each side of her face.

Spencer glided out of the classroom. I stepped back as he approached the door to allow him to leave. "How is he?"

"Good. He's...good."

We pressed our noses against the glass, looking at our little boy, all grown up. Spencer hooked my pinky with his. "What does this remind you of?"

"Tell me about it." I let out a wistful sigh. "I've come this close to losing it a million times already. I mean, I can't believe we were late, despite my amazing planning."

Spencer let out a hearty laugh. "Planning isn't everything."

I shook my head, still amazed at how different he was, how much we had both changed over the years.

"I used to hate the fact that I showed up late for my first day of school," Spencer went on. "So, when I grew up, I did everything I could to make sure I was always on time, always prepared, always one step ahead. But"—with our noses still pressed against the glass, we each turned slightly toward each other—"being late that day was the best thing that ever happened to me."

I craned a little further to get a better view of him, the happiness written all over his features. "It was the best thing that ever happened to me, too."

He threw a warm look my way. "I'm going to tell you something, Cass, and you have to promise me you won't cry."

"I make no such guarantee," I whipped back. "Why? Did something happen in there?"

Spencer nodded. "The little girl James sat down next to." His grip around my pinky tightened. "Her name is...Olivia."

That was it. I spluttered hopelessly into the glass and started bawling like a baby. Spencer gently pulled me away from public humiliation and into his warm body, rubbing my hair as I rained down a flood of tears onto his shoulder.

"It's okay, Cass. It's okay."

After a few moments of crying my heart out in a—luckily for me, still-empty school hallway—we started to make our way toward the entrance.

"Do you think—" I looked over hopefully at Spencer. "That James and Olivia might be like...us?"

"What? You mean, be best friends for seventeen years before going away on a weekend getaway where they realize they are both in love with each other, get married, have a child, fulfill their career passions including an unexpected side hustle that blows up into a world-famous, successful art career, and then live happily ever after?"

God, I loved this cheeky side to Spencer. "When you put it like that, it does seem a little far-fetched that it would happen...again."

The next time I glanced over at Spencer, though, his eyes had gotten a little misty, too. "It would be the coolest thing ever, baby, but let's not start planning weddings just yet. Let's wait and see if they become friends first... That's always a good first step."

He was right. It was.

"Besides"—he nudged his arm up against mine—"we've got a whole bunch of stuff to look forward to before that."

Those words settled in my chest like being wrapped up snugly in a warm blanket on a cold winter's night. Spencer was right. We had a lifetime of things to look forward to together.

We had our son. A beautiful home. Work that fulfilled us.

And the one thing that tied all the strands of our life together.

Us.

Our love.

Our beautiful, ever changing, yet still always constant love. A love that had started exactly twenty-seven years ago.

I glanced over at Spencer's strong profile. The curved tip at the end of his nose. The freckle that dotted his cheek. I felt so much love for him.

My husband.

The father of our beautiful boy.

My partner and equal.

But beneath everything I could see by looking at the man he was today and the impressive collection of memories we had already collected together, I was amazed that I could still be transported back to that first day at grade school and the nervous little boy who threw me a weird little wave and a hopeful smile as he sat down next to me.

Underneath it all, and despite all the changes that had happened, and all those we were yet to face, one thing had remained constant throughout the years.

Our friendship.

We were and would always be best friends.

As we walked silently, hand in hand, down the hallway, I relished in the reason why what we had was so special.

Because the basis of real love was friendship.

And true friendship was one of the rarest and most precious things in the world.

~

What's next for Casey Cox?
Get the latest buzz, a FREE prequel novella to the *ESCAPE* series, and exclusive behind-the-scenes author sneak peeks.

CLICK HERE to get the goodies!

MESSAGE FROM CASEY

Thank you so much for reading *Getaway: An Escape Novel*.

Writing a vacation romance during a global pandemic was an interesting experience. While travel may seem like a dream for many of us (as I write this message in April 2021), I hope you enjoyed this little escape from reality.

Can I ask a small favor? If you enjoyed the book, would you mind leaving a short review on Amazon? It really helps other readers decide whether the book is right for them.

Happy reading!
Casey, xo

ABOUT CASEY COX

Casey Cox is devoted to delighting readers with contemporary MM romance stories that are unique, thoughtful and funny. Casey's books are great to read if you're looking for something sweet and smart, with a side of sass, and a small helping of sexy!

Casey lives on the east coast of Australia, loves the beach and is a proud fur-parent to two utterly adorable, perfectly-perfect French Bulldogs named Ralphie and Lilly.

For more information, please visit
www.caseycoxbooks.com

Made in the USA
Las Vegas, NV
14 January 2025

16332798R00193